*For everyone who's ever broken the rules
and liked it*

# THE ANTI-HERO

## THE GOODE BROTHERS

### BOOK ONE

## SARA CATE

Cover design: Emily Wittig

Editor: Rebecca's Fairest Reviews

Proofreaders: Rumi Khan and My Brother's Editor

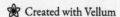 Created with Vellum

# DEAR READER

This is a story of a man who is betrayed by his faith and his father. His relationship with God and the church is complicated and at times, toxic. There are elements of religious trauma, homophobia, child abuse, and violence against women in this story. Please read with caution if any of these listed topics are potentially triggering to you. Your mental health and safety is important to me.

As always in my books, the kink and elements of BDSM are entirely fictional and meant to be read as fantasy, not reality. There is degradation, masochism, bondage, and sex without a condom. Should anything in my novels serve as inspiration to you, you and your partner(s) are responsible for your own research and safety.

I hope you enjoy Sage and Adam's journey of self-discovery, exploration, and religious recovery.

If the idea of getting railed in a church offends you, you might want to pick another book.

Enjoy!

Love always,
Sara

# PROLOGUE

Adam

12 years old

Isaac offers me a bite of his banana, shoving a handful of mush toward my mouth, drool dripping over his chubby little fingers.

"Nom, nom," I say, pretending to take a bite, and he laughs. He's got those big front teeth on the top now, so he looks funny when he smiles, but he's still pretty cute.

With those blond curls and big blue eyes, he looks just like Mom.

"Oh, Isaac, you're a mess," Mom says with a smile as she wipes his hands clean with a damp paper towel. Then she places a kiss on the top of his head, ruffling his hair. "Adam, will you help the twins get their shoes on? We're gonna be late."

She sounds frantic as she scoops my baby brother out of his high chair.

"Of course," I reply, pushing my breakfast away as I stand up. Just as I start toward the living room, she touches my arm, so I turn toward her. She's wearing a proud, loving expression as she touches my combed hair, thick with dried gel.

"You look so handsome." Then she uses her thumb to wipe cereal milk from the corner of my mouth. Grabbing my napkin from the table, I quickly dab my face.

"Thanks, Mom," I say with a smile.

The house is busy today. Mom and Dad have been planning for this day for months, but it's still crazy. The seven-year-old twins are fighting about something upstairs, their footsteps thundering through the house. Dad is still up in his office. I can hear him on the phone, his voice booming with frustration, probably over something going wrong today.

I grab Caleb's and Luke's black loafers from the rack by the door, then I bound up the stairs to find them. I'm only two steps up when I hear Dad hollering.

"Lucas! Dammit! You got this shit all over my pants." I freeze, my blood running cold with dread as I wait for the inevitable— Lucas's howling cry.

"Melanie!" my father shouts, practically shaking the walls. I'm sprinting now, eager to get my little brother away from Dad so he doesn't yell anymore.

In the upstairs hallway, Lucas is lying on the floor, screaming his head off, red-faced and covered in yogurt and tears.

"Come on, Luke. Get up," I say gently as I help him to his feet.

He's holding his cheek as he cries, and sure enough, his hands are covered in white, sticky yogurt. He must have snuck it up here from breakfast, even though he knows that's against the rules. I quickly shuffle him toward the bathroom to get him cleaned up.

His clothes are disheveled and he messed up his hair, so I try to fix it in a rush. Behind me, my dad stomps down the hall, looking furious. In the mirror's reflection, I watch as my mother reaches the landing with Isaac in her arms.

Dad scolds her, shaking the empty yogurt cup in her face, while she nods in agreement with his berating words.

*She shouldn't have let him have food upstairs.*

*She should control these damn boys.*

*She shouldn't have had so many fucking kids.*

It's hard to watch, and I don't like the way Lucas gapes at him with fear. So I kick the door closed and recomb Luke's hair while he cries, complaining that I'm pulling too hard.

"We're going to be late!" Dad yells again.

He shouts those five words at least four more times before we get everyone loaded up in the van. And he mutters them again in frustration all the way to church—the *new* church.

*Dad's* new church.

When we pull into the parking lot in the back, I stare up at the giant building and wonder how on earth this could be a church. It's just bricks and drywall and paint. Our last church had beautiful windows and creaking floors and a comforting smell that you couldn't find anywhere else in the world. Even on cold days, it felt warm.

But Dad looks proud as he walks ahead of us toward the back entrance, so when he smiles back at Mom, I try to smile along. He seems happy. This could be good for everyone.

Then, for a split second, he glances at me, giving me that beaming smile, and I don't have to force my grin anymore. When he turns back to the building, I pick up my pace so I can walk next to him.

There's a man I recognize who opens the back door and welcomes us in as we enter. It's huge in here, but a lot of it is still under construction. Straight ahead is a big open walkway, and I can see the front of the church from here.

We're all walking fast now as more people join us. They're the people who work with my dad, although I don't really know their names or positions. They don't talk to us much. And I don't pay much attention when they talk to Dad, giving him instructions and things to remember.

As a family, we meet together at the front of the church. Large black doors loom ahead of us, and I stare at them in confusion. Those aren't church doors. Not like our last church.

"Okay, so we'll greet them outside before welcoming them in. Melanie, you lead the ladies to the nursery. Let them see you checking your boys in and then they'll do the same."

My father touches my shoulder and stares down at me. "Adam, I want you to stand here and greet the congregation. Understand?"

"Yes, Dad," I reply proudly with a nod. I'm not nervous. I've been the greeter hundreds of times at our last church. I can do this in my sleep. But as one of his employees hands me a box of programs, I stare at them, confused.

This is a lot more than we'll need.

For the next few minutes, everyone seems to be running around frantically. One of the men my dad has worked with a long time, Mark, talks with him in private near the door. With nothing better to do, I eavesdrop on their conversation.

"Make sure to talk about that new club that opened down the street. We need to promote family values."

My father nods while reading the paper Mark gave him. "Yes, yes. House of sin...desecration of our good city. This is great."

"Encourage tidings for this mission. As a community, we can have that club closed down," Mark replies.

"Their donations would fund the legal team we need to pass this bill through legislation," my father says.

"Perfect," Mark says, clapping him on the shoulder.

I turn toward my mother, who's busy fixing Caleb's tie. "Mom..."

She glances up at me.

"What's Dad talking about?" I ask. "What club are they trying to take down?"

When she looks in their direction, I notice the way her features stiffen like she's annoyed. "None of your concern, Adam. Don't worry about it, love."

A moment later, my father rejoins us, but Mark stays on the

sidelines. And when the assistants finally open the doors, my family is all standing together like we're posing for a Christmas card, smiling and waving.

When my eyes adjust to see the crowd waiting out front, my smile fades and my eyes widen. This is a lot bigger than the congregation we had at our last church.

My dad steps out first, waving at everyone with a big, proud smile. Once their cheers and applause have faded, he makes a little speech while I stare in surprise at everyone waiting to come in. Dad had been getting more and more popular at our last church, but I had no idea it was like this. Is this from that book he wrote?

The next thing I know, he cuts the ribbon and then the congregation is all rushing in. They smile at me, thank me, and take their programs one by one. Then Dad positions himself at my side, placing a heavy hand on my shoulder as he helps me pass out programs.

We do that together, and when he glances at me during the chaos of it all, he smiles, and it feels so good because he never looks at me like that.

The crowd of people slows down, and during a quieter moment, he squeezes my shoulder. He's happy, and I wish he could be like this forever.

And I don't know why, but I want to show him I'm old enough now. I'm not a kid anymore and he can include me in things that he doesn't include the younger boys in. "So, what were you and Mark talking about?" I ask.

He responds with a confused expression, so I continue.

"Some club you want to shut down."

His jaw clenches as he inhales through his flared nostrils. I'm nearly as tall as him now, so when he turns me toward him, I can look directly into his eyes. "There are people in this world who threaten the values we hold close, Adam. Temptation our community shouldn't be exposed to. It's our job to protect these good people, Adam. It's our job to protect their souls. Do you understand?"

Silently, I nod.

Then he glances around the giant entryway of this new church. "This will all be yours someday, Adam. You want that, don't you?"

Do I? This wouldn't be so bad. I could get used to all of this attention. Plus, the people are all so nice.

"Yeah, I would."

"Good," he replies, squeezing my shoulder again. "Then, just follow my lead."

In that moment, with my father by my side, I feel so much pride and hope that I never want a single thing to change. It's like the first day of my brand-new life because now I have a purpose. Together with my father, we will save this city. We'll save their souls and make the world a better place.

My father is a good man, and what we're doing is good, *really* good.

For the first time in my life, I feel like a hero.

# APRIL
## THE SON

# ONE

ADAM

The bell chimes over the door of Sal's Diner as I pull it open, immediately welcomed by the scent of frying bacon and coffee. The place is packed, and I let out a grumble as I squeeze through the horde of patrons to reach the hostess stand.

The young woman behind the booth greets me with wide eyes and a flirtatious smile.

"Mr. Goode," she chimes happily as she picks up a menu.

"Good morning, Veronica," I reply with a grin.

She blushes as her gaze lingers on my face for a moment too long, clearly chuffed by the fact that I remembered her name. Then, she spins toward the bar, and her expression falls when she notices that every single stool is occupied, including the one on the corner that I always take.

"I'm...sorry," she stammers, but I hold up a hand to stop her.

"It's okay, Veronica. I can wait."

"I'm really sorry," she repeats, looking apologetic, but I shake my head at her as I quietly ease into the corner of the crowded waiting area, pulling out my phone in hopes that it will hide my face enough to not be noticed here.

Apparently, Sal's has picked up in popularity over the last few months. It doesn't help that Austin is filled to the brim with trendy brunch spots—it would appear that greasy spoon diners are back in because every hipster tourist or college kid within a thirty-mile radius has started packing in the tiny restaurant each weekend.

*My* regular Saturday morning diner.

The only saving grace is that most hipster tourists and college kids don't know who I am. Unless their parents tuned into my father's Sunday morning program, they don't know Adam Goode from Adam Levine.

And my Saturday morning breakfast is the only time I like it that way.

Any other day or time, I'd be happy to smile for selfies or sign their King James Versions, but this is *my* time. This is when I get my writing done, where I can really focus and create my best sermons. I usually watch recordings of old sermons on my phone before digging into writing my own.

I have my own office at the church, but I prefer working elsewhere. When I'm here, surrounded by the white noise chatter of the breakfast patrons, I feel as if I can really tap into something deeper.

Someday I might not have this option. I'll be too busy running the church instead of just writing sermons for it.

Eventually, it will be me at that pulpit on Sunday mornings. But for now, it's still him.

So, until then...waffles and coffee.

"Just one?" a warm voice chirps from the hostess stand, and I glance up from my phone to see a mess of pink waves on a petite frame standing near the front. "It'll be about thirty to forty-five minutes."

The woman's shoulders sag as the look of defeat washes over her entire stance. "Seriously? I just got off the late shift and I'm famished. Can I put in an order to go?"

The girl grimaces. "It'll probably take that long to fill the order, to be honest."

"Fuck my life," the woman groans.

My eyes subtly rake over her body, from her brightly colored hair down to her black boots. She's not wearing much, exposing her belly, back, and limbs all covered in ink. Various tattoos are stamped across her body like someone was bored in class and spent their time doodling on her sun-kissed skin.

The black crop top she's in stops somewhere along the middle of her back, and those blue jean cutoffs leave a gap in the high waistline like she bought a size too big.

Wincing, I curse myself for staring at the woman's ass like some perverted gawker. Biting my bottom lip, I turn my attention back to my phone. I'm watching the broadcast from last year, a sermon about morality playing in the AirPod stuffed in my left ear.

A blur of pink enters my periphery as the tattooed girl takes a seat on the bench next to me. I glance her way, shooting her a polite smile before staring back at my phone.

The girl lets out a sigh, followed by a soft moan as she rubs her forehead. I catch sight of her bloodred nail polish and the tiny tattooed symbols on each of her delicate, long fingers.

"Mr. Goode," the hostess calls sweetly from the stand. My eyes widen as I glance around to see who might have heard her call me by my last name, but the only ones who pause are an elderly couple sitting on the opposite bench.

I smile at them before moving to the front.

"Your seat is ready," the hostess says, clutching the menu to her chest. But as she steps toward the empty seat, waiting for me to follow her, my feet don't move. There's a right and a wrong in this scenario, and even as my stomach growls with hunger, I know what I have to do.

With an internal grimace, I turn back toward the pink-haired girl on the bench. Her eyes are closed as her head rests against her fist, but I step back toward her, tapping her gently on the arm to wake her.

As her eyes pop open, she stares at me in shock.

"Take my seat," I say with a huff.

"What?"

"A seat at the bar just came open. Take it."

"Seriously?" she asks, scrutinizing me like this is some sort of scam.

"Yes, seriously." I step back and hold out a hand, showing her the waiting hostess, whose smile has turned tense.

The pink-haired girl stands up hesitantly before moving toward the empty stool. "Thank you," she calls back, her eyes meeting mine for a brief second before she sits down and turns her attention to the menu.

I take my place back in the corner, watching my phone as crowds of people come and go in front of me.

When the sermon comes to an end, the app immediately loads the next video. Our services are nationally televised and recorded, available to the whole country on nearly any streaming platform they prefer—satellite radio, TV broadcast, or online. For all I know, people in this very restaurant are tuning in to their own personal AirPod sermons.

The theme of this week is virtue, and I need inspiration from sermons in the past because, at the moment, nothing clever is coming to me. But some of these old speeches of his were written by his staff, and they lack appeal. They're dull. That's why my father passed the sermon writing baton over to me. He says I phrase it all differently and in a way everyone can understand. He's a bit old-fashioned, so he grew up on flowery prose and, frankly, boring-as-hell metaphors. But he wants to relate Leviticus to the Dallas Cowboys' last big trade, and that's what I'm here for.

"Mr. Goode," a sweet voice calls, and I look up to find the hostess grinning at me. "Another seat at the bar is open."

I smile at her, my stomach growling with the promise of hash browns and bacon, thankful that my wait wasn't too much longer. Quickly following behind, my grin turns to a frown when

I realize the empty barstool is just to the left of Miss Pink Hair herself.

Taking the seat next to her, I glance her way just as she looks up at me. There's a nearly empty plate in front of her and a half-filled cup of coffee. There's also more color to her cheeks now and a much livelier expression.

"Oh my god, it's you," she proclaims as I take my seat. With a cordial grin on my face, I nod to her. I'm a little surprised she recognized me, if I'm being honest. She doesn't seem like the kind to—

"You're the one who gave me your seat. You are literally a fucking lifesaver. I was so hungry, I thought I was going to die."

I look downward, momentarily humbled as I realize she recognizes me as the Good Samaritan who gave up his seat...and not the son of Austin's most prominent pastor.

"You're feeling better, then?" I ask, without looking at her. My eyes are still glued to my phone while I silently pray that she's not the kind of person to indulge in too much small talk just because I was polite.

"Much. The biscuits and gravy here are good enough to bring someone back from the dead."

"I agree. It was my pleasure. I'm glad you had a good breakfast."

As I glance toward her, getting a good look at her up close, I notice she has her left nostril pierced, not once, but twice. And a gold hoop hanging from the middle of her nose as well. Then there's another on the right side of her bottom lip. It's a pity, really. She has a very nice nose.

And very nice lips. And very nice piercing blue eyes.

Honestly, it's a perfect face overall—even with that tiny star tattoo hovering just over her cheekbone.

It's wrong of me to be so judgmental, but if the girl wasn't so covered by ink and metal, I might have noticed sooner just how beautiful she is.

The waitress comes by and takes my order of coffee and the

waffle breakfast with a side of hash browns. Then I turn my attention back to my phone and try to focus on the sermon, looking for inspiration, but I keep getting distracted.

At first, I blame it on the lively conversation happening between the couple to my left, but in reality, it's her every movement next to me on my right. There's something about those nimble fingers and pierced face and exposed midsection that makes it nearly impossible to focus.

So I give up and place my phone on the counter, pulling the AirPod from my ear. Instead, I focus on pouring four half-and-half packets into my coffee. Then I let my eyes wander over to the red nails drumming on the counter as she finishes her breakfast. When she picks up the ketchup bottle from the metal stand on the counter, I watch in horror as she douses her scrambled eggs with it.

I let out a stifled laugh.

Her pink hair flips as she turns toward me. "Are you laughing at my breakfast?" There's a hint of playfulness in her tone, such that it makes me feel comfortable with a little light teasing.

"I wouldn't have given my seat to you if I knew you were going to desecrate those eggs."

She laughs around a mouthful, covering her pretty pink lips with her fingers as she aims her humor-filled eyes at me. "Don't knock it till you've tried it," she mumbles, chasing down her bite with a sip of coffee.

"I'm fine, thanks."

With a shake of her head, her expression fills with mischief. When our eyes meet for a moment, I realize she might take this for flirting.

When was the last time I really flirted with someone? The last few dates I've had were all awkward arrangements set up by friends or my mother. It's possible that in the last five to ten years, I have completely lost my game.

Not that I should be flirting with this girl. There is zero interest on my part, and even if there was, I could only imagine my mother's face if I brought home someone like this. I remember what happened when Caleb introduced his wife to my mother and had to break it to her that she was a Lutheran.

The next thing I know, Pink Hair is grabbing my napkin-wrapped fork and pulling it out from the sticky paper holding it together.

"I'm telling you. You're missing out."

Then, to my utter shock, she stabs the fork into the untouched portion of her plate and holds it out to me. I could make a big deal about germs and her being a complete stranger and how inappropriate this is, but I'm too shocked and entertained to say no. Those sweet, nimble fingers of hers, holding the fork out to me, are too compelling for me to refuse.

So I lean forward and close my mouth around the repulsive bite of sweet ketchup-covered eggs. And it truly is repulsive, but the way she's watching me is making it impossible to disappoint her. So I dab my napkin on the corner of my pursed lips and nod.

"Not bad."

She sets the fork down with a scoff. "Not bad? You're crazy. It's delicious."

Just then, the waitress sets down my two plates—one piled high with waffles and three dollops of butter on top and the other covered in steaming hash browns.

As she refills both of our coffee cups, there's an awkward silence between me and the girl to my right. When the waitress leaves, Pink Hair turns toward me. "I'm Sage," she says.

"Adam," I reply, putting out my hand. She slides her long, tattooed fingers around mine and shakes it with a firm squeeze.

"Nice to meet you, Adam. Thanks again for giving me your seat."

"Thanks for sharing your breakfast with me." I laugh, nodding toward her eggs.

She blushes, covering her cheeks and looking away from me.

I hate to admit it, but it's actually a little adorable.

"I can't believe I did that. I worked all night, so sometimes when I'm sleep deprived, I might as well be drunk. I'm sorry."

A laugh spills from my chest. "Don't apologize. I should be thanking you for enlightening me about the magic that is ketchup-covered eggs."

She knocks my shoulder with her own. "Stop it."

"Seriously, don't be embarrassed. I normally sit here alone and eat my breakfast. No one has ever fed me at the bar before."

This time when she laughs, it's a feminine giggle, and I get lost in the wrinkles her cheeks make when she smiles so brightly. Her elbow is propped on the bar and she rests her head on her palm, turning toward me and letting her gaze settle on my face as I cover my waffles with syrup.

"You're going to watch me eat now?"

"It's either that or fall asleep?"

"Well then, by all means." With a smile, I lift a hefty bite to my mouth and hum as the sugary sweet syrup hits my taste buds. "Want a bite?" I mumble with my mouth full.

She snickers again.

After a sip of coffee, I start cutting up another bite and glance toward her as I ask, "So, what do you do? What kind of work keeps you up all night?"

"I work at a nightclub. It usually closes at four, but last night was busy, so we stayed open. Which meant I couldn't leave until almost seven. My boyfriend stayed behind to close up."

I swallow down more coffee and a stinging sense of disappointment.

"You need some rest," I reply because I suddenly don't know what else to say. I feel blindsided by this news of a boyfriend, which is ridiculous. This girl is not my type—boyfriend or not.

"No kidding, but the real kicker is that I know I won't be able to fall asleep. I hate sleeping during the day."

"Then I don't think the night shift is wise for you."

With a huff, she shrugs. "I know. It's ridiculous." Almost like a sign from God himself, she lets out a yawn, covering her mouth with her elbow.

"So, tell me about this club of yours. Is it fun?"

A throaty-sounding laugh nearly makes her choke on her coffee. I'm not even sure why I asked that. I have a suspicion I'm subconsciously trying to prolong her stay, even though it's clear she should pay her tab and go home to sleep.

"It's not really your type," she replies, blotting her face with her napkin.

My head snaps toward her after taking a bite of my potatoes. "What's that supposed to mean?"

Her fingers pinch at her bottom lip as she stares at me with a devious smile. "I mean...look at you. You're not a club kind of guy. When was the last time you went to one?"

I feign offense. "Are you calling me old?"

"Not at all," she replies. "I'm calling you...conservative."

"Still offended," I reply with a laugh.

"This club is...not for conservatives."

"Is it a strip club?" I whisper, leaning so close I can smell the flowery scent in her hair.

"No," she whispers, leaning even closer.

I notice that as we both pull apart, we do so slowly, almost begrudgingly. Is it just me? She's really flirting with me, isn't she? Or maybe she's like this with everyone? Bold of me to assume this beautiful and clearly beguiling woman has any interest in me just because she smiles at me.

And ridiculous of me to assume it matters. She might as well be a house cat with how compatible we are.

After the next couple of bites of my breakfast, I notice her hesitating. She's biting her bottom lip and staring at her hands that are encased around the tiny ceramic diner mug. I'm about to ask what she's thinking about when she reaches into her back pocket and produces a black card.

The script on the front is shiny and pink, naturally, as are the edges and logo on the back.

And I let out a laugh as I read the name of the club.

*Pink.*

Ironic.

There's not much more information aside from the website, address, and phone number.

"You should...check it out sometime."

"I will," I reply as I slip the card into my back pocket.

Sage yawns again, so I flag down the waitress. When she approaches, I promptly inform her that I'll be paying my pink-haired friend's tab.

"You don't have to do that," she argues.

"Go home. Get some sleep, Sage."

"Well, aren't you just my knight in shining armor today?" she replies sweetly.

"More like khaki slacks. Now go."

She turns on the barstool so her knees are practically pressed against the side of my thigh. She hesitates before leaving. I'm about to insist she go again when her hand lands softly on my forearm. "Maybe next Saturday, I'll get off late again and we can share another breakfast."

My focus is lost on the enigmatic crystal-blue color of her eyes. And for a moment, I don't see the pink hair or tattoos or piercings. I see a mystery wrapped in beauty, and I start to wonder what might be underneath.

"Maybe..." I reply softly with my gaze on her face.

"Bye, Adam." With that, her hand leaves 1 ; arm, and I feel a cool, empty void where it once was.

"Bye, Sage."

I watch her leave through the front door and disappear down the street before turning back to my half-eaten breakfast, suddenly less interested in waffles and syrup.

For a while, I just sit on the stool and relive every moment of our conversation, committing her scent and smile to memory since I know it's the most I'm going to get. It's hard to decide if I'm really so attracted to her or if she's just the most interesting person I've ever truly met.

Either way, she steals every thought in my head for the rest of my morning—for reasons even I can't understand.

When I finally pick up my phone again, I see the sermon I was watching is now over.

# TWO

## SAGE

"Morning, Gladys," I call as I cross the soap-scented Laundromat toward the door that leads to my apartment in the back. The sixty-nine-year-old owner is sitting behind the tall counter, watching reruns of *Days of our Lives* on one of the last working TVs hanging from the ceiling.

"Morning, Sage," she replies without looking away from the soap opera. "Busy night?"

I pull a can of Mountain Dew from the fridge in the back. Slumping against one of the industrial machines, I crack it open as I roll my eyes. "So fucking busy. We didn't close until seven."

She glances down at her watch. "It's past nine. Where have you been?"

"Stopped for breakfast at Sal's. Met a cute guy who bought me biscuits and gravy."

She glares at me over her glasses. "Good. Dump that loser, Brett, and date this guy. I bet he wants to do more with your biscuits than just pay for them."

I chuckle over my soda. "Eh, he's not my type."

"Why? Does he own a car and pay his rent on time?"

I scoff and act wounded, grabbing my chest like she's stabbed me. "That hurt." Then I stand upright and point at the TV. "Spoiler. It's not Stefano's baby. I've already seen this episode."

"You little bitch," she snaps, throwing a tiny box of detergent at me as I run toward the exit in the back while laughing. "Love you, Gladys!" I call before disappearing through the heavy door and dashing up the dirty cement stairwell toward my apartment.

She's not really mad at me, and if she is, she'll forgive me by closing time. I moved into the apartment above Gladys ten years ago, and she's been like a mother to me ever since. Okay, maybe "mother" isn't the right word. More like...weed-smoking, boyfriend-hating, crass, vulgar, brutally honest, and eccentric aunt. Either way, she's all I've got for family, and I'd probably die without her.

When I reach my apartment, I only have to push my key in the lock before I hear tiny claws clicking excitedly against the wood floors. As I push open the door, Roscoe starts yipping like mad. I quickly lift the six-pound, three-legged chihuahua into my arms and kiss the side of his head.

"Hey, little guy. Did you have a nice night with Auntie Gladys?"

He licks the side of my face while I drop the keys in the bowl on the entryway table. As soon as I see the cozy sofa in my living room, a warm haze of red and purple cascading over the room through the patchwork curtains, it suddenly hits me how sleepy I am. Before I can collapse and sleep for the next eight hours, I take Roscoe out through the fire escape and down to the fenced-in area behind the building. We had a handyman put the small fence back here with an eight-by-eight patch of turf and a bowl of water for Roscoe to use since we don't have a yard.

He doesn't mind it, especially since it was this exact alleyway that I found him in two years ago. I caught Gladys feeding him her leftovers, and after that, he never left. We share custody, which works out since she and I work opposite shifts.

While he does his thing on the turf, I sit down on the metal stairs and pull out my phone. Immediately I think of Adam, remembering how good he smelled and how soft his arm was under my hand when I touched him. He was simply flawless. With nearly black hair, perfectly combed in place, and a neatly cropped beard, he reminded me of something out of a J.Crew catalog. I'd love to grunge him up a bit. I bet he gets even hotter the dirtier he gets.

Worry and regret land hard in my gut like a stone, weighing heavily on my conscience. Is that the kind of guy I should be trying to settle down with? Gladys was right. By the looks of him, he's got a lot more going for him than Brett. If I'm being honest with myself, I know Brett is never going to marry me. We've been dating for three years and we haven't even moved in with each other. Or talked about it. I'm twenty-seven years old. Not to say I'm in a rush to settle down, but the longer I wait, the smaller that dating pool is going to get.

What would my life even look like with a guy like that, though? My nightlife would be traded for what...the suburbs? Regimented and routine monotony. Every day in bed by ten, sex once a week, if we're lucky, a few drinks on the weekends, and our only friends would be some boring married couples that live the same dull lives we do.

Well, when you put it that way...

No, thank you.

Roscoe yips at a passing man at the end of the alley, who instantly gives me the creeps, so I scoop the dog up and hurry back up the fire escape, locking my window behind me. Then, I fill Roscoe's dishes with kibble and water, patting him on the head before unlacing my boots and kicking them into the corner. While I walk into the living room, I unbutton my denim shorts and shimmy them down my legs, plopping down on my cozy sofa in nothing but my panties and loose-fitting crop top.

The moment my head hits the pillow, my body feels like lead. A heavy duvet is draped over the back of the couch and I pull it over me, snuggling up in the cool covers against my warm skin.

I *own* a bed—I just haven't slept in it in months. Or maybe it's been a year already. I'm not sure why, but there's something about dozing on my couch that feels more natural. Maybe it's my erratic sleep schedule or the fact that *going to bed* feels like such a proper, mature thing to do, whereas I generally crash where I land instead.

When I go to Brett's for the night, I sleep in his bed, but that's not often anymore. We see each other at the club all the time, which means that's usually where we have sex. So at the end of most nights, we go to our separate apartments, and that's that. I have Roscoe to take care of anyway, and I feel bad when I leave him with Gladys.

My phone buzzes on the coffee table, so I pick it up and see Brett's name on the screen.

> We did over twenty grand in liquor last night.

I roll my eyes as I read the message, my fingers flying to respond.

> Because Penny isn't limiting the patrons like she's supposed to.

The text bubbles pop up as he responds.

> Why would we limit them if this is our biggest moneymaker?

So much for sleep, I can practically feel my blood boiling.

> Because it's a sex club, Brett. Letting our patrons get drunk is a liability.

I already know his argument before his text pops up.

> They're adults, Sage. What they do is up to them. We have security so no one gets hurt.

> You need to lighten up.

I resist the urge to throw my phone through the window and down to the dirty alleyway below. All of Brett's decisions are motivated by money and profits. He doesn't do the research like I do. He doesn't care about safety or liabilities. He doesn't network with other club owners like I do.

It should be me running that club, but that's a fight for another day.

To him, it's just a club where people fuck and occasionally get kinky, but he has no respect for the safety or lifestyle of our patrons. It's for this reason that most of our patrons are disrespectful, horny assholes who think it's a brothel, not a sex club.

The only reason he forbids them from bringing their cell phones into the club is to keep them from posting incriminating evidence that would get us shut down. Every day, I battle with the impending doom that I'll be stuck going down with this ship, but I refuse.

It's a good thing my name is nowhere on the business, even though I *care* about Pink a hell of a lot more than he does.

> I'm going to sleep. It's your club. Do what you want.

Guilt assaults me as I toss the phone down with a huff. I hate fighting with him, especially about the club. I'm not an owner. I have no real influence. Technically, I'm an employee and not even one with authority.

But I *want* to be.

Same sob story, different day. I love Brett, but the dream I've been carrying of us running that club together is getting hazier by the day. I can either fight for our relationship, or I can fight for the club, but I can't have both.

What's sad is I'm not really sure which one I would choose.

My phone buzzes again, so I lift it to see the screen.

> Baby, don't be like that.

> You gotta trust me. I know what I'm doing.

My jaw clenches tight as I swallow down my resentment. It's not his fault that he doesn't hear just how condescending that sounds.

> I'm going to sleep.

I almost put the phone on the table before adding in a quick, *I love you.*

He responds quickly.

Love you, baby.

He does. I believe he does.

And maybe that's why I've stayed as long as I have. It's hard to leave someone who loves you, even though you know realistically it's not working. Love is stupid like that. It's like drinking poison because it tastes good.

Roscoe jumps up onto the couch, nuzzling himself into the space between the back of my knees and the couch. Then he rolls himself into a little ball like a tiny armadillo and lets out a disgruntled-sounding sigh.

With a laugh, I pet his head and try to force myself to stop thinking about Brett and the club.

Instead, I reminisce about breakfast, reliving the moment Adam smiled at me, really looking me in the eye and not at my tits or my ass. The way I felt being next to him. The way I'd feel if a guy like him liked a girl like me.

# THREE

## ADAM

My mother cooks once a week, naturally, on Sunday. Since my father has the house fully staffed with chefs and housekeepers, there is really no need. But my mother, bless her soul, complains that Sunday dinner doesn't taste the same when someone else makes it.

All this to say, my mother is old-fashioned.

And if my bitter, selfish brothers can offer her one thing in this life, the least they can do is show up for lasagna or chicken potpie once a week.

"Our Heavenly Father, bless this meal and the family at this table. We thank you for all these blessings and for the fortune to be together on this holy day. Amen." My father's voice takes on that deep, commanding preaching tone when he says grace—the same voice he uses in the church each week. But as soon as the blessing is done, he turns to my brother, Caleb, on his right and asks him to pass the sweet tea in a more casual and familiar inflection.

Growing up, I hated to hear my father preach. He didn't start until I was seven, and it felt so strange to me. Like watching your parents be anything other than your parents. His tone, pitch, and even the vocabulary he used when he was preaching all felt so...rehearsed.

With time, though, I grew to appreciate it. I learned to separate my father, the man, from my father, Truett Goode, the most famous pastor in all of Texas.

"The sermon was beautiful today, Adam," my mother mumbles quietly to me as she smears butter over her biscuit. "You're a wonderful writer."

"Thank you, Mom."

"I liked the part about the Cowboys," my brother, Lucas, adds.

I chuckle cynically as I glance sideways at him. "I thought you hated the Cowboys."

"Oh, I do, but I liked how you related their draft pick to the Rapture."

My muffled laughter draws the eyes of my family around the table. Across from me, Caleb furrows his brow as he mouths, "The Rapture?"

"You had to be there," I retort, at which Caleb rolls his eyes.

There are four of us boys, three at this table. The twins, Caleb and Lucas, are five years younger than me. And they both went their separate ways from the church as soon as their tuition was paid and they were officially on their own.

Caleb got married right out of college. A few years later, he and his wife, Briar, had a baby—Abigail. At only five and a half, she's easily the cutest kid this whole family has ever seen. With big brown eyes and perpetually tangled brown hair, she's never not smiling or somehow manipulating the rest of us to get whatever she wants.

My youngest brother, Isaac, hasn't been at this table in years. I quickly do the math in my head as I stare at his empty seat. Eight years. His absence stings, so I swallow down the memory and look away before the burn becomes noticeable.

As I reach across the table to retrieve a biscuit from the porcelain bowl, I'm suddenly reminded of the petite frame and bright smile of my unexpected breakfast companion last week.

To be honest, I've been thinking about her nearly every day since. Like a scent I picked up in the diner that's clung to my clothes, catching a whiff every time I move or inhale.

And it's surprisingly pleasant.

Such a strange woman, and yet, we seemed to get along so naturally. So much so that I wish we could have talked longer. I would have gladly sat next to her for the rest of the day, joking about the appropriate breakfast foods to cover with ketchup or whether I was *too conservative* for nightclubs.

Was this a sign that I needed to put myself out there more?

If she had been a more fitting match for me—and didn't have a boyfriend—would I have asked for her number? Invited her out on a date?

When was the last time I felt chemistry so potent? I've nearly forgotten how intoxicating it is. For one word to turn into an hour of conversation. And then a touch. And then a kiss. And then an explosion of ravenous hunger that lies dormant for too long.

I've been on enough dating apps to know you don't find that sort of spark on blind dates. It's more like lightning, and now I'm forced to wait and hope it strikes again—preferably with a more suitable match.

"Everything okay, sweetheart?" I glance up from the roasted chicken on my plate to see my mother watching me with concerned interest. A comforting smile stretches across my face.

"Of course, Mom. I'm good."

She looks pleased, her eyes wrinkling at the corners as she grins in return. My mother is an angel, sometimes too good for the rest of us. There's even a running joke in the family that the only truly pious one out of all of us is her—silent and sweet Melanie Goode.

My mother would rather sew her own mouth shut before ever daring to utter a negative word about anyone.

"Lucy Clayborn asked about you at the service this morning," she utters quickly before filling her mouth with mashed potatoes.

My smile is forced as I nod. "Oh? How is she?"

Naturally, waiting until her mouth is empty, she finally replies, "She's good. Such a beautiful girl. I can't believe she's not married yet."

*Subtle.*

"Well, she's running a business, Mom. I doubt she has time for dating."

"I know," she replies. "But a business is hardly a replacement for companionship and a family."

My brows rise as I consider that the last I heard, Lucy's cycle studio was expanding with three more locations and a crew of celebrity instructors. I'm willing to bet companionship is the last thing on Lucy's mind.

"I think she's always had a crush on you," my mother adds. I feel Lucas's eyes on my face and I shoot him a quick *help me* glance.

But when he only laughs to himself, offering me no lifeline out of this conversation, I toss him under the bus. "Luke's single."

Of course, this makes my mother uncomfortable, and I instantly regret it. She's not willing to set her church friend's daughter up with the least Christian son she has. Or at least that's what the elephant in the room is screaming.

"Oh, my sweet Luke is so handsome too," my mother says in a singsong voice as she turns to sweep his wavy brown hair out of his face. Then she brushes his cheek before leaning in and pressing a kiss to the spot.

His lips press together tightly to express his discomfort before quietly uttering, "Thanks, Ma."

"It would be so nice to see my boys settle down—especially you, Adam."

Why, in that moment, do I think of my new rose-haired friend? The thought of her at the table with us, striking up a conversation with my mother or Caleb's wife, Briar, is so ridiculous it nearly makes me laugh. Those tiny ripped shorts in our dining room. Tattoos and piercings at this table. They'd all think I lost my mind—especially the man at the head of the table.

I'm sure the conversation would be awkward and hilarious at the same time. She'd make my mother blush and my father scowl. Lucas and Caleb would be obsessed with her if only for the chaos she would wreak on our home. If Isaac were here, he'd adore her.

*Get out of your head, Adam.*

Maybe I should just take Lucy out. I bet dating a successful career woman would be easier anyway. No need to impress her. Things could be simple. Just going through the motions. Sex, intimacy, affection—all surface level, but that would be perfect. It wouldn't require much. It would tick all the necessary boxes.

My father would most certainly approve.

That's what I need—a safe, practical relationship, even if it doesn't sound all that exciting.

"Perhaps you could ask her to the charity dinner next month," my mother adds persistently, just as I take the last bite on my plate.

"I'll think about it," I reply, although I could very well just tell my mother to coordinate it. Like a little matchmaker, she'd have Lucy's mother on the phone in minutes and the whole thing would be meticulously orchestrated without an ounce of effort from me.

But I don't. Something holds me back.

I'm not exactly sure what. Maybe it's the energy required in dating. Or the fact that as beautiful as Lucy Clayborn is, I don't find myself particularly attracted to her. I haven't once reminisced about the shape of her lips or the playful cadence of her voice.

Perhaps what's really stopping me is the pink-foiled business card in my wallet—and the opportunity it represents.

# FOUR

## SAGE

"Your ass looks so fucking good in those shorts," Brett says as he steps into the office.

I'm bent over the desk, running the numbers on this month's expenses for the hundredth time, but they're not adding up and it's making me frustrated as hell.

Brett comes up behind me and grinds against my ass, but I hardly pay him any attention.

"Babe, where is this extra fifty grand coming from?"

He ignores my question and buries his nose in my hair.

"I told you we made a shit ton in liquor sales last night," he replies, mumbling into my neck. Warmth trickles down my spine as I feel him stiffening behind his zipper.

It's making my head foggy as I reply. "But I have the receipts for that. The sales are accounted for."

"You must be missing something then," he replies. His fingers dance along my ribs, and I giggle and squirm in response. He knows how ticklish I am, and he's teasing me on purpose.

"Brett," I whine, my attention wavering from the expense report to the way he's warming my body up.

"I need you, baby." His deep voice growls against my ear, and I quickly lose my strict resolve. Within seconds, I've lost track of the reports, and I'm letting him shimmy down my shorts. Then he thrusts in hard from behind me.

My fingers crinkle the papers on the desk as I hold on to the surface to give me leverage.

"I have the best girl in this whole fucking club. Look at you, princess. So fucking good for me."

He's always been talkative during sex, and I shut my eyes tight as he pounds into me, trying to focus on my own orgasm before he gets his.

I love his praise—I do. It's just...lost its allure.

Every time it's the same. *Princess. Best in the club.* I think it would turn me on more if I believed it...or heard it any other time than during sex.

I'm in my head too much, and before I know it, he's shuddering and moaning through his release and I'm left wishing for my own.

*Fuck.*

I hate when he does this. Revs me up just to let me down. I mean...it's not his fault. He doesn't know because I don't tell him. For a couple running a sex club together, our lack of communication in the bedroom should be a crime.

"Goddamn, princess. I can't fucking resist you." His mouth cascades down my spine before he pulls out and lets his cum drip between my legs. I reach for a handful of tissues on the desk and wipe myself clean before pulling up my underwear and shorts.

As he flops himself down in the chair in the corner of the room, I return my attention to the papers on the desk.

"As I was saying..." I reply with a playful smile. "There is an extra fifty grand in the account, and I have no record of it."

Brett is scrolling through his phone, and I feel myself starting to tense. I've learned over the years with him that if I approach things without too much criticism or condemnation, he's usually pretty receptive. But I can't ever direct blame or...accountability toward him.

"Baby..." I say, getting his attention.

He glances up from his phone with a sigh. "Yeah, what's up?"

*Inhale. Exhale. Smile.*

"The fifty thousand dollars. Any idea where it's from?"

When his expression tightens and I spot a hint of hesitation in his eyes, I know he's not telling me something. My smile fades and my shoulders square up.

"What is it?" I ask, feeling a knot of worry squeeze in my gut.

After a resounding huff, he tosses his phone down as he glares at me. "Don't be mad. But I didn't tell you because I knew you wouldn't like it."

I force myself to breathe.

"I took out a loan on the club," he says.

My face falls, and my voice takes on a low, harsh inflection. "What?"

He stands from his chair and crowds me toward the desk, taking my hands in his. "Relax, princess. I got this under control."

"You got a loan? From where? At what interest rate?"

He chuckles in response to my questions and my jaw clenches at the sound of his laughter.

"Come on, Sage," he replies sarcastically. "You think I went to the fucking bank? Like those assholes would give me a loan."

That's the part I was trying to ask but couldn't do so without sounding offensive. Brett has annihilated his credit from bad loans in the past. The only way we were able to pay off the lease on the club was with the money I got as a settlement when my dad died.

Did I have the good sense to get my name on the deed too, after I helped him pay it off?

No, of course not. I was young and in love...and incredibly stupid.

"So...who gave you a loan?"

He kisses my forehead and strokes my back. "It's confidential."

I nearly snap my head off my own shoulders pulling away from him. "Excuse me? Confidential? I thought we were a team."

"See, you're getting all pissy about this, like I knew you would. Why can't you let me handle things? You gotta trust me, Sage."

"Trust you? How can I trust you when you keep things from me? We're supposed to be a team, Brett." I let out a heavy sigh as I curl a wave of hair behind my ear. I can already feel the fact that this conversation is going nowhere. If I argue with him, he'll shut down. I've done it enough in the past to know. "What is the money for?" I ask as gently as I can.

A smile creeps across his face. "I'm hiring a consultant."

"A consultant?"

"Yeah, this chick who's worked with other clubs, and she knows exactly how to make ours even better."

All of the air is sucked out of the room, making it hard to drag in my next breath. My chest tightens, and my eyes water. "What?" The small word slips through my lips.

"This is what you wanted, princess. You wanted me to do something to make the club better and finally put real work into it, and that's what I'm doing."

I have to look away, running this through my head a few times to be sure I'm not overreacting or putting too many emotions where they don't need to be. But no matter how many times I think this through, there's no version of this news that doesn't stab me like a knife.

I turn back toward him with teary eyes. "You hired another *woman* to help you run this club, but you never, *ever* listen to me."

His jaw tightens. "She's a professional, Sage." His tone is flat, and the implication stings.

"But she doesn't know this club like I do. She hasn't helped you build it from nothing. She doesn't know the patrons and the city like I do." I'm getting irritable and heated.

Suddenly, the room feels so small and I have the burning need to cry. It's building in my throat like bullets, and I will not let him see me break. When he tries to place his hands on my arms, I shove him away.

"I need to get out of here," I snap, unable to keep the shaking out of my voice. When he lays a hand above my elbow to stop me, I turn back toward him, sending him a hateful, angry, *don't you dare* glare. Within seconds, he lets go.

He calls after me one more time just as I tear open the door to the office and rush out.

# FIVE

## ADAM

Lucy smiles politely at me over the table. With her long, blonde hair curled at the ends, so it flows in flawless waves over her shoulders, she really is stunningly beautiful. Tall, thin, fit, educated, and probably most importantly, Christian.

If only I felt as enamored by her as my mother is. All throughout dinner, I keep trying to think of things to ask her to keep the conversation moving as my mom watches from the head of the table like she's rating my skills on a first date—if that's what you would call this.

When I showed up for dinner tonight, I was surprised to see Lucy's Prius parked in the long drive. I silently cursed my sweet mother and her good-intentioned meddling. She's clearly trying to get me to invite Lucy to the charity event next month.

At the head of the table, my father watches without a word, and I take his silence as a sign that he's pleased with how this is going.

As Lucy talks, mostly about the big plans for her cycle studio expansion, I try to see myself with her. Our wedding photos would be flawless. Even our kids would be cute. My life would be picture perfect, as everything from the outside looking in would be exactly as it was meant to be.

But I don't see much when I try to imagine Lucy and me alone. Even if I picture her naked body under mine, it lacks something.

Although, to be fair, sex has always lacked something for me. I like it. It feels good and scratches the itch from time to time, but that's all it is—satisfying. And maybe that's all it's meant to be. For so long, I've been holding out for earth-shattering and mind-blowing, which would explain why I'm still single at thirty-seven.

"Adam, you should go to her studio," my mother says as she pours herself another glass of sweet tea.

"Are you calling me fat?" I ask with a laugh.

Lucy's reaction is a tense, humorless smile.

"Not that everyone who goes to your studio..."

"I was not calling you fat," my mother says, shooting me a stern glare.

"That's not what I meant," I reply, trying to overcorrect. "It was a bad joke."

"It's okay," Lucy replies with a smile.

Abigail sends me an awkward, wide-eyed expression that says, *Good job, idiot.* The rest of the family around the table sit in silence. Even they can tell how painful this date is.

It was an ambush date, really.

"When will we get to see you preach again?" Lucy asks, and I glance up quickly from my plate to stare at her in surprise. Then my eyes dash over to my father at the head of the table, sitting proudly with his hands clasped under his chin with a haughty smirk.

It's been months since I've stood at the pulpit and delivered a sermon of my own creation. Often for special occasions or because my father had prior engagements, but it was never spoken about as if it would become a regular occurrence. And it certainly was never requested.

I clear my throat. "I'm not sure," I reply to Lucy. "Hopefully, soon."

She nods, looking pleased.

"Adam is a wonderful preacher," my mother adds, and I scrutinize the woman across from me for her reaction.

When her eyes meet mine, there's a sparkle there, and a certain excitement inside me starts to grow. Suddenly, I can see so much more of our future. I see her standing next to me on Sunday. Before my sermons, we can greet the congregation together. Serving meals on Thanksgiving. Praying together.

It's promising, but it's still from the outside looking in.

"Pass the ketchup, please," Caleb says, knocking my shoulder, and as I glance over at the bottle sitting next to Lucy, it feels as if I've been abruptly snatched out of a fantasy. And for the thousandth time this week, I think about the pink hair and chipped black nail polish of the woman I shared a fifteen-minute meal with two weeks ago.

"Yes," I mutter, grabbing the bottle and practically tossing it at my brother.

As Lucy strikes up a conversation with Briar, I try to refocus my mind on the possibilities of the woman across from me, but it's like trying to start a fire with wet matches. Nothing comes.

Instead, I think about the way Sage fiddled with the ring in her lip. Or how her eyes twinkled in my direction as she passed me a bite of her breakfast.

Irritability swells behind every memory of her because it's been two weeks and I still go back to that moment when I know in my rational mind that it means nothing and I will literally never see her again.

And yet...the pipe-dream fantasies of her feel a little less perfect from the outside looking in but probably a bit more fun the other way around as well.

Looking up from my empty plate, I notice Lucy's is nearly empty too. She sets her fork down and places her napkin over what's left of her meatloaf, and I seize my chance.

"Would you like to go for a walk?" I ask.

With a tight smile that doesn't reach her eyes, she nods. "Sure."

"Go on, you two," my mother chirps excitedly as she jumps from her seat to clean up our plates. Then I lead Lucy toward the front door. Once we step out into the warm spring night air, she shoves her hands in the pockets of her long, cotton dress.

"It was nice of your mother to invite me to dinner," she says as we make our way down the long brick-paved drive.

"It probably should have been me. I'm sorry," I reply. My hand itches to touch her back or arm.

"Did you want me to come to dinner?" she asks, glancing up at me.

I clear my throat. "Of course I did."

When she doesn't respond, I notice the way she nods to herself, and I wish I knew what she was thinking. Why am I so bad at this? Breakfast with Pink Hair was so easy—

No. Stop it.

"The truth is," I reply, trying for sincerity, "I'm so busy I forget to have a personal life."

She chuckles quietly. "Same."

"But I really like you," I say, forcing the words out in hopes they feel truer when I speak them.

They don't.

Lucy stops and turns toward me. "I like you too, Adam..."

Her voice trails off and I sense a *but*.

My brow arches as I wait her out.

"But..." she says, finally, shuffling her feet and looking off into the distance instead of at me. "I don't really know you."

"Then have dinner with me again. We can get to know each other."

"Will we?" This conversation is taking a strange turn as if she knows something I don't. Something about me.

"Why wouldn't we?" I ask, feeling confused.

She places a hand on my arm and leans toward me. "You're a

nice guy, Adam. Dating me would make your mother very happy, which is exactly why I think you would do it."

When I laugh, she doesn't...which means that it isn't a joke.

"What is that supposed to mean?"

"When was the last time you did something just because you wanted to?" she asks, shooting me a challenging expression.

"I'm walking with you right now," I reply.

Leaning in, she adds, "Is that really what you want to be doing right now?"

Taking this as my opportunity, I let my hand drift over her lower back, tugging her closer before I press my lips to hers. They're soft and pliable, making me want to slide my tongue between them or bite the bottom one just to hear the sounds she'd make. But I hold back.

When I pull away, staring down with a soft smile, she lets out a heavy sigh. "That's what I mean. You're a really good guy, Adam. Maybe a little...too good."

Then she lifts to her tiptoes and presses her lips to my cheek.

"Please tell your mother thanks again from me."

Without another word, she continues the walk down to her car, waving back before climbing into the driver's seat and pulling away.

I watch her go, feeling blindsided and wondering how the hell someone can be *too good*.

✝

"I like her," my mother says as she dips her hands in soapy water to pull out a fork.

"She's really nice," I reply as I set the porcelain plate on the stack in the cupboard. I don't have the heart to tell my mother that Lucy left without exchanging numbers or plans to see me again.

Because I'm *too good*.

"Stay for a drink." My father lands a heavy slap on my back as I dry my hands on the dish towel hanging from my shoulder.

Another nostalgic ritual of my mother's is to clean up the kitchen after Sunday dinner—regardless of the fact that my father pays people to do it for them. I make it a point to dry the dishes every time.

My brothers never stick around this long.

"Go," my mother insists as she takes my towel. There's only a casserole dish left, so I concede.

As I follow my father into his office on the second floor of the house, he shuts the door behind us. He's pouring two glasses of whiskey before I even sit down.

Every time he invites me to his office after dinner like this, I'm anticipating the moment he finally breaks the news I've been waiting for—that he's stepping down.

And putting me in his place.

My father is great at what he does. He's a natural orator, charismatic and engaging. He's changing people's lives for the better.

But at the same time, he's sixty-nine years old. He's growing more and more out of touch with the next generation every day. Our demographic is comfortably fifty-plus, and if we don't make a move to capture those under fifty soon, our legacy will die with them.

I take the seat opposite his desk and let my gaze drift to the mess of papers scattered across the surface. But I'm not focusing on anything as he starts talking.

We riff back and forth for a while, laughing about something said this morning at church or whatever ridiculous joke one of my brothers made at dinner. My dad and I share a somewhat shallow relationship that never delves too deep into feelings or secrets. Not that I think he's hiding any. I'm sure as hell not. But I do pride myself on being the closest son he has, making him proud and doing what's right.

"Damn good sermon this morning, Adam. You work hard on them, and it shows."

"Thanks..." I reply, sensing the ominous *but* from my father's tone.

"You put your heart and soul in each one, and I'm so proud of the writer you've become."

A smug smile stretches across my face as I let his praise wash over me. If making my father proud was an art form, I'd have mastered it by now. Honestly, it feels more like a science than an art, something my brothers never cared much to attempt. I simply do exactly as I think he would, and it pays off.

And yet...I still get the feeling that there's a catch to his comments tonight.

"I like writing them. You know that. But I can't help but feel like there's something you have to criticize." I send him a crooked brow and half smile as I take a sip from my glass. "In short, cut the bullshit."

He laughs, leaning back in his chair. "You're writing them for you, not me."

My jaw tightens and my heart starts to race. Is he implying what I think he's implying?

"I'm writing them for the congregation," I reply proudly.

There's another low chuckle before he shakes his head. "Smart-ass."

"Well, what are you trying to say?"

"I'm trying to say that..." He swirls his whiskey in the glass before throwing it back and emptying the contents. Here it comes. If I'm reading the situation correctly, my father is about to offer me the position I've been waiting for.

"I think your talents would be better suited for your own ventures. We're giving the sermon-writing job back to Mark."

There's a beat of silence as I stare at him, waiting for the punch line of this joke.

My mouth goes dry, and suddenly, I realize my leg is bouncing. We sit in tense silence for a moment longer as his words fill the room like noxious gas.

"Your writing is so good, Adam, and I hate to see you waste that energy on sermons. Why don't you work on your book? Or write for the podcast again."

My knee is bouncing like crazy now. "Everyone loves the sermons. They relate to *real* people and *real* issues. No offense, but Mark's sermons are based on antiquated values."

"Mark's sermons are based on the scripture."

"And mine aren't?"

His brow furrows, but he stays silent.

He can't be serious. This can't be happening, but I bite back my surprise. I refuse to let my father see me falter.

A familiar feeling starts to resurface. Something I've buried deep for years—my whole life maybe. I'm sure it has a name. Resentment. Bitterness. Spite. But I've never voiced it, and I've never paid it much attention.

Not since *that* night.

He's my father. He provides for me and my brothers and has for years, but there's a price for the luxury of his love, and that price is my pride.

"I'm just thinking about what's best for the church, Adam," he says in a casual tone with complete disregard for how this actually makes me feel. "Use this as an opportunity to focus on more important aspects of your career. Did you really plan on writing my sermons for the rest of your life?"

As I let out my next breath, it sounds a bit too much like a disgruntled sigh, but I don't respond. He stands from his seat and goes back over to the whiskey bottle on the drink cart, he keeps talking, but I'm no longer listening.

Something dark and sinister stirs around in my brain.

I wish I could call him an asshole to his face. I think about what it might feel like to sock him square in the nose with my fist. I imagine how delightful it might feel to see him cry or beg for mercy.

These thoughts are vile, and I should feel ashamed.

I *should*, but I don't.

I just do what I've always done when these malicious thoughts and visions surface, I quickly shove them back down. I bury them right along with the memories that triggered them in the first place.

My unfocused gaze is on his desk, but I'm not reading a word typed on the mess of pages. Not until I spot the word *Deed*. My thoughts quiet, and my eyes focus.

Behind me, my father is still droning on and on, and I'm not catching a single line. Instead, I lean forward and try to read as much of the document as I can. The other papers on his desk seem to be things like sermon notes, press releases, printed articles, and proposals.

This page is an official document, crinkled at one edge with a coffee stain on the other. The most I can make out from here is an address I don't recognize and a name I've never seen before.

I peer behind me to see my dad with his back to me, so I move fast, pulling out my phone and snapping a quick pic of the document before he can turn back around.

"Are you listening to me, Adam?" His sharp tone rips my attention away from the paper.

"Yes, sir," I lie.

"Well, aren't you going to argue with me? Defend yourself, for fuck's sake."

My nostrils flare and another growling sigh emits from my chest. "It's late, Dad. I'm tired. I was up all night writing *your* sermon, remember?"

"Watch your tone, *boy*."

When I stand and face him, he lets out another chuckle of laughter, this time darker and more sarcastic than before. Sometimes, I wonder when he looks at me like that if my father even likes me.

Sometimes, I wonder if he hates me.

I don't wonder about my brothers. I *know* he doesn't like the twins.

And I know he hated Isaac.

*Hates not hated.*

But me... I've stood by his side since I was a child. I've doted and dedicated my life to his mentorship. Because I thought that's what he wanted. A son to carry on his legacy. It was the only way to earn his love.

Yet, as the two of us grow older, I can't help but wonder if my father would like his legacy to die with him. Too greedy to share the spotlight, even after his death.

And now this. The biggest slap in the face of my life.

"Get some rest, son," my father says, clapping that heavy hand on my shoulder again. The look on his face is smug enough to punch, but I know that's not possible. So I punch him in my head —hard enough to knock him out.

Then I smile like the good son I am and walk out the door.

# Six

## ADAM

The radio is turned down and the GPS is guiding me through the dark city streets as I grow closer and closer to my destination. The address on that property title is now stored safely in my phone, and I'm too damn curious to let it go. There's something oddly familiar about it, but what's really drawing me to see it for myself is the fact that my father doesn't own any properties outside of the church and his house.

So why, all of a sudden, is he in possession of a deed for some downtown warehouse? And why wouldn't he tell me about it? He usually tells me about all of his business dealings—more so to boast, I'm sure. On occasion, he'll assign me tasks, like organizing a book signing or a public appearance at a soup kitchen.

But keeping me entirely in the dark on whatever this is only feeds into the bitterness I'm already feeling toward him.

My hand squeezes the steering wheel as I replay the events in his office tonight. That smug look on his face when he reassigned the sermon writing to Mark. The way he brushed off my loyalty to him and the church. Because, deep down, I know my father doesn't care about any of it. Not the congregation. Not God. Not his family.

The only thing he cares about is *himself*.

My brothers know that. They picked that up a lot faster than I did, which is why they jumped ship years ago.

Not me. I spent my entire adulthood living up to his standards. While my brothers went to parties and wasted their years away having promiscuous sex and discovering themselves, I was at home writing his sermons and patting myself on the back for being the *good* son.

Did he ever really care? My career and my future mean nothing to him. The only time he ever truly valued having me around was when I made him look good. During the press release of my book, *Footsteps*, he stood by my side, not as support to me, but as publicity for *himself*. He congratulated me when *his* following increased, not when my book, a memoir about growing up as the son of a preacher, hit the best seller's list.

This downtown district is quiet, but as I get closer to my destination, the buzz of people on the streets intensifies. A brightly lit taco truck parked on the side garners a line, and I peer out my window to check out the people standing there. Most of them are dressed in the sort of fashion you'd expect for a night at the club—leather and skin.

There's a chain-link parking lot on the right, and I pull in, backing into a spot as the GPS informs me that I've arrived at my destination. I'm facing a black-brick warehouse on the corner that appears to be some sort of nightclub, judging by the young people milling about on the sidewalk outside.

Another car pulls into the spot across from me, and a couple emerges from the four-door sedan. To my surprise, it's not a pair of twentysomethings but a man and woman who look to be in their thirties. They're not scantily clad either. If anything, they almost look dressed more appropriately for church than a club.

My features tighten in confusion as they walk hand in hand toward the building. The man pulls open the black metal door, ushering his lady through, and they disappear together into the dark abyss of the warehouse.

Why on earth does my father hold the title for a place in the city?

As people come and go from the building, a neon sign above the door catches my eye. I hadn't seen it until now, but the word *Pink* glows against the black brick.

The hairs rise on the back of my neck. In a rush, I fumble for the card still sitting in my wallet. As I pull it out, I suddenly realize why the address sounded familiar. I read it on this very card two weeks ago.

My mind scrambles to make sense of this.

Sage works at this club.

And...*my father* holds the deed?

Is this some ridiculous coincidence?

I pull my phone out of my pocket, and with shaking fingers, I google the name of the club. My head swirls with confusion and disbelief as I stare at the search results.

*Pink is a premier sex club located in Austin, Texas.*

My heart is hammering in my chest.

What...the fuck?

Why on earth does my father, the most prominent pastor in Austin, hold the deed to a sex club? What could he possibly gain from this?

This must be part of his plan to have it shut down. For as long as I can remember, my father's main objective was to clean up the city of any clubs like this. He's had two shut down since he started his church. But I've never known him to take this route...to own it first.

Normally, he'd preach about them in his sermons. Uncover scandals and abuse taking place inside. He has connections in the city who would help him.

So, this just doesn't make sense. There's no way he'd tie himself to a place like this.

My fingers tighten around my phone. Why didn't that asshole

tell me about this? He didn't include me in whatever the hell his plan is here, and that pisses me off more than anything.

Just knowing he has anything to do with Sage only throws fuel on the fire. She and I had a connection. Sure, she's just a stranger, but we had a moment, and it's all gone to shit now that I know her club is *this*.

Before I know what I'm doing, I tear open the car door and march toward the club. I feel the eyes of some of those lingering in groups, seemingly either waiting for rides or socializing. No one stops me as I reach for the door—not that I really expected them to. Doing my best to keep my cool, I pull open the door and enter the dimly lit lobby.

The first thing I notice about the inside of this club is that it's not nearly as loud as I expected and not nearly as dark. There's a hostess stand and two young women chitchatting. When one of them looks up and notices me walking in, she simply holds out her hand, looking mildly annoyed by my presence.

I stare at her open hand in confusion. Does she want to see my ID? Is this for real?

"I need your phone," she snaps in annoyance.

"My phone?"

She huffs out a sigh and reluctantly turns her body toward me. "Phones aren't allowed inside the club. Are you a member?"

"No, I'm not a member," I reply through clenched teeth.

Her eyes rake slowly over my body, and it's at this moment that I tense out of fear that she'll recognize me. The last thing I need is to be seen in a sex club but at the same time...I'm fuming and don't give a shit about my reputation. In fact, at this moment, I'd like to burn it all to hell.

"It's a fifty-dollar entrance fee, then. And I need your phone."

My brow furrows. I pull out my phone and wallet, setting the device on the counter and fishing out a fifty. As I hand it to her, she starts reciting something that sounds like rules, but she talks so fast and mumbles, so I barely make out what she's saying.

I definitely catch a few alarming words—consensual, security, and...*condoms*?

What the fuck am I walking into?

"Thanks," I mutter when she finishes, sliding my wallet back into my pocket. I watch as she puts my phone in a drawer with a pile of others. *Unbelievable.*

As I turn the corner into the main room of the club, my sense of discomfort grows. Music from the giant speakers thumps louder, like a heartbeat, pounding in time with my own.

I survey the darkened atmosphere, taking in the numerous tables and booths that are situated around the bar. There is a random doorway in the rear and a hallway off to the right. The second floor is draped with mirrors, which I assume are transparent from the other side.

And as I catch movement in the booth on the far end of the room—movement that looks too much like a blow job to *not* be a blow job, my stomach turns with anxiety.

I'm in a sex club.

By all reasoning, I should turn around and walk out right now. If I am spotted here, there'll be hell to pay—literally. But I'm too fired up. Still so angry from the conversation with my father earlier and now this. Something inside me aches to rebel, and it's something I've never felt before.

So with that, I head toward the bar.

Finding an empty barstool with a view of the large room, I take a seat and wait patiently for the busy bartender to notice me. As soon as we make eye contact, she gives me an expectant expression, and I quickly blurt out my order for a Tullamore Dew on the rocks. After she passes me my drink, I pass her my credit card and inform her to keep my tab open.

My eyes focus on the room, and I think again about Pink Hair. A feeling of disappointment settles in my chest. The chasm that divides my world from hers just grew to the size of the moon. We might as well be on two different planets at this point.

The first glass of whiskey goes down easily. It's only fifteen minutes before I order a second. The entire time my mind is in a vicious, angry cycle, going round and round from surprise to anger to wanting to do something about it and round again.

To my surprise, the bartender lets me get piss drunk, and the entire time I'm at the bar, watching people around me in the dark space nearly fuck each other in all corners of the room, I don't spot Pink Hair.

What would I even say to her if I did see her? I just want to understand.

My head is heavy, and the voices and music in the room blur in my inebriated brain.

I'm sulking over my whiskey when a flash of pink catches my eye. I lift my head in a rush to see Sage rushing across the room, clearly on a mission. When she reaches someone sitting in a booth on the side, her body language changes. Her arms cross over her tiny frame and her chin tilts downward as she speaks.

It's not the girl full of sunshine and sparks that I met two weeks ago. She's angry, struggling, frustrated.

I know the feeling.

I can't hear what she's saying over the thump of the bass, but it's clear they're having somewhat of an argument. Her arm gestures toward the bar, and she gives an exasperated expression as his head falls back. Then he puts a hand out toward her, palm out like a stop sign, and her posture shrinks again.

The man stands, and I take in his appearance. Slim, black pants, tight black button-down, dark-blond hair to his ears, and tattoos creeping up his neck. When he puts his hands affectionately on Sage's arms, seemingly to settle her down, I look away.

That must be the boyfriend.

My jaw clenches as I glare at him from across the club. I've never met the guy and I already don't like him. He's talking down to her—literally and figuratively.

After Sage storms off, heading toward a narrow hallway on the side of the room, I make my move.

I'm drunk and in no position to be talking to anyone, especially with all the spite and anger mixed with whiskey in my bloodstream. I keep up my pace behind her, coming in hot as she reaches for a doorknob to a room I assume is an office.

Before she can close herself in, I'm there. My hand grips the door with a loud thud, and she lets out a gasp as her eyes turn up to stare at my face.

"What the—"

Before she can finish that sentence, I'm inside the office, slamming the door to close us in together.

# SEVEN

## SAGE

The door to the office slams, and suddenly, I'm standing in close proximity to none other than the man I had breakfast with two weeks ago. If today was trying to throw me for a loop, it succeeded.

The only thing stranger than him being here is the look of utter vitriol on his face.

My sense of danger is heightened, although I'm not entirely worried that this man is about to hurt me. The expression on his face doesn't match the gentleman who gave me his seat at breakfast, but I'm too stunned to properly voice just how confused I am.

"What the..." I stammer.

"Remember me?" he mutters, and I can tell immediately that he's drunk.

Fuck Brett for never listening to me about the alcohol limit. *This* is exactly why there needs to be one.

"Yes, of course. What are you doing here?" I back farther into the room, feeling my way toward the desk, where I have more access to things that could be used as a weapon—stapler, scissors, the rolling office chair.

"You own a sex club," he slurs.

Confusion tightens my features. "Yeah. So?"

"You bragged all morning about your little club. If I'd known then what kind of club it was—"

My face twists in disgust. Here I was, thinking this guy and I had a connection, and now he follows me to my club, only to ambush me and try to make me feel bad about it. I knew I shouldn't have given him the card.

"Oh, you wouldn't have bought my six-dollar breakfast? Get over yourself."

I try to move past him toward the door. This entire day is a fucking waste, and the sooner I can get out of here and wash it all away with cheap beer *alone* in my apartment, the better.

Why are all men so fucking disappointing?

"If I had known you were a pretentious prude, I wouldn't have given you that card in the first place," I snap at him.

"I thought you were different," he mutters, blocking my way.

My eyes narrow as I glare up at him. "Fuck. You."

Just as I reach the door, ready to throw it open and leave him in the office, he says two words that stop me in my tracks.

"Truett Goode."

My hand is on the knob, but I don't turn it. Instead, I spin around and stare at him in confusion.

"Does that name mean anything to you?" he asks.

I know who Truett is, of course. Everyone in Austin knows that self-righteous, hypocritical smug bastard.

As I stare at Adam, waiting for an explanation, he starts to look even more drunk than he was a moment ago when he cornered me in here.

"That's my father."

My jaw drops.

*Of fucking course it is.*

Then, because it's just all too ironic, I start laughing.

"What's so funny?" Adam asks, looking offended.

"Oh, nothing," I reply, crossing my arms over my chest.

"My father is going to have your club shut down," he adds, and I laugh again.

"Is that a warning...or a threat?" I ask with humor. Adam just grows more and more frustrated with my laughter. I find it hilarious to see how angry he is to learn that I own this club. Wait until he finds out his father is one of our most prestigious members.

"I'm serious," he barks. "He has the property title in his office. He already owns this building."

My laughter stops.

The blood drains from my face as I glare at him, humor replaced by fury. The entire conversation with my boyfriend earlier tonight replaying in my mind.

"That fucking asshole," I mutter to myself when I place the pieces together, realizing Brett levied the deed to the club with the *one fucking man* he should not get into business with.

What an idiot. Brett is powerless against him. I'm sure Truett had some trick of charm and allure he used to get Brett to hand him everything we've worked to build.

"I have to go—" I say, reaching for the door handle. As soon as I get out of this office, I'm going to find Brett and tell him what a shortsighted idiot he is. And then I'm leaving.

But my hand freezes when I notice Adam focusing on something near the desk. I let my words trail off as I follow his gaze. When I notice that the thing he's staring at is the security footage on the computer screen, my skin erupts with goose bumps.

Because the man on the screen is unmistakable. Truett Goode is currently in the club, having his way with a young woman in the VIP room.

I quickly glance back at Adam, my eyes wide and my skin burning hot with anticipation. He's glaring at the screen, and I'm surprised there's no actual smoke coming out of his ears.

"That motherfucker," he grits.

The next thing I know, he's pushing past me, marching out of the office and down the hall on a mission.

*Oh fuck. Oh fuck. Oh fuck.*

I'm chasing after Adam, calling his name, trying to get a grip on his arm to keep him from doing anything crazy, but there's no stopping him.

And the neon lights at the end of the hall loom like an omen—VIP.

*Fuck, fuck, fuck.*

He barrels past the spot where a security guard *should* be, slipping right through the black curtain that separates the general population from the exclusive section of the club. It's louder and darker in there, but there's no missing the man in the booth on the other side of the room with his face buried between the legs of the woman on the table.

Adam is practically running toward him, and I can do nothing but watch and wince as he grabs the man by the collar of his shirt and tosses him out of the booth. The woman screams and the VIP room erupts in chaos.

*Where the fuck are the bouncers?*

My hands cover my face as Adam drags his father off the floor by his shirt and rears back his fist. There's a look of such hatred and anger on Adam's face as he hesitates with his arm cocked and ready to fly.

But he never sends his fist coursing toward his father's face. Instead, he stares at him with raw emotion and pain etched into his features. It's almost like he's frozen in place, some sort of internal voice stopping him from doing what he so clearly wants to.

"You..."

His words hang in the air, uttered through an expression of pure hatred.

Finally, *finally*, the six-foot-three bouncer grabs Adam by the arm and hauls him away from Truett. I turn to find Brett and two other bouncers rushing into the room.

"What the fuck is going on?" Brett snaps with his angry eyes on me.

"Well, it looks like the new owner of our club was about to get his ass kicked."

Brett's expression grows tenser.

"What the hell is wrong with you?" Truett growls as he uses the edge of the table to help him get up to his feet, clearly struggling to rise. "You ungrateful little shit."

"How could you do this?" Adam yells in anger. "To us. To *Mom!*"

Truett only laughs as he fixes his suit. "You've got a lot to learn, son."

"Son?" I hear Brett gasp.

"How could you do this?" Adam says, still held tightly in the bouncer's grip. "You were supposed to take it down. You made a promise to the people."

"And that's why you're going to keep your mouth shut about it. What the people don't know won't hurt them. They want a *good* preacher, but what I do in my private life doesn't really matter so long as they have someone who *looks* like a good man. Because if they like me, they must not be so bad."

Adam struggles against the bouncer's grip on his arms. I wince again as his expression contorts from anger to anguish, the pain evident in his features. He looks like his entire world is collapsing, and I'm starting to think it is.

"Hold him," Truett grunts.

The air is sucked from my lungs as I step closer, but Brett's hand on my arm stops me.

*What is happening?*

The bouncer squeezes Adam's arms even tighter behind his back and my stomach drops.

"I'm your father, so it's my job to teach you a lesson. And your first lesson is a little humility because you've frightened that sweet girl and you've embarrassed me at this club."

Truett rears back his fist and lets it fly. The smack as it lands hard against Adam's face is audible, and I let out a scream at the sound.

"Stop!" I yelp.

Brett yanks me toward him as Truett lands another hard punch.

Adam spits blood onto the floor as he lifts his head back up to face his father.

"You never did fight fair," he growls.

"Life isn't fair, Adam. Grow up." With that, he jolts forward, cracking Adam hard in the stomach with his fist. Adam folds over in pain, and I tear myself out of Brett's grasp.

Before he can grab me again, I thrust myself between the two men, putting a hand out to stop Truett from throwing another punch.

"Enough!"

He grimaces at me before glancing over at Brett. My teeth grind together as I see the two men sharing a silent conversation, and I realize, at this moment, I'm really out. Out of this club. Out of my relationship. Out of a lot of money.

"Get him out of here," Truett says darkly as he turns his back to me.

I send one glaring expression toward Brett before I push the bouncer toward the door. He's practically dragging Adam as he moans, looking like he's about to pass out.

*Fucking men.*

As I push open the heavy door that leads to the back of the club, the bouncer tosses Adam out, and he rolls onto the dirty pavement with a groan.

"Are you fucking kidding me?" I argue, but the guy only shrugs as he disappears back into the club.

"Assholes!" I shout in frustration, banging my fist on the heavy metal door. Rage is bubbling up inside me and I let it all out with a wailing scream.

Behind me, Adam groans again.

When I turn around, I find him struggling to his feet. He's

still clearly drunk and bleeding like crazy from his nose. As he gets to a standing position, he sucks in a breath through his teeth, wincing with pain and grabbing his ribs.

Probably bruised a few of those.

I'm standing here with a few choices. Go back inside the club with Truett and Brett and leave Adam Goode to fend for himself.

Or I get in my car and drive home—again, leaving Adam Goode to fend for himself.

*Shit.*

"Come on," I say, sliding my hand under his arm and guiding him toward the employee parking lot on the left.

"Where are you taking me?"

"To my car," I reply.

"Why?" His voice is deep and gravelly, clearly tired and in pain.

"I can't put you behind the wheel of *your* car. Do you have a wife or someone at home who can take care of you? You look like shit."

He manages a small chuckle. "No wife. Nobody."

*Shit.*

"Fine," I reply with a grunt as we reach my car. It's an old Ford pickup that Gladys lets me borrow since she never drives anywhere. Apparently, it was her husband's before he passed. The passenger door creaks as I open it for Adam. Without another word, he slides into the seat, resting his head against the headrest.

As I climb into the driver's seat, he squints his eyes and turns toward me. "Where the hell are you taking me?"

"Back to my apartment," I reply without looking at him.

"You don't even know me."

"I don't like you very much either, but what choice do I have?" I shrug as I start the truck. It takes a few turns before it finally revs up.

Finally, I look at him. "I can't put you in an Uber like that. And if I take you home, who's going to help you bandage up that gross cut on your cheek? Or clean up that mess of blood all over your face?"

His brow is furrowed as he stares at me, clearly struggling with an argument for that.

I let out a tired sigh. "Listen, this is partly my fault. And I feel bad that you had to find out about your dad like this. So just promise you won't rape and/or murder me at my apartment, and I'll make sure you don't die."

After a disgruntled sigh, he nods. "Fine."

# EIGHT

## ADAM

"You live in a Laundromat?"

"I live *above* a Laundromat," she replies as she unlocks the front door and ushers me in. This would be the strangest part of my day if not for that moment back there when my father had someone hold me down while he broke my nose.

I can only assume it's broken by the way it keeps bleeding and has gone completely numb. In the truck, Sage tore off her shirt and handed it to me to stop the bleeding. Now she's prancing around in a bra, and I'm doing my very best to keep my eyes off of the tattoos scattered around her torso and chest.

My eye being swollen shut helps.

I don't object as she pulls me through the dark and empty Laundromat. There's a door in the back that she opens and pushes me through. Then we're walking up some cement stairs when my ears are assaulted by a sound that feels like nails being driven into my already pounding head.

"Roscoe, hush!" she whisper-yells as she unlocks the door of her apartment.

As we enter, she scoops up the small dog, but he doesn't stop his incessant yipping. When I try to pet the tiny demon, he snaps at my hand.

"Jesus," I say with a wince.

"That's not a good sign," she says with a judgmental glare, carrying him away from me. As if dogs can sense evil, and I've just failed the test.

"In my defense, I'm bleeding profusely and I smell like a dirty sex club."

She mumbles something as she walks away, and I realize I should probably feel bad for insulting her club, but I'm too irritated to care at the moment. The pleasantries and chemistry from that morning we met are long gone, and at this point, I've lost the energy to care. If I wasn't covered in blood, I'd turn around and order a ride home.

"Come in here," she barks out the command, and I follow her to the kitchen. If you could call it that.

The apartment is a studio, long and narrow. A large velvet green couch covered with pillows and blankets faces a wall full of old windows overlooking the city. Not a bad view, actually.

To my left is a kitchen *space* with one small counter, a mini-fridge, and a sink. No oven. No range. She has a tiny microwave next to the coffeepot, leaving her about ten inches of usable counter space.

I find myself staring before she snaps at me, and I direct my attention to her. She has some mismatched chairs around a table that looks like it came out of an old diner. She points to one of the chairs, and I meander my way over, wincing at the stabbing pain in my rib cage.

"Sit."

*Bossy.*

As I sit down, the chair squeaks, and Sage positions herself between my legs, tilting my head back and taking a look at my nose. When she makes a pained expression, I know the diagnosis.

"I have good news and I have bad news," she mumbles quietly.

"Let me guess. It's broken."

"Afraid so." When she pinches the bridge, it hurts so bad I flinch, yanking my head out of her grasp.

"So, what's the good news?" I ask. My eyes are tearing up from the pain in my nose.

"I've done this before."

"Done what?" I barely get the words out before her fingers are back on my face, and she's popping the cartilage back in place. She might as well have torn my nose straight off my face for how bad it hurts.

"Fuck!" I shout as I grab my face.

Sage steps away from where I'm sitting, and by the time I blink the moisture out of my eyes, she's roughly tilting my head back again and wiping it clean with a warm, wet washcloth.

I stare up at her, feeling a good deal more sober than I was at the club.

"You enjoyed that, didn't you?"

"Mm-hmm," she replies with a flat expression.

"I was an asshole at the club," I confess.

"You're all assholes."

At that, I nod. She's right. We are all assholes.

"Where did you learn how to do that?" I ask as she presses on the cut on my cheek, which stings as she does it.

She responds with a shrug. "My stepdad taught me when I was a kid because he had a habit of running his mouth and getting punched for it."

Well, that's depressing.

"Where was your mother?"

"Half the time, she was the one who did it," she replies with a snicker.

Thinking about her mother instantly makes me think of mine. She would never lay a hand on my father. And yet, with what I know now...she should.

Nausea builds in my stomach, and pity for my mother makes me want to throw up. Does she know what he's up to every night?

Definitely not.

Sage's hands drift away from my face, and she pulls up a chair to face me. And as my gaze trails to her face, not bothering to hide the melancholia I'm feeling inside, she doesn't say a thing. Instead of a snarky, sarcastic comment, she just shows me a sympathetic expression and rests her hand on my knee.

It's so strange how comforting and unexpected that is. Not a single word. Not a lecture or a line of questions. No lies or words of wisdom. Just empathy and her presence.

"I have a butterfly bandage for your cheek. Stay here."

When she stands up and disappears into the bathroom on the other side of the apartment, my eyes follow her. I try to find the warmth toward her I felt the last time I saw her, but it's gone. In its place is only bitterness and resentment, and it goes both ways.

If I had it in me to apologize for being such an ignorant brute, perhaps I could fix it. But I don't, and not because she doesn't deserve it. But because she does—and I'm just a prideful dick.

Instead, I point out the obvious when she returns from the bathroom.

"Your boyfriend didn't tell you he sold the club."

She glances up at me, a glimpse of confusion on her face before understanding. "Technically, he used it as collateral. For a loan from your dad."

"He's not my dad," I reply, my tone dripping with resentment. "Not anymore."

Sage takes a deep breath, looking sympathetic. "Well, it would seem Brett got a loan from Truett," she says, correcting herself.

I laugh. "Your boyfriend isn't getting that title back. When my father has the upper hand, he keeps it."

She lets out a sad-sounding chuckle before shrugging her shoulders. "Oh well. Not my business anymore."

"Did you just find out tonight?" I ask.

"Shortly before you came in. Yes. He said he was using the money to hire some sex club consultant. Which is ironic because he's never listened to me, so I don't know why he would listen to her."

I stare at her with scrutiny while I silently wonder what the fuck that Brett guy had that was worth so much heartache and pain.

"It seems we were both betrayed tonight." She says it very casually, but I can see the hurt in her eyes. Just two weeks ago, I saw the pride on her face when she gave me the card to the club. Now, it's all been ripped away from her, and I'm curious if that hurts worse than the lost relationship.

"He's so busy taking care of your dad that he hasn't even texted me to see if I'm okay."

I want to tell her I'm sorry, but I don't.

She opens the bandage and stretches it over my skin. I wince from the sting, but after it's in place, I feel like a new man. No more aching nose or dripping blood.

But with my focus no longer stolen by the pain, I'm left to picture the whole scenario again. My father grotesquely tongue fucking some random woman right there in the open at the club.

"It doesn't make any fucking sense," I say, and Sage stares at me in confusion.

"What?"

"How he can go there and do that where anyone can see. After he's been so vocal about closing them down. Why hasn't anyone outed him for that?"

She laughs. "Oh, you mean the VIPs? That good-ole-boys' club? Your father isn't even the most prodigious man in that group of snakes."

"You're joking," I reply, stunned.

"I wish. Your dad feels comfortable in there because as long as he holds everyone else's secrets, his are safe."

"And Brett wouldn't ever use that against him?" I ask, trying to piece it all together.

"Not now that Truett Goode holds the deed."

"Brett is an idiot," I reply before I can stop myself. "Sorry."

"No, you're right. But to all of them, it's a game of power over each other. They probably get off on that more than the sex, to be honest. They think they have each other by the balls, but what they really have is a roomful of powerful men just holding balls."

I let out a laugh.

Once the tiny apartment grows quiet, I look up at where she's sitting across from me. "I should go. I can catch an Uber."

"It's late," she replies softly. "You can take the couch. It's really comfortable. I sleep on it almost every night."

There's something in her expression that has me thinking she *wants* me to stay. It's the only reason I give her a nod and a tight smile. "Okay. If you're sure."

"Of course," she replies, jumping up from the chair. She scrambles around the apartment, putting a new pillow and fresh blankets out for me.

As I stand up to move toward the couch, my ribs scream in pain again. She notices and rushes toward me.

"Let me look at that."

With her fingers on the hem of my shirt, she waits for me to give her a nod of consent before she pulls it up and inspects the ribs on my left.

I wince as she presses on them. Then her fingers slowly cascade down the length of the bottom rib and my skin erupts in goose bumps. I force myself to swallow as I stare at her.

Maybe I'm still a little drunk, after all, but suddenly I feel like the girl I just met and I have bonded more than I've connected with anyone in my life. We were both betrayed, blindsided, and hurt by those we should trust more than anything.

"I think it's just bruised, but even if it's broken, there's not much they can do. Just have to wait for it to heal and hope you don't have to cough or sneeze for the next six weeks."

"Lovely." I groan. As she pulls my shirt down, our eyes meet in a heated and intimate gaze.

She's standing so close I feel the heat from her skin. As she stares up at me, the intensity between us burns, but not in the way it did before. Not in a *good* way.

And when her fingers reach for the buckle of my belt, I stop breathing. With her eyes on mine, she slowly pulls the leather from the metal clasp.

"What are you doing?" I whisper, not entirely sure how I feel about this. I'm somewhere between wanting it and *not* wanting it, lust and virtue battling for superiority in my mind.

This isn't right. I know it's not right, and there might have been a moment today when I wanted this with her, but now...not like this.

And yet, I don't stop her as she unbuttons my pants.

"I don't know," she replies. "I just...need this."

"Because you're mad at your boyfriend?"

Still, I don't stop her. Even when she nods, confirming that it's just a revenge fuck she wants.

I'm frozen in place, my cock growing hard behind my boxers, but my mind still reeling from whatever this is.

Lust. Need. Hate and rage all blurred into one.

Once my pants are undone, she slips her shorts down, and just like that, she's in nothing but a bra and panties, and I'm staring dumbfounded.

Without looking up at me, she presses her hands against my chest. "Come on, Adam. Please don't be a nice guy right now."

*A nice guy?*

Is that what I am? A guy who does everything *right*. Who follows the rules.

Nice guys don't fuck for revenge.

Nice guys don't fuck without emotion.

Nice guys don't *fuck* at all.

Something in me snaps, and maybe it's the alcohol or the fact that I was in a sex club tonight, but I'm real fucking tired of saying no to the things I want. So I grab her by the back of the neck and pull her face to mine.

With our mouths inches apart, I mutter against her lips, "I'm not a fucking nice guy."

She smiles wickedly, almost like a dare. "Then prove it."

Holding tight to her neck, I spin her around and bend her over the back of the couch. She lets out a small yelp and then a moan as I drive my hips against her backside, grinding my hard length against her.

Her pink hair falls over her face as I release her neck and rip her thin satin thong down her legs. I take in the sight of her, bent over and moaning with need. Every little vertebra on her spine moves with the heavy intake of each panting breath. Unable to stop myself, I lean over and roughly kiss my way down, biting and nibbling on her sensitive skin like I need to devour her to survive. As I reach the sweet pink globes of her ass, I bite down hard on her flesh, making her scream. Releasing my teeth, I lick the marks I left and do the same on the other side. This time, she trembles, and my cock twitches in response.

Her fear turns me on.

So I drop to my knees and spread her wide, like an animal inhaling the scent of her. I'm unhinged. Completely undone, dismantled, and royally fucked in the head.

I've never done anything like this. Never so depraved or disgusting.

And I fucking love it.

Burying my tongue in her cunt, I fuck her with it, just to hear her scream again. My dick leaks at the tip from the taste and scent of her.

"I know what I'll call you," I mumble as I nibble my way around the cheeks of her ass, then back into her pussy, spreading her just to take another long, devouring lick of her. As I pull my mouth away, I smile. "Peaches. Because you taste so fucking sweet."

She's humming and moaning, husky and needy, as she hangs her ass in the air. "Please fuck me, Adam."

"I'm not done yet," I mutter. Then I take another bite, and she screams again.

She's still shaking as I stand up behind her and pull my cock from my boxer briefs.

A nice guy would probably find a condom or at least ask her first. But I think we've already established that that's not who I am or what she wants right now.

So I slide the head of my cock through the warm, wet lips of her cunt, teasing the entrance before thrusting in without mercy.

When she lets out a yelp, I thrust in rough again. "This is what you wanted, wasn't it? Then, fucking take it."

I slam in again, and her yelp, this time, is loud and slightly alarming. But then she murmurs a breathy, "Yes. Fuck me."

Suddenly, I hear myself, and I can hardly believe what just came out of my mouth. I'm not like this. I'm fucking her like I want to hurt her, but she likes it, so I don't stop. What the fuck is wrong with me?

Slamming my hips against her ass, I pull out and push back in, fucking her with brutal thrusts. And with each one, she pleads for more.

All thoughts disappear from my mind until all I know is sensation and the feel of *her*. Her body. Her sounds. Her touch.

Or is it mine? At the moment, I don't exactly know the difference. Only that it feels so fucking good. Being inside her. Letting go. Feeling freer than I've ever felt in my life. Almost as if fucking her is releasing the anger and rage I felt today. Which I guess is why she needed it, and apparently, I did too.

Before long, my spine tenses and my dick tightens and I pull out just in time to watch my cum shoot out in warm jets all over her back. The noise that comes out of me as I let go sounds more animal than human. It sounds like a monster, but it feels like freedom.

For a long time, I stand here, waiting for every drop to release, watching her spine move with her breathing again. Minutes go by while I wait for the shame to creep in.

"Get me a towel," she says in a breathless command.

It feels like waking up as I go to the bathroom, not daring to look at my reflection in the mirror before I grab a towel off the rack, returning to wipe the mess from her back.

Then everything becomes quiet and awkward. I can't quite tell if this is shame or disappointment with myself, but I stare at her as she pulls her clothes back on.

Was I too rough? Did she come? Did I do the right thing?

As I stare at her, pulling her pink hair into a ponytail and wiping the running makeup from her eyes, I realize that Sage and I truly are from two different worlds. We couldn't be less compatible, and I'd be an even bigger asshole if I tried to pretend that it didn't have anything to do with status and wealth. It has created two completely different people who will never see eye to eye.

"You can still stay," she mumbles awkwardly as she moves toward her bedroom.

I clear my throat and zip up my pants. "Thanks, but I'm going to go."

"Fine," she mutters with her back to me.

"You're...okay, right?" I ask, wanting to reach for her.

With a huff, she turns toward me with a sad smile. "Don't try to be the nice guy now."

I let my hands fall to my sides as I shrug. "I can't help it."

"Night, Adam," she says, pinching her lips together and backing away, moving toward the door that leads to her bedroom.

"Night, Sage. Thanks again." I awkwardly point to my nose.

Holding her arms crossed in front of her body, she lets her gaze linger on my face a moment, and I can tell there's something heavy weighing on her mind. I wait for a moment before she finally mutters quietly.

"I wish there was a way we could make them both pay."

A short huff escapes my lips.

"I'm not the revenge type," I reply.

"It wouldn't be revenge," she says. Before disappearing through the door, she softly adds, "It would be atonement."

# NINE

## SAGE

**M**y dreams are filled with that word—*atonement*. Ringing through my sleeping mind. I just imagine myself full of rage and power, like a mastermind enacting some act of retribution for what's been done, not only to me but also to Adam. The details are fuzzy, but I can tell that it feels good.

Roscoe wakes me up sometime around eight the next morning, actually in my bed too, which is strange. For a while, I just lie in bed and try to think about nothing, especially ignoring the fact that I cheated on Brett last night.

I should probably feel bad about that. I should...but I don't. Not after the way he brushed me aside at the club, putting his VIPs before me. Leaving me to tend to a battered Adam in the parking lot. What the hell did he expect?

I guess that was my way of revenge, although it didn't really affect Brett at all.

Before any guilt has the chance to creep in, I climb out of bed and shuffle into the kitchen.

As I'm making my coffee and feeding Roscoe, I keep replaying the events of last night in my mind. Everything from the argument with Brett in the office to the cartilage of Adam's nose snapping back into place under my fingers.

And, of course, the quick fuck over the back of my couch. That's the moment my mind keeps getting stuck on. It was easily the most satisfying sex I've had in a long time. Just thinking about the way he flipped a switch has my thighs clenching together with warmth.

In the span of two weeks, I met him, shared a spark for a brief moment, fought with him, and fucked him.

He was betrayed. I was betrayed. And neither of us can do a damn thing about it.

After my coffee is made, I set it on the cherry-red-and-chrome table I picked up in a flea market when I moved to the city. While I carry Roscoe down the fire escape, I wonder if Adam was silently judging the eclectic taste of my apartment. Not a single thing matches, and I'm not sure if *no style choice* is a style choice in itself. But I keep it clean, and I value every single mismatched inch of the menagerie that is my home.

I imagine he lives in a cookie-cutter model home full of things that hold no value other than what some designer paid for them at the home goods store. Not that I'm knocking him for it. I'm sure his home is nice.

After Roscoe does his business, I take him back upstairs and put him in front of his food bowl while I scroll through my phone and drink my coffee. It doesn't take long before I'm putting Adam's full name in the Google search bar and deep diving into the results.

Why? I don't know. I have no intention of ever seeing him again. But curiosity is a tempting bitch sometimes.

It turns out the whole Goode family has a squeaky-clean reputation. Melanie Goode might as well be president of the privileged white Christian wife club. She's chaired tons of foundations and charities, and even though she's in her fifties, she barely looks a day over thirty.

Adam has three brothers—Lucas, Caleb, and Isaac. All as

attractive and prominent. Lucas is a professor at the university. Caleb owns his own law firm.

The only one who doesn't pop up much is Isaac. From what I can tell, he stopped showing up in family photos about eight years ago.

And at the head of the table—Truett.

It makes me wonder how much his family really knows about him. Does Melanie know her husband pays for sex at the club nearly every night of the week, often with a different girl each time? Do his sons know that he has been known to snort a line of blow on the very table he was caught licking pussy at last night?

Probably not.

I wish they did. I wish I could unveil every dirty secret that club keeps, and not because they shouldn't be allowed to have a discreet place to fuck, but because men like Truett Goode abuse that right. He uses his platform to preach about all of the dangers of the very things he partakes in nightly. It's the most hypocritical thing I've ever heard. And Brett lets him.

The club could be so much better. Instead of catering to rich men who manipulate the rest of us to hold their secrets, it could be a club for *real* people. No patronizing assholes or a toxic male-dominated environment.

It's a pipe dream.

I'll never be able to knock Brett and Truett down from their thrones. As long as Truett and his squeaky-clean, all-American family maintain that pure and holy reputation, Brett has all the power. If he didn't hold Truett's secrets in the palm of his hand, that entire club and its filthy VIP membership would crumble to pieces.

I'm deep in thought, my mind starting to buzz with some far-off notion, when a hard knock at the door yanks me from my concentration and Roscoe starts yipping his head off.

"It's me," Gladys calls from outside the front door. "I need your help fixing the TV again. I think someone taped over *Days of Our Lives.*"

With a chuckle, I stand up from the chair and open the front door. Gladys is standing on my welcome mat with a despondent look on her face. With long gray hair and a tie-dye T-shirt, Gladys is exactly what you'd expect a sixty-nine-year-old hippie to look like.

She's as blunt and bold as she is kind and peaceful.

With a shake of my head, I smile while grabbing my keys from the table. "I told you. No one can tape over it. It saves digitally. There are no tapes."

"Then where the hell is it?" she snaps.

Roscoe scurries down the stairs ahead of us as we make our way to the Laundromat. When we enter, I notice a few regulars in the front. People come in almost daily to either do laundry or just enjoy the free TV and AC. I've never seen Gladys turn away a single person in the ten years I've been here.

Roscoe greets the regulars as I send them a quick hello and take the remote from the counter. I don't bother showing Gladys how to find her recorded episodes anymore. I've done it enough to know she's never going to get it. But as long as she doesn't learn, then it means she needs me. And I'll admit—it's nice to be needed.

"So, who was that guy you brought home last night? He's not still up there, is he?"

My eyes nearly bug out of my face. "It was no one!" I answer far too excitedly.

"He didn't look like no one. He looked like the kind of man who owns a car and treats his girlfriends nice."

Gladys *hates* Brett. Hates him so much I've been too scared to even bring him around. I should be more excited to tell her he's probably, maybe, definitely out of the picture. But I already know the *told you so* lecture I'm going to get from that.

So we just skim over it and head directly into *who's the new guy* talk.

"He got into a fight at the club, and I was just helping him out. Were you spying on me?"

"I spy on everyone who comes into my Laundromat at three in the morning. So, what's his name?"

I roll my eyes as I lean on the counter. "Adam."

"He sounds nice."

A laugh bursts out of me. "Did you miss the part where I said he got into a fight at the club? He was literally bleeding."

"Was he beating up Brett?"

"Gladys," I reply, leveling her with my gaze. "No. He was not beating up Brett."

"Too bad."

At some point, I need to tell Gladys that I'm no longer working at the club, which means my income is sort of gone. I don't, of course. Not yet, at least.

I'll find something else by the time rent is due.

"The girls are excited about book club next Saturday," she says as she taps her well-worn copy of the smutty romance of the month on the countertop.

"I can't wait to hear what Mary thinks about the scene on the raft," I reply with a giggle.

Gladys cracks up as she replies, "That was my favorite part!"

About six months ago, a few of Gladys's friends and I started a romance book club.

But not just any romance books.

Old mass-market paperback romances with Fabio on the cover that have titles like *Romancing the Rogue* and *Ravished by the Highlander*. It's honestly more fun than I ever expected it to be.

Especially in the first month when the devoutly religious florist next door had to say the phrase *throbbing member* out loud and ended up in such a fit of giggles, she wound up on the floor. We still call that meeting "Mary's Awakening."

"I can't wait," I reply.

My phone vibrates in my back pocket, so I fish it out and see Brett's name on the screen. My eyes narrow as I stare down at his message.

· · ·

> Why haven't you texted me?

With a huff, I roll my eyes. Then I quickly type out my reply.

> Why haven't you texted me?

> Because I knew you were all pissy. Are you in a better mood yet?

Un-fucking-believable.

I want to type out a million different things to him, but after breaking up and getting back together so many times in the past few years, I'm officially numb to it all. I'd like to fight with him or tell him all the ways he hurt me, but there's no point.

Instead, I just respond with:

> Enough. It's over. Best of luck with the club. I'm moving on.

It feels so final and my finger hovers over the send button for a very long time. When I glance up and see Gladys watching me, I wait for her to give me an encouraging nod before I finally tap the screen.

It doesn't hurt. It probably should. Brett and I were little more than fuck buddies and friends the past three years, but I just always assumed that's what a comfortable relationship was. Someone you could laugh with and screw from time to time.

But he never appreciated me or made me feel seen. Brett invested *nothing* in our relationship, and the standard for him to please me was so low it might as well have been underground.

For him, I was a convenience.

For me, he was my world.

An imbalance I felt every single day of our relationship, so much so that I became starved for his attention and would devour every tiny crumb of it.

"You're free, sweetie."

I don't even realize I'm crying until I feel Gladys wrap her arms around me and hold me against her chest. I breathe in her familiar patchouli fragrance as I fume internally.

I've said all I could say and I've fought all I could fight.

And she's right. Now I'm free.

# MAY
## THE GENTLEMAN

# TEN

ADAM

"You're missing Sunday dinner again?" Luke's voice on the line sounds both shocked and concerned.

My younger brother thrives on consistency and tradition. Any deviation from a well-formulated pattern is liable to drive him into a frenzy. Which is why I've waited an entire week to tell him I won't be sitting at the table again tonight.

"I just can't face him yet," I reply. I refuse to lie, especially to my brothers. But he doesn't need to know the whole truth. As far as he and Caleb know, I've been released from writing duties at the church. Which is a nice way to put it.

They don't need to know about the club or what happened there.

And they don't need to see what a mess I've become since. It feels like my life was completely derailed from the track it was on. I had purpose and direction before. Now I have nothing.

"But what about Mom?" he asks, and I wince.

My mother is a subject that literally pains me every time she crosses my mind. She's called me every week, but I keep the details light and put on my best fake optimism.

To be honest, I never want my mother to know what my father is really up to.

"I'll call her and apologize. It's not like you and Caleb haven't missed a few dinners from time to time."

"Yeah, but you're not me and Caleb," he replies, and I understand what he's trying to say. "And this is three in a row."

As I reach the restaurant, I pause, lingering outside with Lucas on the call.

"Listen, Luke. I gotta go. I'll call Mom later, okay?"

"Okay." He's hesitating, and I know he can sense that there's more to the story, but I don't elaborate.

In fact, I haven't been in the mood to do much at all lately. I spent the last three weeks pretending I would get some writing done. That I would bounce back. But there has been no fucking bouncing. I feel as if I've landed like a lead balloon. I didn't just lose my job. I lost everything I've strived to achieve. I'll never step into his shoes now, and I'm not so sure I want to.

But I hate the idea of moving on.

Hence why I'm here at Sal's on a Saturday morning like clockwork. Old habits die hard, they say.

As I pull open the door to the diner, the first thing I see is bright pink.

*Peaches.*

My heart starts pounding in my chest and my cheeks burn with shame.

But it's too late to turn and run.

Pausing two steps into the lobby, my gaze connects with hers, and we stare at each other for a few long, tense moments.

Immediately seeing her brings back a flood of memories from that night at her apartment. And with those memories, a torrent of disgrace as I remember what came over me in that moment. Perverted, vile, depraved. I desperately wanted to lock up that incident and pretend it never happened.

And yet, I think about it as often as I try not to think about it.

"Morning, Mr. Goode," the hostess says in a cordial greeting.

"Your spot at the bar is open today." With a smile, the girl takes a menu from the stand and starts toward the bar when I stop her.

I have no good reason for what I do next.

"Table for two, actually," I say with my eyes on Sage.

She stares at me, her lips parted and her eyes full of curiosity.

"Oh, okay," the hostess responds, grabbing a second menu and leading me back toward a small two-person booth near the back of the diner.

When Sage stands to follow the hostess with me, I feel a sense of victory course through my veins.

*What am I doing?*

We follow behind silently until we reach our seats and sit across from each other.

"I was wondering if I'd see you here again," I say.

She smiles shyly. "Well, I don't pull any more night shifts, and I don't normally get up this early, so you lucked out today."

"I guess I did." I find myself staring at the ring in her lip and the way she sometimes bites it when she's nervous like she is right now.

Then, from out of nowhere, I'm hit with a memory of the way I acted that night. And the fact that I owe this woman an apology.

"Sage, I'm sorry...for what happened that night." I stammer, feeling uncomfortable.

"Which part?" she asks with one brow arched.

I lean forward, keeping my voice a near-silent whisper. "I didn't use protection. And I left..."

"Oh," she replies, a hint of a smile on her face. Then she leans forward to whisper in return. "I'm tested regularly and on the pill, so it's okay. But I appreciate your apology."

With a sigh, I sit back and let out an exhale. The relief of that information settles some of the worry in my bones. The last thing I need right now is an unwanted pregnancy with a stranger.

Sage and I are sitting in mildly awkward silence when I feel a pair of eyes on me from across the restaurant. A man, roughly my

father's age, is watching me over his newspaper, and it's clear by
the way his eyes dart back and forth that he recognizes me.

Judging by the disgruntled line of his mouth, he doesn't
approve of my company. A month ago, I might have cared.

The waitress scurries over to pour us coffee and take our
orders, and the moment she's gone, I turn my attention back to
Sage. Why did I want to sit with her today? What on earth am I
trying to gain here?

And why the hell haven't I been able to stop thinking about
her since the day we met?

"How's your...?" She points to her cheek, and I lift my fingers
to mine, feeling the scar there. It's mostly healed but still pink and
fresh.

"It's good. Thanks to you."

She shrugs in response.

"So, how are y—" I start to ask before she quickly cuts me off.

"I've been thinking." The words scramble out of her mouth,
and I notice immediately the flustered expression on her face as
she gazes up at me.

"Okay..." I reply carefully.

"It's going to sound crazy, but I just have to get it out, or I'll
regret it."

"Go ahead. Say whatever you need."

Her ring-covered fingers are grasping the coffee mug tightly,
squeezing it nervously. "I've been thinking about this ever since
that night. Which is why I'm here. I figured you might come back
on Saturday mornings, and I didn't have any other way to contact
you that would be discreet enough."

*Discreet enough?*

"I assume you and your father are still on the outs," she says,
leaning forward to keep it quiet between us.

Glancing around, I make sure no one is listening as I nod.

"And you're still pretty mad at him and would like to see him
suffer a little? Maybe even...ruin his reputation?"

My heart starts to pound a little faster. I lean forward. Here I just wanted a nice breakfast date in hopes that she and I could start over and I could right my wrongs. But she's manipulated this entire meeting for what...a revenge scheme?

"I'm not interested in outing him if that's what you're implying. I've thought about it, and I think it would do more damage to my—"

"No," she says, cutting me off again. "I can't out him. I can't out any of them. It would cost the workers at the club too much. It's not their fault."

"True," I reply with hesitation. My curiosity has me laser-focused on every word Sage is saying. Somewhere in the back of my mind, I already know that whatever it is she's suggesting, I won't comply with. I'm not interested in revenge or making my father's downfall my goal in life now, but I am dying to know what she has in mind.

She looks down at her fingers as she chews on her lip, and I wait for her to continue. When her eyes cast upward, they are renewed with purpose.

"You can't control how he'll react or what he'll do. Same with Brett. All we can control is what *we* do."

My brow furrows as I stare at her. "What are you talking about?"

"Your family has a good reputation, right?" she asks, and something about Sage mentioning my family makes me slightly uncomfortable. Swallowing that discomfort, I nod.

"Yes."

"That's what gives Brett all his power."

My forehead creases even more as I lean in. "I don't follow."

She sits back in her chair as she tries to recompose her argument. "If everyone knew how slimy the Goode boys are, no one would be surprised to hear that Truett himself owns a sex club. And if no one would be surprised, then Brett has nothing to hold over your dad's head. And if Brett has nothing to hold over his head, he never gets the deed back, and it's out of his hands forever."

A heavy breath passes my lips as I stare at her. At that moment, the waitress delivers our plates to the table, but neither of us moves to eat. The space between us lingers in silence as her words hang in the air.

I replay them, briefly wondering if Sage is entirely out of her mind or a manipulative genius.

When a few moments have passed, and I'm still mulling over what I think is a major reach in conclusions, I grab the bottle of ketchup from the tray by the wall.

As I pass it to her, I mumble, "Did you just call the Goode boys...slimy?"

At that moment, I can't help but compare this meal with the last one I shared with a woman, the day Lucy came to dinner. It's wildly unfair how there's something *here* where there really shouldn't be.

"Hypothetically," she replies, taking the bottle and immediately dousing her eggs with the sugary red mess.

"My brothers are not slimy," I reply as I cover my waffles in syrup.

"It sort of doesn't matter. If only one of the Goode boys is in the public eye..."

"And that would be me?" I say, finishing her sentence.

With a mouthful of biscuit, she nods. "Mm-hmm."

"You want me to...be publicly slimy in order to tarnish my family's reputation, therefore exposing my father for the snake he is and...I got lost at the end there."

Her shoulders slump in disappointment. "Okay, it's a reach. I know."

When I chuckle, lifting my coffee cup to my lips, I watch for a hint of a smile on her face. As she glances back up at me, I catch a tiny flinch in the corner of her mouth.

"What should I do first?" I ask, teasing her. "Rob a bank? Mug a nun? Sell drugs on the corner? It's a valiant concept, but I don't think any of those things are going to hit your boyfriend where it hurts."

"Ex," she corrects me. "And you're right. None of those things would."

When she takes another bite of her breakfast, I get the lingering suspicion that she has some idea of what *would* hit her boyfriend where it hurts.

I don't say a word as she chews and swallows, chasing it down with her coffee. "I'm waiting," I say with a smirk.

"For?" she teases back.

"What *would* work. You have an idea, don't you?"

My eyes get caught on the delicate movement of her fingers again, especially as she sweeps her pink waves out of her face and places her chin in her hand, resting her elbow on the table.

"Oh, that's where I come in."

I fight a smile again, watching the way her full lips pout theatrically.

"Go on," I reply, sitting back and crossing my arms, doing my best to keep my expression stern and serious.

"Well...what would upset your family's squeaky-clean reputation more than me?"

A scoff bursts through my lips.

"What on earth do you plan on doing to my family?"

"Dating you, of course."

I'm reaching for my coffee cup, my arm frozen in midair. *Dating?*

A lot of thoughts start to swirl through my mind at this moment. The first one is me questioning if Sage is using this elaborate plan as a strategy to get me into bed—again. Although I guess there wasn't really a bed involved at all the first time. But that's where things feel muddled and wrong, so I breeze past that thought and directly into the next.

Does she really think so low of herself that she believes dating her would ruin my family's image?

*Do I?*

For the past month, I've thought about Sage and never once did I make an attempt to contact her. I know where she lives. I could have easily visited that Laundromat to seek her out, to take her on a date, to let myself indulge in staring at all the things about her that fascinate me. Or endeavored for a repeat of what happened in her apartment last month.

But I haven't.

Because even I know that Sage is a round peg and I'm a square hole.

Or is it the other way around?

"Relax, I'm not talking about *real* dating," she says when she notices the expression of contemplation on my face. She's probably thinking I'm panicking on the inside, which I guess I am. But not for the reasons she thinks.

"So, what are you talking about?"

"Being seen together," she replies, sipping her coffee.

I glance around the diner. "We are being seen together."

She lets out an adorable huff. "I mean somewhere your family and the public will actually see us. Somewhere that makes a real statement. Don't y'all have, like, balls and galas and shit?"

I snicker. "We sometimes have galas and shit. We have a charity dinner in three weeks."

"Perfect!" she chirps. "Just imagine the look on your father's face when you show up with me on your arm."

"What makes you think *dating you* will ruin my reputation?" I ask with scrutiny.

"Well, first of all, I'm a full-blown atheist. I couldn't give two shits about church or God or any of that. Second of all, look at me."

My brow furrows. "And?"

She gestures to her tattoos and the piercings on her face. "Are you going to pretend you've ever dated anyone who looked like me?"

When I don't answer, she makes a raised-brow expression. "See, I'm perfect for that gala in three weeks."

Putting my hands up to stop her, I feel my anxiety rising the more excited she gets about this plan. "Now, just wait a minute. I'm not on board with this idea...yet."

"Of course," she replies, her posture slouching. "I mean, think about it. It would drive both of them insane to see us together."

"You're right about that," I say, focusing my eyes on all the little things about her that I like. Her nervous little habits and all the delicate lines of her tattoos. "But do you think it's enough? One charity dinner?"

Her tongue peeks out, running over the ring in her lip. "Well, I have some other ideas too, but we can start small."

The waitress approaches the table to check on us, placing the check face down. I snatch it up before Sage can even move.

As I feel the breakfast coming to an end, my mood dampens. It dawns on me now just how long I was looking forward to this chance encounter happening, living just in the hopes she'd be here. I had no idea all of this would come about. There was no way for me to know she'd have a ridiculous plan for me to almost immediately shoot down.

Because I know already I'm not going through with this. Maybe if she had asked me last week, when my anger was still fresh, I'd have jumped at the opportunity. But now, I realize that once I open this can of revenge, I won't be able to close it back up again. I'll never be able to get back the man I was before I embarked on something so calculating. Lying to my family. Becoming someone I'm not.

And maybe worst of all—kissing any chance of reaching my father's level of success goodbye. If that's even what I want anymore. I'm a mess, and the last thing I need to do now is jump into a fake relationship with a girl I barely know—no matter how much I want to.

# ELEVEN

ADAM

I watch Sage walk down the empty city street until she turns a
corner and disappears. In my mind, I know...that's it.

She and I have no more business together. I need to focus less
on her and more on what I'm going to do with my life now, and it
sure as hell isn't pretending I'm dating someone just to make my
father mad. This isn't high school. I'm not a child.

As I turn in the opposite direction and start my slow stroll
back to my apartment, I think about that night with her again.

That wasn't me. The way I behaved with her was evil.
Wanton. Weak. Years of Bible studies and sermons have taught me
that temptation is like poison to the virtue of a good man.

But at the same time...I finally got to feel what it's like to truly
let go. To finally do what I always wanted to do.

And it *felt good*.

My father would tell me that was the work of the devil. The
temptation to give in to such carnal and sadistic urges can only
bring a man to ruin.

Of course, that is the same man who I caught indulging in his
own *carnal* urges and with no remorse. Without apology or

contemplation. As if it meant nothing to him. As if...everything he taught me my entire life...was a lie.

I'm not a fool. I'm thirty-seven fucking years old, and I have enough self-reflection to know that indulging in vices from time to time does not make me a good man condemned.

But am I a *good* man?

I've never had meaningless one-night stands before. And would have never dreamed of sleeping with a cheating woman. Something came over me that night. I was depraved, and the only thing worse than the way I behaved was how much I enjoyed it.

Not to mention how flippantly I treated her, leaving just after I came and never putting her pleasure before mine. I *used* her.

God, I'm no better than my father.

Fuck—do I want to be?

These thoughts circle round and round as I reach my building, taking the elevator up to the third floor. The moment I step off, I pause in my tracks as I find myself standing face-to-face with the man himself.

Instantly, my blood starts to boil.

I haven't faced my father in three weeks. Not even for church or Sunday dinner. Just the sight of him now proves I'm not ready.

"What are you doing here?" I mutter darkly as I try to pass him by to get to my door on the other side.

My father grabs my arm and gets in my face. "We're going to have a civil conversation. You understand?"

"Fuck you," I reply, seething with hatred as I stare into his eyes. I'm still wearing a light bruise under my eye and a scar where he split the skin of my cheek with his fist.

"Open the door, Adam."

I yank my arm out of his grasp as I plunge the key in the hole, turning it with a click and opening the door before marching inside. He's behind me, shutting the door so we're suddenly alone.

"I have nothing to say to you," I call with my back to him as I head toward the kitchen. I need a fucking drink.

"Too bad. You're going to listen anyway."

I spin on him with my brow furrowed. "You think because you're my father, you can talk to me like this? Get the fuck out of my apartment."

He scoffs with a smug grin that I'd like to punch off his face. "The apartment I bought for you."

Something in me snaps. "I've worked my ass off for you. I've dedicated my life to your church. Your message. Your career."

He rolls his eyes. "You're still throwing a fucking fit over the writing job. Jesus, Adam. Grow up."

"Does Mom know?" I ask as I pull a bottle of vodka out of the freezer, pouring it directly into a glass and shooting it back with a wince.

My father ignores my question, staring at me with a blank expression.

"Does she know you fuck twenty-year-olds every night?"

"Are you done?" he mumbles, looking bored.

"Get the fuck out." I toss back another shot as my eyes narrow at him.

"The reason I came here is to make it perfectly fucking clear that you will come to Sunday dinner tomorrow, and you won't utter a word of this to anyone, Adam. Not your mother, brothers, or anyone at the church."

"Or what?" I reply with a scoff.

His eyes meet mine, and there's something calculating and cold in the look on his face.

Suddenly everything I debated on my walk becomes crystal clear. About how good of a man I am if I'm truly like him, and for the first time, I realize—if he's a good man, then I want nothing to do with that.

It feels as if my shackles are released.

I can be as *bad* as I want.

"Son," he starts with a sigh. "I don't want to see you hurt or struggling. But if you try to ruin everything I've built, I'll have no choice. If word gets out, the ones you'll really be hurting are them. Your family. Our congregation. So from now on, you'll come to family dinners and events for the church, but you'll never speak another word about this."

My teeth are clenched so tight my jaw aches. I *hate* him.

I want to punch him again, but I can't. Sage was right. He's too powerful, and I believe him. If I try to mess with his place at the church with rumors, he has enough power to make my life hell. I know he'd do it.

So without another word, I waltz straight to the front door and pull it open. Then I stare at him with my chin up. "You've said what you wanted to say. Now get out."

"Do we have a deal, son?" he replies without moving.

Looking at the floor, my jaw clenches again. "Yes," I say, seething with hatred. "I won't tell anyone about the club or about who you really are. But that's it. You and I are done."

"The apple didn't fall as far as you think it did, son. We do our job, and we help the people. Stop worrying about everything else."

He presses his lips into a tight smile as he walks confidently out of my apartment.

I don't wait until he's in the elevator before I slam the door closed. My mind is racing and my blood is pumping, boiling with my hatred for him, and I'm far too restless to let it rest now.

So I pace my apartment for fifteen minutes, waiting until I'm sure he's gone before I snatch my keys from the counter and bolt out the door.

I'm too hyped up to walk and too buzzed to drive, so I order myself a quick ride before I reach the street level. Then I pace anxiously as I wait for it to pull up. Within about five minutes, it's there and I climb in.

The entire conversation replays in my head the entire way over. This new energy surges through me, and the ideas that burn in my mind feel like gasoline on the flame.

As the driver pulls up to the Laundromat, I shoot him a quick *thanks* and bolt from the car. A bell above the door chimes as I pull it open and enter the Laundromat. It smells like fabric softener and incense, and there's a thin, gray-haired woman standing behind the counter, her eyes glued to the TV hanging from the wall.

I meander my way to the back, where the heavy black door is that leads to Sage's apartment. I nearly make it all the way before she stops me.

"I hope you're nicer than the last one."

Turning back to the woman, my face pinches in confusion as I send her a curt wave. When she doesn't say anything else, I shake off the strange encounter and enter the stairwell, bounding up the steps until I'm standing in front of her apartment door.

I rap on the wood, and Roscoe starts barking immediately.

"Would you just chill out?" she snaps at him before pulling open the door. Then she's staring at me in shock. "Adam."

"Fuck it. I'm in." The words fly out of my mouth without warning because the quicker I say them, the less chance I have of backing out.

"Um...okay. Great!" she replies with her adorable bare shoulders lifted in excitement.

"But being seen at the gala isn't enough. We need more. I want there to be nothing left of my reputation when we're done."

Her lips part as she stares up at me in surprise. "Are you sure?"

"One hundred percent. I want nothing to do with him for the rest of my life, and I'm tired of being so fucking good. So tell me your plan."

"Okay..." She opens the door wider to let me in. I step into the small space as Roscoe bounces around my feet. Reaching down, I pet him softly on his tiny head. To my surprise, he doesn't try to bite my hand off this time, which I take as a small victory.

"So, what did you have in mind?" I ask, turning toward Sage.

"We're going to need drinks for this."

"Can it be coffee?" I reply. "This isn't about being impulsive to me. I want to take this seriously."

Her brows crease together as she moves toward her tiny kitchenette. "Sure. Can I ask what changed since I saw you...like an hour ago?"

"My father was at my apartment when I got home. Told me to stay quiet about it. Threatened me. It just...set me on edge."

She watches me as she prepares a pot of coffee in her tiny drip machine. "Threatened you? Jesus. Has your dad always been such an asshole?"

I lean against the counter with my arms crossed. "Yeah, he has. But he hid behind his ministry. I always knew he had it in him, and honestly, there was this look in his eyes today... It made me think he wanted me to push his buttons. Like he wanted to prove just how fucking tough and powerful he is."

"Stupid toxic masculinity," she mutters as she pours the water in the machine.

I laugh silently to myself. "Everything about him is toxic."

"Well, if it makes you feel better, I can tell you're a much better person than he is."

Her nimble fingers hypnotize me through each step of the process, finally pushing the button that lights up red. A moment later, it starts spurting and bubbling to life. When she finally glances up at me, I work up the courage to say the exact words hanging on my tongue.

"That's the thing, Sage. I don't want to be a good person anymore."

Confusion morphs her features as she stares at me. "What do you mean?"

"I mean... My entire life, I have behaved. I've been righteous, virtuous, holy, God-fearing, and loyal. Look what it got me. He's been none of those things, and he has enough power to manipulate everyone in his life."

"But that's not—" she starts, but her words stop there.

"That is what I want, Sage. He didn't follow any of the rules, and God blessed him anyway. I want to be done with all of it. And I need you to help me."

We're bathed in silence, and I'm so enamored with staring at her that I don't even realize how much time has passed. The coffee maker beeps, and she turns to pour us each a cup.

When we take our mugs and sit down on opposite sides of the couch, she just blurts out two words that have me instantly choking on my coffee.

"Sex tapes."

I sputter and cough, feeling the burn of the hot liquid down my windpipe as I try to recover and understand what she's implying at the same time.

I mean, of course I know what she's implying. What's one step further than fake dating? Fake sex tapes. It makes perfect sense.

Except she didn't say *fake* sex tapes. She just said *sex tapes*.

"Sorry," she says, handing me a paper towel to clean up the coffee now staining my shirt. "I guess I shouldn't have sprung that on you."

"It's fine," I reply. "To be honest...we were on the same page. Or at least...I think we were."

As I glance up at her with desperation in my eyes, she seems to catch my implication and holds up her free hand in surrender. "Oh, I didn't mean that you and I would sleep together again... I mean, not *really*. In fact, I think for this to work, we should keep our...hands—and other parts—to ourselves."

Why do I suddenly feel disappointed by that? We've already fucked. Why not do it again, but this time for the camera?

Solemnly, I nod. "Of course, I understand what you meant. We could make them look real."

"Yeah, exactly."

I muddle through the idea for a moment as I attempt a second sip of my coffee. There's something about the idea that feels weak. Sex tapes are great if you're a national treasure or major celebrity, but I'm barely known around Austin, let alone far enough to have any sort of impact on his reputation. I'd be lucky if that made a few local Twitter threads.

"I don't know, Sage. No one will care about me."

"They will. I'm sure hardly anyone will actually see them, but if we make sure *they* see them, it will have them clawing each other's faces off. I know Brett. If he finds out Truett's son is banging his girlfriend, he'll lose his mind."

I scrutinize her for a moment as I take a sip of my coffee, stuck on the word *girlfriend* instead of ex-girlfriend. "You just want to incite chaos, don't you?"

With a sinister smile over her mug, she nods. "Yes, I do."

# TWELVE

## SAGE

"Holy shit." Adam is standing behind me, and I wince when I feel his eyes scrutinize my bedroom closet. I use the term closet lightly here because it's really more of a room lined with clothing racks that also has a bed in it.

"Yeah, it's a lot," I reply as I slide the hangers on the dress rack, looking for the bright-pink minidress I have in mind.

"How does one small person have so many clothes?"

"Focus," I say, leveling him with a terse glare. "Okay, so how fancy is this gala?"

"I don't know..." he replies as he pulls out a black lace top. "I wear a tuxedo. The ladies wear ball gowns."

"Hmm..."

We came in here a few minutes ago to decide on my wardrobe for this event, and I'm honestly torn between making a scene or discreetly pissing off his dad. The minute he sees Adam walking in with me on his arm will be sweet enough. I just don't know how far Adam wants to take this.

When I spot the neon-colored dress at the end of the third rack, I know right away it's not the right choice.

Adam's arm brushes mine as we reach for the same hanger, but I catch the way he instantly recoils, pulling his hand away, like touching me might give him some communicable disease.

I saw his face when I suggested the videos. The apprehension was clear as day because, in his mind, he was panicking at the mere thought of having to have sex with me again—as if that one fleeting night was too insane as it was.

I'm not offended by that. It has nothing to do with me and everything to do with all of that brainwashing he was subjected to that made him believe good Christian women are the only people his dick is allowed to respond to.

When he stares in confusion at another strappy dress, I take the hanger from him with a laugh. "Okay, how about I try on a few things, and you pick what you want me to wear to this thing?"

With a sigh, he nods and makes his way back to the couch.

When I walk out two minutes later in the bright-pink minidress, his jaw is hanging open like a fish. And not necessarily in a good way. The mermaid tattoo on my right thigh is showing, and so are her beautiful tits.

"I don't know if they'll let you in wearing that. It needs to be a little more formal."

"Fair enough," I reply, turning back to the room.

I pull a purple gown off the most unused rack in the corner. I wore it to one of the club's formal evenings, but since it was marketed so poorly, I was the only one dressed so nicely. Now I hate this dress, but I figure it might work for this occasion, so I slip it on.

When I walk out this time, Adam is staring at his phone. When his eyes drift upward to assess this option, his reaction is a little lacking. He gives a shrug. "It's pretty, but I don't know if he'd even recognize you in that."

"I have pink hair," I reply with a laugh.

"It's not quite...fierce enough. I want him to *know* we're trying to piss him off."

My fingers drum on the sequins of my dress as I think about what I own that could pull off something like that. Realization dawns as I remember the *perfect* piece I bought not too long ago.

"I got it," I shriek, lifting the hem of the gown as I shimmy back into my bedroom.

It takes a few minutes to get into, mostly because of all the straps and harnesses, but when I see myself in the full-length mirror, I know this is the one. It's elegant *and* kinky. It's giving Dominatrix wedding dress vibes.

With black, shimmery fabric hanging from my shoulders and hips, it covers enough to be classy but shows enough to be provocative. There are black leather straps across my torso and thighs with a deep plunging neckline that exposes just enough of my tits to make them look sexy.

The skirt of the gown has slits on both sides so that my legs peer through the material as I walk. And it's just see-through enough to leave very little to the imagination.

"I think I found the one," I announce as I walk out to the living room. Adam's eyes do a double take, glancing up for only a second at first before shooting right back up my body. His gaze rakes over every inch of me as I wait for him to say something.

His lips are parted and he quickly runs his tongue over the bottom one before he swallows his nerves. "That's a good choice."

"Think so?" I ask, spinning once. When I come back around to face him, I swear I notice him shifting and readjusting himself in his seat. He's staring at my body, and I can't tell if he's looking at my tattoos or my breasts—or my mermaid tattoo's breasts.

I can tell how much he's struggling with this, so I get an idea. "Stand up," I say, and he furrows his brow at me before doing it. Towering over me in a tight black T-shirt and snug-fitting jeans, I get a blast of heat to my core at the memory of him that night, bending me over the couch.

*You want this? Then take it.*

I almost don't recognize him now.

Stepping close to him, I turn my back as I brush my hair off to the side. "Unzip me, please."

His fingers brush the nape of my neck as I tilt my head for him. The back of my dress opens with an audible *zip*, but instead of holding it in place, I let it fall to the floor, so I'm standing in front of him in nothing but a thin cotton thong.

He sucks in a breath, and I feel him tense behind me. My bare flesh breaks out in goose bumps as I turn around and stare at him. His gaze lands heavily on my breasts and I watch something change in his expression. Shame warring with lust and desire. There's something in Adam's reaction that I've caught a few times now, like he's so worried about keeping a part of him hidden that it's tearing him apart.

And while I didn't do this to seduce him, I admit to myself now that if he let that part out again, I wouldn't stop him.

But that's not the plan.

Instead, I grab his bare hands and press them to my breasts.

When his eyes widen and he gazes up at my face in shock and confusion, I speak. "Listen, if we're going to do this, you have to stop acting so uncomfortable around me. I see you struggling."

"I'm not struggling," he retorts with hardened features.

"You are. We've already fucked, Adam. You had your face buried in my pussy for a half hour. So let's just accept that it happened, but it was just a one-time thing. Don't be afraid to touch me now because no one is going to buy us as a couple if you can't even look me in the eye or touch my tits."

"I am touching your tits."

"Because I'm *making* you touch them."

"No one has ever *made me* touch their tits before," he complains, averting his gaze.

"Well, I am because I want you to lighten up. In three weeks, I'm going to be your girlfriend. And if we go through with the tapes, then you'll have to do a lot more than touch my tits, so let's just get the awkwardness out of the way now."

"You're the craziest person I've ever met," he replies, and I can't quite tell if he's serious or teasing.

Either way, it stings a little. I hate being called crazy. Maybe that's what Brett did to me. Made me *feel* crazy for so long that I started to believe it. Made me not even believe myself sometimes.

"I'm not crazy," I reply through clenched teeth.

His hand squeezes my breast as his eyes meet mine. Something in them darkens. "I like crazy. I *need* crazy."

My thighs clench as warmth assaults my core again. And I feel as if I'm floating, high on his nearness, not quite sure what it was I was trying to accomplish with this or why I'm suddenly wishing he'd go a little crazy on me.

Instead, he pulls his hands away from my tits and puts distance between us. "I'm glad you did this. It did break some of the tension. And I think it's good that we just...lay everything out now."

"Okay..." I reply, stepping back.

"Full transparency, always. I need to know I can trust you."

"Of course. Same."

"And we have to agree that this...is fabricated. None of it is real. We can't... Especially like...that."

When he gestures between us, I get the message loud and clear, but my eyes narrow at that last part—like *that*. Something tells me Adam Goode isn't used to being so dirty, but rather than push the issue, I nod. "Of course," I say, repeating myself. "We don't want things getting complicated."

"Exactly."

"But we obviously can't be sleeping with other people at the same time, or it could ruin everything." I cross my arms over my chest, still standing in front of him, mostly naked.

"Agreed," he nods astutely. "Three months. If it's not working, we let it go. Call it quits." His air of confidence is infectious and a little disarming. For a man that struggled to touch my tits a moment ago, I find Adam's introspective nature refreshing. I don't meet a lot of men who can truly look me in the eye the way he does and listen to what I have to say without saying something condescending. That wild, unhinged night in my apartment aside, Adam truly is a gentleman—a secretly perverted gentleman.

"I can do three months."

His eyes drift around my apartment for a moment before coming back to my face. "Do you need any help...since you lost your job?"

I can't even keep my eyes from rolling at that not-so-subtle dig. "Don't worry about me. I can take care of myself. I've been doing it since I was seventeen."

His pure-brown eyes stay on my face for a moment too long, almost as if he doesn't believe me. So I snatch the dress off the floor and march to my room. After hanging the black dress on the hanger, I pull on a T-shirt and jeans before walking back out to the living room.

Adam is holding Roscoe in his arms, petting his head as they both look out the large window in my living room. Illuminated by the afternoon light, I take a moment to admire him. With his dark hair and trimmed beard, he seems almost too perfect. But every-thing about Adam seems perfect, and I can't help but wonder if there's something imperfect that he's hiding.

And I find myself wishing I could be the one he allows to see those imperfections.

# THIRTEEN

## ADAM

It's been three weeks since the start of this little plan, and every single day since she brought it up, I've been tempted to cancel. Every time I sit down at my desk to get some writing done or make a goal for my mysterious and bleak-looking future, I get caught up in this scheme we hatched like a couple of revenge-hungry high schoolers. Nearly every day, I've typed up a message to Sage to cancel. I'm a grown man, for fuck's sake. I don't need to be *pretending* anything, let alone pretending to date a woman, just to piss off my dad.

And yet, here I am.

I park my Audi outside the Laundromat and pull out my phone to text Sage. I only get two words in when the front door opens and she strides out.

*Holy fucking shit.*

That dress—and I use that term loosely—looks ten times better than it did in her apartment three weeks ago. Her pink hair is in curly waves over one shoulder and her exposed skin is shimmering like she's wearing some sort of thin layer of glitter.

Scrambling like an idiot, I jump out of the car and rush

around the back to open her door, but she's already climbing in
by the time I get there.

"What are you doing?" She laughs. Her lips are dark, the
shade of Merlot. And her eyes pop even more than they usually
do with thick fan-like lashes and silver shimmery eyeshadow over
her lids.

"I was being a gentleman," I reply with my hands out.

She waves me away as she pulls the door closed. On my way
back to the driver's side, I have to adjust my thickening cock in my
pants. This effect Sage has on me is just annoying at this point.
I'm not doing any of this to get closer to her or to get laid. It's not
about her and me. It's about causing as much grief and pain for
my father and her ex as possible. So I really need to keep my head
in the game.

If only I didn't have the feel of her breasts etched in my mind,
haunting me every day since.

As I climb into the car, she turns my way with a contempla-
tive expression. Instantly, my car smells sweet and flowery, and it
doesn't help my dick situation.

"Damn, Peaches. You look nice."

"You too, Church Boy. I like your suit."

"Thanks," I reply as I put the car into drive.

We're not far from the gala, which is being held at a botanical
garden just outside the downtown city area. We're going to arrive
about fifteen minutes late, which is exactly what we planned. I
need to make an entrance, and I really want to see the look on
Truett's face when I walk in with Sage on my arm.

My mother's reaction...I'm less excited about.

I wish I could clue her in on everything, but there's no way to
do that without her getting hurt. I just know that seeing me act
out is going to disappoint her, and I literally lose sleep every night
thinking about it. My mother didn't do anything wrong. She
doesn't deserve to be lied to.

*I knew I should have canceled this.*

Sage is typing away on her phone when my eyes cascade over

to her. Her leg is exposed all the way up to her hip, and I shift in my seat again at the mere thought of those pretty little thighs of hers wrapped around my waist. She's so tiny I bet I could fuck her up against a wall, holding her in place with nothing but my cock.

I mean, obviously not, but I love the idea.

I can't seem to help how lewd my thoughts get when I'm around her, and I'd be more proud of all the gross and filthy things I'd like to do to her if I wasn't so worried about myself at the same time. This isn't like me.

"Nervous?" she asks, and my eyes dash to her face.

"No," I lie. The truth is, I'm nervous as hell. There's a good chance we'll walk in and my father will have us escorted right out. Then all of this would be for nothing. At that point, we'll have to move right on to phase two of the plan, which I'm equally nervous about.

"So, we go in. Listen to some rich people speak about something. Eat our dinner. Dance. And leave." Sage has run through this plan so many times I'm starting to wonder if she's the one who's nervous.

"What are you so worried about? You have the easy part tonight. Brett won't be there."

"The easy part?" she asks, leveling me with a tense stare. "I have to walk into a giant roomful of people dressed like *this*."

I nearly slam on the brakes as a feeling of guilt washes over me. "This was your idea. You're not comfortable with it?"

"I'm comfortable with it," she argues. "I'm just...nervous."

I swallow down my rising shame as I let out a deep breath. "Well, if it's any consolation," I say, glancing over at her, "you'll be the most beautiful woman there, by far."

Her gaze softens as her eyes linger on mine. "That's very sweet of you."

The closer we get to the event, the more my anxiety grows. This is so out of character for me I'm trying to disassociate from it entirely. I normally either come to these alone or with some nice churchgoing girl my mother sets up for me. So I just do my best to shed the *good boy Adam* persona for one night. With her at my side, it doesn't feel so unnatural.

I pull the Audi into the valet line and Sage wrings her hands together in her lap. "Ready or not," she says.

*Ready or not.*

A moment later, our doors open simultaneously and we each step out into the warm Texas night air. Standing, I readjust my tux, pulling my tie from my neck before putting my arm out for her. She loops hers through mine and squeezes herself close to my body as we make our way to the entrance.

I can already feel people staring. Out here, it's mostly just guests and the valet attendants, but as we approach the door, I start recognizing the members of my father's team. His manager, publicist, event coordinator, assistants. Each of them beams at me and then turns their eyes toward Sage. That's when their smiles fade.

They're staring. And not in a good way.

It's an alarmed sort of staring, and I feel my blood starting to boil. They're silently judging her with their eyes. So I squeeze her tighter against me.

We step into the building as I softly mumble, "Here we go."

"Where's the bar?" she replies, and I find myself smiling as we enter the ballroom.

In any large event, it's always easy to spot my father because of the enthralled people that typically surround him. Tonight is no different. There's a crowd at the front of the room, and I can already hear his booming voice from here. Haughty laughter and a smug arrogance permeate the room like noxious gas.

"A drink is a good idea." I pull Sage toward the bar on the left. We get in line, standing in awkward silence until we reach the front and I order myself a whiskey on the rocks and her a vodka martini. Just as we get our drinks, I spot my brother, Caleb, with his wife, Briar, each holding drinks and looking miserable on the edge of the room.

I study their expressions as their eyes settle on Sage at my side.

Caleb appears instantly surprised and intrigued, unable to keep the confusion off his face. With his brows pinched together, he glances at me as if he's trying to place where he knows me from.

Briar only stares at Sage for a moment before quickly looking away, never one for confrontation.

As we approach them, Sage stays close to my side. I put out my hand to greet my brother. He shakes it with a look of amusement. "What are you up to?" he mutters quietly, but I ignore his question.

"Caleb, this is my..." I clear my throat as the words get caught. "My date...Sage."

*Fuck.*

I botched that one. I should have called her my girlfriend, not *date*. We're not trying to just make waves; we want to cause a tsunami. But it's okay. It was only the first try. I'll get better.

On my arm, I feel Sage squeeze me as if to say, *Nice job, asshole.*

Then she smiles politely at my brother and takes his hand as I continue the introductions.

"Sage, this is my brother Caleb, and his wife, Briar."

My chest feels tight with anxiety as Sage puts her tattooed hand in theirs one at a time. I notice Caleb's hesitation as if he can already sense that something is off. As if he knows it's all a lie.

But I can't tell him it's a lie. Sage and I went over the rules in her apartment, and I've been replaying them in my head ever since.

*Rule #1: No one can know the truth. Everyone needs to believe we're a real couple.*

That means brothers, friends, strangers, everyone. I don't normally keep secrets from my brothers, but lying to Caleb and Lucas should be easy. It's my mother I'm worried about.

If we want this to be effective, we have to sell it. To everyone.

Caleb's scrutinizing gaze finds my face. "So...where did you two meet?"

*Rule #2: Get the story straight.*

"He bought me breakfast at the diner. Last week." Sage is

wearing a bright smile, and I have to admit—it's convincing. Her arm slides across my back as she settles herself against my chest, her head nestled in the crook of my arm. She fits perfectly, and she's not a bad actress. Or not a bad liar, depending on how you look at it.

They don't need to know Sage and I shared our first breakfast over a month ago. It was my idea to go with a fake anniversary to avoid the date of our meeting lining up too precisely with the day my father fired me.

"Last week?" Briar asks, taking a sip of her champagne.

"Well, you move fast," Caleb adds.

My gaze slides down to Sage's face. "What can I say? It was instant chemistry."

Her cheeks dimple as she scrunches up her nose, smiling up at me. So far, so good. We're sort of killing it, if I do say so myself.

*Rule #3: PDA is key. Be as public as possible.*

Which means I should kiss her. We're definitely in one of those moments when I should lean down and press my lips to hers, but I hesitate a moment too long, and Sage's smile fades. She turns away, putting her vodka martini to her lips and taking a drink.

Clearing my throat, I glance back at my brother, who is still staring at me as if I've sprouted a dick on my forehead. With his eyes narrowed and his lips pressed together tightly, he looks about two seconds away from calling bullshit. My temperature starts to rise.

Just then, his eyes track over my shoulder, and his demeanor changes. I can tell by the way his mouth slackens and his shoulders tense that our father is somewhere behind me. He turns his eyes away and takes a large drink from his glass.

And when I turn around, I watch Truett Goode cross the room toward me.

This is the point of no return. First, he sees me, and he looks furious.

Then he sees her, and he looks terrified.

# FOURTEEN

## SAGE

The look on Truett's face is probably enough for Adam. I'd say if nothing else happens from this little charade, the expression of pure panic and terror his father is exhibiting probably makes this whole thing worth it.

I feel it in the way Adam pulls me a little closer, squeezing me tighter against his side as Truett approaches.

"Son," the man says by way of greeting as he reaches us. It's not exactly a warm greeting either, more of an emotionless acknowledgment.

"Dad," Adam replies, giving him a nod.

"Who..." he starts, clearing his throat to regain his composure, "who is this?"

Of course, Truett knows exactly who I am. I watched him enter that club nearly every night. I was there the first time he fucked someone in the VIP room, and I was there the night his son caught him with his face between another woman's thighs.

I know Truett, and he knows me.

When I glance up toward Adam, waiting for his answer to the

man's question, I expect him to falter again. I expect him to hesitate and uncomfortably call me his date.

But he doesn't falter at all.

"This is my *girlfriend*, Sage," Adam says with an air of smug confidence—head held high, arm proudly draped behind my back, eyes laser-focused on the man in front of him. There's a flinch in his father's expression as he utters that word.

"Girlfriend?" Truett replies with astonishment.

I can hardly contain the grin on my face.

"Nice to meet you," I say as sweetly as possible, extending my hand toward him. Adam's father stares at it a moment before a tall, thin blonde woman I recognize as Melanie Goode joins him at his side. Her reaction is not nearly as trained as everyone else's. She gapes at me with shock, her eyes scanning me from my pink hair down to my strappy black heels.

But just as I expect her to verbally belittle me with disgust or contention, she takes me completely by surprise as she smiles sweetly. "Well, aren't you a vision? I don't believe we've met. I'm Melanie."

She puts her perfectly manicured hand out, and I shake it nervously, waiting for Adam to jump in with the introductions. When he doesn't, I glance up at him and, for the first time, notice a sense of apprehension on his face. He's staring at his mother with softness and remorse written across his features.

"I'm Sage," I say to Melanie, but this time, my smile isn't forced.

Truett's scornful gaze is directed at me, and just as he opens his mouth to say something, there's a booming voice over the loudspeaker. A man in a blue suit at the front of the stage warmly welcomes all of the attendees and invites us all to find our seats.

Without a word, Melanie smiles tightly at me before turning her back and pulling her husband toward the front of the room.

As I glance back up at Adam, I notice that the confidence and satisfaction are gone from his face.

We make our way over to the tables in the middle of the room.

They're large and round, big enough to fit eight people at each, which means we're seated at the same table as Adam's parents, his brother and his wife, along with two empty seats.

Adam is tense beside me as we wait in silence for the others to join us. Melanie Goode keeps glancing my way and every time I catch her staring, she gives me a polite smile and looks away.

Briar Goode looks like she's on a mission to get drunk before everyone else. She's already halfway through a new glass of wine.

A man who looks more like Adam and Melanie is sitting on the other side of Briar. No one greets him and he doesn't speak. Just leans back in his chair as if he's already bored, and the event hasn't even started.

"That's my brother Luke," Adam whispers in my ear. "He hates these things."

"I can see that," I reply under my breath. Then I glance at the empty chair. "Who is that seat for?"

The muscles in Adam's jaw clench, and I sense that I've just touched on a sensitive topic. "My youngest brother Isaac."

"Is he coming?" I ask.

"No." Then he takes a drink and averts his eyes. "He doesn't come...to anything anymore."

With that, I drop the subject. The last thing I want to do tonight is get on Adam's nerves. He's my lifeline, the only person I can rely on in this den of wolves.

"How are you feeling?" he asks. His lips are so close to my ear I can feel them brushing my hair. If I were to turn my head, we'd be mouth to mouth. Something tells me he was about to kiss me earlier after the introduction with Caleb and Briar. But he hesitated a second too long and the moment passed.

I'm cursing myself for not practicing the kissing before tonight. I had him touch my boobs. Why didn't I just kiss him too, to get it out of our systems? Because before tonight is over, we're going to have to kiss at least once. That was the deal.

"I need more alcohol," I reply in a whisper with my nearly empty glass up to my lips. "Everyone is staring at me."

"That's the idea, remember?" His voice is low and authoritative, sending a wave of chills down my spine. I hate how good he smells and how nice it feels to be seen with him. To be seen *as* his.

Adam always looks clean-cut and well-dressed, but tonight is next level. In a dark-charcoal suit with a coral-colored tie, he almost looks like he dressed to match me. Not to mention the pink in the silk around his neck brings out the warm-brown tones of his eyes. And the soft-pink hue of his lips.

"You're not going to stop me from drinking too much, are you?" I ask with a coy smirk as I finish my martini.

"Fuck no," he snaps. "Get as drunk as you want. Give them a show."

With that, he waves down the waiter.

We don't actually get all that drunk. Although when one rich white man after another takes the stage to talk about the foundation, almost as much as they talk about themselves and how *generous* they are, I wish that waiter would make his trips a little more frequent.

After what feels like hours of torture, they serve dinner and the music plays. I barely pick at my meal. It's a pecan-crusted chicken breast that's bland and tastes a little too much like this place feels—smug and snobbish. The charity they're supporting is literally for feeding children in third-world countries while they sit here and gorge themselves on a three-course meal, patting themselves on the back for how benevolent they are.

The longer I sit, the more bitter and cynical I get.

So when I notice the conversation around us growing quiet, I turn to Adam. With my lips against his ear, I whisper, "I'm bored. Let's cause a scene."

His brow twitches as he fights a smile. There's vitriol in his eyes as they glare across the table at his father, who's talking to some old guy.

Adam's eyes find mine for a moment before he tosses down his napkin and takes my hand.

"Let's dance," he says out loud.

Everyone at the table glances our way as we stand up and move toward the dance floor. There are already a few couples out there, but they're mostly very old and very boring. The music is some nameless, instrumental song I don't know, and definitely not the kind of tune anyone should be grinding to.

Not that Adam and I are *grinding*, but as he pulls my body against his, my right leg slips through the slit in my dress, exposing my tattooed leg all the way up—mermaid tits and all. I'm practically straddling his thigh as we start to sway in gentle circles around the dance floor.

To my surprise, Adam is actually a pretty good dancer. He's got rhythm and grace, leading me with strength, so all I really have to do is hold on to him and let him guide the way.

I scan the room as we move, noticing the way people stare at us with confusion before leaning in toward each other as if to gossip about us. It gives me a strange sense of satisfaction to know I'm disrupting this whole stupid charade of theirs.

"People are watching," I say to Adam, but as I turn my head to look up at him, I find him staring softly at me. Not with condemnation or judgment. Almost like he's...*admiring* me.

With a blink, the look is gone, his expression tightening and his jaw clenching.

"You should have seen the look on my father's face when he recognized you. Scared shitless."

"Good. Let him sweat a little," I reply. "Do you think he suspects it's fake?"

With a subtle shake of his head, he says, "No. He has no reason to think it's fake, but we might need to sell it a little more."

"Then kiss me," I reply bluntly. Adam's eyes grow serious, and I notice the bounce of his Adam's apple as he swallows.

"Now?"

"Are they watching?"

He glances back at his father's table. "Yes," he says with trepidation.

"Then do it," I say, trying to encourage him. His arm is

wrapped around my lower back and we're still moving in harmony with the music, but I can tell Adam is struggling with this part. And I don't understand why.

We shuffle around the room for another turn and I can see him trying to find the right time. Just then, the song comes to an end, and the dancers around us freeze in place, clapping for the orchestra on stage.

"Now," I say as we come to a stop. His grip on my back tightens, and I feel the hard planes of his chest against my breasts as he squeezes me tighter. I also feel the swell of his dick in his pants, and while it's not a raging hard-on, it's not exactly soft either.

Just as our eyes meet and he leans down toward me, I brace for the kiss—

"Can I cut in?"

Our movement stops and we both freeze, our lips only an inch apart. Adam's fingers squeeze mine so tight it almost hurts.

The clear, Southern drawl of the man behind me feels like a cold drip of fear cascading down my spine, and as much as my body is telling me to run, to get away and hide—I can't.

Instead, Adam and I make brief, intense eye contact before turning toward his father, who is waiting to take my hand like it's the casual, expected thing to do.

My stomach turns when Adam tightens his grip on my back.

"It's just a dance," Truett mutters darkly.

He can't tell his father no. Not when hundreds of people are watching. He can't cause a scene here and now, painting Truett as the victim. It's not part of the plan.

I hear the tightness in his chest as he replies to his father, "No."

"Of course," I say, interrupting Adam. My smile is as fake as it's ever been and probably looks more cross than I want it to. And when Adam squeezes me again, I fear the confrontation might be inevitable after all.

So I peel his hands from my back and look him in the eye. "Of course," I say through gritted teeth. "It's just a dance."

Adam's molars grind as he reluctantly places my hand in Truett's and steps away. The old man gives me a sickening smile that makes my skin crawl. His heavy-scented cologne replaces the sweet and subtle scent of Adam's as he pulls me against him. I have to force myself to look natural, to smile and move my feet when the music starts playing again.

Even though we're on a dance floor surrounded by couples in a room packed with hundreds of people, I feel alone with Truett, and it's not a pleasant feeling at all.

He tugs me closer so my body is flush with his, and bile rises in my throat. Fear and panic create a tremor deep in my bones, and I keep my eyes unfocused as he grins at me.

"Just keep smiling," he says in a low tone.

"I am," I reply. Even I know my tight-lipped expression is probably not selling anything. But right now, I don't care.

"You think you're so clever, don't you? How good is that pussy that you've seduced my son?"

It dawns on me at this moment that he doesn't suspect us of lying. He believes Adam and I are a real thing, which means he believes Adam...and blames me.

*Just stick with the story, Sage.*

"I didn't even have to try that hard," I reply, my smile growing wider as I manage to look him in the eye. "I had him worshiping me just hours after you nearly knocked him out."

"I bet you did."

"Does it make you sick to know how easily I won him over? How fast I convinced your son to put pussy before God?"

He pinches my back, and I bite back the urge to yelp as tears sting behind my eyes.

"Watch yourself, you little slut," he mutters lowly, keeping his expression warm and kind as he insults me.

"No, I'd rather not," I reply, glancing around the room for Adam. But with the crowd on the dance floor now, I can't seem to find him.

I want to make sure he hasn't abandoned me with this

monster, but also because I don't want him to hear this next part, where I go a little rogue.

"You know, Reverend Goode," I say, forcing my voice to stay kind. "I'd stop seeing Adam...for a price."

"Whores always have a price," he replies. "Name it."

My face grows solemn and serious as I level my gaze at his. Being this close, I notice that he looks so much more fragile and weathered in person than he does on TV. When he's behind that pulpit on the stage in front of a crowd, he appears indestructible. But seeing him like this, I'm reminded that he's not. He's a vulnerable little man with a fragile ego and more to lose than the power to protect himself.

"I want the deed," I say, and there's a flinch in his eyes as I say those words. I already know he won't take the bait, but I have to try.

"The deed to the club, you mean," he replies.

"Of course. Is that how much your son's virtue is worth?"

The song comes to an end, and Truett only smiles at me. "That's what I thought," I say with a wink. But as I start to pull away, he snatches me by the waist and yanks me against him. My blood runs cold as he holds me in place, putting his mouth against my ear as he mutters darkly.

"Don't you dare fucking threaten me, you vile slut. You have no idea who you're fucking with. If you don't leave my son alone, I'll find a way to ruin you, understand me? If I ever see you with him again, I won't play so nicely next time."

I'm practically shivering as he releases his hold on me, letting me stumble backward. Before I know it, I'm in Adam's arms, and he's staring down at me with concern etched in his features.

"Thank you for the dance, beautiful," Truett says with a beaming grin. The people around us watch with rapt appreciation, and they all start clapping as he strides away from me.

Adam turns me so I'm facing him, his thumb stroking over my cheek.

"Are you okay?" he mouths silently.

For a moment, I feel so full of rage and anger I could cry on the spot, but Adam's eyes are tethering me to the moment. Instead of crying, I grab his arms and pull him closer. I don't know how many people are watching, but I know we have an audience as I plaster a big fake smile on my face.

Then I lean in and mutter through my teeth, "I fucking hate him, and I want to make him suffer."

Satisfaction washes over Adam's eyes as a grin stretches across his cheeks. "Me too," he replies.

"Then fucking kiss me, and make it good."

With that, he crashes his lips against mine without an ounce of hesitation or doubt.

Game fucking on.

# FIFTEEN

## ADAM

Sage's lips are soft and taste like chocolate with a hint of vodka. And considering this is supposed to be a fake kiss for show, it's strange to me that that's the first thing I notice. But as she melts against me, leaning her weight into my arms, I find myself wanting to deepen the kiss from more than a peck on the lips.

The eyes of those around us burn against my back, watching as I hold her, my mouth pressed to hers. If only they knew my heart was beating wildly under my suit and my dick was struggling to control itself. Making out and popping boners at elegant events is definitely frowned upon, but I don't care.

Having to stand idly by while my father had her in his grasp made me irritable and out of my mind. I didn't know what they were talking about or what he was promising her. The feeling of being out of the loop, and having her out of my reach, had my blood boiling like a fever.

That's why I'm feeling so desperate and frantic now.

After a moment, I gently pull away from the kiss and my eyes meet hers. Warm sky-blue orbs gaze up at me and I lose my sense of time and space. I forget I'm surrounded by my parents' friends. I forget about the plan. For just a second, I want to kiss her again.

So I do.

With my hands on either side of her face, I drag her mouth back up to mine and press my tongue against the seam of her lips. I think, for a second, she's going to fight me. Instead, she opens gracefully, letting me lick my way into her mouth. Our tongues brush together in soft friction as she lets out a gentle hum.

On my back, her fingers are gripping tightly against my jacket, pulling me closer. And somewhere in my mind, I keep reminding myself that this is for show. We're doing this for a reason that has nothing to do with my heart or my dick.

However, my dick doesn't seem to get that message. She brushes against it, and a hot buzz of arousal shoots through my body. I'm painfully aware of just how hard I am and how much she keeps shifting against me, which has me wanting to fuck her right here on the dance floor.

I'd love to see the look on my father's face then.

There's a bright flash distracting both of us from the kiss. Sage and I flinch at the same time as we pull apart and stare into the eyes of a young man holding a large camera with a flash bulb attached to the top. He gives us an awkward grin.

"Can I get your names for the publication?"

My brow furrows and he notices, shrinking into himself.

"Sage Astor," she says proudly, and I have to relax my clenched jaw.

"Adam Goode," I add.

"I know who you are," he replies with an awkward chuckle.

This is what we wanted, right? Publicity. Proof. Exposure. So why does it still feel so strange? He's going to post that picture somewhere and then the world will know. I have a pink-haired, pierced, and tattoo-covered girlfriend. It feels like the one thing I've been taught to avoid since childhood and I didn't even realize it. All the while, my mother was trying to set me up with quote, unquote "good Christian girls," but what she was really accomplishing was teaching me to never look twice at a girl like Sage.

And now I'm intentionally breaking that rule.

Sage and I stand in awkward silence for a moment before I realize I'm still holding her affectionately. My hands drop away as she takes a step back.

"Can we go now?" she whispers, turning her gaze away from mine. Judging by the frigid chill in her voice, the unexpected photographer killed her buzz.

"Yes," I reply flatly.

My hand moves to her lower back as I guide her to our table to say our goodbyes. She's tense under my touch. As we reach my family, I make the announcement that we're leaving, and I notice the smug look of victory on my father's face. I hate the idea that he thinks he's won somehow.

I want to yank him up by his collar and tell him that this is only the beginning. I'd like to spit in his face and remind him what a royal piece of shit he is, but I can't do that here.

Instead, I kiss my mother on the cheek and wave goodbye to my brothers as I escort my date to the exit.

"I'm starving," she mumbles in the passenger seat. As I pull the car out onto the main road, I glance over at her and feel my stomach growling like she summoned it.

"Didn't you eat the chicken?" I ask.

She shrugs. "The chicken was fine, but that rice tasted like rotten dirt." She twists her face up in disgust and I bite back a laugh.

"That was truffle risotto," I reply.

"I thought truffles were chocolate."

"Truffle is a dessert, but truffles are an exotic mushroom that, yes, taste a little like rotten dirt."

"Rich people are weird," she replies, scrolling through her phone. With another laugh, I glance sideways at her, noticing that she's typing the charity name into the search bar.

"Looking for that picture already? It's a little early."

"I know. I just want to see if we're in any pics yet."

She's still scrolling as I come up to the intersection leading to her apartment. There aren't any good restaurants in this part of town. It's mostly businesses and clubs. So I make a right instead.

"You like burgers?" My voice is low, almost like I don't want her to hear me.

"Huh?" she asks, looking up.

"I know a good burger joint over here."

At the mere thought of greasy ground beef covered in cheese, my stomach starts to growl louder this time, and Sage giggles next to me.

"You're taking me out for burgers?" she asks as if it's so hard to believe.

"*I* am going to grab some food. You mentioned you were hungry. Would you like to go with me or not?" My voice is a little too loud as I snap at her, but she only reacts with a tight-lipped smile and humor in her eyes.

"Yes, please."

With an audible huff, I pull into the run-down parking lot of the place Caleb introduced me to a few years ago. It's clearly popular because the inside is packed to the brim with people. After finding a place to park, I hop out and make my way toward Sage's side to open her door, but she's already climbing out before I get there.

We walk together to the window, where we place our order for two cheeseburgers, an order of onion rings, and two chocolate shakes. Sage is bouncing eagerly on her toes as we wait in silence for the food to come out. And when they call our number, she lets out a growly hum, inhaling the scent of fried onions wafting from the paper bag.

Instead of trying to fight for a table inside, we walk out to the car and place our food on the trunk.

"Go ahead," I say, patting the surface. "Have a seat."

With an onion ring perched between her lips, she tries to hop up but fails on account of her small size and awkward heels. Grinning to myself, I place my hands under her arms and hoist her up until she's sitting on the back with her legs dangling over.

"Thanks," she mumbles with a smirk.

I reply with a silent nod. Then we dig into our late-night, greasy meal together. The sounds she makes as she devours her cheeseburger have my dick twitching, so I turn my body away from hers, afraid of a repeat of what happened tonight on the dance floor.

"Oh! Look!" she shrieks, staring down at her phone with wide eyes.

Moving to stand next to her, I glance at the screen and notice it's her and me standing together near the bar. She's tucked perfectly under my arm as we talk to my brother and his wife.

"Golden boy, Adam Goode, seems to have found himself an interesting girlfriend for once!"

"It says that?" I ask, leaning closer, and sure enough, it's an Instagram post from someone who looks like they screenshot the photo from another source. "What do the comments say?"

Sage drops her phone in her lap and glares at me. "Adam, we never read the comments."

"Why?"

"Because that's where the trolls are," she replies.

"There're already twenty comments. I want to see what they say."

"Have at it," she says, tossing me her phone.

I don't know what I'm even looking for as I hit the button that reveals everyone's comments. I think I want proof that this fake dating scheme is as controversial as we want it to be. It's the uproar and shock that I need to see.

What I get in the comments chills my blood instead.

*He could do better.*

*How much did he rent her for?*

*What on earth is he doing??*

*Why, Adam. Whyyyyyyyy?*

My face falls and I fight the urge to respond to each one of these assholes. What on earth would I even fucking say?

I harden my features and close out the app, handing the phone back to Sage. She's holding her burger in one hand, a dot of ketchup on the side of her cheek. With a flex of my hand, I shove it in my pocket to keep from wiping the ketchup away.

She continues scrolling as she eats. When I notice the way her shoulders tense and goose bumps cover her arms, I shrug out of my jacket and wrap it around her small frame.

"Thanks," she mumbles, glancing up at me with uncertainty in her tone.

"So, are there any more posts about us?" I ask casually as I fish my burger out of the bag. She reads a bit as she scrolls. It seems there are a lot of posts about us together, making some pretty generous waves in the Goode church and Austin community. It's the validation I think I needed.

But am I ready to take it to the next step? Because being seen together and being seen *fucking on camera* are two very different things.

There's a buzzing vibration in my pocket, so I shift my burger to the opposite hand and pull out my phone. It's a text from Caleb, and the message makes my stomach drop to my fucking balls.

. I like your girlfriend.

With a twinge of guilt, I struggle with how to respond. What would I say if she was my real girlfriend? Thank you? Plus, with

Caleb, I can't exactly tell if he's being serious or not. So I don't say anything at all, and a moment later, he texts again.

> Dad seems pissed.

And there it is. That's why Caleb likes my new girlfriend, because she ruffles Dad's feathers, and while Caleb has never had the balls to do it himself, he loves anything that pisses our father off. If only he knew that was my plan all along. If only I could tell him that Dad is pissed because my new date is a threat to his name and reputation. But I can't. I promised to follow the rules, which means everyone has to believe it's true.

*Good.* I respond without explanation.

"You were right," Sage says, stealing my attention. "This place is the best."

I glance up from my phone to see her sitting on my car, in my jacket, with ketchup on her face, looking infuriatingly cute and sexy at the same time.

Letting out a tense sigh, I pick up a napkin from the trunk and lean in, wiping the mess from her cheek. "You're a mess," I mumble.

She smiles in return, dimples piercing her cheeks. I narrow my eyes at her in a grimace as she beams.

I fucking hate it when she does that.

# SIXTEEN

## SAGE

The car is quiet as Adam pulls up to the front of the Laundromat. His jacket is still wrapped around my shoulders. It's past eleven, but I've been a night owl for so long that late hours barely affect me anymore.

He puts the car in park and lets his hands settle in his lap. I don't climb out of the car just yet. I feel like he wants to say something, and part of me wonders if it's going to be him backing out of the plan.

"Are you sure you want to go through with this?" I ask, my voice level and quiet.

"I'm sure." His response is quick, which I don't expect. I glance over to stare at his silhouette in the dark car, half of his face illuminated by the streetlights and neon signs.

Adam is always so stoic. Like he's holding in his anger, burying it deep within himself, so now it's etched into his DNA. This is the only way he knows how to be, which makes me want to rub my thumb into the crease between his brows until he lets that worry and anxiety melt away.

At times, he's sweet. Charismatic. Like the morning in the

diner or tonight as he proudly held me by his side. I have a feeling that was the *real* Adam, but he's been so conflicted with duty and obligation his whole life; he's been tricked into thinking he's someone he's not. And now that his father has pulled the morality rug from under him, Adam has turned into a powder keg ready to blow.

I wish I could heal him of all the pain he's radiating.

"Will this make you feel better?" I ask. When he glances my way, I continue, "When you ruin your reputation to spite him. Will it make you happy? Able to move on?"

The crease in his brow deepens. "Does it matter?"

His tone is cold, reminding me that even after those small gestures of kindness and the bone-melting kisses tonight, Adam Goode still refuses to let me in. Ever since seeing his dad tonight, his entire mood's darkened, and I can't seem to get him back.

"Of course it does," I reply.

"We're not doing this to make ourselves feel good, Peaches. We're doing this to tarnish his reputation."

Reaching across the seat, I place my hand on his arm, my fingers sliding over the rich fabric of his black tuxedo. "It's okay to do things because they feel good. That doesn't make you a bad person."

He looks first at my hand and then my face. Hearing what I just said, paired with how I'm touching him...I realize now that it looks like I'm soliciting something. So I quickly take my hand away.

Clearing my throat, I look out my window as I speak.

"We'll start filming tomorrow. We can do it at my place."

"Okay," he replies, and when I glance back at him, I notice the angry crease has softened.

"Noon," I add. To which he nods.

"Good night, Adam."

Before he can even try to get out and open my door for me, I climb out. I barely make out his saying *good night* before the door shuts and I'm alone on the street.

As I make my way to the front of the Laundromat, unlocking it with my key, I expect him to drive away. But he doesn't. He waits for me to be safely inside before he takes off into the night.

✝

"Why are you watching porn in my Laundromat?"

I nearly spit out my Mountain Dew as Gladys leans over my shoulder and stares in shock at the video playing on the screen of my phone.

My finger swipes the app closed as my cheeks heat with embarrassment.

"One month without a boyfriend, and you're that horny already?"

I let out a laugh as I pocket my phone and get back to work loading coins into the sorting machine.

"Fun fact, Gladys. I'm always horny."

Her laugh is hearty and warm as she tousles my hair. "I believe it."

"And second of all, that wasn't porn. It's an app where people can upload videos of themselves and people pay to watch them."

"Oh...like porn," she replies sarcastically. "Is that what you're going to do for money now?" Then she holds up her hands in surrender. "Hey, no judgment. I support sex workers."

With a smile, I shake my head. God, I love Gladys.

"Actually...maybe." My eyes squint with unease as I watch her face for a reaction. I've been looking for a new job since I left the club, but no one is hiring at the moment. Instead, I've been helping around the Laundromat and Gladys has been flexible with my rent to allow me more time to look.

To my surprise, she only looks mildly uncomfortable with the news that my new job venture might be porn.

"But not by myself," I continue. "That...new guy I'm seeing—"

"The rich, older one," she replies.

"Yeah, him. He and I want to make some videos. For...fun."

Yikes, this feels forced and uncomfortable. Is she even buying any of this? I mean, I did work in a sex club, so it can't be that much of a stretch for her to see me doing this now.

She's folding towels as she seems to be mentally chewing on what I've just told her. Her face tenses in scrutiny before she glances my way and shrugs.

"Hey, make money with him if you can, I guess. Harold and I used to record ourselves all the time. But he would have never, ever let me post them anywhere. It would have been nice to at least make some money with them."

"Oooh, so kinky, Gladys. Do you still have them?" I ask with a giddy smile.

"Somewhere in a box, I'm sure. If I die and you find a video-tape labeled *Hawaii vacation*, burn it."

Gladys and I are both laughing so hard now neither of us hear the front doorbell chime. It's not until I feel his gloomy presence hovering three feet away that I realize Adam is here. God, his dad really did a number on him last night.

My laughter dies as I turn to stare at him. His sudden presence sends a flutter of butterflies to my stomach because I know exactly what comes next.

"Oh, hi," I mutter.

"Hi," he replies flatly.

He's in a pair of dark-gray joggers and a V-neck T-shirt that hugs his chest and shoulders. His dark hair looks a little wet at the tips like he just got out of the shower and came straight over. I can smell the potent scent of his cologne from here, musky and rich. I don't know if it's laced with pheromones or if that's just the effect of expensive cologne, but it has me noticing just how ridiculously handsome he is today.

And how badly I want to rub my face all over his pecs.

And feel those thick biceps wrapped around me.

Jesus, maybe Gladys was right. I am horny as fuck.

"Ready?" he asks, nodding toward the door. Has he totally forgotten that we're supposed to be selling it as a couple?

I can feel Gladys staring at me, so I widen my eyes at him, glancing toward Gladys as if to remind him we have an audience.

Instantly, his cold, detached demeanor morphs into a forced smile as he crosses the room. Without warning, he leans down and presses his lips to mine. It's a quick peck, but it takes me by surprise. As he stands upright, he smiles at Gladys.

"Hi again."

"Hi again," Gladys replies with a playful smirk on her face.

"I'll finish these later," I tell her as I stand from my chair.

"Go. Have fun," she says, waving us away.

"Mind if I send Roscoe down?" I ask.

"No, I'll watch him," she replies, shooting me a wink. For a moment, I feel terrible about lying to her, even if it is a small, harmless fib.

"Thanks, Gladys!"

Grabbing Adam by the arm, I tug him toward the door leading up to my apartment. He seems as tense as I'm feeling today, which is good, I guess. I don't want to be the only nervous person in this scenario.

After we reach my apartment, I carry Roscoe down the stairs, hearing Gladys call for him before I set him down and shut him out in the stairwell.

Then it's just me and Adam alone in my apartment with heavy doses of anticipation and awkwardness.

"Got anything to drink?" he asks.

I scurry toward the kitchen. "Is beer okay?"

"Yes," he replies as I pull out two, one for each of us.

After a long drink, he looks determined and ready to work. "So, how are we going to do this?"

"Okay, so I've been thinking," I say, pulling out my phone. "We can upload the clips on FanVids—you've heard of it, right?"

"That amateur porn app?"

"Yeah. We can start with short clips—fifteen to thirty seconds.

Then we share them anonymously on socials and try to get subscribers. Then after it's created some buzz, we post longer videos. *Real* videos. Well...real-*ish*."

His brows are scrunched together as he stares down at my phone, the FanVids app open to show him how people can scroll the feed. Guessing by the confusion on his face, he's not familiar with the app and doesn't quite know how this is going to work, but that's okay. I'll handle the distribution; I just need him to be *him* and play the part.

"So people can see these short clips for free?"

"Basically. But we have to show your face. We need people to see that it's you."

As I scroll through the app, video after video popping up, my skin starts to grow hot. Maybe it's the suggestive nature of the clips, or maybe it's the realization that *we're* about to post stuff like this too. Either way, I'm struggling to even hold still at this point.

"Let's do it," he says at last, and I bite my lip as I stare up at him.

Our eyes meet for a moment, and I get a whiff of his cologne again, my body growing excited at the prospect of getting to touch him again. The room fills with tension while neither of us moves.

Finally, I clear my throat and walk toward the couch. His eyes follow me before landing on the tripod I have set up already.

"Have you done this before?" he asks.

"No," I reply. "Well, not like this. I just bought this because I thought it would make things easier." Then I show him how I clip my phone onto the tripod and point it at the couch. Suddenly, we have a hands-free device for shooting videos.

He swallows without moving toward me. He's definitely nervous. "So, now what?"

There's an audible silence as we each take a long drink of our beer, both of us clearly needing the liquid courage to go through with this. After letting out a heavy sigh, I roll my shoulders back.

If we're going to do this, we should get it over with, right?

"So I'm thinking for the first clip, we can be on the couch, me straddling you." I grab the tripod and place it in the center, facing the couch. "Here, sit."

He hesitates.

Then, after a heavy sigh, he grabs the back of his T-shirt at the nape of his neck and whips it over his head in one fast swipe. I swear my mouth goes dry as I stare at his chest, lightly dusted with dark hair down to the ripples of his abs and the V-shape leading into his gray joggers.

*Holy shit*, I curse silently in my mind as I stare at him.

"Pants too?" he asks.

I force myself to swallow. "Maybe just...underwear for this shot," I stammer. "They won't be in the frame, but even if they are, I'll be on top of you." My voice cracks.

*Why am I so nervous?*

One by one, he slips off his shoes and pulls off his socks. Then he drags his sweats down his legs, and I turn away. Why the hell must Adam Goode be such a perfect specimen of a man? Why can't he just be as repulsive as his father?

"My turn," I whisper to myself before I yank my Van Halen T-shirt over my head and slide my shorts off. Suddenly, we're standing in our underwear, both of us trying to awkwardly cover ourselves as if we haven't already screwed on this very couch. Why does this feel so much stranger now?

"All right, sit," I say, pointing toward the sofa. Suppressing his nerves, he rounds the couch and drops down in the middle.

I quickly open the camera app on my phone and aim it at him, making sure to get him centered so his face doesn't get cut off. I can crop more later.

With that, I climb onto his lap, one leg on each side of his hips. For a moment, my brain seems to short-circuit from this proximity. His face is just inches from mine and he's definitely sporting a half-staff erection, pressing against my panties.

But I need to stay professional about this. Taking a deep breath, I try to center myself to focus.

*Fuck, he smells so good.*

"The camera can't see my face if you're in front," he says. Which is a good point—the camera is pointed at the back of my head. So, I grab the tripod and maneuver it to the side, catching us at an angle. I'm still slightly covering his face, but I lean my head back a little so he's in plain view.

"You're gonna lean back like that?" he asks with a wrinkle in his brow.

"Umm...no. That's awkward. Here, grab my hair," I say, picking up his hand and putting it against the back of my scalp. Immediately, he takes a handful and pulls, so my spine arches and my head hangs.

We both glance at the screen. It's perfect. Adam is taking up most of the frame, my body only in one-third of the screen, just enough to be suggestive and honestly, hot as hell.

"Okay, so I'm going to press *record* and we're going to move like we're fucking. You keep pulling my hair, but make sure to make a sexy face."

"A sexy face?" he asks with a laugh.

"Yeah. Don't just be, like, dead-faced. You need to scowl at me."

"*Scowl* at you?"

I let out an exasperated sigh, and he lets go of my hair. "Listen, Adam. If we're going to do this, you're not going to fuck me like a good little Christian boy. You're going to fuck me like you hate me. You're going to fuck me so dirty your grandkids will have to repent for it. Spit on me. Pull my hair. Slap me around. Make it the dirtiest fucking thing you've ever done. Okay?"

His face is frozen for a moment, his pupils slowly dilating, and that half-staff turns into a solid staff—which I guess means he gets the message.

"Okay," he says with a crack in his voice.

"Okay," I reply, leaning back to press record.

"Wait," he says, stopping me. Then he reaches around to my back and with one hand, he quickly pinches the clasp of my bra and it comes free effortlessly. He slides it off before tossing it across the room.

As he glances quickly at my breasts, I feel momentarily ashamed that my nipples are already hard and tight—and have been since he walked into my apartment, looking and smelling so damn good.

Shaking off the embarrassment, I reach behind me and hit record on my phone.

"Action," I say, turning to face him.

Our first shot is a mess. He fumbles for my hair and I struggle with where to put my hands. I start to bounce on his lap, but my rhythm is off and his thrusts don't match mine. Nothing about this is hot at the moment.

"Okay, cut," I say, sitting upright and hitting the red circle on my phone to stop the recording.

"That was terrible," he replies with a despondent sigh.

"Yes, it was."

"Will they be able to hear us in the video?"

"I can cover it with music, or we can leave the sound on."

"Leave it on," he replies, suddenly looking as if he has a plan of his own.

"Okay... Take two."

As soon as I hit the red button on my phone, the camera beeps for three seconds before it starts recording. Then, without warning, Adam's hand is back in my hair, but this time, he pulls so hard I let out a yelp.

His hips jerk upward, sending me toward his chest. Then his mouth is next to my ear.

"Fucking ride it," he mutters with control. I nearly gasp, just from the shock of his sudden change of demeanor. Where the hell did this come from?

With a bruising grip on my hip, he squeezes me tightly as he guides my movements, bouncing me on his lap.

I'm momentarily struck speechless as another gasp and cry escapes my lips. Because of the angle of my head, I can't quite see his face, but I don't need to see to know he's really in the scene this time. He's clearly selling it, and I'm caught off guard, so I start to worry if I'm acting the part well enough.

"Faster," he growls, and my momentum picks up speed.

Fuck, I'm getting so hot from this. It feels...real.

Arousal blooms between my legs every time I land against his hard length, and I feel a slow build toward something that is definitely against the rules, but I can't help it. The noises coming out of my mouth are not acting. And when the hand in my hair moves until it's wrapped around my throat, I'm struck silent.

*What the fuck is he doing?*

*And more importantly, why the fuck do I like it?*

He yanks my face toward his, putting our lips inches apart as he sneers. "What did you say? You want me to fuck you like I hate you? Well, here you go."

My eyes are wide as I stare into his, my hands grasping for his arm or shoulder as I keep up the rhythm of my bouncing. I manage one last yelp just before he crashes our mouths together, kissing me hard as he tightens his grip on the sides of my neck.

His tongue invades my mouth, and I forget how to breathe. Melting into the moment, my body tingles with the deprivation of air, and just when I start to feel as if I might pass out, everything stops.

His hand drops and I fall away from his kiss.

I'm gasping for air and waiting for my vision to focus when he says, "That should be enough, right?"

"Huh?"

"Jesus, are you okay? You told me to be rough."

I feel as if I'm dangling at the top of a roller coaster, waiting for a rush of wind that never comes. Instantly, I snap out of it and turn around to grab my phone to hit stop on the video.

"Um...yeah, that should be perfect."

With trembling fingers, I replay the video. My heart is still hammering in my chest, and there's still a slight throbbing need between my legs. The minute Adam leaves, I plan to relieve that. Maybe more than once.

We're both leaning over the phone to see the video, and it's only slightly uncomfortable to watch. But it's honestly...perfect.

His face is so carnal and erotic, nothing like the virtuous church boy we see on TV. And his words are so titillating that every time I rewatch it, hearing him say *fucking ride it*, I feel my panties moisten more.

"Yeah..." I say, clearing my throat, "I think that will do just fine."

# SEVENTEEN

ADAM

"**D**amn, I look pretty fucking hot," I say, watching the video on my phone.

Sage has done an impressive job of editing the short ten-second clip by adding a filter, cropping, and putting some soft music with a heavy beat in the background to match the action in the video.

She scoffs at my remark, rolling her eyes from across the room.

As soon as we filmed that scene, we both got dressed and I put in an order for some Chinese food to be delivered to her apartment. She's curled up on the couch, eating lo mein out of the box, as I sit at the mismatched table in her kitchenette area with a box of fried rice.

"How many views does it have?" she asks.

"Four thousand already. Is that good?"

"Not bad," she replies with a mouthful. "I'm sharing it on some burner accounts to get the buzz going. Let's see if we can get this to go viral."

Watching her from across the room, I replay the scene over in my mind. As hot as it looks on camera, it was even hotter in the moment. The way her body responded to my dominating her like that—it was more than I expected. Those sounds she made had my dick harder than it's ever been.

Man, I really need to get laid more often. And if it wasn't for rule number four, I would.

*Rule #4: No sleeping with anyone else for the next three months.*

The rule makes sense, but it's going to make for a rough three months. I've never been rough with women in bed. Mostly because the women I usually sleep with don't really seem like the *choke-me, spank-me, pull-my-hair* types. And that's not exactly the type of thing you assume without asking first.

Fuck, am I into that shit now? I'm not *that* guy. I don't want to *hurt* Sage, so why the hell does my cock seem to love the sound of her whimpers?

Is she into that shit?

Judging by how soaked her panties were, she seemed pretty into it. My cock twitches in my pants at the memory of how good she felt on my lap, those pretty little thighs clenching around me, and her perky little tits bouncing as she pretended to ride my cock.

For the first time since that night, I actually consider fucking Sage again. I mean...why not? It's not like we'd ever date for real, so we might as well just screw and get the authentic thing on camera, right?

Then I remember rule five.

*Rule #5: Keep it fake.*

It made sense when we proposed the rule. Three months of faking a relationship, never letting things get real to keep it from getting complicated. We have to keep the end goal in mind. Fuck with Truett and Brett a little, make things tense between them, and hopefully get the club away from my father in the process. With Truett's son publicly fucking Brett's ex, it should be easy.

"What do you think Brett will do when he sees it?" I ask.

Immediately, Sage fidgets and looks uncomfortable. "Umm...I don't know. He'll probably call me to tell me what a ho I am. Or find some way to make me feel like shit for what I choose to do with my own free will."

"He won't...hurt you, will he?"

Her brows pinch together as she stirs the noodles in the carton, not looking up at me as she shakes her head. "No. He wouldn't."

As worry starts to creep its way up, I'm about to say something to Sage when my phone rings on the table. I see my brother's name on the screen, which is strange because Caleb never calls me.

Hesitantly, I pick it up and swipe the screen to answer it.

"Hey, Caleb—"

"Holy shit, Adam," he barks into the phone. "Tell me this is some deep fake photoshopped bullshit."

I drop the food carton on the table as my eyes widen. I'm not sure why, but I bolt out of my seat and stumble for a response to my brother's accusation.

"Dude, answer me," he yells.

"It's real, Caleb."

"What the fuck, Adam? Did you leak this shit on purpose?"

Across the room, Sage is staring at me with alarm on her face. This is what we wanted, right? This is what happens when you post a sex tape online. People see it.

"Yes, I did it on purpose," I reply. My heart is pounding in my chest as I start to pace the room. My phone beeps and I pull it away from my face to see that I have another incoming call, this time from my father's publicist. I quickly hit decline.

"Why the fuck would you do it on purpose? What is going on with you?"

"Because I'm sick and fucking tired, Caleb. I'm tired of being so perfect and doing everything he wants us to do for his image, his reputation, his ministry."

"Jesus, Adam. This is about him firing you as his writer?"

"It's about a lot of shit, Caleb. Shit you wouldn't understand. He's manipulated us long enough, and I'm fucking done. I posted that video because I wanted to. I started dating Sage because I wanted to. I brought her to the gala last night because I *fucking* wanted to."

The line goes silent for a moment, and I can tell by the background noise that Caleb is in his car. After a moment, he responds.

"Damn. He's going to lose his shit, Adam. Are you ready for this?" His tone is softer now as if he understands me a little more, but it's laced with worry too.

"Yes, I'm ready. And if he thinks I'm not going to do it again, he's wrong."

Caleb sighs. "This isn't like you."

"No, brother. This *is* me. My entire life up until now...*that* wasn't me. It was him."

Silence again. I didn't realize until this moment just how much I want my brothers on my side for this. How much I need to hear at least one of them say how much they hate that motherfucker so I'm not so alone. Not just for me. For Isaac too.

"Good for you, Adam. Fuck that asshole."

I'm struck speechless for so long I don't even realize the call ends, and my phone is buzzing with texts and messages.

"The video is already at two million views," Sage says quietly, looking down at her phone.

"Good," I reply, feeling motivated and ready to do some damage. "We can film another one tomorrow."

She stares up at me with surprise. "Okay..." As her voice lingers, I know she's about to say something else. "Is everything all right?"

"It's better than all right. The video is working, and we've only just begun."

I cross the room to the door and glance back at her, sitting on the couch with her pink hair shining with the afternoon sun. She looks beautiful from this angle, and I feel sort of...proud of her now. Proud of what we're accomplishing.

So proud I almost...smile. But that's against the rules. Not one of our rules, but one of *my* rules.

*Don't let Peaches know how much I like her.*

It's easier this way. No feelings. No strings.

Before I let a smile slip, I grimace instead. As I turn the knob on the door, I glance back at her, quietly muttering a cold *goodbye* before slipping out of her apartment.

# EIGHTEEN

## ADAM

Checking the app becomes obsessive. Watching the number of views climb is like a hit of ecstasy, and soon, I'm an addict. Every like, comment, and share is a serotonin boost I didn't know I needed.

These comments are a lot different than the Instagram posts from the night of the gala. Maybe because they're filled with more praise than shame.

*Jesus, this is hot.*

*Who knew that Goode boy had it in him?*

*I don't know who this guy is, but he's making me want to go back to church again.*

I've also watched the video itself about a hundred times too. Not to brag, but I can't get over how good I look, how hot *we* are together. Sage really does appear like she's riding my dick and enjoying it. And that filthy expression on my face is something I didn't even know I could do.

My mind is racing when I get back to my apartment. Texts, DMs, and calls have been coming in like crazy. Apparently, this video went viral fucking fast. I had no idea so many people even cared, but once it got out that Truett Goode's oldest son made a sex tape on FanVids, the media went wild with it. People who had no clue who I was before today are suddenly following my social media accounts in droves.

Everyone loves a scandal.

The one person I haven't heard from yet—who I expected to —is my father. And that might be the call I'm most anxious to get. Dread and excitement are warring for control in my head as I anticipate his reaction.

On the one hand, I can't fucking wait to hear how pissed he is.

On the other...I've spent my whole life pleasing him. Being the perfect son. His protégé. Doing everything right, the way he wanted. Playing the role of the well-behaved son is my entire identity. It's all I know.

So yeah...shedding that responsibility is like crawling out of my own skin.

The incoming message notifications get overwhelming, so I put my phone on Do Not Disturb as I drop onto the couch in my apartment and watch the video again. I wish I knew why this is so addicting and why I can't stop watching it.

Opening my text message thread with Sage, I type out a message with a smile on my face.

Three million views.

She types back her response immediately.

Everyone loves a good boy gone bad.

. . .

Grinning at her message, something strikes me about it—
something not right.

> It's because of the way I acted in that video.
> Not because you're bad. You know that, right?

I'm blushing.

You're too sweet, Church Boy.

> Well, I just wanted to make sure you knew
> that.

Um, hello.

Duh, Mr. "Fucking Ride It."

> Now it's my turn to blush.

I reply. My smile stretches across my face as I stare at her messages,
hearing them in her voice.

I didn't know you had it in you.

She replies.

> Neither did I.

> I take it you've never been rough with a girl before.

> Not like that.

> Well, you should try.

> You clearly have a knack for degradation.

I hover over the keys before I type my response. I can't tell if I'm being forward or if this is inappropriate to ask. But something about typing over text makes it easier to discuss.

> Is that how you like it?

While the bubbles bounce on the screen, indicating that she's typing, I shift in my seat. My dick is growing thick in my pants just thinking about it. Today was clearly tense and I'm feeling very high-strung at the moment. A cool breeze on my shaft might be enough to send me over the edge.

Then her response nearly knocks me out of my seat.

> Well, considering I've watched it twice now with my vibrator handy, I think the answer is yes.

My mouth is hanging open as I stare at the screen. What the fuck is this woman doing to me?

I don't respond because what the fuck would I even say?

Well, actually...that's not true. I know the old Adam wouldn't know what to say, but this new Adam, the one who made his sex tape debut today, knows exactly what to say.

With a devilish grin, I type out my response.

> Tell me you recorded that.

Sorry, that was a private showing.

If you had just stuck around for a few more minutes.

I know she doesn't mean that. That would be breaking the rules. But still...it's fun to flirt with the idea.

You really are a horny slut, aren't you?

So you haven't rubbed one out yet?

> Nope.

You're lying.

No one is that good.

> I am.

No, you're not.

Not really.

You've just been pretending for a very long
time.

The texts stay quiet for a moment. Biting my bottom lip, I grow
restless in my seat.

So I pull up the video again.

My thumb brushes over the curve of her breast on the screen,
and when that little yelping cry she made hits my ears for the
hundredth time today, I let myself replay the whole thing in my
mind. My cock twitches in my pants, reminding me that it's been
neglected since I put it through so much this afternoon. I'm not
embarrassed by how hard I was as she was bouncing on my lap. I
mean, any man would have popped a hard-on in that situation.

Clearly, she was feeling it too. Her nipples were hard as fuck,
and it was *not* cold in her apartment.

For a moment, I consider opening a porn site on my phone to
get off to, but I can't stop watching this clip. Hell, watching
myself choking her is clearly getting the job done because my dick
is aching already.

Reaching into my sweats, I wrap my hand around my hard
length, eliciting a deep moan from my throat. Even dry, this feels
good as fuck.

Rolling down the top of my pants, I ease my cock out. Then, I
pause the video as I start to stroke. Letting my head hang back on
the sofa, I let my imagination paint a picture some porn site never
could.

I picture that today wasn't fake, and I let myself remember
what it felt like to sink my cock into Sage's warm cunt. To feel her
riding me like she was today, fucking her so deep, she cries out
with every thrust, torn between pleasure and pain.

In my mind, I squeeze her throat again, watching her face as a hint of fear and arousal floods her bloodstream. She likes it. Loves being used. Loves being the thing I use to get off.

My imagination paints the picture of her in her bed just now, getting herself off to the video of us, and I nearly come right away.

Then another text from her pops up on the screen.

> Uh-oh. You've gone quiet.

> What are you doing???

I let out a groan. The head of my cock is tight, throbbing as a drop of precum slips from the tip.

"Oh fuck," I mutter as I squeeze on the upstroke as if just a text message from her is enough. I'm so close. But as the vision in my head starts to fade, I text her back.

> I'm watching our video.

> Right now?

> Yes.

My hand is moving fast now but doing just enough to keep my climax at bay, dragging out the inevitable and enjoying every torturous second. While I wait for her text response, I open the video again. Instead of watching, I hold the speaker close to my ear and focus only on her moans and cries. Then, I let my imagination take over again.

She's on my lap right now.

The hard bud of her nipple is in my mouth, and her wet heat is snug around my cock instead of my hand. With every thrust, she's getting closer, and when I feel her pulsing with her own orgasm, I unload, filling her up as I come.

*You want me to fuck you like I hate you?*

My ears are buzzing like static as my own voice replays on the video again. Closing the app, I drop my phone on the sofa and stare down at the mess I just made.

"Jesus." There are white globs of cum all over my shirt, nearly up to my neck and covering the hand still wrapped around my cock.

I desperately need to get laid. But oh yeah...I can't.

"It's going to be a long three months," I mumble as I grab a tissue from the end table and wipe up the mess from my hand. It's not like I was having so much sex before, but with all of this fore-play, it's going to be that much harder.

My phone buzzes with a text. Smiling, I pick it up and read her response.

> Are you done?

> Did you record it?

> The girls would pay good money for that.

I laugh as I type up my reply.

> Seriously?

> Would you?

Oh, hell yeah. That shit is hot.

With a scoff, I shake my head. It seems hard to believe that that's what women want.

Standing up, I tear my shirt off and throw it in the laundry room on my way to the sink to wash up. Just as I'm drying my hands on the towel, there's a heavy bang on the door. My heart nearly flips its way up through my throat as I stand there in shocked silence.

"Adam, open up," my father bellows from the other side.

As I make my way toward the door, I prepare myself for what I know is coming. The likelihood that he's here for a casual conversation is pretty slim.

He bangs again before I turn the dead bolt to unlock it. Then I swing the door open and he comes charging into my apartment, his wrinkled face red with fury, slamming it behind him.

"You motherfucker." He growls with rage, and I notice the way his fists clench at his sides as he paces the room. "What the fuck are you thinking?"

My face stays passive and uninterested during his rant. Crossing my arms over my still bare chest, I watch with satisfaction as he fumes.

"Say something, Adam! Goddammit."

"What's wrong, Dad? You didn't bring any bouncers to hold me down while you beat the shit out of me?"

His eyes narrow. "Oh, so this is about me? Is this your way of getting revenge, Adam? Do you have any idea what this is doing to your mother?"

I laugh. "So now you care about her?"

"Don't start with me, boy." He has a finger pointed in my face, and I notice the way it trembles. "First, you show up with that slut at the charity event, and now you post some video of you two fucking all over the internet? Are you out of your fucking mind?"

"I'm thinking pretty clearly for the first time in my life, actually."

My cool temper only makes him angrier, and I love having that power over him. His anger fuels something inside of me, pushing me to fight back. For the first time in my life, I don't feel like apologizing or playing the good son. Seeing how my rebellion enrages him only makes me want to do it more.

"Do you have any idea what this is doing to our family? To me? Your reputation? Any chance of taking over after I'm gone is dead now, son. Do you understand that?"

"I don't care," I reply coolly, even though it feels like a lie. "I don't care about my reputation or the family's. And least of all yours." I let out a chuckle as I lean against the counter, staring at him with humor.

"What about that little slut of yours? Do you care about her?"

Something in me tenses at the mention of Sage.

"We're just having a little fun," I reply with a smirk. "And we met because of you, so thanks for that."

"Don't get too attached, Adam," he says like it's a threat. At which I laugh again.

"You let me worry about my love life, old man."

His anger morphs into something far more menacing. "If you care about her at all, you'll end this now. Because I can't ruin you, but I sure as hell can ruin her."

Before I know it, I'm charging toward him. His back slams against the front door loudly with my forearm pressed against his windpipe.

"It'd be so easy too," he mumbles as he struggles to push me off of him. "She has no one, Adam. No family. No money."

I release my arm against his throat and clench my fists with the desire to punch him so hard he'd be out cold.

But like the brainwashed coward I am, I don't.

"Do it," he says in a cruel dare. When it's clear my fist won't leave my side, he laughs. "You always were a pussy. Couldn't think on your own. Couldn't fight on your own. Couldn't do shit on your own. At least Isaac had the nerve to leave."

With rage boiling to the surface, I grab him by the back of his shirt and tear the front door open, tossing him out in one quick motion. Just before I slam the door on him, I hear him laughing, and it chills me to the bone.

Then I pace my apartment in anger. I let him get to me. And I said I wouldn't do that.

Why didn't I say something? Why couldn't I open my fucking mouth and threaten him right back? And why the fuck couldn't I punch him? It's like he has me so trained I can't utter a single word against him or lay a single hand on him. And I *hate* him for that.

Flipping the dead bolt closed, I pick up my phone and call Sage.

She picks up on the first ring. "What's up?"

"Let's film another," I say with urgency. She senses my anxiety immediately.

"Now?"

"Yes, fucking now. Bring your tripod and come over."

There's a second of silence before she responds, "I can't right now."

"Why?" I reply in a dark mutter.

"Because I have plans." Her tone is weak, with a hint of sweetness. And it's grating on my nerves.

"What plans?" My teeth are clenched and it's bugging the hell out of me that her first response isn't, *Yes, Adam. I'm on my way.*

She clears her throat. "I have a book club meeting."

"You have to be fucking kidding me."

"You're welcome to join," she replies jokingly. "This week, we're discussing *The Rake and His Reluctant Bride.*"

"Are you fucking with me right now? Because I'm really not in the fucking mood."

I expect her to argue back. Give me some quippy, sarcastic

reply, keeping the conversation light on her end, even though—
I'm aware—my attitude fucking sucks.

But she doesn't.

Instead, the line goes dead.

# NINETEEN

## SAGE

The margarita machine whirs loudly behind us as Gladys, Mary, Sylvia, and I set up the card table with various dips and snacks, our single, shared copy of *The Rake and His Reluctant Bride* in the center.

Sylvia crocheted the blue-and-gold doily in the middle on which the book sits. Gladys is whipping up the margaritas, which I already know will be so strong I'll be drunk in minutes. And Mary is arranging potato skins on the tray like she's about to present them to the king of England.

As for me, I sit curled up on the black folding chair, watching the three of them setting up, wearing a smile on my face because book club night is my favorite night of the month. And the start to my day wasn't so bad either.

Even if I did have to hang up on Adam just now for being a pompous, self-righteous, bossy asshole. Instead, that moment this morning on the couch, when he had his hand around my throat and his rough words in my ears, has been playing on repeat all day.

And yeah, I did let out all of that built-up tension with the magic wand after he left, but the effect it had on me lingers. Brett was never very *rough* in bed, but then again...Brett was never very *anything* in bed. Sadly, the same goes for nearly every other guy I've slept with. There was the occasional ass slap or hair pull, but the dirty talk was never anything more than "Fuck yeah" and "Don't stop."

But the way Adam looked me in the eye and told me he wanted to *fuck me like he hated me* altered my brain chemistry. Even if it wasn't real. I felt those words in my bones.

I've never wanted to be so *used* before. Like that night in my apartment, I got off on him getting off. And that's something I could never say for Brett. Does it have to do with the fact that Adam is slowly getting corrupted? Am I the one corrupting him?

Do I want to be?

The flutter of butterflies in my belly answers that question.

"Okay, let's get started," Gladys says, clapping her hands together. The rest of the ladies gather their chairs and circle around the table. Then, Gladys dives immediately into her personal likes and dislikes of the book, just as she does every month.

As for *The Rake and His Reluctant Bride*, she loved it. But then again, Gladys always loves the broody alphas.

"He was so...cruel to her," Mary replies, looking a little uneasy.

"He only acted that way, but deep down, he really loved her," Sylvia adds.

"I just don't understand why. If he was on that ship for so long, why was he so mean to her when he returned? It doesn't make sense."

"Men don't make sense," Gladys says, popping a chip into her mouth.

"It added conflict," Sylvia replies, making a scowling expression. "If he had come back to her happy and ready to marry her, there wouldn't have been a story."

I let out a laugh. "I think it's deeper than that."

"How so?" she asks.

But as I remember the rake in the story and how cruel and dismissive he was of the heroine, I'll admit I'm struggling to find the depth I'm looking for. "I don't know. I just think there was more to his brutish attitude than just a lame story device. He was broody and rough, but he wasn't a *bad* guy. Besides...I think the baroness liked it."

"Yes, let's talk about the good stuff," Gladys adds with a wink. "Like that scene in the garden."

We all hum in unison.

"That was pretty hot," I say, taking a long sip of my margarita.

"Not as hot as their wedding night," Sylvia replies. "The way he tied her to the bed with the ropes."

Mary is blushing across from me, so I stifle my laugh with my lips around my glass.

"He must have learned how to tie those knots on the pirate ship," I joke, and we all erupt with laughter.

"My husband was in the Navy for twenty years and he never did that with me," Gladys adds. Now we're all howling, and my cheeks are burning from laughter. As I wipe away the tears falling from my eyes, I notice Mary quickly compose herself and stare wide-eyed at something over my shoulder.

"Can we help you?" she asks with a small voice.

Under the table, Gladys nudges my knee, so I quickly spin around and stare at Adam, standing near the extra-large dryers and watching us with confusion.

It's weird how my mood instantly brightens at the sight of him before remembering how rude he was on the phone, like some toxic mixture of excitement and bitterness.

"Hey," I mumble.

"What are you doing?" he asks, glancing at the ladies around me.

"I told you. Book club."

His only response to that is a flinch of his brows. "Can we go upstairs, please?"

"No," I reply sternly, "I'm in the middle of something."

"Well..."

"Why don't you join us?" Sylvia asks in her sweet Southern drawl.

"Yeah, pull up a chair." Gladys's voice is a little smokier and less cordial, but the invitation is still there.

"No, thank you, ladies. Sage..." His eyes are piercing as he stares at me. There's not a single chance in hell he's going to get me out of this chair and up those stairs before the end of this meeting. I have half a mind to tell him that right now, but I don't want to let my harsh response ruin the fun we were having.

"Come on, we could use your input," Gladys adds, breaking the tension between Adam and me.

"My input?" There's that deepening wrinkle between his brows.

"Yeah. We need a man to explain this to us, so you're right on time."

Sylvia jumps up to grab Adam a chair, unfolding it and placing it next to me. Meanwhile, Mary is loading food onto a paper plate and handing it to him as he shuffles hesitantly toward the empty chair. I watch him with amusement, biting my lip, as he awkwardly takes a seat and smiles politely at the ladies fawning over him.

On the other side of the table, I notice Mary staring at Adam like he's the greatest thing she's ever seen. He must notice too, because, after a moment, he gives her a tight-lipped grin.

"You recognize me, don't you?"

"I have all of your father's books," she replies, launching into full-on fangirl mode. "And yours too!"

"Thank you."

"I didn't know you wrote a book," I reply, staring at him over my margarita glass.

"Two," he replies.

"What are they about?" My interest is piqued. I guess I've had Adam pegged as his father's son for so long I forgot to wonder what he actually does on his own. Somehow on my Google search, I got so distracted by his family that I missed his personal accomplishments.

"They're devotional," he replies, brushing it off like I wouldn't care, but Mary quickly cuts him off.

"Oh, they're so much more than that. I gave your first book, *Prodigal*, to my son when he came home from Afghanistan. It saved his life."

Aside from the tumbling of clothes in the dryers behind us, the room is silent as we all stare at either Adam or Mary. It's like seeing a whole new side of him, kind and warm and humble. Suddenly, I realize there's probably a lot about Adam Goode I don't understand.

With grace, he nods at Mary as he says, "Please thank your son for his service. And thank you for sharing that with me. I'm glad it could help."

I glance at her, seeing the tears welling in her eyes as she smiles warmly back at him. Mary is always smiling. She's like a warm glowing light wherever she goes, but to see her react to Adam in this way, as if *he* is the one emitting light...makes me feel strange inside.

The room is bathed in quiet tension for another moment before Adam clears his throat. "So, what book are you discussing tonight?"

Sylvia hands him the worn paperback, and he looks it over with interest.

"It's about a baron who is kidnapped as a boy and raised by pirates. When he returns home as a man, he has to marry the woman he was betrothed to, but they hate each other," Sylvia explains. Adam looks mildly interested as he reads the back of the book.

"But what we can't understand is *why* the rake hated the baroness so much," Mary adds.

Gladys grabs a handful of chips and drops them on her plate. "He didn't *always* act like he hated her," she says with a laugh.

"Maybe you can help us understand," I say, glancing playfully at him. "Why would a man hate a woman he's so attracted to?"

Adam's forehead wrinkles. Then he glances down at the book, looking deep in thought for a moment.

"Maybe he doesn't understand her. I mean...they grew up in different worlds, right? And it seems that everything in his life is out of his control, even the woman he's supposed to marry. So, the only thing he can control is how he reacts to the situation."

He glances up at the ladies around the table, and I notice the way he won't look at me as he continues.

"So I imagine he was pretty frustrated to find that the woman he was forced to marry was someone...he also *wanted* to marry. I'm sure it felt as if he had no power in his own life. And the only person he could take that out on...was her."

Finally, his gaze falls my way and our eyes lock for a brief moment before I turn my eyes downward.

"So, he never hated her at all. Not really," Mary says wistfully.

"I don't know. I didn't read it, but I'm willing to bet he didn't," Adam replies.

"Men are always shit at expressing themselves," Gladys says, and I can't help but laugh. Next to me, Adam chuckles too.

"I agree," he says, taking a bite of the potato skin from his plate. He seems deep in thought for a moment, and when he reaches for a drink, I hand him my margarita. He takes a swig and winces from the strength of it. Then takes another drink.

I glance around the table, and the women seem enamored by him. Even Gladys is smirking. For once, I can feel what it's like to have a boyfriend people actually *like*.

But then the guilt creeps in because Adam is *not* my boyfriend. Lying is so much worse when it runs this deep. It's not our words that lie, but our actions. And it feels wrong.

"All right," Adam says, passing my drink back to me with a smirk. "Now tell me about this garden scene."

Immediately, Sylvia launches into a very descriptive retelling of her favorite scene in the book.

# TWENTY

## ADAM

It's nearly ten at night when we've finally cleaned up the leftover food from the card table. I help Gladys place it in the storage closet in the back, along with the chairs.

Sylvia keeps starting up a conversation as we try to say our goodbyes, and Mary hugs me for the third time. But we eventually usher them out the door, and I turn my attention to a clearly tipsy Sage, who is holding a platter of cookies with a beaming smile. She stumbles, knocking her shoulder into an industrial-sized washing machine.

"Better get her to bed," Gladys mumbles under her breath.

"On it," I reply with a huff. Peaches giggles at me as I take her by the arm and steer her toward the door that leads up to her apartment.

"You're not scowling," she says with a slur in her voice, tripping over the first step and sending the cookies flying onto the floor.

Rolling my eyes, I help her pick them up and wrinkle my face in disgust as she pops one into her mouth.

"You're a mess," I say. "And I am scowling."

"No, you're not," she replies with a laugh. "You're smiling. Ever since that gala, you stopped smiling."

I pause for a moment as I let that sink in. Of course, it's true, and I hadn't even realized it. He did ruin my mood. And I've been a bit of a jerk ever since.

But that's what I want, right? For her to keep her distance, to never cross a line or let anything grow between us. The longer she sees me as a broody asshole, the better. Right?

Once we get the cookies picked up, we finish the climb up her stairs, and as soon as I hear Roscoe yipping on the other side, I realize that she's right; I am smiling.

I'll blame this one on the tequila.

"Roscoooooe," Sage croons as the front door opens and the three-legged rat-sized dog starts bouncing against our legs. She picks him up and he starts kissing her face affectionately.

When she looks up at me again, she stops and points with wide eyes. "See! You're smiling again."

"Stop it," I grumble as I take the cookies to the kitchen and dump them into the trash before she can eat any more.

"He needs to go out," she says, walking toward the fire escape. I step in front of her just as she stumbles again.

"I'll take him," I bellow, stealing the dog from her arms.

"Thank God," she replies with a hiccup. "I have to pee so bad."

As soon as he's out of her arms, she turns and sprints toward the bathroom on the other side of her apartment, pink waves bouncing as she runs. When I know she can't see me, I let myself smile like it's a secret.

Then, I carry Roscoe down the fire escape and wait for him to do his business. Once he and I are back in the apartment, I stop frozen in the kitchen area as Sage stands in nothing but her bra and panties near the couch.

"Where should we do it this time?" she asks nonchalantly.

"Do what?"

"Film the scene you wanted," she replies with innocence.

Scoffing, I place Roscoe on the floor. "Absolutely not."

"Why not?"

"You're drunk."

"So? It's not like we're really doing it."

I only consider it for a moment before immediately shaking my head. "No. Still doesn't feel right."

The look of disappointment on her face is obvious as she crosses her arms and lets her shoulders slump forward. Then she rounds the sofa and plops down on the cushions, pulling the blankets up to cover herself.

As I'm standing there staring at her, I realize I could just leave. But I don't.

Instead, I take the seat opposite her on the couch. She's lying down with her head on the pillow as she looks up at me.

"Why didn't you tell me you wrote a book?"

"You never asked," I reply. "Besides, I didn't think we were sharing personal stuff with each other." Which feels like a lie. No matter how fake this relationship is, I'm dying to know everything about her. I've been intrigued since the moment she entered that diner.

"Well, you *are* my boyfriend," she says before letting out a yawn.

"Okay, so what else do you want to know?" I ask. "My favorite food is waffles. I'm a Capricorn. I've never had a dog or any pet, really. And my best friend is my brother, Caleb." Turning toward her, I add, "So what about you?"

Her lips twist as she goes into deep thought. I bite back a smile, watching the way her nose crinkles.

"My favorite food is Mary's green chile enchiladas. I'm a Leo. Roscoe is my first pet and probably my best friend too, if I'm honest."

The corner of my mouth lifts in a crooked smile. How is it possible that she's even cuter when she's drunk? Then the smile fades as I realize just how alone she is. The Laundromat owner downstairs and the three-legged stray dog are the only family she has. She lost her job at the club because of me.

"Do you like writing?" she asks, distracting me from the depressing realization. But honestly...the question makes me a little uncomfortable. As if it's too personal.

"I do like writing."

"Would you write another book?" She yawns again.

"Yes," I reply without hesitation.

"Good." Her eyes softly close and she stretches her legs out so I pull her feet into my lap, rubbing her cold toes with my hands. Then I slip off my shoes and prop my feet up on the ottoman.

I stare at her for a moment as she sleeps, and I try to remember how I felt about her when we first met. All the misconceptions and assumptions I made about her feel so flat and shallow compared to the person I've discovered she is.

Then as I stare at the tattoos traveling up her arms, I imagine what it would feel like to be Sage's *for real*. What would my life look like?

What if I posted pictures of us online and held her hand in public? Not as a fake girlfriend, either. I do that already, but how would I truly feel if it was real?

No matter how hard I try, it doesn't fit. She doesn't fit in my life.

But at this point, I don't even fit in my own life.

Maybe if I wasn't me and my world wasn't defined by my father's career, I could make her fit. If I truly had feelings for Sage, I could see myself kissing her in public. Holding her under my arm. Waking up next to her every day.

Our lives would be an eclectic mix of church, tattoo shops, sex clubs, and Sunday dinners. It would be so chaotic and strange... but it would be mine.

When she's fully asleep, I pull out my phone and open up the camera. Propping it on the coffee table, I aim it at her sleeping face and hit record. Then, I ease myself off the seat and crawl over her, dipping my face down to press my lips against her cheek.

She smells so good, and I wish for a brief moment that I could just lie here with her and fall asleep with her in my arms. After brushing my thumb over her jaw, I sit up and hit the stop button on the phone.

With some quick trimming of the video and a couple soft filters, I post the five-second clip to my social media with the caption, *Her gentleman.*

It's fake, I remind myself as I hit send. But even with it being fake, I suppress a sense of vulnerability from posting something so personal for the world to see. Even if that's the point of this whole thing.

I'm dismantling every single expectation anyone ever had of me, one video at a time. The whole thing feels very liberating— and terrifying.

After the clip is posted, I set my phone on the coffee table and pull Sage's feet back into my lap. With my legs propped up, I rest my head on the back of the sofa and fall asleep with ease.

# TWENTY-ONE

## SAGE

The first thing I register before I peel my eyes open is the familiar scent of rich cologne. The second thing I notice is that I'm not alone. Normally I have space on this deep-set couch, but today, I'm sandwiched between a hard body and the cushions.

As I open my eyes, I see his familiar dark beard and tan skin. Then I realize that I'm almost naked, in nothing but my bra and panties.

Although I vaguely remember Adam sitting at my feet, he must have moved in the night. He is now holding me tight in his arms as he sleeps, and the events of last night come flooding back to my mind.

*Dammit, Gladys and her strong-ass margaritas.*

Very carefully, I try to maneuver into a sitting position, but there's no room, and I don't want to wake him. So I just surrender and fall back against his body, swallowed up by the couch and his tall frame.

While lying in silence, I stare at Adam, wondering what version of him I'll get when he wakes up. Will I get the version that looks as if the world is breaking down around him? Or the one that smiles, with the dimples and soft wrinkles around his eyes instead of between his brows? Or the dark side that lets me wear his hand like a necklace? He's been so broken by someone he was meant to trust. I can see the torment radiating from him with every mood swing, every grimace, and every smile. His world has been ripped out of his hands, his self-identity with it, and I can't help but wish I could just wrap my arms around him and put him back together.

Only a few minutes pass before he starts to stir too. And he seems just as perplexed by this unexpected sleeping arrangement when his eyes open and he notices my half-naked body pressed against his.

Leaning back, he stares at me for a moment before letting out a yawn. "Morning."

"Morning," I reply. "Thanks for taking care of me last night."

"Of course," he says. He climbs off the couch and turns his body away from me. "It was...interesting."

"You mean the book club?" I ask.

"Yeah."

It would seem I'm getting the guarded Adam, who keeps his emotions walled up and secret, achieved with a blank expression and one-word answers in a flat tone.

"You can just say it was fun, Adam," I say as I climb off the couch and head toward the kitchen.

I only make it two steps before a hand grips my arm, steering me around to face him. His face is only inches from mine as he stares down into my eyes as if he's ready to say something. I wait one long second after another before he finally gives in and mumbles quietly, "It was fun. Thank you for letting me stick around."

I'm lost in his eyes, feeling them look right into my soul.

"Well, we have to look like a couple, right?" I say, quietly. My eyes dance from his eyes to his lips and back up. Morning breath be damned. I think he might kiss me right now, and I'm not entirely sure how I feel about that.

I need to know what to expect. Maybe that's why I've stuck around with shitty boyfriends for so long—no surprises. They were simple, predictable and made my emotions easy to define.

But with Adam, nothing makes sense. Desire and attraction have always felt very one-sided. Of course, I like him. Of course, I want him. Look at him.

But he never lets himself want me—even when he clearly does. And now...lines are getting blurry and it's making me panic.

His hand drops away from my arm as he steps backward. "That's right. We have to make everyone believe it."

I slip away, going quietly to the bedroom to get dressed.

The apartment is tense and quiet as I start making coffee. Adam uses the bathroom and comes back with Roscoe in his arms. Then, without me even having to ask, he climbs out the fire escape window and takes him outside.

While he's gone, I pull out my phone. The scent of brewing coffee fills the room as I start to scroll. And the first thing I notice is that I have more notifications than usual. It only takes a moment before I realize it's because I've been tagged, and when I click on *what* I've been tagged in, my heart nearly stops.

It's a video of me sleeping on my couch. Subtle light filters in from a small lamp in the corner. Then, Adam's face enters the frame, and he leans down, pressing his lips to my cheek.

My jaw nearly hits the floor.

Adam took this while I was sleeping. People are sharing it, tagging me, clearly invested in our relationship.

*Fake relationship, Sage. Fake.*

I have to keep reminding myself of that because I swear my heart doesn't know the difference when it sees stuff like this and starts fluttering in excitement regardless.

Being on Adam's account suddenly has me scrolling, and I can't help but notice how hard it is to hold back my smile as I pass picture after picture of him looking handsome as hell every time. Some of the photos are clearly modeled by a photographer and some are candid of him and his brothers or his mother.

There's one of him that's clearly a selfie, wearing a pair of dark sunglasses, holding a cup of coffee in some outdoor café. He looks like the kind of man supermodels fight over and absolutely *nothing* like the guys I date. He doesn't even have a single tattoo on his body.

For no reason at all, I screenshot that photo and keep it in my camera roll. Then I scroll a little further and come across a video on his feed. Immediately, I press play.

It's Adam in a deep-blue button-down shirt and dark-brown slacks. He's standing at the front of the church, holding a microphone in his hand. As he walks, he preaches, and while I'm not focusing so much on his words, I can't take my eyes off the way he looks in that role. He's so natural, pacing around the stage, inflecting on all the right words, keeping the attention of his audience. He's clearly gifted in public speaking. Hell, even I want to believe in God after listening to this.

"What are you listening to?" he asks as he climbs back in the window, setting Roscoe down on the floor.

I hold up my phone to show him. "I didn't know you were a preacher too."

His face tightens in a grimace. "I'm not."

"This looks like preaching to me."

Without letting the expression relax, he walks over to me and takes my phone. Staring down at his own video, he scrutinizes it for a moment. "I've only done it a few times."

"Did you like it?" I ask.

A beat of silence goes by before he nods. "Yeah, I did."

Then he lifts his head and looks at me as if he's been struck by an idea.

"You know...I was thinking," Adam says. "We should film somewhere different."

I slip my phone into my back pocket. "What's wrong with my apartment?"

"Your apartment is fine, but I just figure we need to mix it up. Really give them something to talk about."

I pour coffee into each cup on the counter, then a little cream in each, handing Adam's to him. "You sound like you have something in mind," I say with a playful smirk.

"I do."

"And?"

I take my coffee to the linoleum table, where he's already sitting.

"It's a surprise," he mumbles, blowing on his coffee.

"I love surprises," I reply with a smile.

"It's not enough to be fake dating and making sex tapes. I want to really hit him where it hurts. Spit in the face of everything he loves."

His voice is dark and serious as he talks, and it pulls on my heart to see him struggling so much. Adam is going through something major. The nice guy who bought me breakfast last month would have never said anything so menacing. Reaching across the table, I place my hand on his.

"What happened yesterday?" I ask, remembering the way he called me in a panic, clearly upset by something.

"He came over."

"And?" I gently pry.

His expression darkens as he stares downward at the coffee. "I wanted to knock him out. He tried to threaten me, control me, intimidate me."

"Did you?"

He looks up at me, and there's something burning in his expression, his gaze holding mine for a moment before he shakes his head and stands up. "No. I didn't. But it's clear he knows how to push my buttons, so I want to push his."

My heart breaks for him again.

He takes a sip of his coffee, places the cup on the counter, and nods toward my bedroom. "Get cleaned up and let's go."

"So bossy," I reply, taking another drink.

Within minutes, I'm dressed, and we're both heading out the door.

# TWENTY-TWO

## SAGE

"You must be joking."

As Adam turns down the access road, avoiding the long line of traffic ahead, I realize he is, in fact, taking me to his father's church.

On a Sunday morning.

"I am not," he replies.

He reaches into his visor and pulls out a laminated card, rolling down his window as we pull up to a security station blocking the entrance to the back of the church.

"Morning," he greets the guard waiting there.

"Morning, Mr. Goode," the man replies. Adam waves his card at him while I try to duck down in my seat. As I sneak a peek through the window at the guard, he gives me a terse, furrowed glare.

"Morning, miss," he says politely.

"Morning," I chirp in response, trying to feign confidence, like I'm *supposed* to be here—which I'm not.

After a moment of clear hesitation, the man finally waves us through as the bar rises. Adam pulls into the massive parking lot behind the church.

"How on earth are we going to get through here unnoticed on a Sunday?" I ask.

Just as he pulls into the spot labeled *A. Goode*, he turns to me and gives me a devilish grin. "Who says I don't want to be noticed? What's he going to do? Beat me up in front of the congregation?"

My stomach turns as I imagine walking into that building. I haven't been inside a church since I was thirteen and my aunt dragged me to Sunday school after I got in trouble at school for kissing a boy in the bathroom during PE.

She thought I needed Jesus. Like *he* could somehow make me not love making out so much.

It didn't work. I ended up getting to second base with a boy in Sunday school instead.

"And where exactly are we going to film this video?" I ask.

Adam appears far too cocky about this and I'm slightly concerned that the wheels are coming off the tracks of this plan. As if his anger at his father is clouding his judgment.

"I have an idea..."

He opens his driver's side door and hops out. Meanwhile, I take a long, heavy breath before following him. As we walk up to the back entrance of the church, I scurry along to keep up with him.

"Please tell me we're not doing it on the altar during Sunday morning service," I say.

He scans his card on the door lock and it unlocks with a click before he pulls it open.

"It's called a pulpit, and no. I wish," he replies with a laugh.

The inside of the church, from this perspective, seems more like an office building with doors on either side that are labeled *Marketing Director, Treasurer, Outreach*. The ceilings are enormous, giving the entry space alone a grand, larger-than-life sort of vibe.

It makes me instantly uncomfortable.

So far, there are no other people around, but I hear chatter in the distance. When we turn a corner at the end, I spot a group of people with headsets on who are dressed up for church but seem to be frantically speaking about something I can't make out.

Adam grabs my hand and pulls me in the opposite direction. Before long, we hear a "Mr. Goode!" in a woman's surprised-sounding voice.

Adam turns around and waves toward them. "Morning, Beverly. Good luck with the service today."

She hesitates, and I don't need to turn around to know it's me she's looking at. What are the odds any of these people here have seen the videos of us going viral at the moment?

"Uh, thanks," she calls out.

My hand squeezes Adam's. I hate this. I want to leave right now.

He glances down at his watch and then back at me. He does a double take—and then he stops.

"What's wrong?"

"What's wrong?" I shriek just above a whisper. "I don't belong here, Adam. I feel like a freak, and I don't like it."

His expression softens as he pulls me down a hallway, pushing me toward the wall and stepping so close it makes it hard to breathe.

"It's a church, Sage. Of course, you belong. Everyone does."

"That's what *you* think, Adam. You were practically born here. Not everyone feels the same sense of comfort in this place that you do."

"Do you really not feel comfortable here?" he asks, like there's something wrong with me. My temper rises.

"No. These people *hate* me, and I know, I know...that was sort of the point. But it doesn't feel good to see the way they look at me."

When he steps a little closer, he draws my attention out of my own head and onto him. I'm focusing on the planes of his chest in that tight shirt and the feel of his hands on my arms.

"Why do you give a fuck what these people think about you?" he asks.

"I don't," I stammer, looking down to avoid eye contact.

He puts a finger under my chin and lifts it until I'm staring into his eyes. Then he opens his mouth as if he's about to say something, but nothing comes out. His eyes search mine for a moment, and I'm waiting on bated breath for something, *anything*.

Finally, he quietly utters, "Take a deep breath."

And I try to obey, pulling air into my lungs, although it feels heavy and difficult. When he sees me struggling, he says it again, this time with a deep, authoritative tone.

"Take a deep breath, Sage."

I freeze, staring up at him with surprise. Suddenly, I'm able to pull long, slow breaths into my chest, and my panic slowly subsides.

It's the first time Adam has ever *commanded* me like that, and I think it might be the first time I've ever obeyed *anyone*. But there was just something soothing and safe in his tone that made it almost impossible not to obey.

When he notices me starting to settle down, he leans closer and softly whispers, "I don't think you're a freak."

"Yes, you do," I reply with a laugh. "But I *really* don't care what you think."

As I smile up at him, he doesn't return the expression. Then I regret saying it.

"You are not a freak," he says, this time using that cool authority again. And like a fool, I start to believe it.

"Okay," I reply, just to please him, hoping it means he'll take the intensity of his gaze off my face.

"If you want to leave, we can."

"No," I reply. "Let's get the shot you want to get."

After a moment of hesitation, he grabs my hand and pulls me

down the hall. There's a murmur of voices in the distance, like a crowd of people creating a low hum of energy. We stop at an intersection of hallways, and Adam glances anxiously around before continuing straight ahead. As we reach a heavy wooden door, my stomach drops as I notice the name on the golden plaque above it.

*Reverend Truett Goode.*

*Oh fuck.*

My hand squeezes Adam's as he pulls a set of keys out of his pocket, scanning the hallway one last time before shoving the key in the door and twisting it to unlock.

"How do you know he won't be here?" I whisper.

"Because the service is set to start in thirty minutes. He's in makeup."

"Are you sure he won't come back?" I sound panicked, mostly because I *am* panicked.

Adam glances my way and lets a playful smile tug at his lips. "Come on, Peaches. Live a little."

Then the door opens and he pulls me inside. He turns and locks it behind us.

Truett's office is ginormous. There's a massive oak desk with ornate embellishments and a giant cross etched into the front. Behind the desk is a throne-like chair and a large framed photo of Jesus on the wall at the back of the room.

Adam rushes toward the desk, positioning himself behind it. "I want him to recognize his office, so maybe you can put your phone over there and record from an angle."

I hurry and open the camera app, propping the phone on one of the heavy ornate chairs positioned in front of the desk. It puts Adam in plain view and Truett's nameplate front and center on the desk.

And...well, Jesus.

Fuck, I'm going to hell in a handbasket.

Without thinking too much about it, I hit record and yank off my top, so I'm in just a bra and tight jean shorts. Adam's eyes flicker down before he catches himself and looks back up at my face.

"Where do you want me?" I ask.

"Here," he replies, gesturing for me to stand between him and the desk. At first, I'm facing him, breathing in the scent of his cologne and getting momentarily lost in the warmth of his honey-brown eyes.

He stares at me a moment before placing his hands on my hips and spinning me around.

"I'll...fuck you over the desk like this," he says, a tremor in his voice. Then he presses himself against my backside and heat assaults my core. It's so fucking cruel that we can pretend to have sex so much but can never have any actual sex. We've just guaranteed ourselves three months of the worst blue balls in history.

As he moves to take off his shirt, I stop him. "Leave it on," I say.

He pauses. "What? Why?"

"Because it's hotter if I'm naked and you're not." With that, I reach back and try to unfasten my bra. When my fingers fumble for a second too long, his touch sends chills down my spine as he unclasps it himself. My bra falls to the desk, and I try not to think about it too long as I reach down and unbutton my shorts, shooting them down my legs.

My thong stays on, but as I check out the view on the camera, I realize it can be seen on the screen.

"You'll have to take that off," he mutters quietly.

We don't have time to think too much about this or formulate a new plan. The sooner we get the shot, the sooner we can leave. So, I nod. My fingers tremble as I drag my underwear down my legs.

There's something different about this time than last. For one, I feel much more exposed, and not just because I'm naked and bent over a desk, revealing everything for him.

But also because we're in *his* domain. I'm the outsider here.

And most of all, I feel exposed because my feelings for Adam are changing too quickly. I'm afraid he can read the desire on my face. Like it's written all over my body in the way my nipples pebble from the slightest touch and how my belly warms every time he looks at me. And how, right now, with him positioned behind me, and the very thought of him fucking me here and now, has me so aroused I'm afraid he can see it.

My fingers grip the desk as I lean over it, my belly touching the cool surface as my small breasts hover just above the various papers Truett has scattered across it. And the sound of Adam's belt coming undone makes the pooling arousal even worse.

The silky fabric of his boxer briefs presses against my backside, and my fingers clutch the desk tighter. I wince as I imagine the mess I must be making there.

When we both glance at the camera screen, there's a moment of awkward silence, because his boxer briefs can be seen clear as day.

"Should we change the angle?" he asks.

"No," I reply without looking at him. "This angle is perfect."

"You want me to take them off?"

"Just do it," I say.

As he slides off his boxers, I glance at the screen to see just how hot and real it looks, but he's still not pressed all the way against me.

"I'm going to get hard and I won't be able to help it."

"It's fine," I reply in a mumble.

"Are you sure?" he whispers. I can hear the concern in his tone.

"We've done worse already," I reply. "Let's just get the shot."

He clears his throat. "Action."

The camera timer beeps—three, two, one.

With that, we both start moving. He thrusts toward me, slamming his half-hard cock against my backside, and I moan with pleasure. But as his motion starts to pick up in speed and intensity, I start to feel more and more connected to him. With each thrust of his hips, my moans feel less and less like acting.

He's not inside me and he's nowhere near my clit, and still...
something about this feels *so good*.

"Harder," I say with a breathy yelp, and Adam slams against
my backside with such force I knock a pile of papers onto the
floor.

I squeeze my thighs together as I bite my lip to keep from
embarrassing myself. It's pretty obvious now how much I desperately need to get laid. I feel like I might come from some fake sex
dry-humping, and that's just humiliating.

But then his fingers dig deeper into my hips and the softness
isn't so soft anymore. He's growing hard, and I can't help but
notice that the motion of his hips is taking on a less fake, more
real rhythm.

My thighs clench even tighter.

"Go ahead, Peaches. Come on my father's desk." His voice is
husky and strained.

"Yes," I cry out, pressing my hips back toward him.

Suddenly, I feel his stiff length slide between my thighs,
rubbing against my aching clit, and I let out a gasp and a moan
that is very, *very* real.

Glancing up at the camera screen, I see his expression in the
video. There's a look of feral determination on his face. His grip
on my hips tightens, and his breathing grows shallow with a grunt
on every exhale.

"Keep going," I whisper, clenching my thighs tighter around
his cock.

"You're so wet, Peaches," he says with a growl, and I shame-
lessly drop my forehead against the desk as I thrust back against
him. The moisture of my arousal coats his cock as he fucks the
space between my legs.

And with every stroke against my clit, I grow closer and closer
to my climax.

"Don't stop," I beg.

"Look at you," he mutters through clenched teeth. "So
fucking needy for my dick."

I cry out louder at his filthy words. The muscles of my thighs burn as I squeeze them together, urged on by the hardening of his cock. Which means he's about to come too.

With church music playing in the distance, we grind our bodies together until we're both breathless and shuddering out our releases. He groans loudly as I feel his cock pulse against me, spilling his cum all over my legs and his father's desk. My own climax drives pleasure into every extremity of my body.

For a few long moments, we stay in that position, recovering from the heat of the moment. When Adam releases his claw-like grip on my hips, I lift my head and stare directly at the video still recording on my phone.

As Adam snatches a tissue from the box on the desk, I reach over and grab my phone, stopping the recording. Still, it's silent as he turns away from me and cleans himself up. After I do the same, I grab my clothes and start to redress.

Nothing about that quenched this new craving. Instead, I think it just made it worse.

Adam clears his throat and tosses the cum-stained tissue into the trash can in the corner of the room and then our eyes meet for the first time.

He opens his mouth to say something and I have no idea why I feel the need to speak before him. Maybe because I expect him to say he's sorry and I don't want to hear an apology. Nothing about what just happened requires one in my eyes.

"Well, the viewers are going to love that," I say with a smile.

His mouth closes as he fights a smile. "You'll have a lot of editing to do."

With that, he pulls me toward the door. When I try to pick up the papers on the floor, he touches my shoulder.

"Don't," he says, "I want him to know we were here."

"Oh, he's going to know," I reply with a laugh as I glance back at the mess we left on his desk.

# TWENTY-THREE

## ADAM

We're in the car, driving back to Sage's place, when I realize I want to take her to dinner—at my parents' house. My fingers grip the steering wheel as the idea enters my head, and I know that even though it's fucking crazy, there's no way I can let it go now.

Glancing over at her in the passenger seat, my cock twitches in my pants as I remember what her body felt like in my hands. How perfect that little ass is and how hard I came just from rubbing my dick on her.

My memory of the night we had sex is hazy from alcohol and adrenaline. I want to remember what it feels like to really sink my cock inside her. I want to feel how tight she is, how warm, how sweet, and how dirty.

What happened just now in my father's office was crossing the line, but at least we crossed it together. I could read the expression of need and desire on her face. She came at the same moment I did. That's just how in sync we are. How mind-blowing would the sex have been if we let ourselves truly give in?

What kind of man does that make me if I treat this girl like she means nothing more to me than a quick fuck? If I've disregarded her for so long but suddenly find myself wanting to know how she feels from the inside.

It makes me a piece of shit. It makes me no better than *him*.

My head is getting flooded with guilt when I truly need to keep my focus here. Take down Truett. Ruin the man who took everything from me.

I've fucked with his work. Now I'm ready to fuck with his home.

"Will you come to dinner with me?" I ask, glancing sideways at her. My eyes catch on the way her soft-pink waves blow across her face, revealing the constellation tattoo on the side of her neck.

"Dinner?" she asks, curling her hair behind her ear. "Sure."

"Perfect."

We pull up to her apartment and sit in silence for a moment, and it feels like that moment in the office is lingering in the air, thick with tension.

"Do you want to come up?" she asks softly as she stares out the window. "I'm going to edit the video for the app."

Something is pulling me up to her apartment. A force that promises more than just sex. I see the way she looks at me. How she wants to *fix* me. Comfort me. Offer me more than my family could.

Fuck. It's really messing with my head. And messing with my head is not part of the plan.

"No. I'll go home, but be ready for me to pick you up at five for dinner."

She's opening the door before I even finish my sentence. Hovering over the open door, she leans in with a sympathetic expression as she nods. "Okay, Adam. See you then."

Then she closes it and walks away.

✝

My afternoon was spent tossing and turning on my couch, sleep evading me until I let my mind wander to the tattoos on her skin, tracing each one in my head like my own form of meditation. That's what finally helped me nod off, and I slept so soundly that I barely woke in time to pick her up for dinner.

As I pull up to her apartment, I take out my phone and text Caleb. I've been an asshole brother for not talking to him more lately, but I can't possibly bring him into this.

> I'm bringing my girlfriend to dinner tonight.

He texts back almost immediately. I'm grinning at my phone with confusion as he responds.

> Fuck yeah.

> You seem to really like her. Which means Mom will like her.

Well, this is feeling too fucking real all of a sudden. And it settles heavily in my gut like dread as the passenger door opens and Sage slides into the seat next to me. She has on a pair of black chunky boots with a short green corduroy skirt...and a bra.

"You forgot your shirt," I mutter as my eyes rake over her petite frame in my passenger seat. The only thing covering her bra is an open flannel shirt that's so long the sleeves hang over her wrists. It's an atrocious outfit...and she really should not look so good in it.

"I thought you'd like it," she replies, beaming at me with her perfectly straight white teeth. When she catches me staring a moment too long, her smile fades. "What?"

I clench my jaw as I look forward, fighting a smile as I put the car into drive. "Nothing. I'm just..." My voice trails.

"Just what?"

"Just wondering what you'd look like," I say, finishing my thought with a wince.

"What I would look like if...what?"

Glancing sideways at her, I start to feel bad for even bringing this up, but now I know she won't let me let it go.

"If you were...normal," I reply sheepishly.

Instead of pouting or getting mad, she laughs. "You mean, you wonder if you'd be attracted to me if I looked *normal*," she says, using air quotes.

*I am attracted to you*, I think but don't say.

"No," I say, quickly avoiding that accusation.

"Yes, you do," she persists. "Here." She pulls out her phone and scrolls through some apps as I drive. Then as I pull up to a stoplight, she thrusts her phone in my face. There on the screen is a blonde-haired young woman with a button nose, a dimpled chin, and straight white teeth in a cheesy grin. She's wearing an oversized green sweater and tiny shorts that barely peek out the bottom. She's holding a key chain in her hand.

"I was seventeen. I got the keys to my first apartment. Out of my mother's house and on my own for the first time."

A smile creeps across my face against my will as I stare at the girl in the photo and see Sage.

One question answered. Would I still be attracted to her if she *looked normal*? Yes.

It's too bad she had to go and fuck it all up with that ring in her lip that her tongue is constantly fiddling with. And those tattoos all over her pretty skin, from her neck to her toes. And that pink fucking hair that looks like cotton candy in the sunshine.

"Answer your question?" she asks, giving me a mischievous grin.

I clear my throat, tightening my grip on the steering wheel.

"Was that scary?" I ask, changing the subject. "Moving out on your own at such a young age?"

She scoffs playfully. "Scary? No."

Glancing sideways at her in the passenger seat, my eyes catch on the thick lashes as she blinks down at the photo on her phone.

"Not at all?" I ask.

"No. Sure, it was a struggle, but to me, the struggle meant I was free."

"Was it so bad living with your mom?"

She shrugs. "We fought a lot. And I felt like I had to fight for her love. It was like she always wanted me to be grateful to her for the simplest things, things she should have done because she loved me. So I just decided that I was better off without it."

The car grows quiet for a moment as I stare ahead at the road, thinking about what she just said. It strikes me how much I can relate to that, and not just about my father, but maybe about my faith too.

"So, where are we going?" she says with eagerness. I know I'm probably about to crush that excitement.

"My parents' house."

Her head snaps in my direction as her eyes widen in surprise. "What? Why?"

"Because I go every Sunday. Well, I *used* to. I haven't been to Sunday dinner in six weeks, and I think it's time I return...honey," I say, adding on the romantic pet name with a teasing smile.

The shock on her face slowly morphs into frustration. An adorable little divot appears between her brows as she glowers at me. I can tell she's working herself up, and I love that Sage doesn't hold back. She's not like the women I date: quiet, compliant, shoving their feelings down to avoid confrontation.

"Adam, *dear*," she replies with grit. "The whole plan was to tarnish your reputation to ruin your father's. But you're using me to irritate him. I know that was the plan, but you're taking it all too far. When are we going to get to torturing my ex with our fake relationship? So far, it's all been about you."

Tendrils of guilt and shame creep their way up my spine as I stare straight ahead, letting her words sink in. Then I snake my hand over to her thigh, resting it there as I look into her eyes.

"It's just a casual family dinner," I say softly, feeling tethered by her bright-blue eyes. "It's really special to my mother, and I've missed it."

The wrinkle between her brows slowly disappears. The tension in her shoulders melts away and she slides down against the seat.

I wasn't going for sympathy and I wasn't trying to manipulate her. What I said is true. I miss family dinners, and I don't want to go alone. I don't want to face my family's scrutiny without someone by my side.

As we pull up to the house, I place the car into park behind Caleb's SUV. After shaking off my nerves, I open the door and Sage does the same. We meet on the driveway, where I put out my hand and she slides hers into it.

When we reach the front door, I open it like I always do, feeling the eyes of the security camera on my back the entire time. Leaving the front door unlocked on Sundays is another one of Mom's wholesome traditions. Normally this place is locked down like a prison, but she finds something symbolic in leaving it open one holy day a week, and not just for her children, but for anyone. Of course, no one knows it's unlocked, but she does. And that's all that matters.

There's chatter coming from the dining room as we step into the grand foyer. Sage squeezes my hand, pulling her plaid shirt a little tighter around her chest to cover herself. And as we take two steps inside, I catch sight of our reflection in the giant mirror over the entryway table.

Sage sees it too, because we both stop. For a moment, we stand there and stare. There's something about the sight of us together that holds my interest. It's like I can't look away. Like I love the way she looks by my side. Full of color and her skin speckled with art, she is far more interesting than my drab black-on-black appearance.

I slip my phone out of my back pocket and tuck her under my chin, both of us facing the mirror as I snap a pic. Neither of us is smiling, and honestly, we both look sad and yet beautiful as well.

"For the socials," I whisper as I slip my phone back into my pocket.

"Did someone come in?" my mother calls just before appearing at the end of the hallway. She freezes in place as her eyes land first on Sage and then on me.

"Adam," she mumbles softly.

"Hi, Mom," I reply. Just seeing her feels like a punch to the gut. "You remember Sage."

It takes my mother a moment before she can react, still in so much shock either from me showing up after so long or from Sage's presence in general. But the woman standing in front of me doesn't have a rude bone in her body.

"Of course." She greets Sage with a smile, walking toward us with arms wide. "I'm so glad you came, sweetie."

My mother hugs my date first, a warm embrace that doesn't appear uncomfortable or forced in the slightest. In fact, even Sage squeezes my mother in return in a way that almost appears to be a surprise to her.

Then my mother hugs me, reaching up on her tiptoes to kiss me on the cheek as she does. Suddenly being in her arms makes me feel smaller and all the filthy and hateful things I've done in just the past month come coursing through my mind like a tsunami of shame.

"I was hoping you'd come. I made your favorite," she says with a smile as she takes our hands and pulls us across the house toward the dining room. I laugh to myself as she does because she thinks my favorite is her lasagna, but the truth is, they're all my favorites. She couldn't cook a bad meal if she tried.

As we reach the dining room, all the gentle chatter stops and a clang of forks hitting plates replaces the sound of their conversations. I feel my father's heated glare on my face as I pull Sage under my arm.

"Uncle Adam," Abigail shrieks, stealing my attention and forcing a smile on my face.

"Hey, Abby," I reply, tousling her messy brown hair. Then, I realize my fake girlfriend hasn't met my real niece yet. "Sage, this is my niece, Abigail."

"Hi," Sage says, awkwardly waving to her and then to the entire table. My brothers return the greeting while my mother busies herself, setting another place at the table. "I hope it's not too much trouble," Sage mutters delicately.

"Of course not," my mother argues. "There is always room at the table."

Meanwhile, my father and I are in a hate-filled stare-down, his nostrils flaring with his rage as my face remains stoic and calm, like a dare. He can get as angry as he wants. Hell, that's the whole fucking point. But I refuse to break.

"Please, sit," my mother calls as Sage and I take our seats next to each other between Abigail and Luke.

My niece grins up at me excitedly, and I feel another sucker punch of guilt for missing out on six weeks of this.

"Sorry I'm not really dressed for Sunday dinner," Sage says in a soft apology. "Adam didn't tell me we were coming."

My mother laughs. "You look beautiful." Then she gives me a pointed stare. "Adam Matthew Goode, communicate with your date a little better next time. I taught you better."

The smile that tugs on my lips feels like a relief. "Yes, ma'am," I say with a nod.

"We were just about to say grace," a dark voice from the head of the table says in a cruel, muttering tone. We all turn our attention to him as he puts on his best fake smile. "Perhaps our guest would like to lead us tonight."

Sage's eyes widen as she shakes her head. "Oh, I can't. Thank you, though—"

"I insist," he argues.

"I can say it," I interject, but he only holds up a hand.

"Son, we let our guests say grace. You know that."

Shivers tingle their way up my spine as everyone stares at Sage, and I feel every bone in my body tense. My hackles rise as I frantically try to find a way to protect her. I never should have brought her here, and just as I'm about to push out my chair and yank her from this table, she clasps her hands together in front of her.

"I've never said grace before, but I can try."

"Thank you," my mother whispers.

Sage glances up at me through a side glance. Our eyes meet for a moment, and I give her a reassuring nod before she turns her eyes downward and clears her throat.

"I never sat down with my family for a meal. I've never sat down with *any* family for a meal like this," she says, and I notice the eyes around the table lifting to glance in her direction. But Sage continues, "And I'm so incredibly thankful to be here. I'm thankful for Mrs. Goode for cooking this delicious meal. I'm thankful for the entire Goode family for allowing me to sit here with you, and I'm thankful for Adam's brothers for being so nice to me, even though I'm an outsider. And mostly, I'm thankful for Adam—"

"That's enough," my father barks from the end of the table.

Abigail flinches next to me, and my anger grows as I glare at my father.

"Truett!" My mother scolds him in a harsh whisper.

Still, Sage continues, "I'm thankful for Adam for showing me what a real good man is, without judgment or hypocrisy."

"I said enough!" Truett snaps again.

"Thank you," she finishes, and before my father can interject any more, I hear Luke from across the table.

"Amen."

"Amen," the others follow.

My niece's small voice is last as she softly mumbles, "Amen."

A fist lands on the table with a bang, rattling glasses and plates. Then he points a finger at Sage. "Young lady—"

"Don't," I snap, my fierce gaze on his face. "Don't talk to my girlfriend like that. She did what you asked her to."

He ignores me and looks back at her. "Grace is meant to thank God and God alone for the blessings in our lives. My *family* is well aware of that," he says through clenched teeth, his eyes scanning the room.

"Well, you asked me to say it, and that's how I say it," she replies, her chin held high. Something warm and affectionate settles in my chest at the sight.

"It was lovely," my mother replies.

"Yes, it was," I say with my hand on the back of Sage's chair. I move it to rest at the top of her spine, just under her neck, and I move on instinct alone. My mind hardly registers what I'm doing as I gently nudge her toward me. As she spins to look at me, our eyes meet. Then our lips.

It's a quick kiss, but it feels monumental.

As our faces part, her gaze stays tethered to mine. When I finally face forward, I avoid the curious and shocked stares from the rest of my family.

"Let's eat," I say to break up the tension. As I reach for the lasagna in the center of the table, I'm feeling particularly pleased at the moment. Truett is unhinged, thrown completely off guard, and angrier than ever. And the beautiful woman at my side is the one responsible.

# TWENTY-FOUR

## ADAM

"Is this your room?" Sage asks as I click on the light to the large bedroom at the end of the massive hall.

"This is my childhood bedroom," I reply as we both step inside. I shut the door behind us, mostly to get five minutes to breathe and step out of our roles. Although, to be honest, stepping in and out of the fake-dating scenario feels less and less like much of a change at all.

"Oh wow," she says as she scans the room, walking to each wall to examine the photos hanging there. Most of them are of me and my brothers in various stages of our lives. "Look at how cute you were," she says with a smile as she comes across one of me when I was twelve, holding baby Isaac on my lap.

I remember that day when Mom and Dad brought him home. After feeling like the odd one out with the twins for so long, I finally had a brother to myself. Or at least that's how it felt. It was my job to protect him, to keep him safe, to be his equal.

Subtly in the back of my mind, I wonder if I failed him—a thought that's plagued me since the day he left. I never realized in all of my years that the one person I was supposed to protect him from was our own father. Now I have no idea if he's safe or alive or happy. He might as well be dead, but even with death, we get closure. When Isaac ran away, all we got was emptiness.

Sage turns back toward the bed and stares at it with a smile, distracting me from my gloomy thinking. "How many girls did you feel up on that bed?"

I laugh. "Zero."

"Bullshit," she says, cackling. "You guys have your own fucking wing in this ginormous house and you never once brought a girl in here?"

I can't hide my mischievous smirk as I drop my ass onto the mattress. "Okay...two. But that's it."

She sits next to me with a teasing smile. "That's disappointing."

"I know, but back then, all I wanted was to be like my father. I thought I was on the right path."

It's quiet for a moment as she lets out a sigh and then places a hand on my thigh. "I'm sorry for causing a scene at dinner. There's nothing wrong with saying grace. I was just trying to piss him off."

"You did just that," I reply with a lopsided grin. "Your grace was just fine, and you don't need to apologize. But, Sage..." I turn my head to face her. "Is it true you've never sat down at a family dinner?"

She lets out a huff and avoids my eyes. Then she leans back on her elbows. "Sort of. I had a friend in high school who used to invite me over to dinner. We sat at a table like that. Sometimes Gladys and I eat together too."

"What about your family?" I ask, leaning down on my side beside her.

"My mother had me when she was really young and when I was in high school, she remarried and had a few more kids. Her new husband was an asshole, and he hated me, so I emancipated myself at seventeen and moved away. Then, we just...lost touch. It's sort of sad how easily she was able to let me go."

My heart lurches as she speaks.

"I'm sorry," I whisper. As she turns toward me, our eyes meet and our faces are impossibly close. I let my gaze trail from her stunning blue eyes, down the gentle slope of her button nose, to the ring in her lip. And I find myself swallowing, almost as if...I'm nervous.

The tension grows as we stare at each other from just a few inches apart. And just when it feels unbearable, she turns away.

"I'm not gonna lie, Church Boy. It's a little weird that your parents have kept your room so immaculate after all this time."

I let out a sigh and shift on the bed. "It's my mother. She thinks we're going to need it again someday. So she keeps all of our rooms the way they were when we left. Even Isaac's."

Her eyes find mine again, and I instantly regret bringing him up. *Please don't ask me about him.*

"Want to film a scene?" she asks, and I stare at her with confusion. Just like that, she breaks the tension.

"In here?"

"Yeah. It's kind of hot. Fucking in your childhood bedroom."

Blood rushes to my cock at the mere thought of getting to actually fuck her in here like we're teenagers. "No..." I say, glancing at the door. "Someone could walk in, so let's keep our clothes on."

She bites her bottom lip. "Now I really feel like some girl you snuck into your room."

A laugh bursts through my lips. "Just a couple of horny teenagers."

"So let's make out. I'll let you feel me up like you did with those girls from high school."

"Seriously?" Suddenly she's asking to make out with me? Where the fuck did this come from?

Then she holds up her phone. "For the viewers."

*Oh. Of course.*

For the viewers.

*Jesus, Adam. Get your head on right.*

"Sure," I reply casually.

With excitement, she scoots up the bed until her head is near the pillows. Then she turns on her camera and places it on the nightstand, finding a good angle before lying down on her back and waiting for me.

Something about this feels wrong and right at the same time. I mean, there's no way to really *fake* making out so, like it or not, this will be real.

The sight of her lying on my bed, waiting for me, is something I'd like to etch in my memory forever. I can't even remember the names of the girls I kissed here twenty years ago, but I'll remember the way Sage is looking at me right now, in that black bralette and green skirt forever.

After taking a mental picture, I crawl over Sage's body and nestle myself between her legs. With a smile, she whispers, "Action."

But I don't kiss her, not right away. Instead, I brush a tendril of hair off her cheek with my thumb, and I stare into her eyes for a moment. And I think about that moment at dinner when she thanked me during the grace, and I can't help myself.

"Was that real?" I ask.

Her face falls. "What?"

"When you thanked me during grace for showing you what a good man is? Were you being truthful?"

Recognition dawns on her face. And it takes her a moment to answer.

Fuck, I'm an idiot. *Of course it wasn't real, you moron. After everything you've done to her and how you've used her, why would she thank you for that?*

Without an answer from her, I start to climb off, but she wraps a leg around my hips and holds me in place. Then she runs a hand across my cheek and down to the nape of my neck.

"Yes, of course it was truthful, Adam."

I don't care if she's lying. I really don't care.

Without another word, I dive in, pressing my lips to hers. She opens for me, and I slide my tongue between her lips, gliding against hers until she hums in response.

And I pretend it's real.

Resting on my forearm above her head, I kiss her like I mean it. Like it's not fake.

Her fingers grip the fabric of my shirt, tugging me closer as I hungrily devour her mouth in a torrent of passion. For a moment, I forget about the phone recording us.

I just taste *her*. Feel *her*. Need *her*.

I suck on her bottom lip and then pull it between my teeth for a small nibble. Releasing her lip, I lick the gold ring there, and she hums again.

"Adam," she whispers against my lips as our kiss grows more intense.

My mouth trails from her lips to her neck as she hikes her skirt up to wrap her other leg around me, pressing me against her in delicious friction. I kiss my way along the constellation drawn on her tender skin, licking every star until she is trembling in my arms.

Her tight fists drag my shirt up, finding the exposed skin of my back, clawing her nails along my rib cage in slow, torturous scratches. Following her lead, I tear down the bralette covering her tits, and once her supple breasts are exposed, I latch my mouth on the tight bud of her nipple and bite enough to make her cry out.

Her fingers scratch my scalp as she digs her nails in my hair, pulling me closer. Then I switch sides, biting the opposite nipple until goose bumps appear along every inch of her skin. My cock is painfully hard as I grind it against her.

There is too much fucking fabric in our way, or so my dick says.

But I've lost touch with reality somewhere. This isn't happening. I'm not going to fuck her here on my childhood bed with my family just downstairs.

I'm not going to fuck her *anywhere*. Because this is all for show. She and I will never truly be together like that. Never.

Even if this feels so good and right.

"Peaches," I whisper against her skin as my mouth trails back up to her mouth.

"Yes?" she breathes.

"Tell me this is real." I bite my way along her jawline, up to her earlobe, but she doesn't answer right away. It's stupid of me to even ask this, but I need to hear her say it. I need to know it's not just me. "Tell me you feel it too."

She hesitates, and I nearly lose hope. But then she drags my hand between her legs, pressing my fingers to the moist center of her panties, and I get my answer. "Feel how real it is."

A low, hungry growl of need and overwhelming lust climbs from my throat, and I'm already pulling her panties aside, ready to feel her arousal for myself when there's a knock on the door.

My hand freezes as I pull my body away from hers. She stares up at me with worry in her eyes as my brother's voice calls through the door.

"Hey, Adam, Mom is looking for you." It's Luke.

"Thanks," I reply loudly. "Be right out."

There's a chuckle from the hallway as he retreats down the hall, and I glance down at Sage before we both break into a fit of laughter.

"Now I really feel like a teenager."

"Me too," she replies with a blush on her cheeks.

After I climb off of her, averting my eyes from her while she shimmies her skirt back into place and I rearrange the hard-on in my pants, I realize just how close we got to crossing the line.

We set rules to stop ourselves from doing this, but when we're in the moment, it's so hard to say no to what we really want.

We take a moment to compose ourselves, mostly to wait for my dick to soften before we walk back out to the living room, where my family is waiting. Everyone is there but my father, who generally retreats to his office rather than socialize with the rest of us. Normally, I'm there to join him.

"Your father asked for you to come to his office," my mother says with a cup of tea in her hands.

As I stare at her, seeing something heavy behind the facade of comfort in her eyes, I decide to shake my head.

"Sage and I have to get going."

Her expression changes. I don't know if it's alarm or surprise, but she looks slightly unsettled as she processes the fact that I'm disobeying him. Even at thirty-seven, I'm ignoring his request. Something I've never done in my life, at least not until lately.

Without another word, she stands from her chair. "Okay, sweetie. Another time then."

She gives me a tight hug, tighter than before, and I wish for the first time that I could have an honest conversation with my mom. I wish I could tell her the truth about my father.

But I can't. Not yet. So I accept her hug and watch as she embraces Sage after me.

"It was so lovely to have you," my mother says to her. I'm amazed at how real it seems.

"Your lasagna was delicious and I loved being here with all of you," Sage replies—again, selling it really well.

"Anytime, dear."

Then Sage and I leave through the front door without another word.

"That was nice," she says sweetly as we reach the car. "I really like your mom."

I pause as I unlock the driver's side. Then I glance up at her as I reply, "She likes you too. I can tell."

Which isn't a lie.

Sage seems pleased with this response. Warmth and pride color her features as she opens the door and climbs inside.

# JUNE
## THE ANTI-HERO

# TWENTY-FIVE

SAGE

"Why are the views so low on our latest videos?"

Adam is hovering over my shoulder as I lean against the counter, scrolling through our feed. Our feed is full of videos by now, but he's right—views have been down. The first one that went viral, the scene in his dad's office and one of us making out in his childhood bedroom. None from the last two weeks are as popular as we anticipated.

And I think I know why.

"Well..." I say with a wince as I stare down at the screen. "I have an idea."

"What?" He leans back on the counter and stares down at me with his arms crossed.

I pull up the first video, specifically the part where he's choking me from the front. "This," I say, pointing at the image.

His brow furrows as he stares at the feed, and after a moment, realization dawns on his face. "Oh. That makes sense."

He hasn't so much as choked me or smacked my ass since, and viewers miss the degradation.

And honestly...so do I.

"So, I think in today's video, we should throw in some more of that. They really seem to like it," I say as I cross the room toward the couch where the tripod is already set up.

Adam has been spending more and more time here since we started filming these. Some nights, he even sleeps over—on the couch, of course. Nothing has happened between us since that confusing make-out sesh on his bed. It was real—of course, it was real. But my wires are still a little crossed and I can't quite make sense of whether it's just physically real or if I'm the only delusional one who's sensing more here. Either way, I'm keeping it all in my head.

Adam has been in a better mood too. It's like watching him piece himself back together, slowly, one piece at a time.

"But do you?" he asks, throwing me off. I was so lost in my thoughts I missed the original question.

"Huh? Do I what?"

He slowly crosses toward me. "Do you like it? The degradation? Me choking you, pulling your hair, calling you names?"

I swallow my nerves, turning my gaze down and away from him as I try to hide my facial expression. "Does it matter? It's not real."

"It's real enough," he replies.

Is he really worried about my well-being here, or is he trying to get a read on my sexual interests?

"Do you?" I ask, trying to turn the attention back on him.

"I asked first," he replies.

When it's clear he's not going to relent, I let out a huff and throw my shoulders back. Staring up at him, I give him an exasperated look. "Fine. Yes. I do sometimes like it. Don't judge me for that."

"Why would I judge you?" he asks, sounding offended.

"Because that's what you do, Adam. You judge me. You don't like the way I look. The way I dress. The way I act. The way I live, so I sure as fuck don't expect you to like the way I fuck."

I throw my arms up and stare at him, letting my heated words permeate the air, and it's quiet after I utter them. He only stares back, no expression on his face.

And for a moment, he has the nerve to appear as if *he's* the one offended.

Then when I turn back to the couch, he steps a little closer. Until he's standing just over my shoulder. Not close enough to feel his breath, but close enough to feel the energy emanating from his skin. Like a warm ray of sun I want to bask in.

"I don't judge—"

"Let's just shoot this," I say, interrupting him.

"Where do you want me?" he asks as he tears off his shirt.

My lips twist in thought as I maneuver the camera on the tripod downward, hitting record. Then I kneel and stare up at him.

His eyes widen in surprise as he takes in this prime blow-job position I'm in. "It's going to be hard to fake that, Peaches."

"I want you to slap me."

He forces a laugh. "Absolutely not."

"Just do it. Not too hard."

"I'm not slapping you, Sage."

With a roll of my eyes, I stare up at him in frustration. "Stop trying to be so chivalrous, Adam. Slap my face, grab my throat, and spit in my mouth."

"Jesus Christ," he stammers, grabbing his hair at the scalp. "You're really asking me to do that?"

"I'm telling you to," I reply stubbornly.

"And what if I don't want to?"

"But you do," I say, narrowing my eyes at him. "I know you do."

He looks mentally worn and frustrated as he paces around me. Clearly at war with himself, and a little part of me starts to feel bad for it.

"Okay, look," I say, trying to calm him down. "If you really don't want to, I'm not going to make you."

"This shit isn't normal, Sage. It's not...right."

"Why not? If I'm giving you consent, and we both want it, then who's to say it's not right?"

"I don't know..."

"God?" I ask with a tilt of my head.

He gives me a flat, unamused expression. "Stop. I just need a minute to think this through."

I let out a sigh and rest on my heels as I wait. Adam's been raised to believe that anything kinky must be evil. He's been internally punishing himself his entire life for all the shit he gets off to in secret. I know he does. I just wish I could help him let that shit go.

"Adam, it's okay if you like it. As long as I like it, and I'm literally telling you I do—"

He lets out an exasperated huff as he crowds me. "Fuck it," he mutters. "Sage, look at me."

There's that authoritative tone again that makes me weak. So I stare up at him obediently.

The next thing I know, the fingers of his hand are smacking me on the cheek, making me gasp and my eyes clench shut. A moan flies out of my mouth. Then his hand is around my throat, and he's jerking my attention up toward him.

"Open your eyes, Peaches," he mutters with a tight jaw.

My lids pop up just in time to see him lean down toward me. Arousal burns in my belly as I stare up at the ferocity in his eyes. His guard is down like I've picked a scab so long I've made it bleed. And now it's gushing.

Then, with a firm grip on my face, he slides two fingers into my mouth, making me gag and choke as he pulls them out. Spit flies from his mouth, landing on my face. But then he's there, running his tongue along the length of my cheek.

His face is inches from mine as he grits his teeth in my face. "You fuck me up. You make me want shit I know I shouldn't want. You know that?"

Disoriented, I nod.

"But I love it, Peaches. I fucking *love* having you like this."

He hesitates a moment before adding, "Like the dirty slut you are. Aren't you?"

Again, I nod. This strange, all-consuming sensation washes over me. Like adrenaline and arousal mixed together, and as ridiculous as it sounds, it all feels so...intense.

Then his mouth is crashing against mine, as the grip on my throat tightens, so much so that I start to feel my pulse in my own ears.

I'm lost in his dizzying kiss and all too quickly, it's gone.

He pulls away, leaving me swaying on the floor. He's walking away again, pacing frantically. "Cut," he barks loudly.

I don't rise from the floor. I can barely move. So I stare at him until he finally freezes and glances back my way. The features on his face melt into unadulterated shame and sympathy combined as he rushes toward me.

"Fuck, Sage. Get up," he mutters as he lifts me to my feet.

"I'm fine," I mumble.

Grabbing his own discarded shirt from the couch, he uses it to wipe down the surface of my cheeks, lips, and chin. Then he holds my face in his hands, forcing me to look at him. "I'm sorry. Are you sure you're okay?"

Turning my face in his hands, he examines my cheek, where he slapped me. "I said I'm fine," I argue, regardless of the fact that my voice quivers as I force the words out. Why the fuck do I feel like I'm about to cry? I *did* like that. I liked it *a lot*. But suddenly the feel of his arms around me and the gentle touch as he dotes on me has me wanting to bawl.

So I shove him away. "Adam, stop!"

"You made me do that. Now I'm going to make you do this," he says in a commanding tone.

"It was a ten-second clip, Adam. It's hardly grounds for aftercare."

"I don't give a shit," he snaps. "Sit down." His words are sharp, sending chills down my spine as I suddenly find myself doing what he says. A moment later, he's handing me a glass of water and holding a cool rag against my face.

I stare up into his eyes, growing more and more emotional at the sight of this pure and kind version of Adam. And all the while, the camera records on the tripod, catching every second of his aftercare.

And I let it.

✝

"Have you still not heard from that asshole ex-boyfriend of yours?" Adam asks, sitting across from me at the same diner we met at. It's become a bit of a Saturday morning ritual, but considering that we've spent nearly every waking minute together since all of this went down, it really doesn't matter which day of the week we eat here.

"No," I mumble with my lips against a cup of coffee.

"Do you think he's seen the videos?"

Setting the cup down, I think it over. Has he seen them? Probably. I mean, how could he miss them? The little degradation snippet we posted is already doing better than the first video. Viewers love a little slap and spit.

"I think I'm afraid he *has* seen them and just doesn't care," I say, without looking him in the eye.

Adam hums out his disapproval and it's quiet for a moment before he speaks again. "So, let's go to the club."

"Ha," I say, stabbing a bite of his waffles with my fork. "Very funny."

"I'm serious. Let's go rub our relationship in his face. We can even record a video in there."

He makes it sound so simple, as if Brett wouldn't throw the biggest fit in the world, acting as if he is somehow the victim here. And how I'd somehow fall for it.

"No, we shouldn't," I reply.

"Why not?"

"First of all, recording in the club is incredibly unethical. And second of all, I have no desire to see my ex or rub anything in his face. I'm moving on."

Even I can hear how unconvincing I sound.

"Come on now. You said you wanted revenge on him and that it was part of the deal. Besides, if we want to fuck up his relationship with my father, I think us showing off ours is a big part of that."

Letting out a long, annoyed-sounding sigh, I lean back in the seat. "Fine."

He shoots me a wicked-looking wink from the other side of the booth, and I hide my own smile behind my coffee cup. As he continues to talk, going on and on about how well this new video is performing, I let my eyes take in the sight of him.

Adam has changed a lot in the last two months since I met him. His clothes are grungier, his posture is more relaxed, and his demeanor is softer. Like he's becoming more himself, or maybe I'm just rubbing off on him now.

Either way, he's changing.

And it's like the worse he behaves, the better he gets.

# TWENTY-SIX

ADAM

Sage's hand feels so small in mine as we walk across the parking lot toward the club, her heels clicking on the pavement. I have a bit of déjà vu, remembering what it felt like pulling up to this place for the first time.

It still feels as strange and as foreign now as it did then, only this time, I'm not alone.

"We're just going to go in and let him see us together, and then we're leaving," I say to comfort Sage. Her usual confident and headstrong demeanor is changing with every step closer to the building. It's like she's shrinking before my very eyes.

The girl at the hostess stand waves her right through without making either of us pay or check in our phones like she did to me on the first night. So either this girl is her friend, or word doesn't travel very fast in sex clubs.

As soon as we enter the main room of the club, we both pause near the outskirts of the dense crowd and look around for a familiar douchebag with blond hair. When there's no sign of him and we start growing uncomfortable, I tug her toward the bar.

I have to squeeze through bodies just to get close enough to get the busy bartender's attention.

A strange tingle travels up my spine while I wait for our drinks, and it's the indistinguishable feeling of being watched. Subtly I glance around the room, looking for a camera or a pair of watching eyes, and what I find is far more than a pair. Damn near every set of eyes in this place is either glancing at Sage and me or rudely gawking at us.

Sage must feel it too, because she squeezes my hand.

"What is going on?" she whispers.

Just as I turn to answer her and suggest we get the fuck out of here, a girl from across the bar leans forward on the surface and points directly at us. "Oh my god, it's you!"

*Jesus Christ.*

Now, literally everyone is looking at us, some with confusion and some with recognition. So she continues hollering through the noisy club.

"You're that hot couple from FanVids!"

A collective gasp of awe fills the room as throngs of people turn toward us. Sage and I are suddenly bombarded with requests for photos and autographs, which we both do our best to politely decline. I don't like the way the men are looking at her, hovering too close, so I put her body between mine and the bar.

Someone hands us drinks, and when I notice Sage lifting the straw to her lips, I nearly smack it out of her hands.

"Don't drink that." I tear it away and set it on the bar, giving her a stern glare.

When I hear more than one person asking to *watch us*, I lose my patience. I grab her hand, ready to make our way out of the club. But just then, a woman with wavy red hair and a face full of makeup steps up close to us and calmly directs us to *follow her*, and for some reason, I listen.

I let the beautiful girl pull us out of the crowd, across the dance floor and straight into the same VIP room where my father and his goons beat the ever-loving shit out of me two months ago.

As soon as the sign on the door comes into view, my heels dig into the tiles and I stop the woman from pulling us in there. She turns back toward me with sympathy on her face. "Relax," she says with a smile, "your dad's not here tonight."

My body relaxes as I let her drag me the rest of the way. As we enter the VIP room, I notice that it's far calmer in here than the last time I came barreling through these doors. I keep my eyes forward as I follow the redhead to the bar.

I glance back at Sage, who gives me a quick shrug, which I take to mean she doesn't know this woman. There's no sign of Brett either, which grates on my nerves. We're here to ruffle his feathers and he's not here to let us do that, so the only one with ruffled feathers is me.

"I bet you two didn't expect that," the girl says with a smile. She's a bit taller than Sage, with round curves and her cleavage spilling from her thin dress. As her eyes travel the length of my body, down and then up, I pull Peaches even closer to my side.

"We didn't," I reply flatly.

"Who are you?" Sage asks.

"I'm Sadie," she says, putting a hand out toward each of us. "I just started working here in April."

Sage's expression changes in the blink of an eye. Curiosity morphs into resentment as she stares intensely at Sadie. Has Sage spoken about this woman and I wasn't listening? Am I missing something?

"You're the one he hired," Sage mutters.

Sadie doesn't seem fazed by the change in temperament. In fact, she looks pleased with it.

"Don't worry," she says to the girl at my side. "I know who you are too. Wanna get a drink?"

"Please," I interject. Sage nods and the three of us make our way to the tall booth in the corner, *not* the one I caught my father at.

With our beverages in hand, Sadie tells us everything, essentially catching me up to speed. And I see the hurt in Sage's eyes as she replays the entire thing—Brett casting her aside, dismissing her ideas and hard work, hiring someone else before giving his own girlfriend the credit she deserved. It makes me hate him even more.

Then she looks at me. "And I know all about your father too. He hasn't come back in since you started filming those videos. Brett's been scarce too. Something about you two together really freaked them both out."

"Why?" Sage asks, leaning forward.

"Because it's unhinged," Sadie says with a laugh. "Those videos are the last thing they expected out of Mr. Inspiration over here. Everybody fucking loves you guys. And that freaks them out because you hold all their secrets. They're not the kings of their domain anymore."

"Don't you...like working with Brett?" Sage asks with resounding unease.

"Fuck no," Sadie snaps in reply. "I've seen great clubs and I've seen sleazy clubs. When I came here, I could tell it had a woman's touch, but that's not what he wanted from me. Once my contract is up, I'm out of here."

"So, I take it Brett's not here," Sage replies.

"Oh, he's here." Sadie's gaze travels upward to the second-floor balcony covered by mirrors. "He's just too chickenshit to show his face."

I let out a grumble of annoyance. "Well, coming here was a waste."

"Was it?" Sadie asks, peering at me with curiosity. "You're at a sex club and you have an eager audience. I think if you want to make a real scene, you know exactly how to do it."

I feel Sage's eyes travel to my face and I only glance down at her for a moment, alarm written on her features. But I'm not entirely sure what I'm feeling, so I quickly look away.

For one, there's no way Sage and I can *fake* live sex. There are too many people around who would see that certain things aren't going where they're supposed to.

But I can't hide the part of me that hopes what we do isn't really fake. The thought of taking Sage to one of these rooms and having my way with her, audience or not, makes my dick nearly jump through my pants. It's already uncomfortably hard behind my zipper.

And I know without a doubt in my mind that I'm not fucking Sage in this club tonight. Even if she tells me to. Even if she fucking begs me to, how could I trust that she truly wants it and isn't just feeling the pressure?

While I'm sitting here having my existential crisis, Sadie leans over to Sage and whispers something in her ear. It takes everything in me to keep from yanking my date away, afraid of what ideas Sadie might be planting in her head.

Then Sadie waves at me and struts away from the table. Sage and I are left alone, still with a few lingering eyes from around the VIP area on us.

"What did she say?" I ask, curiosity burning.

Her lips purse together uncomfortably. "She told me to take you to the playrooms."

"Why don't we just leave?" I reply without asking anything further.

"Do you want to leave?" she asks, leaning close to me and gazing up into my eyes with something like hope and fear.

*No, Sage. I want to fuck your brains out in every stupid room of this place until it's covered in us, and then I want to burn it to the fucking ground.*

But I don't say that. Which is good because I really shouldn't, but I can't bring myself to lie and say I really do want to leave. And my dick is doing most of the thinking at this point. It's that little silver dress she has on and the way her lips look so fucking kissable with that dark stain.

Being around Sage makes me feel so goddamn vulnerable. And I can't explain why. So I can't come out with it and admit all the filthy things I want with her in this place right now.

But I can follow her lead.

"Take me to the playrooms," I whisper, leaning in and pressing my lips to her ear.

I feel her tremble.

"Are you sure?" she replies softly. "It's all in the open back there. There won't be any faking it."

"We won't be fucking," I say, noticing how the edges of her mouth drop a little at that admission. So I rest a hand on the small of her back and pull her closer as I continue, "But if he can't see you, then let's make sure he hears you."

Her weight gives in to my touch a little as she nearly falls into my body.

And I take that as a yes.

# TWENTY-SEVEN

## ADAM

The *play*room is essentially an open area with strange furniture and strobe lights so intense it makes it hard to see. The walls are mirrored and the floor is black. It's oddly crowded with the sounds of sex surrounding us, and that immediately makes me want to leave.

That on top of the eyes following us.

But my only focus is on her and our task at hand. If Brett wants to try and pretend we don't exist, I'm going to make sure he can't pretend for long. I'll have all eyes in this club on her in a moment.

For now, I'm just trying to get my bearings enough to make a plan. We meander through the room, and I keep my eyes on our surroundings until I spot a mirrored wall with a pair of soft leather cuffs hanging from the ceiling.

I pull Sage toward them and stop her until we're both staring at our reflection in the mirror. Much like at my parents' house, I savor the look of us together. She fits under my chin so nicely. But then, in the flashing lights, I catch a glimpse of myself in the mirror.

And I realize just how different I look. My hair isn't coiffed the same way. My clothes aren't as neat and pressed as they once were. I look like a different man with her in my arms, and for the first time in a long time, I like the man staring back at me.

So I imagine for a brief moment that it's my job to protect her. My job to care for her, to fulfill her needs, to make her smile, and to make her come.

Am I good enough for that? Do I even deserve that much? How can I when I don't even know who I am anymore?

"People are staring?" she whispers. "What are we doing?"

I straighten my spine. "Do you trust me?"

She nods.

"Just tell me to stop and I will, okay?"

"Okay," she replies.

Something about her so eagerly agreeing hits me. Which means I can't fuck this up.

Still facing the mirror, I turn Sage until her back is against the glass and lift her hands until she reaches the cuffs. She has to stand on her toes to get there, but once she's high enough, I secure each wrist in the leather and hear an audible gasp from her lips.

With her arms pressed to her ears, she hangs from the cuffs, slowly swaying with her gaze still settled on my face.

Once I'm sure the cuffs will hold her and she's safe, I grab her by the jaw. A hint of a smile lifts the corners of her lips. Maybe it's the audience, or maybe it's the environment, but I feel free to let things slip that I usually keep to myself.

"I've always wanted to have you at my mercy like this, Peaches. I can do anything I want to do to you now."

"So do it," she replies in a challenging tone.

People have gathered around us, but I'm not worried about them. My focus is only on her and how fucking exquisite she looks bound up like this. With just her arms above her tiny frame, she's completely *mine*. And I really could do anything to her. If I wanted to lift her dress and fill her with my cock, I could.

And the thought is tempting.

But I have other plans for her at the moment.

With her face in my hands, I stare down at her before taking her lips with my own. I lick my way into her mouth, rough and dominant, so she knows this mouth belongs to me.

All she can do is hum and struggle to breathe as I kiss her. Then I drag down the neckline of her dress, exposing her breasts and moving my mouth to bite her already tight nipple.

She cries out as I bite too hard. Then I pull my lips away from it and slap it enough to make her gasp. Her wide eyes find my face and I panic for a moment that I've gone too far.

"Do it again," she whispers, and I can't keep my lips off of hers after she says that. Something about Sage just seems to wake up every nerve ending in my body. She makes me realize all the things I want aren't so far out of reach.

And that I shouldn't feel so bad for wanting them.

But for now, I'm only focused on her body and getting her to make that face again, so I rip down the other side of her dress, exposing her other breast. I take a minute to admire it first.

It really is perfect. So small, yet perky, and just enough to squeeze my hand around.

When I slap the other side, making her gasp again, it takes everything I have to keep from losing my mind.

"You're gonna have to be louder than that, Peaches." My lips devour every inch of her skin from her neck down to her collarbone, biting and sucking until she's moaning and gasping with every breath.

"Are you as wet as you were that night in my bed?" I whisper when I make my way back up to her ear.

She sucks in a short gasp at my question. Everything I've said up to this point, I've said loudly so everyone can hear. Like this is a performance.

But that last line I whispered because I want to know. I *need* to know.

"Why don't you find out?" she replies, her eyes burning into mine.

Without a response, I slowly tug on the fabric of her dress, lifting it until she's fully exposed. Then with our eyes still locked, I reach between her legs and slide my hand down the front of her panties. She trembles from my touch, but when I ease between her folds to find her soaked with arousal, I'm the one to react.

She feels even more perfect than I remember. Warm and soft and ready for me. Her cunt leaks like it needs my cock, like it's *crying* for it.

"You can't keep doing this to me," I growl as I hold on to the cuffs above her head and lean into her. "I have my hand between your legs, Sage. And you feel so fucking good."

Her lust-filled eyes stay on mine as she bites her lips.

Sliding my finger through the pool of moisture, I keep my eyes on her as I ease my way inside her, wishing so badly that it was my cock fucking her and not my finger. With every thrust and glide of my hand, she moans and hums, tilting her hips to keep with the pressure of my hand. We exist in our own little world, and right now, that world revolves around her perfect pussy.

"I need to taste you, Peaches."

"Please," she whines, her head hanging back as she writhes with need.

Pulling my hand from her panties, I quickly work them down her legs. She carefully steps out of them, and then I shove them into my pocket. With her dress pulled up, I get a good look at her, and she fidgets as she waits, clearly anticipating my mouth on her cunt.

Instead, I touch her, running my fingers through her folds and getting her warm and relaxed. And then I rear back my hand and slap her hard between the legs. A high-pitched gasp bursts through her lips and she stares at me with shock. Her chest heaves up and down with her heavy breathing.

So I do it again. And again. I turn her pussy red with my hand, each gasp and moan from my strikes getting more desperate sounding. She's swaying now, hanging from her wrists while her legs tremble.

She's had enough, so I finally ease to my knees at her feet and stare up at her, loving the way goose bumps ripple along her breasts and across her bare skin. With my hands on her thighs, I steady her, and she stares down at me with excitement and need.

"Don't worry. I'll kiss it better," I say with a smile. Then I turn my attention to her soaking cunt in front of me. Easing some of the weight off her feet, I spread her thighs and take a look at just how perfect she is up close. After one more glance up at her face, I lean in and run my tongue along the length of her folds, and she immediately responds with a long, soft moan of pleasure.

"Fuck, I love the way you taste," I mumble. So I dig my face between her legs and lap at her pussy like a man dying of thirst, and I don't come up for air even once.

I am not the man I was before. Now that I allow myself to indulge in all of the dirty, sexy, beautiful things I never let myself do before, I feel free.

And starved.

With a growl, I lift Sage from the floor and wrap her thighs around my head on my shoulders. With her back against the wall, she rides my face closer and closer to her climax.

I get lost in savoring the taste and feel of her against my tongue. Sucking hard on her sensitive clit makes her legs buck and her spine arch. Within seconds, I have her squirming and panting for air. I'm going to make her come, and on the one hand, I can't wait, but on the other...I don't think I'm ready for this to be over.

Releasing the suction from her clit, I use my fingers to spread her wide again, and I feel the audience behind me now, desperate for a view of what's *mine*. So I put my mouth back where it was and watch as she gives them a show, looking more exquisite than I've ever seen. As I slide my finger inside her, I curl it in a *come here* motion while still sucking on the spot that makes her squirm.

She comes undone.

"Oh god, don't stop," she cries out. And I make it my life's purpose to make her come right here on my shoulders. I'm relentless, sucking and nibbling while thrusting so hard that she tries to practically climb out of my grasp.

"Adam!" she screams just before I feel her body seize up in my arms, so I know she's in the throes of her orgasm. I let her ride out the wave on my tongue, and it's the best thing I've ever experienced.

When I finally ease her off my shoulders, I feel like I've lost a sense of reality. In some ways, I have.

Something changed in me while I was touching her, tasting her, feeling her.

And I never want to go back.

# TWENTY-EIGHT

## SAGE

My wrists burn and my arms ache, but I can't feel anything other than his mouth between my legs. Who would have thought Mr. Church Boy himself had such a talented tongue? Not me, that's for fucking sure. I thought that first night was a fluke or a moment of passion, but tonight proved me wrong.

He's just that good.

When he finally pulls his mouth from the apex of my thighs, I'm hanging in a cold sweat and my heart is still hammering in my chest. Our eyes meet as he wipes his mouth with the back of his hand, and suddenly I'm melting all over again. Then he fixes my dress, covering my naked breasts. Carefully, he unbinds my hands and rubs at my wrists when he notices the red marks left behind.

As he sets me on my feet and stares down at me, I feel as if we're seeing each other for the first time. His Adam's apple bobs as he swallows, brushing my sweat-soaked hair out of my face.

And I want to kiss him. I want to worship those exquisitely talented lips. I want to get lost in a connection so intimate that none of these people standing around us exist. There is only me and Adam. *My* Adam.

Pressing upward, I reach for his mouth, mere inches away when we're bombarded.

"Let me buy you two a drink," an older voice says in a gravelly mumble.

"My girlfriend and I would love to take you both to a room," a female voice interjects.

"You two are so hot," another voice joins in.

Soon, it's a cacophony of sexual invitations, voices blended together as bodies crowd us. Adam pulls me closer as I sense his patience growing thin. His jaw clenches as he pushes me through the crowd toward the door.

It's chaos until we finally reach the door, sucking in fresh air when we get to the parking lot, running hand in hand until he's practically shoving me into his car. As he slams the door with me safely tucked inside, the cool leather against my ass reminds me that I'm not wearing any underwear. The panties I came here with are now in Adam's pocket, and I don't know if I should remind him of that or if I should let him keep them. If he even wants them.

What even are we now? I still don't know if I mean anything to Adam Goode, which is frustrating because, with every passing moment, he means more and more to me. This broken, splintered man is slowly coming back to life right before my eyes.

Sure, he just tongue-fucked me to oblivion in front of a crowd, and he seemed to really enjoy it, but that was just playing the part. It doesn't mean he cares about *me*.

All of this runs through my head in the time it takes for him to shut my door and walk around the car to the other side and climb into his own seat. By the time he slams his own door and glances my way with a strangely warm expression, I'm feeling hopeless and confused. And he can sense it.

"I should get you home," he says, almost making it sound like a question.

Awkward silence fills the car, and I can't stand it, so I turn toward him and address it head-on.

"Should we talk?"

His brow furrows. "About?"

"About what just happened back there. That wasn't pretending, Adam."

There's a look of contemplation on his face for a split second before he responds, "It's all part of the plan, isn't it?"

"It was supposed to be fake. That wasn't fake. And what happened at your parents' house wasn't fake either. And in your dad's office—"

"Okay," he snaps, and I close my lips, letting a wave of heat flush my cheeks. Inside, I'm begging Adam to do anything but shut me out. Don't leave me hanging here with my heart on my sleeve just so he can avoid facing reality. Don't make me look and feel like a fool.

I understand this is a big change for him. I understand that he's behaving in a way he never would have before, but it still feels like he has one foot in his past life and one foot in this life. I just wish he'd step all the way in—for me.

When it's clear he's not going to say anything other than *okay*, I turn forward and stare out the windshield, silently fuming. "Never mind. Just take me home."

I approached the subject too fast. Why did I have to push him so hard?

"What do you want me to say?" he argues. "We got carried away, Sage. You want me to confess something personal and profound to you just because I got off a couple times? Everything is *fake*, okay? The relationship. The sex. The way I treat you in those videos. I'm not really *like this*. It's all *fake*."

"Fuck you," I mutter as I yank on the car door and move to climb out.

"Where are you going?" He grabs my arm to keep me in my seat.

"I'll get a ride home, Adam, but I'm not going to sit in this fucking car with you while you make me feel like an idiot."

"What did I say that made you feel like an idiot?" He jerks me backward until I'm facing him, and I suddenly feel so angry with him I want to hit him. He and Brett and all the other assholes who stomped all over my feelings and used ignorance as an excuse.

"You can keep lying to yourself, Adam, but I'm not going to let you lie to me," I yell. "Rule number five. Keep it fake, right? But what did you say that night, just before you put your hand up my skirt? You told me to tell you it was *real*. And what happened this morning, the way you love to degrade me? You can pretend all you want, but *that* is not fake. But you're so hung up on believing a good man can't like that you put all the shame on me. So, what is it, Adam? If we're truly breaking the rules, why can't we at least talk about it?"

He looks away and my anger only grows more intense, so I grab his face and turn him toward me. "I'm trying to help you, Adam. I *see* you."

For a moment, his expression softens, and so does mine. For a split second, I have *my* Adam back. The one who doesn't care what anyone thinks, who sees me for me, and who gives me the attention I so desperately crave. Who doesn't mind being a little bad to be good.

But as quickly as it came, it's gone. His expression deadens as he mumbles, "It was the heat of the moment. It was all for show, Sage."

Everything inside me turns to ice. None of it was real. This whole time I've been growing these feelings for a man who's incapable of changing or feeling anything. He can't stand to be vulnerable for a single moment.

I yank my arm out of his grasp and fight back the tears that threaten to come.

"You're such an asshole," I mutter as I climb out of the car.

"Why am I an asshole?" he argues as he gets out and shouts over the hood. "Because I followed the rules?"

"That's all you ever do, Adam," I yell, throwing my arms out. "You follow the rules, so you don't have to feel anything. When was the last time you ever stuck your neck out for anyone, Adam?

You've been following the rules your entire life and look at where it's gotten you. No one truly knows you, so no one truly loves you."

Those words come flying out of my mouth, and I watch as they hit him like an assault. If I had pulled out a gun and shot him in the chest, it would have hurt less. Instantly, I regret it and wish I could unsay what I just said.

His mouth falls into a straight line and I know I've struck too hard. Shame and guilt crawl up my throat, nearly making me sick. I'm about to apologize when I notice Adam's gaze scan to something over my shoulder.

The sound of shoes jogging against pavement steals my attention, and when I turn to see Brett running toward me, my emotions get all jumbled up inside. Anger, desire, guilt, fear, comfort—they run together, feeling all wrong, the way different colors blend to make an ugly brown sludge.

"What's going on?" Brett calls from behind me, and I turn back to see Adam's face, looking for something I can't quite put my finger on. He freezes in his spot, a grimace etched in his features.

"Nothing. We're fine," I reply, taking a step back toward the car.

And then Brett touches my lower back and long-forgotten feelings come floating to the surface. I know his touch. It's familiar and comforting and safe.

"Why the fuck are you yelling at her?" Brett asks, putting a hand out toward Adam, treating him like a threat.

"He's not—"

"I don't know," Adam replies, looking at me. "All I know is my life was fine until one morning when I walked into that fucking diner. Now..."

Tears sting my eyes as I glare at him. "Now what?"

"Now I don't know anymore. I don't know who I am. I don't know what I want."

As I blink, a tear slips across my cheek. This feels as close as

I'm going to get to a confession from Adam. He'll never be able to truly express himself, and I'm clearly wasting my time if I expect him to ever admit anything more.

"Let me take you home," Brett says, running a hand along my other arm. A moment ago, I wouldn't have dreamed of ending this night with my ex, but that's how easily a beautiful moment with Adam turned to shit. What on earth was I expecting?

"Fine," I mutter, turning away from Adam.

"Sage," he calls after me, but I don't turn back.

It's clear I mean nothing to Adam Goode. So I'll try to pretend he means nothing to me.

# TWENTY-NINE

## SAGE

Old habits die hard. I can't exactly explain why I'm letting Brett hold me, allowing him to run his hands down my back and press his lips to my cheek, but I'm letting him anyway. I'm convincing myself that it feels nice. That I need this. That this is where I'm meant to be.

Maybe I'm no better than Adam, unable to let go of the past, trudging through bad choices over and over again, doomed to relive the same misery again and again, but we just never learn and refuse to change.

Like how I pressured him to open up to me, so desperate for his love and attention, that's what I've been doing since I was a kid. Giving people the chance to love me and blaming them when they don't. Just setting myself up for disappointment again and again.

After Adam got in his car and drove away, I came back inside the club with Brett. We went to the office, where we always used to hang out. I'm sitting on the desk with him between my legs like we used to.

But I can't stop thinking about Adam. How I put all of my feelings on the line for him and he threw them away. How I've started growing attached to a man who will never allow himself to feel the same for me.

I feel like the world's biggest fool.

I'm lost in my own head as Brett pulls my face toward his and stares into my eyes just before leaning in to kiss me. With a flinch, I pull away.

"What are you doing?"

"You're still my girl, Sage. You always were."

I pull farther away, pushing a hand to his chest to get some distance. "I need some space right now."

"Space from me?" he asks, looking wounded.

My brows pinch together in confusion. "We broke up, Brett. I...started seeing someone else. Why aren't you mad? Didn't you see what we just did?"

He lets out two heavy breaths with his eyes on my face before he responds. "Of course I did. It was for me, wasn't it?"

A chill runs down my spine.

*It wasn't for you.*

"Sure...I guess. But why aren't you mad?"

"Because I knew you'd come back to me. I knew he couldn't keep you." His eyes are dark and hooded as he stares at me with a menacing expression. Brett is so handsome but loses all of his good looks with his cocky and detached attitude. For years, I've been trying to burrow myself in his heart the same way I did with Adam and look where that got me.

"But...I'm still with him. We just had a little fight."

"You're in here now, aren't you?"

A sob lodges itself in my throat. "I'm in here now because I got in a fight with him. Because I need emotional support. Is this some kind of competition to you?"

I try to hop off the desk when he presses against me to hold me in place. What have I done? I've cornered myself in a room with a man who has every right to be furious with me. Brett would never really hurt me, but he would also never pass up the opportunity to make me hurt if he thought I deserved it.

He grabs the back of my neck and I let out a yelp from fear and a hint of pain. Then he crashes his mouth against mine, and I let him kiss me because it's all I know. Not because I want to but because I *have* to. This relationship is all I know.

As he pulls away, his dark eyes focus on mine. "For over a month now, I've had to endure those videos, Sage. Seeing you two together. Seeing him fucking you like that. It killed me."

"Brett..." I plead as I lean away from his grip.

"But you're back, Sage. You're back with me, and I just need to hear you say you're mine."

"Brett..." I repeat, my voice growing tense at the tightening of his hand.

"Guys like Adam Goode get everything. The perfect family. The perfect home. Money, fame, even the perfect women. I can't *stand* the thought of you with him. So please, baby..." His forehead is against mine and I can feel him trembling, as if he's teetering on the edge, ready to explode without warning.

When he lets go of my neck, I feel a moment of relief.

Then I'm blindsided. His palm comes crashing against the side of my face, nearly knocking me off the desk. I'm too stunned to even gasp or cry or react. I just hold my hand to my cheek and stare at him in shock.

"I thought you liked it rough. I saw the video where he hit you."

"That was *consensual!*" I cry out as my chest shudders with a sob.

Terror and frustration mingle through my mind as panic sets in. Is this a joke to him? Brett would never truly hurt me, but does he really think I want it like *this*? Because of how he's seen me in those videos?

When his hand holds my hair at the scalp, something in me

snaps. I swing my hand hard until it lands with a resounding smack against his face, and he freezes, staring at me with the same shock I wore a moment ago. As if I'm somehow the offender.

For a moment, I'm afraid I've only angered him more and we're about to have an all-out brawl, one I will surely lose on account of size and strength alone, but fuck it. If I die fighting, I die fighting.

To my relief, he doesn't hit me back. Instead, he steps away.

"So that pretty boy can slap you around, but I can't?"

"It's not like that, and you know it."

He's staring at me with hurt and anger written in the hard, contoured shape of his eyes and nose. "No, I don't think I do know, Sage. The truth is, I don't understand anything anymore. You were *my* girl. Then you just left, and a week later, you're making waves with that guy? The guy who's gotten everything handed to him. Everything we had to work for, fight for, claw our way out of poverty for, he never had to do shit for. You let *that* guy have his way with you."

Tears stream from my eyes like a faucet. I'm a sobbing mess as I let it all out. "You never cared about me, and you still don't. How could you watch those videos and never call? Never text? Because I'm nothing to you, and I know that now."

He doesn't say a word as I wipe at the tears sliding over my aching cheek.

"You think Adam Goode only gets perfect women?" I say through my chest-racking sobs. "Well, for a moment, he had *me*, and I'm perfect too, but neither of you seems to think that. You turned your back on me, Brett. Then he turned his back on me. You can both go to hell."

When I climb off the desk, he reaches for me, but I slap his hand away. "And for the record, I don't let him slap me around for his pleasure. I do it for *mine*. Because it's *consensual*. And I shouldn't have to explain that to you."

I keep my head down as I stumble out of the club, and the tears won't stop. Every time I think I get my emotions under control, one single thought starts the onslaught again. Standing in front of the club, I keep to myself as I order my ride.

But the minute I get inside the older woman's blue station wagon, I remember that feeling I had earlier tonight with Adam. The softness in his eyes and how I was so sure there was a spark there when there wasn't. Only to find out he is still too broken to see me.

Then we turn onto my street, and I remember that night he came to the book club, and I feel murdered by his betrayal again. He called me *his*. He looked into my eyes and asked me to trust him. Touched me and took pleasure from my body like it was his to take, and I'm fuming with anger.

As she comes to a stop in front of my building, I feel almost too weak to even get out of the car.

"Thank you," I reply with a sniffle as I tear open the door and stumble into the Laundromat. I hide my face from Gladys as I scurry toward my door.

Taking each step in a desperate race to get into my apartment, my safe space, my *home*, I nearly miss the huddled mass sitting at the top of the stairs.

I let out a scream as I lock eyes with him.

"Sage? Jesus Christ." Adam's frantic voice fills my ears. I barely have a second to utter a word before he pulls me into his arms. And the tears return.

"What are you doing here?" I whisper.

"I didn't know where else to go." His voice is raspy and tired sounding. It's full of remorse.

As he pulls away from our hug, he holds my face in his hands and his brows fold inward at the sight of my tears. "What happened? Did he hurt you?"

First, I shake my head. Then, with a sob, I nod.

He did hurt me. And not just the slap across the face. The betrayal hurt. The name-calling. The attacking tone. Everything hurt.

For years, it all hurt so much and I swallowed that hurt like medicine. Taking every ounce of that pain in stride like I was supposed to because taking the pain in silence was the only way to *be good.*

Any form of defense was an offense.

Adam's soft touch brushes my hair out of my face and I wipe at my face with the back of my hand, but he grabs my wrist to stop me.

"Don't wipe them away. Just cry. I've got you."

With another sob, the tears continue to pour out. I barely register what's happening as he unlocks the door and pulls me inside. We don't stop at the kitchen or the living room. He takes me directly to the bathroom.

There he holds me against his chest. And I can sense how paralyzed he is with indecision. He has no clue what to do, but he also has no idea that *this* is all I need.

When my tears have stopped and my face feels raw and swollen, he gently pulls me away from his chest. Instead of speaking, he moves toward the large claw-foot tub and turns on the faucet, pouring lavender-scented bubbles under the stream of water and checking the temperature.

Then he delicately pulls me toward the tub and sits on the edge as he carefully pulls my dress over my head. And since my panties are still in his pocket, I'm fully naked before him.

His hands are on my hips, and his eyes are on my face. The quiet moment stretches wordlessly before he leads me to the water, holding my hand as I climb in, sinking quickly under the bubbles like it's my safe haven.

He disappears for a moment, coming back with a washcloth. Instead of handing it to me, he dips it under the suds and uses it to gently wipe the tearstains from my cheeks. Then he squeezes the water over my head, dousing my hair with it.

And I just lie there, letting him dote on me, feeling entirely at peace because I can't remember the last time anyone ever took care of me. And I might still be angry at him, but it's impossible to tear myself away from his attention.

When his hand sinks under the surface, gently cleaning every inch of me, I let my eyes close. He runs the washcloth over my chest and down my belly, over my hips and across the length of each leg. Even giving his attention to each of my toes on both feet.

As his hand travels up the inside of my leg, my eyes open. But just as I expect him to touch me, he pulls his hand away. He wrings out the washcloth and drapes it over the side of the tub. Then he drops into a sitting position and rests his back against the wall, staring up at the ceiling.

After a moment, he finally speaks.

"You were right. I fucking hate that you were right."

"About what?" I whisper.

"I've followed the rules my entire life. I've always said what I'm supposed to say. I behaved the way I was supposed to behave. And now...I don't know what the fuck to say half the time. I don't even know who I am."

"Adam, that's not—" I whisper.

"I didn't stick my neck out for my brother. When my father berated him, belittled him, humiliated him, I said nothing. Isaac was seventeen when he came out." His voice trembles as he speaks. "He was just a kid, and I was a man. Why didn't I defend him? I could have helped him. I *should* have protected him, but I was too focused on being *the good son.*

"Then, the day before his eighteenth birthday, he just...disappeared. It broke my mother's heart, and I did nothing."

These tears sting because these are the ones I don't want to cry. I don't like hearing Adam's pain. I hate knowing that he's beating himself up for something that is really his father's fault.

"I'm sorry..."

"I'm afraid I can't give you what you deserve, Sage."

I don't respond as I swallow down what feels like knives in my throat. But just the acknowledgment that Adam thinks about my needs, that we could be an us, stops me from speaking.

He turns toward me with bloodshot eyes.

"It was real, and you deserve a man who can admit that."

"You just did," I reply with a teary smile.

I can tell by the look in his eye that it's not enough for him. That he still doesn't feel worthy.

# THIRTY

## ADAM

The rain drums quietly against the window as I stare at the moon through the drizzle. I can't sleep. Sage is breathing quietly next to me, cuddled under a heavy blanket, looking peaceful, and all I can think about is every cruel and depraved thing I've done to her.

I'm no better than him. And by him, I'm not even sure if I mean Brett or Truett, but it doesn't matter. Because the three of us are the same.

My entire life, I considered myself a *good* man, and now I don't even know what that means. I followed all the rules. I read the gospel. I lived the life my father and God set out for me to live and everyone I truly cared about ended up hurt. My mother. My brother. And her.

If I ruin my father's life and go to Brett's apartment now to beat the ever-loving shit out of him, does that make me the hero?

I won't. And not because I don't want to, because I really, really do. But I won't because the honor and integrity that's ingrained in my bones won't let me. The same honor and integrity that has stopped me from every single thing I've wanted to do.

Perhaps we can never truly be good and protect the ones we love at the same time. Maybe it takes a bad man to truly keep them safe and happy.

I think about that night Truett hit my brother. The night he laid his hands on a scared seventeen-year-old boy and the way I watched from the hallway. I flinched. I tried to move, but I was a gust of wind against a mountain.

And I thought I was the righteous one.

Everything replays in my head, not just the last night with Isaac but the very minute I met Sage. I actually believed she was different than me as if I was sewn from a different cloth. And she was somehow...less deserving. Who the fuck did I think I was?

She deserves the fucking sun. The moon. The stars.

And the thought actually makes me laugh. Out of every righteous, God-fearing person I know, this girl might be the best one I've ever met.

I left her with him. I got in my car and I drove away while she cried in the arms of her abuser. Because I did the *right fucking thing*. She got hurt because of me, and it could have been so much worse.

I'm no fucking hero.

And I never truly was. So why have I been acting like one?

Before I know what I'm doing, I'm out of bed, slipping on my jeans. Anger boils under the surface, growing hotter and hotter with every step I take, and it feels like I'm breathing life into a part of myself that I've been suffocating.

I don't even fully know what I'm doing. I just let my instincts carry me without thinking about it too much.

Once I'm fully dressed, I glance back at Sage sleeping in her bed. I don't stop to question if I'm doing the appropriate thing. I've done that enough in my life. This is the wrong fucking thing, and it's the first thing that's ever felt right.

Without another word, I slip out of her apartment.

The roads are quiet as I drive. The rain has slowed to a drizzle, painting the dark asphalt in reflecting light. My fists are tight around the steering wheel, and I let the buzzing heat of anger inside me sizzle and grow until it feels like I'm on fire.

I don't mentally acknowledge where I'm going, but deep down, I know.

When I reach the club, I park in the same exact spot I was in earlier. And I wait.

There are a handful of cars still parked in the lot, and I have a good view of the back of the club from here. I know a few things about Brett that I can count on for certain. He's cocky, and he's stupid. This means I know he's going to walk out of here without security at some point, and I've got nothing but time.

While I wait, I don't bother talking myself down or rethinking this situation. I let the simmer turn into a full boil. And I don't have to wait as long as I thought I would. It's nearly five in the morning when I spot him walking across the back of the lot behind the club with a young woman under his arm.

I jump out of my car and cross the asphalt in a fast-paced walk. He hears my footsteps first, turning toward me just as I find myself within punching distance.

"Hey, asshole," I mutter before throwing a right hook that lands with a satisfying crunch against his nose.

The girl screams and runs away as Brett falls to the ground, holding his face as blood pours from his nostrils.

"What the fuck?" he bellows, but before he can try to get back to his feet, I grab him by the collar and jerk him upward to land another punch against his cheek.

"You think you're fucking tough?" I grit out with a sneer as I hit him again. "Did you think you could hurt her? She came home in fucking tears, you piece of shit."

I punch him again, and this time, he goes limp. My fist aches but not enough. I want to tear it open, crack my knuckles, and break the bones in my hand on his face.

Am I fighting fair? No, but I don't care. I'm done with fair.

I just keep thinking about how scared she was. I think about her tears and her anger, and it makes every assault of my fist against his face feel *so fucking good.*

"Wake up, Brett," I bark before shaking him again. His eye is already swelling shut, but as he slowly peels it open, I hit him again and again and again.

Everything starts to blur around me. Somewhere there's a girl screaming and sirens in the distance. I can't hold my hand in a fist anymore, so I drop his limp body on the pavement.

When I stand up, a sick and twisted feeling of satisfaction washes over me. As I stare down at him, hearing his moans and watching him struggle to move, I feel as if I've made a wrong thing right. Which is fucking juvenile, I know that, but I'm not doing this to be mature.

I'm still breathless, with a cold sweat running down my spine, when the night turns into a flash of red and blue around me.

When the police shout at me to put my hands in the air, I do it—with a smile.

# THIRTY-ONE

ADAM

"**G**oode. Adam Goode," a deep, unfamiliar voice calls. When I peel my eyes open, my head pounds with the assaulting bright light. And when my eyes finally adjust, I recognize my brother, Caleb, standing next to the officer who processed me sometime this morning after I was hauled in.

Caleb is wearing an expression that's somewhere between smug and amused. His hands are in his pockets and he's staring down his nose at me as I peel myself off the bench and move to stand. My broken hand is wrapped in medical gauze, and I remember the medic giving me strict instructions to have it looked at once I was released. But I probably won't. I hope it leaves my hand fucked up and scarred forever. The pain feels good, like it's the first thing I've ever felt in my entire life.

After I sign the papers clumsily with my left hand, I walk out of the station in silence with my brother at my side. He doesn't say a word as we climb into his Volvo SUV, and I don't bother complaining about my head or my hand. I just give him the address of the Laundromat and ask him to take me there instead of my apartment. With a quizzical expression, he does.

Maybe she'll fix me up like she did before. And it makes me wonder if she'll be mad or proud.

"I think I like this new version of you," Caleb finally says as we pull up to a stoplight. "And I feel weird saying that, but causing a little trouble might actually be good for you."

"Why am I the one causing trouble?" I ask, turning toward him.

"That's a good question," he replies with a laugh.

"No, Caleb. I mean...why have we been following that asshole our entire lives? Letting him treat us all like shit. Why am I the *only* one causing trouble?"

"So this is about Dad."

"Isn't it always?" I reply with a grimace.

"What did he do this time?"

"I found out he owns a sex club," I mutter, staring out the window. The car nearly comes to a complete stop as Caleb stares at me in shock.

"What the fuck?"

"I found him there. Face buried between some woman's legs." As I turn to look at my brother, I'm actually sort of pleased to see the horror on his face. At least someone else can feel it too.

"He'll ruin us all," he says. "He's really willing to risk everything he's built for what? Sex?"

I don't reply. Suddenly I'm feeling sick, like I have a hangover from the events of last night. And from this whole conversation.

"Is that what this is all about?" he asks as he pulls up to Sage's apartment.

"Sort of," I reply because I just don't know anymore. It started out about him. Then it became about me. And now... it's about her. And I don't care that my car is still parked at the club or that my broken hand is throbbing. I just want to see her.

"Jesus, Adam. This is insane. Why didn't you tell me sooner?"

"I don't know," I reply, turning toward him. "Because he's in my head, I guess. I don't know if he'll ever get out."

"What about her?" he asks, and I know he's talking about Sage. "Is that real, or is that just..."

"It's real." With that, I pull open the passenger door and stumble out. Every step makes my head pound. Before closing the door, I look back at Caleb, seeing the way this news is hitting him. The same way it hit me. And I almost feel bad for him. He never put as much faith in our father as I did, but it's still hard to accept that the world doesn't work the way you think it does.

"Thanks for picking me up," I say with a grimace, and after he nods in return, I shut the door and cross the street toward her apartment. The entire way up the stairs, I'm silently praying she's not mad at me. Of course if she is, I can't blame her. I took off in the middle of the night.

I'd be no better than Brett if I kept her after what I've done. After the way I treated her. In fact, no man would ever truly deserve her, so what the fuck gives me the right to even try?

As soon as I rap my left hand against the door, it opens, and I'm so fucking relieved I can hardly move. She lets out an audible gasp when she sees me.

"Oh my god, Adam," she shrieks with fear and relief. Then her arms are around my neck, my face pressed to the crook of hers, and I breathe her in like this is somehow the most pivotal moment of my life. The epicenter of my entire existence in this very moment as I come back to her a changed man. I've shed the lies and deceptions. It took more than the last few hours, but giving in to that darkness, feeling the cuffs around my wrists and the flash of the mug shot camera, I changed.

I fed the beast last night, and now it feels as if that beast is me.

"I was so worried about you," she whispers into my neck. "Why did you do that?"

I pull away from her embrace and stare down at her as she pulls me into the apartment, closing the door behind us. "I have to tell you what I did," I mumble, but she's already shaking her head.

"I know exactly what you did, Adam. You don't think I

couldn't figure it out? That I would just sit here and wait for you to come back?"

My brow arches in confusion as I stare down at her. "How did you..."

"Does it really matter? How about you tell me *why* you would do that?"

Taking a step toward her, I reach for her with my good hand and she comes to me, letting me put my fingers on her arm and on her lower back. "Because...I wanted to." It's the only response that makes sense. Simple and to the point.

"You wanted to beat the shit out of my ex? Because he made me cry?"

"Yes," I reply intently.

"You're better than this, Adam. You put Brett in the hospital. He might lose the sight in his eye."

"Good," I say through clenched teeth. My hand leaves her skin as I take a step back. "Sage, you should know I'm not *better than this*. I'm not the good guy you thought. I'm not a gentleman or a hero. What I did last night felt fucking good, and I realize I'm no better than your ex for kicking the shit out of him, but I'd gladly beat the piss out of anyone who hurts you. I may not be good at communicating or admitting my feelings, but I'll admit that. You're the first thing in my life that I'm willing to protect, and I don't care who the fuck I have to hurt to do it."

She nearly cuts my words off as she leaps into my arms, pulling my face down to hers and latching those silky soft lips against mine. My hand screams in pain, but I don't care as I wrap my hands around her thighs and lift her off the floor. Eagerly, she tightens them around me, and I let out a growl.

Carrying her to the wall, I grind myself against her with a long, deep moan. Pulling away from her kiss, I press my forehead to hers as I whisper, "Being between your legs is like heaven to me, Peaches."

"Then fuck me, Adam. For real this time."

I attack her lips again with my own, kissing her harshly as I carry her to the bedroom. I've never felt so close to another person in my life. Her kiss is fervent and hungry as she digs her hands in my hair and pulls me so close I'm practically breathing her in.

As I drop her on the bed, I let out a wince of pain and realize I can't hold myself up with my broken hand. She lets out a laugh as she cradles it in her hands and kisses the exposed skin of my bloody fingers.

"Why don't you just relax and let me take care of you," she says with a smile, and I find myself growling with pleasure again. As I flip onto my back, she straddles my thighs and works on the button of my jeans. I quickly slip off my shirt and lift my hips to allow her to shift my pants down, pulling my boxer briefs with them.

My cock is already hard and dripping for her when she takes me in her hand, biting her lip as she strokes the stiff length.

"You have no idea how long I've wanted to do this," she whispers before leaning over me and placing her lips softly at the head. I'm nearly trembling with anticipation.

I want to reply and tell her she has no idea how long I've wanted her to do this, but as she parts her lips and takes my cock into her mouth, I cannot form words. Only sounds. Guttural, animalistic, euphoric sounds.

There's not a single camera rolling or phone pointed in our direction. This isn't for an audience or for revenge. This is for us. The way it should be.

She takes her time wetting my shaft, licking her way up and down until I'm coated. Then she locks her gaze on mine as she lets my dick slide across her tongue all the way to the back of her throat.

"Oh fuck," I groan as she chokes herself and comes back up for air, heaving a little from the gag reflex. "Do that again, Peaches."

She bobs her mouth up and down on my cock and it feels so fucking good I forget to breathe. Sage always seems to have this way of making me lose control. She makes me feel safe enough to lose control. So when I find myself wanting to pin her to the mattress and fuck her throat until I come, I know she'd love it as much as I would.

But that's not what I do—not this time.

Instead, I yank her mouth off my dick and pull her lips to mine for a kiss. Without putting weight on my bad hand, I scoot myself backward until I'm sitting against the headboard. Then I grab her face in my hand and pull her close.

"Put that pretty pussy on my cock, Peaches. Before I lose my fucking mind."

On the last word, I swat a palm against her ass. She lets out a yelp and tears off her shirt before pulling her shorts and panties off until she's naked. My mouth waters at the sight as she scurries onto my lap. She's straddling me chest to chest as our lips fuse again. Then she eagerly lowers herself onto my cock. Just an inch inside, I feel her tense. So I take hold of her hips and slowly work her down, an inch at a time.

And the exact moment I have her fully sheathing my cock, she settles her weight on my lap and we let out a long groan in harmony. I'm finally inside her, and I almost don't want her to move because this feeling right now is greater than God himself.

My arms wind around her waist and hers around my neck. And we just sit here like that for a moment, breathing the same air, hearts moving to the same beat.

When she tilts her hips, grinding herself, the hunger inside me grows. I lift her up and let gravity take her back down. Then we quickly find a cadence together, her body bouncing on my lap. With one hand latched on to my neck, she leans back and finds the spot that feels best to her and I let her use me, watching in awe as her tits rock with the motion of her body.

I could easily commit every sound, sight, and sensation to memory to keep this moment in the forefront of my mind forever. She is utterly perfect.

Her pounding on my lap grows more and more intense, and I can feel by the seizing of her muscles that she's getting close. And

I desperately need to make her come because I'm not going to last much longer myself. Reaching down between us, I strum my thumb on her clit, and she lets out a high-pitched cry as I add pressure.

"Scream for me, Peaches."

"Don't stop," she says breathlessly, her bounces picking up speed. "I'm almost...there."

Even as her muscles tighten and her breathing pauses, her hips keep grinding through her orgasm until she's shuddering and trembling on my lap.

When I know her climax has peaked, I let myself lose control. Flipping her onto her back, I grab the headboard with my good hand and I drive my hips into her so hard she has to brace herself against the headboard to keep me from crushing her.

I feel the sweat dripping down my neck as I fuck her into the mattress, watching the place where I disappear inside her. With each bruising thrust, I get closer and closer to flying over the edge. When her hands grab the sides of my body, holding on to me as if we're swept up in a violent storm, I let out a deafening yell as I come. My entire body is racked with tremors through my release.

When I finally come down, I open my eyes to find Sage wrapped around me with her face buried in my chest. I let go of the headboard and fall on top of her, pulling her into my arms.

She finally looks up and finds my lips with her own. Then I hold her like that, doing nothing but kissing her and feeling every inch of her body I can get my hands on.

There are no more words in my head, only emotions.

Some of them too frightening to name.

# THIRTY-TWO

## SAGE

Adam winces, sucking in through his teeth as I dab at his knuckles with the alcohol again. The skin is broken on every one of his knuckles, but they're so swollen and red it's hard to tell what's bone, cartilage, and skin.

"How many times did you hit him?" I ask to distract him from the pain as I rewrap it with clean gauze.

"I lost count."

I bite my bottom lip to keep from smiling. We're sitting in my bed, still naked from the amazing sex we had less than an hour ago. I caught his hand trembling and I knew he needed it looked at again.

"All because he hurt me?"

He turns his head and looks into my eyes. "Yes," he replies confidently. I nearly lose my breath for a moment.

"Are you going to break the faces of everyone who hurts me?"

"Yes."

After his hand is clean and bound, I hold his aching fist against my chest. Then I lean forward and press my lips to his. It feels good to kiss him, for real.

"Want some aspirin?" I ask.

"Yes, please."

"Be right back," I reply as I let go of his hand and climb off his lap. When I open the medicine cabinet in the bathroom, I see the extra-strength pain reliever. After dropping three into my palm, I go to the kitchen to get him a glass of water. Then I sit next to him on the bed, watching as he takes them.

Staring at him for a moment, I think about how much he's changed since I met him. He was the church boy do-gooder. Mr. Perfect. But he was also lost and confused. He didn't even know who he was. And now...

Adam seems free. He looks...like himself. The version he was always meant to be.

There are still so many things that separate us. Things we might never overcome. Not entirely.

And these changes won't last forever. It would be stupid of me to assume they would. Nothing ever does.

After the water is gone from his glass, I crawl into his arms, and we lie together on the bed, staring at the plaster on the ceiling.

"Can I ask you a question?" I whisper.

"Of course," he replies, his lips against my head.

"Do you believe in God?"

He tenses, pulling away to look down at me with a guarded but scrutinizing expression. Almost as if he's afraid to answer. Finally, he softly whispers, "Yes." Then he stares at me a moment longer and I wonder if he thinks I'm going to get up and leave based on that response.

"I'm not like my father if that's what you're implying."

Hearing the coarse tension in his voice worries me, so I turn onto my stomach and stare at him. "I know you're not like him. I was just curious. How much of that was really you and how much of it is you now?"

His brow furrows, but I can tell he knows exactly what I'm asking. As he rests his head on the pillow, his eyes locked with mine, I place my head on his arm and stare into his eyes.

"I don't know," he whispers. "But I still believe in something bigger than myself. I was never really like Truett, but I used to believe that if I could stand where he stood, I'd be closer to God somehow. That I'd be worthy."

I touch his face, running my fingers through the short-cropped beard. "You are worthy."

"I was never good enough for my father. But I believed that if I was a holy, righteous man, I'd be good enough for God. Now..."

"Now what?" I lean forward, pressing my lips to his for a brief moment. His pain is written on his face, and although I know this is part of his transformation, the change he so badly needs to endure to be happy with himself, it's hard to watch. Like I'm growing to care for him more than I'm ready to.

"Now I just want to be good enough for you."

It feels like all the air in the room has been sucked out, and I stare into his eyes as tears spring up into mine. "Do you really?" I whisper.

He nods.

"Then let's stay here. Let's not go to their galas or dinners. Let's not even go to the club. Fuck the whole plan, Adam." As I blink, my throat stings with emotion. "Fuck them."

"Okay," he says, and a smile cracks across my cheeks as I take his face in my hands and kiss him hard.

"You're good enough. You're more than good enough," I mumble against his lips.

I don't even know what time it is when I finally emerge from my apartment. After the talk this morning, Adam and I showered together, had sex again, and then he drifted off to sleep. Since I couldn't sleep myself, I climbed out of bed and cleaned my apartment for a while, scrolling the app for updates on our videos.

I said we were done faking it, but I hope this doesn't mean

we're done posting videos. There's a part of me that really loves that part, and now that we get to do it for real, it should be even better.

The sound of voices coming from the front of the Laundromat makes me pause as I close the stairwell door behind me. It's a man's voice, and he's speaking loudly. For a moment, I pause.

Then I hear Gladys and Mary break out in laughter and my shoulders melt away from my ears. It takes me a moment before I recognize Dan, one of the regulars, telling an animated story like he always does. Walking through the rows of washers toward the front, I smile as I reach the crowd gathered there.

At the front of Gladys's Laundromat is an eight-foot white folding table covered in food. Around the table are mostly regulars and a few newcomers, quickly devouring the meals in front of them.

For many of them, this might be the first warm one they've had in months.

"Hey," Gladys calls when she sees me coming. "Come get some enchiladas. They're delicious."

"Sure," I say with a sleepy smile as Mary hands me a plate. Waving to the guys and one girl sitting around the table, I lean against the counter and take a bite of Mary's famous chicken enchiladas. When one of the guys gets up to offer me his seat, I shake my head and insist he take it.

While I eat, they continue their conversation, and I feel Gladys's eyes on me.

"You okay?" she asks, turning her back to the conversation.

"It's been a long weekend," I reply with honesty.

"Adam's treating you right, I hope."

As I take a bite, I nod at her with a smile.

"He showed up here last night looking like a mess. I tried to tell him you weren't home, but he just sat in the stairwell for over an hour and waited."

"Yeah...I know."

For a moment, she just watches me, and I wait for the nugget of wisdom I know is coming.

"He seems like a good guy," she says.

To which I immediately reply, "He is."

"But..."

I glance up at her, not quite understanding why there has to be a but. When she doesn't say anything, I realize there's a big but I've been harboring. Aside from everything Adam has been going through and this whole fake dating scheme, there is still a lot that's keeping me from saying, *Yes, this is the one.*

I set my plate down and turn toward her. "He and I are so different, Gladys. We come from different worlds. And I know. I know...love conquers all—and I'm not saying that's what this is. But...eventually, the honeymoon period will fade and reality will set in and all the things that separate us will be insurmountable."

Pressing her lips together, she nods. Then to my surprise, she agrees.

"You're right. They will."

"Wow, that's encouraging," I joke.

"But it's true, Sage. Those differences will never go away and love will not make them any easier to ignore. I was married to Walter for forty-seven years. He was in the Navy for twenty of them and I burned my bra and went to Woodstock."

I laugh, biting my lip at the image of a young Gladys running around high on everything she could get her hands on.

"There were fundamental things we could *never* agree on. Things we were raised to believe that would never change. Good things and bad. He could be a stubborn, pigheaded asshole, and so could I. But I *loved* him more than anything in the world."

Tears moisten her eyes as she speaks, shutting them for a moment as she gets lost in a feeling.

"How?" I whisper. "How could you get past all of that?"

"Because," she replies, "we built a life together. A life we loved. And underneath all the bullshit and all the things out of our control, we agreed on the things that mattered. And no one had to change."

Reaching out, I touch her hand. "That was beautiful, Gladys. Thank you."

"Sage, baby. You deserve all the happiness in the world, whether it's with him, someone else, or all alone."

"I love you," I whisper as she pulls me in for a tight hug.

Just as we part, I look up and see Adam emerging from the stairwell. He's dressed in the same bloodied clothes he wore last night because he doesn't have anything else at my apartment.

As soon as he sees me, he smiles. Then he crosses the room with his disheveled hair and sleepy eyes.

"What's going on?" he asks, running his hand over his head.

"Mary made enchiladas," I answer as I scoop a bite from my plate and lift it to his mouth.

"Who are all these people?" he whispers before wrapping his lips around the fork. Immediately, he makes a satisfied face as he chews.

"Just...people in the community," I reply.

"We had extra food, so we're sharing," Gladys adds.

His eyes are on my face, and his expression is warm. Something like surprise and pride radiates off of him. "You do this a lot?"

I look at Gladys and we both shrug. "I don't know. Like... once a month or so."

His smile grows. Then, it slides away like melting wax, as if he's retreating into a memory.

Before he can start to beat himself up, I tug on his shirt. "You need to get out of these clothes so we can wash them."

Then I pull him toward the back of the long room. "Where are you taking me?" he asks mischievously.

"Getting you something to wear."

That wrinkle between his brows deepens, watching me as I open the large closet behind the industrial dryers. Inside, we have a folded array of clothes. "This is almost as bad as your bedroom," he mutters, and I laugh. "What is all this?"

"Oh, just clothes that got left behind over the years. We keep it all clean and folded here in case anyone needs something."

I pull out a dark-blue T-shirt and hold it up to his frame. When he glances down, he lets out a chuckle. "You must be joking."

"Hey, it fits," I reply, stifling my own laughter. Then, I pull his bloodstained polo over his head, watching so as not to hit his bad hand. Then I slide the blue T-shirt on, running my hand down the front and over the words *World's Best Grandpa*.

He holds his hands out, letting me admire his new look. I'm trying not to grin too much as I nod in appreciation.

"Okay, unbutton those now," I say, gesturing to his pants.

Laughing to himself, he shakes his head as he does. As he pulls them off, glancing around the corner to make sure no one else is coming to see him in his boxers, I riffle through the closet, looking for a pair of pants that will fit.

When I find a pair of green joggers in what I assume is his size, I pull them out and hold them up for him. He laughs again but doesn't argue as he snatches them from my hand and slides them on.

Once he's fully dressed in a stranger's clean, lost-and-found clothes, I wrap my hands around him and reach on my tiptoes for a kiss. He presses his mouth to mine and gently slides his tongue between my lips. Before I know it, it's getting heated, and I have to peel myself away to keep from doing something very illicit in the back of Gladys's Laundromat.

"Gladys should be able to get these stains out," I say, picking his dirty clothes up off the floor. Then we walk hand in hand out to the main area of the Laundromat, and I catch Gladys staring at him in surprise.

"I hardly recognize you," she says with a laugh.

"Thanks for...uh, letting me borrow these," he stammers.

"Anytime," she replies, patting him on the back.

"Hungry?" Mary asks, already busy making him a plate.

"Very," he replies before taking it from her with a smile. "Thank you so much."

Then he takes the newly empty seat at the table, smiling at the man sitting next to him. The two of them strike up their own private conversation, and I can't seem to tear my eyes away as something swells inside my chest at the sight.

Adam wanted to feel closer to God, and I can't help but wonder if he realizes how close he is now.

# THIRTY-THREE

## ADAM

Sage holds open the black garbage bag as I scoop the remaining paper plates and plastic cups in. I don't even know what time it is. After I woke up to find her gone, I came down to an unexpected gathering.

And honestly, I haven't been tempted to even check my phone in the last two hours, so I really have no idea what time it is.

I can't remember the last time I had so much fun. There's something so authentic about Gladys and Mary—right along with every person who joined them for dinner. I don't know their situations, but it is obvious that that's not what this is about. It isn't about feeding the homeless to feel better about themselves or to fulfill some promise to God.

It's about feeding them because they are *hungry*.

My mother would have loved this.

For the first time in a while, thinking about my mother doesn't incite an immediate stabbing pain of guilt in my chest. Instead, I just focus on the memories, mostly of a time before the megachurch and Dad's big career. Back when things were simple.

And then I look at Sage. Without any makeup, her cheeks take on a natural hint of pink to match her bubblegum hair. Even without those fake lashes and thick black lines around her eyes, they still pop with a deep ocean blue.

I have no idea what this thing is between us now. And I don't think she does either. But it's real. At least that much we know is true.

This morning she asked to stop the fake dating scheme, but even though I agreed, I'm not sure I'm ready to let it go. I can't let my father get away with his lies just like that.

But do I still need Sage to do it?

I don't want to think about that right now. So once we've cleaned up the Laundromat and closed its doors for the night, I stop her before she goes back upstairs.

"I want to take you somewhere," I say. She stops in her tracks and turns back toward me with an arched brow.

"Where?"

"It's a surprise," I reply with a lopsided grin.

"Will I like it?" she asks.

"Maybe."

"Is it dangerous?"

"Could be."

"Will you wear that?" She points to my borrowed outfit.

"If you want me to." I laugh.

She saunters toward me, pressing her index finger to my chin. "Will there be sex involved?"

My laughter fades away. "I'd like there to be."

"Okay, good. I'm in. Let me just run upstairs and grab my keys," she says as she bounces away from me toward the stairs. My eyes follow her every step of the way until she disappears up into the stairwell.

†

Twenty minutes later, I pull into the dark parking lot and Sage turns to stare at me with confusion.

"How is this dangerous or sexy?" she asks, gesturing toward the dark and empty church looming before us.

"I lied," I reply with a sheepish smile. The parking lot is littered with potholes and weeds growing up through the cracks. Last thing I heard, the church facility is used sparingly for functions but doesn't operate the way it used to when I was a kid.

As I put the truck into park, I just stare at it for a moment.

"Why did you bring me here?" she whispers, clearly noticing the melancholy nostalgia on my face.

"This is where I grew up. This is who I am," I reply in a near-silent mumble. "Not that big fancy megachurch or the TV broadcasts. You asked if I believe in God, and the answer is yes. This is where I first met him."

I notice her smile slightly in my periphery as she reaches out and touches my hand. "Let's go inside."

My head snaps in her direction. "What? You can't be serious. That's trespassing."

She rolls her eyes theatrically with a scoff. "Come on, Goody Two-shoes. Let's go get in some trouble." With that, she hops out of the truck and walks toward the dark church.

"I've already been to jail today," I call, but she ignores me. "Fuck," I mutter to myself before following behind.

As I jog up to her, I glance in all directions. We're no longer in the city center, but we're not really out of the city enough to feel entirely safe. There's a good chance we're not the only people looking to break into this place tonight.

"There aren't even security cameras," she says as she pulls on the front doors. "This will be a piece of cake."

"Sure," I reply skeptically. Then, I meander my way around the back, getting hit with another wave of memories as I see the dilapidated playground on the back side. They seriously haven't updated that thing in twenty-five years?

The back door that leads to the kitchen is locked too, but

when Sage tugs on the large sliding door to the nursery, it budges.

Holy shit, we're really going to break into this place.

Why? I have no fucking clue.

With some strength, we're able to shimmy it open enough to slide inside. And just like that, I'm transported back in time. Everything from the walls to the floor brings back an onslaught of memories and suddenly, I'm moving through the church, making my way to the center like it's calling to me. A siren song from my childhood.

The moment I walk into the main space, I stop in my tracks and stare ahead. It's like reattaching my own shadow or taking a breath I've been holding for twenty-five years. I feel a part of my childhood I forgot even existed.

Suddenly, Sage is at my side, her hand drifting down my arm and lacing her fingers with mine.

"Do you smell that?" I whisper, barely able to even move.

"The dust or the mold?" she replies with a cough, making me smile.

"I haven't smelled that in over two decades. It smells like home."

Her hand squeezes mine. Then she pulls me up to the front. Lit only by the bright exterior lights shining through the windows, the first thing I notice is that the carpet that once lined the aisles has been pulled up, leaving exposed concrete below. The pews seem to be in disrepair and the windows above the pulpit have been boarded up.

*How could they let this happen?*

This place used to be beautiful. People worshiped here. This was God's house and we let it fall into decay.

When we reach the front, Sage nudges me toward the pulpit. I stare at her in confusion, so she nudges me again.

"Go ahead."

"And what?" I ask.

"Stand up there. Pretend this place is yours."

I laugh, but then I do as she says. I walk up to the dusty

podium and I place my hands against the surface, staring out at the empty pews in the dim light.

"What would you do?" she asks, sitting in the first pew and resting her hands in her lap. "If this place was yours."

Thinking about it for a moment, I push away everything with my father and his church. I let twelve-year-old Adam, who had been torn away from the life he knew, answer her question.

"I'd...fill the rec room with Mary's enchiladas and I'd feed as many people in Austin as we could."

I can barely see her smile in the darkness. So I go on.

"I'd look every member of the congregation in the eye. I'd learn their names and I'd make sure each and every one knows they are all worthy and loved by God."

My throat stings and my eyes grow moist as I struggle to speak the next one. With a quiver in my lip, I mutter with conviction, "I'd hang a rainbow flag above the door so Isaac knows *everyone* is welcome."

Sage's smile grows brighter, the light outside catching a glint of moisture in her eyes.

"I'd make this place feel like home."

Slowly, she stands and walks toward me, squeezing herself between me and the pulpit. "I like the sound of that," she whispers as she lifts onto her toes to kiss me.

Before taking her lips with mine, I look her in the eye. "Would you be there?"

Her expression changes as she lowers to her feet without a kiss. Averting her eyes, she presses her hands to my chest. "I don't know, Adam."

And I understand. This chasm between us isn't something we can cross easily. How could you build a life with a person so fundamentally different? What could our future possibly hold when our pasts are so vastly contradictory?

But for now, I love the feel of her in my arms and the comfort of her in my life. For now, I'll savor that much.

Putting my fingers under her chin, I lift her eyes until she's staring at me. "It's okay," I whisper, so she knows. We may not be forever, but we can be for now.

Grabbing the backs of her thighs, I swiftly lift her onto the surface and position myself between her legs. She wraps her arms around my neck and goes in for the kiss again. This time, I take it, reveling in the warm sweetness of her lips and how much I love playing with that ring with my tongue.

Before we get too hot with this kiss, I pull away. "So what about you?" I ask, leaning away to look into her eyes.

"What would I do if this church was mine?" she replies with lifted brows. "Probably turn it into a sex club."

This time when I laugh, I lean my forehead against her shoulder and squeeze her ass, pulling her closer. The sound of her giggles against my ear is sweet and calming.

When I pull away, I clarify my question. "No, what would you do if Pink was yours? What would you do with it?"

"Oh." Her eyes light up with excitement. "First thing I would do is reinstate the two-drink limit and stick with it."

"Good."

"Then I would fire every one of those lousy bouncers and hire a whole new security staff."

"Excellent."

She takes a deep breath, gazing off into the distance as she thinks. "And then...I would find people who could teach real courses on sexuality for men and women. Couples could come in to find a new spark together. Assault survivors could have a place to feel safe and empowered. Members could learn how to practice BDSM *safely*. And I'd abolish the VIP section entirely."

With excitement, she tightens her arms around my neck. "It would be more than just a sex club. It would be like...a sex church!"

I laugh again, tugging her even closer. "A sex church?"

"I want people to feel at home there too," she says, relating my dream to hers. And maybe they're not really so different. Except they obviously are.

"Would you be there?" Her voice is soft and gentle as she asks me, and that chasm between us grows.

Because even she knows it's impossible. Even with this rampage against my father and this mission of ruining my reputation, at some point, I'll stop. I think that was always the understanding beneath this whole plan. I might rebel now, but eventually, I'll come back.

"Preacher by day, Dom by night," she says, tugging my neck toward her. Then as her lips touch mine, I slip my tongue between them, feeling for that comfort only her kisses seem to offer me anymore.

Even if I do feel torn in two. Broken and shattered until I don't recognize myself. And my only anchor is her.

With our foreheads still pressed together, she whispers, "Those two things can coexist, Adam. We can be both."

Then her hands slide from around my neck and slowly down my chest and stomach. Then over the stiff erection in my pants. "This is not a sin," she whispers, giving it a gentle squeeze.

It doesn't matter that my mind is arguing with her. She's wrong. It is a sin. But that's what we are, sinners.

As she grinds her hand over my cock, I let out a low, growling hum, pressing back against her touch. She doesn't stop there. Sliding her fingers under the elastic of my ridiculous green joggers, she finds my dick and strokes it like it's something to worship.

It still feels like a sin, but one I'd gladly burn for.

"Feel me," she whispers in the dusty darkness of this nearly abandoned church. And we shouldn't. We *really, really* shouldn't. But right now, this overwhelming hunger to be inside her feels more powerful than God himself.

Reaching under her thin cotton dress, I massage her through her panties, and sure enough, the moisture of her arousal seeps right through.

"Always so ready for me, Peaches."

At the first moan that slips through her lips, I lose my composure. I tear off her panties and throw them on the floor at my feet.

Then I grab her under the knees and yank her to the edge of the pulpit, staring down to watch where my thick cock prods her wet heat.

"Watch it with me," I tell her.

Together we gaze down in awe as I sink inside her. She lets out a small gasp as I fill her completely, latching her arms around my neck again and yanking my lips to hers for a kiss.

"What could be more godly than that?" she whispers through heavy gasps.

As I move out and back in, savoring the sensation of being inside her, my hunger growing with each thrust, I let myself feel what it's like to fuck her without shame. Even here in my childhood church, on the same pulpit my father once preached from. I imagine God is here, not condemning this but celebrating it.

Without all the rules and doctrines, we are just two bodies finding the most divine and explicit pleasure two people can find together.

She cries out for me, so I hold her tighter, moving faster and harder. The podium rocks against her weight as I fuck the heavenly spot between her legs. Our moans echo through the empty building, and just like last night, I let myself go, indulging in what I truly want.

And what I truly want right now is her, filling her up, hearing her cries of pleasure, and fucking her as many times as I can before this ends.

My hips are pistoning against her now as I grow closer and closer to my climax. She's hanging on to me for support with an expression of rapture on her face.

I pick up speed, pounding into her relentlessly as she lets out a deep, husky moan, seizing up in my arms as she lets out her cries of pleasure. When I finally feel myself releasing my own climax inside her, it feels like heaven.

And, like she said, what could be more godly than that?

# July
## The Hero

# THIRTY-FOUR

SAGE

"Holy shit." The alarm in Adam's voice pulls me out of my sleep. My head is against his bare chest, lying in my bed with Roscoe on his lap.

"What?" I mumble sleepily.

"We're making headlines."

I feel the bright light of his phone screen on my face, so I peel my eyes open and stare at a news article, an old photo of Truett and Adam together, front and center.

"What does it say?"

He pulls it away from my face as he reads.

*"Prominent Austin-based preacher, Truett Goode, faces scrutiny from followers due to his oldest son's risqué behavior on the amateur porn app, FanVids. The famous preacher and author has lost more than twenty thousand social media followers and is being publicly criticized for his silence on the matter. Loyal followers are still awaiting a statement from the preacher and his family. No word yet from thirty-seven-year-old son, Adam*

*Goode. The longer Truett Goode withholds his public condemna-*
*tion of his son's actions, the more he risks losing.*

*"The Goode family patriarch is worth more than forty*
*million dollars and has a seven-figure publishing deal with Good*
*Shepherd Press on the line."*

When he stops reading, I sit up and stare at him with confusion. "They didn't even mention me."

He smiles and kisses my head. "Then they're definitely
missing the best part. But Peaches, this is huge. Truett is losing
status as we speak. All while he sits on the deed for a sex club. He
has to be sweating."

This piques my interest. "Brett can't possibly pay him back the
loan he took out. What do you think your dad will do with that deed?"

My mind is turning with ideas and it feels like there's an
opportunity there. If I were to make the same bargain with Truett
that I did at the gala two months ago, would he take it this time?

"I don't know," Adam says with a dark smile creeping across
his face. He looks so proud of himself. And I sort of love that.

So I touch his arm. "This is good news. It means it's
working."

He's staring down at the article as he nods. "Yeah, it is."

Something about this bothers me, though, because if we've
accomplished what we set out to do, does that mean we're done?
What more could we do? We set out to do this for three months,
and it's already been two. Even if we aren't *fake* dating anymore, I
still don't know what we are and if that deadline still exists.

"We should celebrate," I chirp excitedly. I hop onto my knees
and Roscoe takes this as a sign that we should *all* get excited, so he
starts hopping on Adam's lap and barking at us both. We laugh
when he gets so worked up he starts gnawing on Adam's hand.

"What did you have in mind?" he asks.

I jump off the bed and find my underwear littered somewhere
on the floor. "Well, last time, we went to your church..."

"Yeah..." he replies, sounding uneasy.

When I give him a salty look, his brow furrows. "I think it's time we take it to *my* turf."

"I know you're not suggesting that we go to the sex club owned by the guy I put in the hospital."

"Listen," I say carefully, "I know all the back entrances in that place. I could smuggle you in so easily."

"Sage, no." He barks with the tone of a father disciplining his petulant child.

"Why not?" I whine, crawling on the bed and sitting on my knees to face him. I still haven't put on my top, so I'm hoping my bare tits will help sell the plan. "There's so much I want to show you."

"Like..."

I press my lips to his. "So much, Church Boy."

With a pained-sounding moan, he kisses me back.

"Can you be more specific?" He climbs up to his knees so we're facing each other, and I can feel just how aroused he is by this idea. Grabbing my hips, he grinds himself against me.

"You could tie me up," I mumble between kisses. "Make me your little fuck toy."

His mouth freezes before he pulls away. "Jesus, Sage."

I notice the way he winces as I drag him back against me. Adam still struggles so much with the really dirty, kinky things, and I know the reason he feels so bad is because of how badly he wants it.

I just wish he'd let go and give in to what he truly desires.

"Don't tell me that doesn't sound fun," I say, leaning close for another kiss.

He pulls away again. "Does it sound fun to you?"

"Yes," I reply without hesitation.

"Being my fuck toy sounds fun to you?" This time when he asks it, it sounds more like he's challenging me than asking.

"Yes," I answer again, more emphatically.

He climbs off the bed in frustration, reaching for his boxer briefs on the floor and dragging them up his legs as we sit in awkward silence. His movements are rapid and full of tension, radiating anger.

"Just say what you want to say, Adam."

When he spins around, his expression is tight. Thin lips, flared nostrils, wide eyes. "Why do you want me to treat you like shit? You're the *one fucking* person I don't want to hurt, but I feel like you keep pushing me to. I don't get it, Sage."

I hate it when he calls me Sage. I've just now realized how much I hate it. Because it means he's not being intimate. It means he's cross, either with me or someone else.

"You think I understand?" I reply, lowering until I'm sitting on my feet. "I've never wanted anyone to degrade me like that, Adam, but I *desperately* want it with you. I think...because you're so good all the time, I want to be the person you're comfortable enough with to let go of all of that. I want you to be *bad* with me. And I refuse to feel ashamed of what I want. I just...thought you liked it too."

"I do like it," he bursts out, looking far more frustrated as he drags his fingers through his hair. Then he climbs back on the bed and cradles my face in his hands. "I *love* the idea of making you my fuck toy. I love the idea of fucking you so hard you scream. I love the way you look when you're gagging on my cock, tears running down your face."

His thumb runs along my cheek before his hand closes around my throat. Then he pulls my face against his in a way that's both rough and romantic.

"Hurting you turns me on, Peaches, and I hate myself for that. Please don't ask me to do it."

His fingers relax from around my throat as he peppers my face with delicate kisses. I practically melt in his arms.

I feel his torment in the tremble of his fingers and the tender way he holds me like something fragile and valuable. For so long, I've tried to help fix all of the broken things inside him and now I'm asking him to do something that could break him even more.

Or would it heal him?

His entire life, he's been trained to believe these lustful cravings are wrong. That he's sick and depraved and sinful. If Adam learns to control these things he wants and experiences *real* trust, would it help repair everything his father taught him was wrong with him?

"You're not really hurting me, Adam. You know that. It's all an illusion that turns us on, and that's okay. Besides..." I whisper, looking into his eyes. "I trust you."

I can see by the way he stares back at me that this is what he needs to hear. His ability to trust has been shattered, so telling him that I trust him might be the one thing he needs most.

So I continue.

"You could tie me up. Spank me. Hurt me, and I trust that if I told you to stop, you would."

"And I can trust you to tell me if it gets to that?"

"Yes," I say with conviction. "You can trust me."

I feel the conflict in him burning like fire as he stares into my eyes. He's on the verge of something and the progress we've made so far means the world to me. And I want to make the rest of that progress together.

"If you *really* don't want to, then we won't," I say gently. "I'd never pressure you into something I didn't think you truly wanted, but I see the way you're struggling, Adam. And I just want you to learn to let go of the lies you've been fed your entire life that these things you want are bad. Stop telling yourself that fucking me is hurting me."

I press my fingers to his chest, feeling his heartbeat.

"Okay," he says, and by the intense eye contact between us, I know he means it. That *this* means something special to him, and my heart swells with pride.

It's a Tuesday night, which means the club is a tad bit quieter than if we tried to do this on a Saturday. There aren't any stragglers lingering on the street outside the club and security is slacking.

Even then, I'm not confident enough to just try and walk right in. Instead, I make a few calls. And by calls, I mean I send a text to Lacey, one of the girls who bartends in the VIP section.

This is why I'm shocked when, moments after my text, it's Sadie who opens the door in the back to let us in. She's standing in the doorway with a smile on her face and her arms crossed.

I'm frozen midstep, staring at her in shock and wondering if she's about to tell me to fuck off or hug me.

"Hi..." I say with unease. Adam is standing behind me, a firm hand on my arm, ready to drag me back to the car and tell me what a bad idea this was.

"I'll admit," Sadie says, "I knew your plan all along. Piss off your ex by fucking the preacher's son and posting it online. I did not foresee beating the shit out of him, though."

I roll my eyes and turn back toward Adam. "It wasn't exactly part of the plan," I say.

She laughs and looks at Adam with a shake of her head. "Well, it seems to have worked."

"What do you mean?" I ask.

"Brett left town. He keeps saying he's coming back, but I doubt it. And our VIP membership is down by fifty percent. Every prominent member who felt safe keeping their dirty secrets here has left, which, if you ask me, is good."

"Even my father?" Adam adds in.

"Oh yeah," she replies, "I haven't seen him around in months. The last thing he needs is to get caught here after what you've pulled."

"So..." I say. "Are you going to let us in?"

"Sneaking around now? Last time you were *trying to get* attention. What changed?"

Adam and I glance at each other, but neither of us answers

that question. She doesn't need to know that *we* are what changed. Instead of pressing us for an answer, she smiles and opens the door wider to let us walk in.

"The Blue Room is open," she says as we slowly pass her by. "Unless...the Black Room is what you're looking for. That's open too."

"Thank you," I mutter as I take Adam's hand in mine, leading him straight to the back stairwell and directly down the hall where the Black Room looms at the end.

# THIRTY-FIVE

## ADAM

Everything that exists behind the door labeled "Black Room" reeks of both salvation and ruin. The moment Sage opens the door, I feel everything inside me suddenly at war. The things I want battling the things I know I shouldn't have.

The man who wanted to be a hero against the man who knows heroes don't truly exist—not like that. Not the way my father trained me.

The excitement of uncovering this new side of myself at war with the fear that I won't ever become the good man I sought to be.

The terror of losing myself in unlearning the indoctrination I've been brainwashed to believe.

And the strongest battle of them all—this unyielding and intoxicating lust-fueled desire to dominate her against the shame of being a monster if I do.

I'm pretty sure I know which side is going to win.

Sage squeezes my hand as we walk inside. I try to focus on her because looking around the room is getting to my head at the moment. As she locks the dead bolt on the door, she keeps her eyes on me, and I force myself to breathe.

My cock is already throbbing in my pants, and I'm dying to touch her and relieve this ache inside me. Before she can say a word, I pull her into my arms, lifting her from the floor until she wraps her legs around me.

"I want you to take the lead," she whispers against my lips. Her eyes are still focused on mine as if we're shutting out everything else. Until we're ready to acknowledge them.

I drop her onto the elevated bed, leaning over to kiss her. When we pull away from the heated exchange, she looks at me again. "I'm yours, Adam. You can do whatever you want to me, and if I need you to stop, I'll say *red*, okay?"

"Red. Got it."

Then she strokes my face as she gazes into my eyes, and it's like she can see everything happening inside my mind. Like she's staring right into the battle that's taking place there. As she touches my cheek, she whispers, "It's safe here."

I let my eyes close, kissing her again. All I feel at this moment is relief and immense appreciation. How this woman seems to always know how to comfort me and bring me peace is either a sign that she's simply perfect or simply perfect *for me*.

Do I bring her the same feeling? The last time I cared so much for another person's well-being, I fucked it up. I don't intend to do that again.

Sage needs me to protect her, keep her, *own* her. So that's what I'll do.

"Lie down," I say in a low, assertive command.

Letting out a sigh, she releases her hold of my neck and lets her legs fall from around my hips. Then, she does as I say and reclines on the bed, staring up at me for her next instruction.

As I stand up and stare at her laid out before me, I let all the noise in my head silence. I'm not thinking about shame or fear. I'm focused only on her and how exquisite she looks.

In her thin cotton sundress, I run my fingers along the length of her bare thighs, lifting the fabric to reach her blue lace panties hiding beneath. Then I take my time, slipping off each of her shoes and drawing my touch all the way back up to her dress, lifting it up until it exposes her petite, perky breasts.

She shudders as I run my thumb over the hard bud on the right side. I love seeing Sage like this. Like she's *mine*. She is perfect and beautiful and sexy, and she belongs to me. Not because I've taken her but because she's offered herself up to me. Because she sees me as *worthy* of that.

*Because I am worthy.*

"Come here," I say. So she sits back up and lets me pull her dress all the way over her head. Then I press her back down as I drag her panties down her legs. She's lying naked in front of me, and it feels like I have the whole world in my hands.

I continue to play with her, teasing her with my touch until she's practically writhing on the bed. My fingers cascade up her legs, tempting her to move but demanding she stay still. I want to cherish every perfect inch of her body before I wreck her. Because when I'm done here, I won't be as gentle.

When she lets out a whine from my fingers sliding through her folds, I pull away. She's fidgeting on the bed as I undo each of the buttons on my shirt. After I slip it off and hang it over the chair in the corner, I take a look around the room. There are so many different kinds of restraints displayed—cuffs, rope, gags, but when my eyes land on a long black bar with two leather straps on either side, I take it. Then I decide on the two black ribbons hanging from a hook on the wall.

Her eyes are settled on mine as I instruct her to hold her wrists out for me. While I tie her two hands together with one, she keeps her gaze settled on my face, the look of lust growing stronger with each second. As if the more and more she becomes restrained for me, the more aroused she gets.

Wrapping the other ribbon around her eyes, I watch her lips part as I take away her ability to see.

Then, I pick up the long metal pole, and I slip one of her

ankles into the cuff, clipping it with ease. She shudders with anticipation.

"You said you want to be my fuck toy, didn't you?"

She nods, biting her lip.

I move to the other ankle, drawing it out wide until her legs are spread for me. As I click the other one in, I give her a wicked grin she can't see. "Because you're a filthy little slut, aren't you?"

She writhes a little, adjusting to the bar. "Yes," she murmurs, and something inside me stirs at the sound of that.

She lets out a loud, frightened yelp as I yank on the bar, dragging her to the edge of the bed. Then, I grind my cock against her as I mutter, "You're *my* filthy little slut."

Humming with need as she tries to twist and writhe against me, searching for friction, I hold the bar in my hand, her legs high in the air.

"Say it again, Peaches. Tell me what you are."

"I'm your filthy little slut."

My cock threatens to spill just from those words alone. I love her like this, vulnerable and dirty and *mine*.

"Hold your legs up. Let me look at you."

She does as I say, keeping her wide legs held upward, exposing her beautiful pink pussy to me while I slowly undo the belt of my pants. The entire time I'm removing them, I'm just thinking about how good it's going to feel to be inside her.

In this moment, there is no shame. Only trust and desire. Because, as she said, it's safe here, and I'm well aware she wasn't referring to this room or this club but to *us*.

Her bound wrists rest above her head while her legs start to shake from the effort of holding them up for me. All I want to do is fuck her. There are a million things in this room I could use on her, but there is only one place I want to be, so I can't focus on anything else.

Grabbing the pole that holds her legs apart, I press it toward her, practically folding her in half as I line my cock up with her wet, needy cunt and thrust myself inside her.

She lets out a desperate sound, somewhere between a scream and a groan, as I pull out and force myself back in. And just as I expected, she feels like heaven. Just the sight of her, bound and blindfolded, offering her body to me like some sort of sacrament, is the most beautiful thing I've ever seen.

Slamming into her relentlessly, I feel like I'm binding us together with each thrust until we are one.

"This cunt feels so fucking good, Peaches."

I pound into her even harder, making her cry out.

"Louder," I command, and she responds with another scream.

Without any warning, I pull out of her and grab the bar on either side. Then, I flip her and she gasps when I take her by surprise. Yanking her backward until her feet are on the floor, still spread wide, I push her head down into the mattress as I fill her up again.

It feels so good to let go. To let this darker side of me take shape, like meeting a part of myself I've kept hidden my entire life. Trusting that she *actually* likes it. I'm giving her what she wants, and it's not just for me or for her, but for us.

Fucking her into the mattress, I lose control, smacking her ass hard with the palm of my hand just to hear her scream again. The entire time I'm just chanting in my mind—*mine, mine, mine.*

Then my internal thoughts come slipping through my lips with every thrust.

"My filthy little slut. My beautiful, sexy fuck toy. My Peaches. My god."

With that thought, I let go. I come and come and come. Losing track of time and myself, I let my body take over, grinding against her as I fill her up, imagining that while she takes my cum, she takes a piece of me—my sacrifice.

I'm hunched over her, my heart pounding against her back as I listen to her breathing. For a long time, we lie there together, catching our breaths, letting our hearts slow, and letting the post-sex haze settle over us.

When I finally pull out of her, I stand back and watch the cum drip from between her legs. I let it drip all the way down like it's some sort of dirty ritual. Then I lower to my knees to unclasp each cuff, releasing her ankles from the bar. While I'm down there, I press my lips to the mermaid tattoo on her thigh.

Standing up, I lift Sage into my arms, cradling her against my chest while her eyes are still blindfolded and her hands are still tied. Carrying her around to the top of the bed, I place her there with her head on the pillows.

Then I settle myself between her legs, my face buried between her thighs. When she feels my tongue lapping at her cum-soaked core, she tries to close them and gasps in surprise. "What are you doing?"

I ease her thighs open as I kiss each one. "I'm rewarding my good little slut."

Then, I lick her open again, tasting the saltiness of what I left behind mixed with her familiar flavor. I'm perverted and sick for how much I love it.

When she finally relaxes her knees to the sides, she arches her back and eases into the pleasure of my mouth. Her breathing turns shallow, letting out tiny sounds with each exhale. Then, I slide two fingers inside her, curling them to find the spot that makes her legs buck and her spine curl.

Taking my time with her, I hum against her, my lips around her clit. Just watching her writhe and squirm with pleasure has my cock thickening again. Already I miss being inside her. I'd stay there for good if I could.

My hips grind against the mattress as I watch her body slowly morph with her climax. Her skin glistens. Her muscles clench. Seeing her come feels like my reward as much as hers.

After she's come down from her high, I slowly crawl up her body, kissing my way over her stomach and chest. Then I lift the blindfold from her face.

"Since you told me once you love to watch," I say as I wrap my hand around my stiff length and stroke with fast, eager strokes.

Settled between her legs, I fuck my fist as she watches with rapt, hungry attention. She bites her lip and moans along with me as if she can feel it too. With the taste of her on my tongue, it doesn't take me long before I'm grunting out my release, spilling warm, salty jets of cum over her naked body.

I'm left gasping, my skin buzzing as I wring myself dry. Exhausted, I nearly collapse on top of her.

When our eyes meet, we share a smile.

"Not too bad, Church Boy," she whispers.

I find myself laughing as I lower myself over her, letting her tiny body wrap its way around me. After pulling the ribbon from her wrists, I settle into her arms as I let her embrace silence every warring thought in my mind. For the time being, I'm at peace.

# THIRTY-SIX

## ADAM

It turns out Sage's favorite form of aftercare is cheeseburgers and onion rings on the trunk of my car. After I spent an hour forcing water down her throat and cuddling her until I was sure she was okay, I insisted she eat, and this is what she chose.

She groans around a mouthful of burger, a dollop of ketchup at the corner of her mouth. I smile before licking it off her face. With a laugh, she shoves me away.

"You're so obsessed with me," she teases, and I smile, leaning toward her.

"Maybe I am," I reply, stealing a bite of her cheeseburger. Then I press my lips to her cheek.

A few months ago, I thought this was impossible. I couldn't see myself with a girl like Sage. Hell, two weeks ago, I was sure that whatever this is would be temporary. A fling.

And now...I'm stuck. Blissfully stuck.

She's like glue and with every touch, I'm more and more unable to pull myself away. And honestly, at this point, I've just stopped trying. Everything about the church and the sex club feels so arbitrary. Like she said, those things can coexist, and so can we.

I think I might be falling in love. If this is what love feels like. Infatuation. Obsession. I always assumed that love would feel more painful, and I'm not sure why. But nothing hurts when I'm with her.

"So..." she says as she balls up the empty foil wrapper.

"So?" I ask.

"How are you feeling? After that whole thing?"

My eyes narrow in confusion. "How am *I* feeling? Shouldn't the question be, how are you feeling?"

"You've already asked me that a hundred times while we were still at the club, and I told you—I'm fine." She knocks her fist against my shoulder playfully. "Good job, Church Boy. You've mastered aftercare."

With a chuckle, I reply, "Thanks, Peaches. But why are you asking me how I feel?"

"Because that matters too. What we did was intense and new for you. I know you struggled with it, so I just want to see how you're feeling afterward."

I settle myself between her knees. Then I take a long, deep breath before replying. How am I feeling? I've been considering this question ever since we finished up at the club.

Dragging my hand up her spine, I wind my fingers in her hair at the scalp and I tug on it, loving the way she moves with my commanding grip. Looking down my nose at her helpless body in my hands, I groan. "Feeling so good, I want to do it again."

"Oh yeah?" she replies with a wicked smile before biting her lip.

My hand relaxes as it eases down to the back of her neck, touching her with tenderness this time. "I can be myself around you. You make it safe for me to let go."

Her smile reaches her eyes as she nods. "I feel the same."

"My upbringing would have me believe this is the devil's hold on me, but I don't think that's it."

She lets out a quiet laugh. Then she wrinkles her nose. "Yeah, I don't think so either."

After we laugh for a second, I brush a lock of pink hair out of her face and delicately run my fingers along the constellation on the side of her neck.

"I think you and I needed to play these roles, especially for each other. And I don't think I could ever do that with anyone else."

"Neither could I," she whispers, and I feel my blood pressure start to rise as it moves through my veins. My heart is pounding with hope—hope that I'm not alone in these feelings.

I pull her a little closer. "I can't believe I'm saying this, but I think we might be perfect for each other."

Immediately, she smiles, easing the worry in my chest. Then she leans her head closer so our lips are mere inches apart. "I get that feeling too."

"I don't just mean for sex," I reply in a low whisper.

"Neither do I," she says just before our lips touch. Suddenly, Sage and I exist only in the intimate space of our kiss, and it feels ethereal. My hands wrap around her, gently pulling her closer until we're practically one.

This has to be love. There's no other name for it, but it sure as fuck doesn't hurt. It feels like the greatest thing I've ever felt.

It's too soon to say it. I'd be an idiot to say it so fast, but it's enough to know I feel it.

When our tender kiss ends, I stare into her eyes as I remember something.

"At the end of the month, my mother is getting an award. A Good Samaritan award, and there's going to be a ceremony. I'd love for you to go with me."

Immediately, she starts to look uneasy. The last time I took her to an event, my father threatened her, and she was publicly ridiculed, but everything feels so different now. With a calming hold of her arms, I quickly quiet her worries. "I don't mean like a charade or part of the plan. I mean... I want you to go as my date. My *real* date."

"I don't know..."

"I'll keep you by my side the entire night, and I'll make sure that asshole doesn't even look in your direction."

She lets out a disgruntled huff. "Your family is so fucked up."

"I agree," I reply with a nod.

"Why does everyone just pretend everything is okay?" she asks, but then quickly shakes her head. "I'm sorry. It's none of my business."

"No, you're right," I say, running my hands along the bare length of her thighs to keep her warm. "I wish I didn't, Sage. I wish I could turn my back on him for good, but I've already lost my brother. I can't bear to lose my whole family."

"So *expose* him," she says. "Isn't it worse to let your mother stay with someone who actively betrays her?"

"It's not that simple," I reply.

"Why not?"

I love what a challenger Sage is. I do. Just not when I'm the one she's challenging. I don't always appreciate the mirror in front of my face when I don't like the reflection.

"Because..." I mutter with frustration. "She'd stay with him. And I don't know if I can bear that. I think it might actually be worse."

"You don't know that, Adam. You don't know for sure she'd stay. Doesn't she at least deserve the benefit of the doubt?"

"I know you're right, but what you're suggesting..."

"Feels impossible," she says, finishing my sentence. "Trust me. I've been there. When my mother stopped caring about me, I thought it'd be impossible to leave her. I blamed myself for months for being a bad daughter, but it took time for me to realize that blame was never on me. I didn't deserve having to make that choice in the first place, so I sure as fuck shouldn't have felt bad for making it."

She takes my hands in hers, rubbing a thumb over my knuckles. "The guilt of telling your family the truth shouldn't be on you, Adam. Not when he's forcing you to make that decision in the first place."

What she's saying is true, but being true doesn't make it any easier to accept.

"Let me get through my mother's award, and then I'll tell her. I promise."

"Of course," she says with a smile, pulling me closer so she can wrap her arms around my neck. "And I'll be there when you do."

I bury my face in her neck and find my comfort there. If she is with me, then I have nothing to fear. With her, I can do anything.

# THIRTY-SEVEN

## ADAM

"You're not even dressed yet?"

Sage comes barreling out of her bedroom, her long, shimmery black gown gathered at her bare feet. She's pushing her earrings into place before showing me her back, which I take as a sign that she needs me to zip it. Meanwhile, I'm still in my boxers on the couch, petting Roscoe while he sleeps and scrolling through the comments on our latest video. It's a fifteen-second clip of me thrusting into Sage's mouth as she gazes up at me with teary eyes. This one is doing almost as well as the last one and we've gained another ten thousand subscribers. I love that we can make *real* videos now.

"Holy fuck. You look amazing," I stammer as I take in the way the fabric clings to her hips, making her look elegant and sexy at the same time. This dress is nowhere as revealing as the last one. The neckline is straight across her chest, from one collarbone to the other, and the sleeves hang delicately from her shoulders.

As much as I appreciate her in leather and lace—or nothing at all—I can appreciate this too.

"Thank you," she mutters as she finishes attaching her

earring, bouncing in place and clearly nervous. "We're going to be late, though, if you don't hurry."

With a laugh, I ease Roscoe off my lap and stand to zip up her dress, pressing my lips to the back of her neck as I do.

It's cute that she's so nervous tonight, attending this as my real date, or rather, my *real girlfriend*. Although we never really made things official, I don't think we had to. I've barely been to my own apartment in the last two months. I sleep here, eat here, and sometimes even write here. My place just feels cold and lifeless, even on the rare occasion she's stayed there with me. This place feels more like home, which is strange.

After one kiss to her neck, I slide my hand around her waist and inhale the feminine scent of her perfume, going in for a nibble on her earlobe.

"Adam," she whines, enjoying my lips too much to want to pull away. "We have to go. Don't start this."

I grind my hips against her backside, sliding my hands down her sides just to feel her through the fabric.

Fuck, now I'm having a hard time dragging myself off her.

"Okay, okay," I say, stepping away. With a shake of my head, I move toward the bedroom, where my suit is hanging in the garment bag.

As I slip into the rich black fabric, I think about how good this is going to feel, and not in the retribution sort of way. But having her on my arm for real. Seeing her with my mother again. Feeling her presence beside me as we face my father. I can't remember the last time I felt this happy, but Sage has had that effect on me since the day we met.

I still haven't told her how I feel about her, but I don't hide my obsession either. It must be obvious to her how infatuated I am. I'd do anything for her. *Anything*.

"Ta-da," I say five minutes later, as I walk out into the living room of her apartment while fixing the cuff links on my sleeves.

She whistles when she sees me. "Damn, Church Boy."

"I told you I was fast."

She's still adjusting the strap on her heels by the time I've finished tying my shoes. Five minutes later, we're out the door, dropping off Roscoe with Gladys at the front desk. Then, hand in hand, we walk to the lot across the street where my car is parked and she lets me open her door for her so she can climb in.

The moment we're inside, I glance over at her in the passenger seat, looking so stunning I can barely stand it. Reaching over the console, I run my hand along her jaw and pull her toward me for a kiss, sliding my tongue over the gold hoop piercing on her lip.

"Let's skip it. I want to fuck you in that dress instead."

She laughs as she pulls away. "Who said we can't do both?"

"Oh, we're doing both," I reply assertively as I start the car and pull out of the parking spot.

Fifteen minutes later, we're pulling up to the winery where my mother's ceremony will be held. It's a much smaller gathering than the gala I took Sage to, which makes it feel more intimate. After dropping the car off at the valet, I take Sage's arm in mine and lead her down the paved walkway toward the large event area. It's under a canopy of trees covered in white lights, giving it a romantic vibe.

"This is beautiful," she whispers, looking around. In the distance, there is a string quartet playing, and the warm Texas sun hovering just below the horizon gives the air a pleasant heat that puts me at ease. Tonight could truly be great.

But there's something less tranquil lingering just beyond the peace that tonight promises. It's the reminder that, after tonight, I have something truly impossible to do. I have to reveal my father for the man he is to my family.

It still feels impossible. Telling my mother about his transgressions might be the most unthinkable thing I can think of because it means I'm hurting her. But deep down, I know it's the right thing to do.

Before the looming deadline of that conversation can sour my mood, I force it down and try not to think about it. Instead, I focus on the beautiful woman at my side and this perfect night together.

As we approach the party, I spot my mother at the front of the gathering. She's surrounded by women, who all seem to be holding a cordial conversation with her.

Scanning the crowd, I spot my father in the corner, a mass of men standing around him.

My teeth clench as I force my eyes away.

"Hello again," Briar, my brother Caleb's wife, says as we approach her, standing by the bar.

"Hey. You look amazing," Sage replies, going in for a hug. Briar looks momentarily taken aback by this gesture but wraps her arms around her anyway.

"Thank you. So do you," she says in response, letting her eyes cascade up and down Sage's dress. I can tell she's a little surprised by how *appropriately* she's dressed this time.

Caleb and Lucas approach a moment later, and we repeat the greeting process with them. Then the five of us fall into a casual conversation. The entire time, I'm struggling to hold back my satisfied grin because this all feels so goddamn perfect. We started as a ruse, but we somehow became the most real thing in my life. And she fits in so well, laughing with my brothers like she's part of our family now.

In some way, I guess she is.

My hand slides across her lower back, and I tug her against me. Lucas notices, his gaze dancing down to where I'm holding her and back up to my face. As our eyes meet, he gives me a subtle smile, and I wish I could tell him just how good this feels. How he should try harder to find someone like this. I've never even known him to date. But I know it's because he struggles with expressing himself. He's not as outgoing or as social as Caleb or me. He's devoted to his work at the university, and that's it. That's his life.

When we reach a lull in the conversation, I find myself glancing around the event space. I'm getting restless already and desperate for a quiet corner, somewhere to take my hot-as-fuck date to. Just the thought of lifting her dress and fucking her senseless has me itching to ditch this party already.

This is the effect she has on me. I never considered myself so sex-crazed before. But being with Sage has opened my eyes in ways I couldn't imagine. Sex isn't just sex anymore. It's harnessing a part of me that feels natural and liberating. We play roles, tap into a deeper part of ourselves, and connect with each other all at the same time.

And I'm fucking addicted to it.

But that mood is quickly killed as soon as my mother finds us all standing together. I shove the sex thoughts away as we all congratulate her. She looks so happy, and it makes me feel like a monster for both holding secrets from her *and* eventually revealing them.

"Go take your seats," she tells us in her gentle, motherly tone. "You need to eat before you all drink too much and make fools of yourselves."

"Us?" Caleb asks as a joke before looking at Lucas, who only shakes his head with a furrowed brow.

"Not us," he replies.

My mother rolls her eyes and turns her attention to my date. Taking Sage's hands in hers, she gives her a warm expression that makes my heart melt.

"I'm so glad to see you again, Sage. You look beautiful tonight."

"Thank you for inviting me," she replies. "Congratulations on such an honorable award. You deserve it."

My mother smiles, tears welling in her eyes. "Thank you."

Then she pulls Sage into her arms, hugging her tight for a moment longer than the rest of us. My mom might be the kindest person on earth, but this display of affection for my girlfriend is real. I can tell.

And I am renewed with purpose.

I will make this right.

When their hug ends, I take Sage under my arm and walk with her toward our table. With my lips pressed against her head, I mentally prepare myself for the man we're about to face. But I'm not afraid or nervous, and judging by the confidence in her step, neither is she.

# THIRTY-EIGHT

## SAGE

Truett Goode barely looks at me as I sit down at the table across from him. He merely glances at his own son, offers a barely cordial greeting, and then spends the next two hours focused only on his drink, his food, the table, and the trees. His attention is almost never offered to the *people* seated around him, but I guess that's on brand for him at this point.

The tension between him and Adam is thick.

I know I'm not the only one who feels it, and yet, no one will speak about it. The family would rather smile, sweep their feelings under the rug, and pretend Adam's reputation isn't actively ruining his father's career. Of course, none of them truly know how much Truett deserves it. But it's still so ridiculously odd to me how they will go about their small talk and pretend that none of this is happening.

Truett Goode is looking ragged. His eyes have heavier than normal bags under them, and his cheeks are a little more gaunt. Not to mention, he's had two drinks delivered in the time I barely sipped down one glass of red wine.

He's not doing well, but no one else in his family seems to be as concerned.

And that gives me satisfaction because that's exactly what he has coming to him.

Adam keeps his promise and holds me close to his side all night. Even when I have to use the restroom, he sends Briar with me, giving her strict instructions not to let me out of her sight. She takes it as a romantic gesture rather than a real concern for my safety—which it is.

But Truett is still staring down at his whiskey when I return. I don't even get the chance to sit down when Adam stands, practically dragging me to the middle of the dance floor.

His happiness is contagious. It makes me think that this might actually work. For the first time in my entire life, I feel as if the person I'm getting attached to is getting attached right back. I've never had my feelings so requited before.

It's wonderful...and terrifying.

I'm in love with Adam. It's so obvious and visceral. And if I'm judging the situation correctly, he loves me too.

I breathe in the rich scent of his cologne as he pulls me against him, swaying softly to the music. The safety I feel in his arms is blinding. I never realized how much I needed this.

"Sage," he whispers, and I pull my face away from his chest to stare up into his eyes. Something romantic plays instrumentally at the front of the party, and it's created the perfect moment for one of us to say what I know is on our minds.

"Adam," I reply in a breathless whisper.

Neither of us speaks for a while. We just share intense and intoxicating eye contact as we sway in circles to the delicate music serenading us as we say with our eyes what I know we're both feeling inside.

*I love you.*

Maybe he knows this isn't the place or isn't the time. Or perhaps saying it like this is somehow more powerful than bringing those words to life, but we keep quiet as we continue our dance.

His hand squeezes mine before he lowers his head toward me. Instead of a kiss, he rests his forehead against mine. We close our eyes, breathing in the tender moment.

*I love you. I love you. I love you.*

I could be a serious fool for falling for a man like him. Maybe no one can truly pretend to love someone without their heart mistakenly falling when it wasn't supposed to. We come from different worlds with different paths and different values, but it doesn't stop the fact that our hearts beat as one. Regardless of our differences, our souls are the same.

My fingers run through the cropped hair on the back of his head before I pull his lips to mine. The more I feel his love, the more I want his body.

"I need you," I whisper against his mouth.

He pulls away from the kiss and glances around before taking me by the hand and hauling me off the dance floor and toward one of the three large structures on the property.

"Where are we going?" I whisper as we reach the back side of the main building. When he continues to pull me farther away from the event, I realize where he's taking me.

Goose bumps erupt down my arms as we enter the moonlit vineyard. We are completely alone out here, the sound of the party in the distance now.

As he gets a few yards into the rows of grapevines covering us on either side, he spins around and takes my mouth in a bruising kiss.

"Fuck, I need you," he says breathlessly as his lips travel down from my mouth to my neck.

"Then take me," I reply, gripping and pulling at him in a frenzy of passion.

My hands find the hard bulge in his pants, and I rub him hard through the fabric. Letting out a deep groan, he buries his hands in my hair and bites my bottom lip.

"I want this mouth on my cock, Peaches. I might go crazy without it."

Eagerly, I drop to my knees, not giving a shit about my dress in the dirt. Under the moonlight, I undo the button of his pants and tear down his zipper, desperate for the hard length waiting for me.

As soon as I have his dick in my hand, I stroke it as I stare up at him. My mouth opens, my tongue hanging out as I slide the head across the warm, wet surface I'm offering to him.

He groans again, and I can tell by the desperation in his voice that our time in this vineyard will be fast and filthy.

Holding the back of my scalp, he shoves his cock so hard into my mouth, I feel him at the back of my throat, cutting my airway and making me gag. Swiftly he pulls out, staring down with satisfaction.

"That's my girl," he mutters. "Gag on it."

He shoves it back in, holding it there a moment before pulling out again. A string of saliva hangs from my lips, and I smile up at him before he fills my mouth once more. I can already feel the head of his dick swelling on my tongue, but I know he's not ready to come yet.

A moment later, he pulls out and takes a second to compose himself before dragging me to my feet. Spinning me around, he pushes me toward the wooden poles stationed along the grapevines, each strung with wire to hold up the massive plants. I wrap my hands around the wood as I feel him drag up my dress, revealing my bare pussy for him to find.

"Such a filthy girl, Peaches. You wanted me to fuck you tonight, didn't you?"

"Yes, sir," I reply with a wicked smile.

The next thing I know, I feel the palm of his hand land hard and loud against my ass, and I stifle a scream. His hand clamps around my mouth as he leans toward me. "Keep it down, Peaches. This is our dirty little secret."

He spanks my ass again, this time harder, then quickly

massages the tender flesh when he's done. I moan into his palm, squirming with my bare ass in the air. Three more times, he strikes me, each time feeding the arousal between my legs.

When his cock finally pushes at my entrance, it feels like I've been waiting forever. He has to hold my mouth shut as he enters me with force because I try to cry out even louder. With one hand over my lips and the other on my hip, he fucks me in quick, forceful thrusts.

As my body starts to tingle with desire, I feel a quick and intense orgasm cresting at the pinnacle of this sensation. Just as I'm about to come, the fingers on my hip slip between my legs, rubbing hard at my throbbing clit, and I practically scream into his hand.

"Come on my cock, Peaches. Give me all you got. Then, I'm going to come inside you and I want you dripping all the way back to the party."

I'm buried in pleasure from the tips of my toes to the top of my head. The orgasm seizes control of my limbs as I tremble through the climax. With just a few more relentless pounds of his cock inside me, I feel him jerk and shudder out his own release, filling me up like he promised.

We are breathless and panting into the quiet night air. He releases his hand from my mouth and slowly pulls out of me. As his cum drips down my legs, he drags my body to his. His lips press to my ear, cheek, neck. Then his arms wrap around me, and I cover them with my own.

It's another perfect moment for us to utter what we're both thinking, but we don't. Silence ensues.

Then he quietly mumbles, "Thank you for coming with me. Thank you for...just being you."

I smile to myself before turning to gaze up at him. It's enough. For now, it's enough.

# THIRTY-NINE

## SAGE

A fter Adam brushes the dirt off my dress and we've composed ourselves enough to return to the party, I drift away from him as we pass by the bathroom.

"I really need to clean this mess up. It's not nearly as comfortable as you think to have sticky cum covering my thighs."

He shoots me a displeased expression, but I laugh it off. "Don't worry. You can put it back later," I whisper before kissing him.

We're still behind the biggest building, using the less obvious bathroom. It's probably a good choice for me at this point since it won't be easy cleaning this up discreetly with other women around.

"I'll meet you back at the table," I say, pushing him toward the party.

"I'll wait for you," he says, but I quickly shake my head.

"We can't be seen returning together, or they'll know our dirty little secret. Just go. I'll be fine."

After some contemplation, he agrees and reluctantly leaves me to enter the bathroom alone. Locking the door behind me, I grab a handful of paper towels from the dispenser and wet them under the water in the sink. Then, I not so gracefully prop my shoe up on the sink and do my best to clean the slowly drying mess along my inner thighs. The entire time, I curse his name with a smile, reliving every sexy moment in the vineyard.

After I've used the toilet and washed up, fixing my hair in the mirror, I smile at my reflection one last time before unlocking the bathroom door and stepping into the warm night air. This bathroom is still quite a ways away from the party, so I nearly scream when I hear footsteps along the path behind me.

I spin around with a yelp as I notice Truett Goode sauntering behind me. My blood turns ice cold when I notice the stumble in his step, signifying that he's drunk. And I'm alone with him.

Turning back toward the party, I pick up my pace.

"Now, now," he slurs. "Don't be rude. I just want to talk to you."

"Fuck you," I mutter, walking faster.

His slow steps turn quick, and I nearly scream with fear. His fat, clammy hand wraps around my arm, stopping me and spinning me until I'm facing him. I get the urge to spit in his face when I catch a whiff of his whiskey-scented breath, but I'm too frozen in fear.

"I ain't gonna hurt you," he grits out in a deep Southern drawl. "Will you stop tryin' to run from me, dammit?"

My breath comes out with a tremble as I stare at him. Frozen in place, I wait for him to speak.

"What do you want?"

"I want to take your offer," he replies with a twisted smile.

"My offer?" I reply in confusion.

He nearly falls over, his drunk legs struggling beneath him. He grabs my shoulder for balance, leaning against me as he recomposes himself.

With an exasperated sigh, he looks annoyed as he speaks. "You don't remember? At the gala, you offered to stay away from my son in exchange for the deed to the club. Well...I'm ready to take your bargain."

My lips part as I stare at him, wondering if this is some inebriated drunk talk or if he's serious. It makes me sick to think I ever made that offer in the first place, but back then, Adam wasn't what he is to me now.

Shoving his hand off my shoulder and holding my head up high, I spit on his suit. He stares down at it in confusion.

"Fuck you," I mutter angrily. "I don't give a shit about that fucking club. I hope it burns to the ground. The only one who should be leaving Adam alone is you. I'll *never* leave him. Never."

With his brows pinched inward, he crowds me. As I try to step back, he grabs at my dress, clenching the fabric in his fists and sneering in my face.

"You're nothing but a trashy slut. You think you're good enough for my son? You'll never be worthy. No one will ever accept you, and once he's grown sick of you, he'll throw you away, just like your mother did."

I manage a strangled sob as I try to tear myself out of his grasp, but his hold is too strong.

"Yeah, well, I'd rather be a trashy slut than a man hated by his own children. But your son *loves* me. And he can't fucking stand you."

"You little bitch," he says, spitting in my face as he makes me stumble in my retreat.

"Let me go," I cry out, louder this time.

His drunk weight becomes too much, and I stumble on my heels, falling to the ground with a crushing impact, his heavy frame covering me.

He's muttering something cruel, but my mind has stopped registering his words. He's taunting me, telling me to burn in hell, wishing me death, and all I can do is fight back.

As his hands fumble their way over my body, pinching my flesh and attempting to dig their way between my legs, my stomach turns with dread. Still, I fight, kicking my legs against his assault, trying to push him off of me. Then, I scream.

To shut me up, he clamps both hands around my throat, putting his weight on my windpipe until it feels like he's crushing me to death. Fear and panic fill my bloodstream as my vision turns hazy and black around the edges.

All I can think is that I'm going to die. And it's going to break Adam's heart.

My legs turn heavy and my hands can no longer find the strength to push Truett away.

I can't move, I can't fight, and I can't scream.

So, I pray.

# FORTY

## ADAM

S he's taking too long.
As my brother drones on and on about his latest course load, I can't focus. I'm still staring into the dark night, waiting for Sage to round the corner with a smile.

Caleb mentioned he saw our dad heading toward the valet at the front, but I'm too nervous to believe it.

The very thought of him finding her chills me to the bone. He wouldn't hurt her, would he? He may be a liar and a hypocrite, but is he really a monster?

"Where's your date?" my brother asks, taking another sip of his drink.

"She's in the bathroom," I reply. "But she's been in there a while. I should go see what's taking her so long."

"While you're back there, check on your father," my mother calls from beside my brother. "He said he was going too, and I'm ready to get home."

I'm frozen, staring at her in confusion. I assumed my father went home without my mother and she would get the driver to come back for her, but knowing he's still here, possibly threatening or bullying Sage, *my* Sage has my blood as cold as ice.

Without warning, I take off in a run toward the place where I just left her. My mother calls after me, the entire group of them probably alarmed to see me sprinting in such a panic for no reason.

I know she's fine. It's ridiculous to think he would actually hurt her, but I've been fooled by that man before, and every ounce of instinct inside me is telling me that she needs me.

As I turn the corner behind the main building, noticing movement on the ground in the distance, I stop. It takes my eyes a moment to adjust, and when they do, all I see is red.

My father is hovering over her, his hands around her throat and her hands weakly fighting against his grip.

Everything starts to blur, and it's like something in me snaps. It's the same feeling I had the night I attacked Brett.

All of the good inside me turns black, and in its place is only rage.

I don't register charging toward him, and I don't recall dragging him off of her. The only thing I know is I'm holding him by the collar, a drunken mess of a man sobbing for forgiveness as I hold my fisted hand in the air, ready to *kill* him.

"You're...a monster," I growl, my nostrils flared and my mind sick with madness. I imagine myself watching him die, bleeding out on the concrete path. I picture it with gross satisfaction.

"I'm sorry," he cries. "I'm sorry, Adam."

My fist shakes, ready to strike again.

I remember how good it felt to hit Brett. How I promised her I'd make anyone who hurt her pay, and it's an easy bargain to make. No longer worried about my soul, I'm free to inflict my vengeance with pleasure.

"I lost control," he sobs, drunk and hysterical. "I didn't mean to hurt her."

His hands are held in front of his face to defend himself from my fist, but if I kill him right here, what does that make me? Vindicated?

If he is a monster, and it's his blood running through my veins, then what does that make me? I'm not better than him. The best I can do for her now is to rid her world of this vile man and seal my fate. She's worth it. I'd gladly burn in hell for her, so going to prison is a simple sacrifice.

To be the hero in her story, I would.

My fist shakes in anticipation, and I'm ready to break it all over again, this time on his face.

But then I hear a sound that pulls me from the twisted ramblings of my mind.

She coughs. It's a painful, desperate, wheezing sound that makes me pause.

Turning my head, I see her rolling to her stomach, coughing desperately into the ground as she gasps for air.

I drop my howling father onto the ground, relax my fist, and rush to her side.

"Adam," she says, but her voice sounds shattered into a million pieces.

"I'm here," I reply, scooping her from the ground and holding her in my arms. Her hands clench my suit tight in her fists as she continues to fight for each breath, letting out a painful-sounding cough every time she does. Her throat is already swollen, and I'm starting to panic.

When I take off with her toward the crowd, I look up to find my mother standing under the white lights, watching this unfold with horror. Her hand is resting over her mouth and I send her an expression of anguish.

"Call 9-1-1," I cry out. "Please."

She scrambles for the phone in her purse, quickly pulling it out and dialing the number as I rush toward her, carrying Sage in my arms. When my eyes meet my mother's, she starts crying hysterically into the phone, giving the person on the other end everything they need to know.

Her hand reaches out, taking Sage's as she calls for help.

Soon, my brothers and others from the party are there, but I don't focus on them. I'm only staring down at Sage, watching her struggle for each breath, tears streaming down her face as I carry her toward the road where the ambulance will meet us.

Behind me, I hear my father cry out for his wife and his sons, but no one goes to help him.

By the time I reach the road, where the valet driver let us out of my car, the red and white lights of the ambulance flash through the sky. Sage stares up into my eyes, each of her inhales sounding more and more like wheezes than breaths. Her lips are an unnatural shade of blue, and I just stare at her and pray.

*Please let her be okay. Please don't take her from me.*

What if he crushed her throat so bad it swells on the way to the hospital and I lose her?

It would be all my fault. I let that man roam free because I was too scared to reveal what a devil he truly is. I let her die because I'm a coward. Because I showed up too late. Because I left her alone in the first place.

Her face twists in pain and I pray to God to take it from her and give it to me.

"I'm so sorry," I whisper, kissing her head. The ambulance parks on the curb and the paramedics jump out, but at the last moment, just before they take her from my aching arms, I press my lips to her ear. "I love you."

Then, my arms are empty and they're strapping an oxygen mask on her face, taking her vitals. I stand helpless on the curb as they treat her on the stretcher in the back of the ambulance. I'm hit with earth-shattering satisfaction as her chest starts moving with the intake of her breath.

I keep my eyes on her for as long as I can. Distantly, I feel a warm hand clutching my arm, and when they finally slam the doors closed, it's like a punch to my heart.

And suddenly, I feel all the pain I expected to feel from being in love. The fear of losing her. The regret of letting her down. The guilt of knowing she's in pain because of me.

So, as the ambulance drives away and the police pull up, I make a silent promise to myself and to her. If I'm given the chance to make this right, I'm going to take it.

Starting now.

# FORTY-ONE

## ADAM

"Adam, stop," my mother calls after me as I spin away from the road and march back to where I left my mess of a father on the ground.

Caleb's hand winds around my arm first, but I simply give him a severe expression and he loosens his grip. Somewhere in the distance, the party continues, but I'm too focused on *killing* the man who hurt Sage before the police arrive and take him away.

"You know what he's done. You know he deserves this," I mutter through my teeth.

"What are you talking about?" Luke asks as he catches up to us. I continue my walk toward the grassy area where I found him with Sage. My mother trails behind us, still hysterical.

I can't answer my brother's question. Not yet.

When I see my father struggling to his feet in the distance, I move with purpose.

"Adam!" my mother shrieks behind me, but it's all muddled now. Rushing toward him, I wrap my hand around his throat and slam him against the brick wall of the building. He fights me, but he's too drunk and too weak.

When I feel my brothers ambush me on either side, I can sense their hesitation. They're trying to push me away from him, to keep me from hurting him. Behind me, I hear my mother sobbing.

And I realize, now is the time. I waited too long already, and while it would feel *really* fucking good to hurt him with my fists, serving him the justice he deserves is going to feel even better.

Releasing my grip on his neck, I take a step away from him. With a scornful glare, I meet his eyes with mine.

"Hold him," I mutter to my brothers. The look of fear and surprise on my father's face is gratifying.

"What?" Lucas replies.

"I said hold him," I bark at my younger brother.

Caleb moves first, snatching our father by the arm and holding him in place. Then Lucas follows his lead.

"Boys, stop it!" Mom shrieks.

"How does that feel?" I ask him, my voice low. Sirens blare in the distance and I know I'm running out of time. I want him to be here when I expose him. I want him to watch as I ruin his life with his own lies.

"Son, don't do this," he pleads, and I'm not sure if he means punch him or tell them everything. But as his terror-filled eyes glance toward the red and blue flashing lights in the distance, relief washes over me. He's about to pay for what he's done.

"I found out everything he's told us is a lie," I announce to my family. "He holds the deed to the very sex club he's been claiming to take down since we were kids. I caught him there."

"What?" Lucas mumbles, staring at the old man fighting against his hold.

"He's been cheating on Mom. He broke my nose when I found him."

My mother cries louder behind me.

"This is who he really is. A fraud."

Surrendering, he stops struggling, and he stares at me with remorse. My brothers loosen their hold of him, but he doesn't

THE ANTI-HERO                              299

run. A moment later, the police are there, and when they ask for the man responsible for the attack tonight, each member of my family points to him.

I thought it would feel better seeing my father taken away in cuffs. I wanted the satisfaction of knowing that he was finally paying the price for his sins, but not like this.

Not at Sage's expense.

As the police haul him away, the vineyard is quiet. I turn toward my mother to find Caleb and Lucas already by her side, consoling her as she cries into her hands.

I feel so lost. I know I should get in my car as fast as I can and rush over to the hospital to see Sage, but at the same time, something is stopping me. Why would I go? To inject myself even further into her life, so she can get hurt again? Haven't I caused her enough pain?

I've never felt more worthless in my entire life.

Walking over to my mother, I touch her shoulder. "I'm so sorry about your ceremony, Mom."

"I don't give a shit about the ceremony," she snaps, lifting her head. "That poor girl." On the last word, her voice shakes and she cries some more. "She must have been so scared."

My throat tightens, stinging with emotion as I listen to my mother cry for the woman I love.

"This is all my fault," I say, feeling the weight of my family's eyes on my face as I begin what I know is about to be the impossible confession.

"Oh, Adam," she murmurs, her fingers hovering over her lips.

"The entire charade was for him. The sex tapes. Showing up with Sage. I just wanted to ruin his reputation, but I never wanted anyone to get hurt. And I never expected to fall in love."

My mother lifts her head in surprise. "You used her?"

That guts me. How can I explain? I feel my image deteriorating in my mother's eyes, and it no longer matters what anyone thinks about me when I realize that my own mom thinks I'm an asshole.

"Yes," I mutter, a tear slipping down my cheek. I quickly wipe it away. I don't feel worthy of these tears at the moment.

"Then nothing with her was real? Adam, how could you do this?"

"Everything with her was real," I whisper, barely able to get the words out. The heavy truth in them feels like blades, cutting me as I speak them. "I love her more than anything."

"Then what are you doing here? Who gives a shit about your father or the club or his lies?"

I don't move, staring at her and forcing myself to swallow. "I don't deserve her."

My mother steps toward me. Then she places her hands on my face and I stare into her tear-soaked eyes, makeup running down her cheeks. "You're not like him. You saved that girl's life. You're not the kind of man to leave a hurting woman alone in the hospital. I saw the way you wanted to hurt him. I saw how much you struggled with that anger, but you didn't, Adam. You're a good man, and even good men make mistakes. The important thing is that you make it right when given the chance."

Another tear slips out as I let her words settle over me. "Thank you," I mumble. Then my mother's arms wrap around my neck, pulling me into a tight hug.

Suddenly all I can think about is Sage alone in the hospital. Scared, lonely, waiting for me. And a new sense of urgency washes over me.

✝

The nurse leads me down the hall of the hospital, stopping at the last room on the right. As she opens the door, and I see Sage sitting on the bed, thick gauze wrapped around her neck, I brush past the nurse and run to her side. Sage's face contorts in a sob when she sees me, latching her arms around my neck when I reach her.

"I'm so sorry," I whisper into her ear. Brushing my fingers through her hair, I breathe in the relief that she's okay. And I try not to think too long about how close we got to what could have happened.

They'd be hauling us both off in cuffs if she didn't make it—if he had killed her like he was so clearly trying to do.

"I'm sorry it took me so long to get here," I say, sitting on the side of the bed to hold her close. "And I'm so sorry he hurt you."

When she doesn't respond, I pull away and stare into her eyes. She points to her throat and mouths, *I can't speak.*

"Ever?" I reply in a panic.

She smiles and shakes her head. Then she points to the pad of paper and pen on the table next to the bed. She's clearly been using this to communicate with her nurses because it's already scribbled with the words *thirsty* and *Adam Goode.*

She wanted me.

My fingers stroke her arm as she rips the top paper, tossing it to the side before writing something on the fresh one underneath.

*It hurts too much when I try to speak. No surgery though.*

She forces a tight smile and holds up her thumb at the *good news.*

I'm both relieved and sick with guilt. My father did this to her. He nearly killed her, but it's so hard to feel blessed when I know it's my fault this happened in the first place.

"I hate this," I mutter, brushing her hair from her face. Seeing her in this hospital bed, in pain. It kills me. "I'm so sorry, Peaches."

Her brows furrow inward. "You saved me," she mouths, her voice nothing but air.

"If it wasn't for me, you wouldn't have been there in the first place."

Shaking her head, she looks dissatisfied with that argument. "Stop," she whispers, holding her hand out. Then she scribbles on the pad again, and my heart breaks at the words she shows me.

*You were there.*

Then she scribbles below them.

*I love you.*

When she glances back up at me, her eyes are moist with tears, so I pull her mouth to mine for a tender kiss, careful not to hurt her. Shifting over on the bed, she pats the space next to her for me to sit.

I stretch out in the empty space and pull her into my arms, kissing the top of her head and stroking her arm with affection. For a while, we lie there in silence, mostly because there isn't much to say that would outweigh the severity of this moment. But also because Sage can't talk and I don't have anything worth saying.

Eventually I'll tell Sage how I came clean to my family. And how my father cried while the police cuffed him. But for now, the moment belongs to us. And there's nothing fake about it.

It was never fake to me.

I don't even remember drifting off, but sometime later, the nurses come in to check on Sage. When she complains about the pain, they offer her something in her IV, and I pressure her to take it. I notice how gentle they are with her, careful and nurturing in their treatment.

It's another few minutes before the doctor comes in. He tells us that she should be cleared to go home in the morning as long as they can keep the swelling down. When he mentions having to scope her again, Sage grimaces, and I pray that that's not the case. Then I'm assaulted with shame for not being here the first time she had to endure that.

I step out into the hall for a moment to make some calls. First, my mother to assure her that Sage is stable and should be able to go home tomorrow. Then, I call Gladys. It hurts to make the call, but I know she's the closest thing Sage has to a mother, and she deserves to know that someone she loves is in the hospital. Telling her that it was my father makes me feel like the lowest piece of scum on the earth.

"That sonofabitch," Gladys barks into the phone. Her voice is laced with anger and pain when I break the news, but it feels strangely nice to know someone cares about Sage so much. That Sage is never truly alone, even if her own mother isn't there for her.

"If you could keep Roscoe tonight, we'll hopefully be home in the morning."

"They're gonna let you stay all night?" she asks with hope in her voice.

"They're going to have a hell of a time trying to get me to leave," I reply with a dry laugh.

"Give 'em hell."

"Thanks, Gladys. I'll keep you posted."

"Thank you, baby. And, Adam..." she says.

"Yeah?" I reply.

"You're lucky to have each other."

Truer words have never been spoken, I think as I stare into the hospital room at Sage on the bed.

"I agree. Night, Gladys."

After I hang up the phone, I drop it on the table next to the bed. Then I climb back in next to her, kissing the top of her head.

She's already written a message on the paper, so she holds it up for me to see.

*Discharge tomorrow around 3.*

I nod at the message, looking down at her and noticing the expression of concern etched into her features. She puts the pen back to the paper and writes out the rest.

*Will you be there?*

My breath comes out of my chest in a heavy exhale. Remembering that night in the church, we shared our biggest dreams with each other, feeling then as if a future was impossible together. The idea that we would just *be there* was such a lofty wish, but now it feels so trivial. There's not a single thing on this earth that could keep me from *being there*. Truly nothing else matters more than this, than her.

So I grab the pad of paper from her hands and I toss it on the table. Then I wrap her up in my arms, and I press my lips to her forehead.

"I'm not going anywhere, Peaches. I'll be there. For as long as you want."

Then she wraps her arms around my midsection and burrows herself against my chest. We lie like that for a while until exhaustion takes us and we fall asleep together.

# AUGUST
## THE BOYFRIEND

# FORTY-TWO

SAGE

"Biscuits and—"

Adam holds up his hand. "Stop it. You're supposed to be resting your voice." Then he looks up at the waitress. "She'll have biscuits and gravy with a side of eggs, please. Scrambled. And I think we'll need another ketchup bottle. This one is empty."

I smile at him, holding the coffee cup tight in my hands to warm my fingers.

"Thank you," I whisper.

I've been out of the hospital for four days now, and my voice has almost completely come back, except for a slight rasp, which makes me sound like a chain-smoker, but other than that, I'm fine. Still, he's doting on me. And I know it's just his way of making up for what happened.

If only I could make him understand that it isn't just the damage to my throat that I need to worry about. Every time I close my eyes, I see Truett's hate-filled sneer as he presses his weight into my neck. He wanted me dead, and that's not something you just get over with some pain meds and a night in the hospital.

I think more than anything, it's the *why* he wanted me dead that won't stop harassing my ego. I didn't pose a threat to him. I didn't hurt him or take anything from him. I was a problem to him because of who I am, and that's the thought that keeps me awake at night. He wanted me dead because his son loves me.

Never in my life have I ever felt the need to apologize for who I am. Being on my own at seventeen, I was like a kid in a candy shop. I had the freedom to be as wild and free as I wanted with the added responsibility of also keeping myself alive with a roof over my head.

I lived for me by my rules and never with anyone else in mind. But what about now?

My eyes settle on another couple across from us at the diner. Everything about them appears compatible, from their matching black shirts to their matching egg-white omelets.

Adam reaches across the table, touching my fingers. I turn my attention toward him.

"I'm thinking about dying my hair," I whisper, touching my pink strands.

He looks immediately affronted. "What? Why?"

I shrug. "I don't know. Maybe I'm getting too old for pink hair."

The worried line between his brows grows even deeper. "How many painkillers did you take this morning?"

I roll my eyes before holding up an *O* shape with my fingers.

"Then, don't be ridiculous," he replies, taking a drink of his coffee. "You're twenty-seven. You could be sixty-seven and it still wouldn't matter."

I try to let his words of encouragement settle in, but all I keep thinking about is his promise in the hospital to be there for me for everything. And I wonder if any of that fantasy talk at the church still applies. What if I worked at a sex club? What if he had his own church? Would my lifestyle ruin his? Or the other way around?

I love him, but do I love him enough to change for him?

Does he love me enough to change for me?

As he sets down his coffee cup, I can practically feel the concern radiating from him as he stares at me.

"Peaches, look at me."

Leaning back in my booth, I gaze across the table at him.

When he sees tears well up in my eyes, his jaw clenches and his nostrils flare. It's still so incredible to me to be with another person whose emotions are so easily affected by my own. When I cry, he hurts. When I'm happy, he smiles.

It's romantic but also...overwhelming. I've never been so responsible for another person's state of mind before.

"One day at a time," he says, touching my hand again. And I let those words calm me. Silencing the thoughts of the future or of the past, I try to just focus on his presence here right now.

When his phone rings, he doesn't even budge. His eyes are on me.

"Answer it," I whisper, glancing at the screen to see his mother's face.

Reluctantly, he picks up the phone and I hear Melanie's voice on the other end after he swipes to answer the call.

The press has been all over her since Truett's arrest. The minute the news went public, Adam had security increased at their residence and canceled service at the church on Sunday, the day after the attack.

People are angry, confused, and want answers. I hate that so much has fallen on Adam's shoulders, even though he claims to be taking it all in stride. He said there are some other guys at the church whose job entails cleaning up after Truett's mess, but he still has his mother to worry about.

"Yeah, she's feeling better," he says to his mother, his eyes on me.

I smile when I think about how compassionate she's been through all of this. She visited me in the hospital before I was discharged, and she's been sending food to my apartment every day since.

One of Truett's employees posted his bail less than two days after the attack, but as far as we know, he's been staying in a hotel somewhere since. I don't know the details of what happened between him and Melanie, but from what Adam said, she wouldn't let him back in the house.

In my head, I picture her standing by that front door, shotgun in hand, defending her home and forcing him away. While I'm not exactly sure that's how it went down, I love the image.

When Adam's face takes on an expression of worry, I lean forward.

"What's going on?" I mouth.

"He does?" Adam asks his mother.

"Who?" I whisper.

"I'm not ready," he replies.

I bounce anxiously as I wait for him to finish the conversation so he can catch me up on what they're talking about.

Finally, he tells his mother he loves her and hangs up the call. I'm staring at him with anticipation before he finally takes a deep breath. The worry line is still positioned in the middle of his forehead, which means whatever this is, it isn't good.

"He wants to meet with me."

"Who?" I ask.

"Who do you think?" he replies. "My dad."

"Fuck that," I rasp, and Adam gives me a scornful expression for trying to speak.

"I'm not ready," he says, chewing his bottom lip. "I'm just... afraid of what I might do if I see him."

This time it's my turn to reach across the table to touch his hand. "You're not a bad guy for wanting to kick his ass," I whisper. "Good people sometimes do bad things for the people they love. Bad people do bad things for themselves."

The corners of his lips lift in a crooked grin. With those stunning, kind eyes and laugh lines framing his mouth, I admire him for a beat, realizing just how perfect this man is. So I squeeze his fingers with my own.

"I wonder why he wants to talk to me," he says.

"To apologize?" I ask.

Rolling his eyes, he lets out a scoff. "Very funny."

"I don't like it," I reply, to which Adam nods.

"Neither do I."

We're still holding hands and staring at each other across the table when the hostess seats a couple at the booth across the aisle from us. Within seconds, I feel their curious stares on us, but I only glance their way briefly.

I don't know if they recognize us from the videos or Adam's latest family scandal, but either way, it's exhausting. And it feels like being draped in shame I don't deserve, like there's some sort of scarlet letter on my chest.

"I want to go home," I whisper.

Adam quickly waves down the waitress, asking her to box up our breakfast, then pays the bill. A few moments later, we're heading out of the restaurant, bags of food in hand and Adam's arm draped protectively across my shoulders.

It's a short walk to the apartment, but we're quiet the whole way.

And quiet still as we eat our cold food at the linoleum table in my tiny apartment. I don't get much down and by the time my stomach starts to turn, the food lands heavily in my gut, the sky has turned gray and rain pelts the large window in my living room.

I point to the bedroom and toss my uneaten food in the garbage. Without another word, I crawl under the heavy duvet in my room and beg my mind to quiet so I can sleep.

Just as recurring images of that monster with his hands around my windpipe start to play across the insides of my eyelids, I feel the bed dip with Adam's weight. He settles himself behind me, wrapping an arm around me as he holds me close, his lips in my hair.

"I'm here," he whispers, and my hands tighten around his forearm.

It sounds silly, but it makes me feel safer. Not that Adam can scare away my nightmares, but with his firm embrace, I'm able to drift off to sleep with ease.

# FORTY-THREE

## ADAM

I'm helpless. My mother told me a good man makes it right, but I have no clue how to do that. If holding her and being there for her is enough, it doesn't feel like it. Sage is in pain, and it's all my fault.

I was a fool to assume it would pass when her throat healed.

It's been three weeks since the attack, and she's lost the glow she had the day I met her. There is no more bounce in her step and the sparkle in her eyes has dimmed—and there's nothing I can do for her.

I just keep waiting for her to wake up feeling *better,* but no amount of rest seems to help. In fact, some days, she hardly gets up at all.

I've prayed just as much as I've cursed God. I'm desperate *and* angry. Out of all the people in the world to be hurt, why her?

As I pull up to my mother's house, I'm pleased to see the extra security still in place. The media has died down. There are no longer hordes of cameras and reporters stationed around the gate of their house. My father, as far as we know, has secured himself a short-term living situation, and according to the judge at Austin

Municipal Court, he has been ordered to stay at least one thousand feet away from this residence and Sage's for the foreseeable future.

I should be relieved.

But I've never felt more unsettled.

My mom is standing by the side door, her hands on her hips and flour on her apron as she waits for me. When she notices that I'm alone, her mouth sets in a thin, worried line. I pull the bouquet of flowers and the bottle of wine from the passenger seat and pass them to my mother as she pecks me on the cheek.

The good Christian woman she is, my mother never drinks much. Well, never *drank* much. She's made an exception as of late, a decision I fully support.

I'm early for Sunday dinner, but I'm here mostly because I just need to talk.

"How is she?" are the first words out of her mouth.

"No change," I reply, hating that answer.

"Did you call the counselor Luke suggested?"

"She saw her two days ago," I reply, stepping into the kitchen.

"And? Nothing?"

I shrug. Everything feels so uncertain. I know Sage is suffering from the trauma of what happened, and I can't help but feel as if there's more to it. More she's not telling me. More worrying her and more threatening to tear us apart. And it kills me that I could be losing her without even knowing it.

The wine bottle pops as my mother pulls the corkscrew from the top. Then she pours two glasses and hands one to me. Together we walk to the front porch of the house. It's a beautiful late summer evening, and here in Texas, that means it's still humid enough to choke on the air but cool enough to withstand it.

We each take a seat, but I'm too upset to relax. So after a long drink of the dry red Cabernet, I hold it in my hand while leaning forward, my unkempt hair hanging over my eyes. Everything in my life feels *unkempt* at the moment.

"She's healing, Adam. And healing takes time."

"What if she's not healing?" I ask. "What if...my presence is keeping her from getting better?"

With a tsk, she shakes her head. "I was afraid you were thinking that."

"I mean...it was my father who did this to her. Does she think of him when she looks at me?"

When my mother remains silent, her thin lips pressed into an apologetic expression, I know the answer. And it's not what I want to hear.

*I* could be the reason Sage isn't getting better. Or at least healing slowly. As much as she says she's not mad at me and she loves me and wants me with her, resentment buries itself deep. There's a good chance Sage doesn't even know it's there, slowly poisoning her until, eventually, she'll break.

"What do I do? Leave her?"

"I think patience is the only thing that's going to work right now, Adam."

I love that my mother's knee-jerk reaction to this isn't God or prayers or grace. I love that her faith can take a back seat to logic when needed.

But I still don't love the answer, *patience*. Because every minute I spend waiting is a minute I spend worrying. And if I wait too long, I'm afraid it will be too late.

The last time I saw someone so shattered in grief and pain was my mother...the day we realized Isaac wasn't coming back. It feels impossible to even bring it up, but the last time I thought something was impossible to talk about, it ended in Sage getting hurt. I'm not shying away from the impossible anymore.

"Mom..." I say, delicately approaching the topic. She sets down her wineglass and stares at me expectantly. Bringing up my brother feels like I'm hurting my mother intentionally, but I have to do it. "When Isaac...ran away. How long did it take you to recover?"

A slow, sad smile pulls across her face as tears gather in her eyes. "Honey, I never really recovered," she replies. "Not from him leaving. Not from the way your father treated him."

"Then why did you stay with him?" My voice cracks as I ask the question that feels like an assault.

As a tear slips over the pink blush of her cheek, she shrugs. "I was scared. And I have been so codependent on your father that I don't know how to decide anything on my own."

"I'm so sorry," I reply, blinking salt trails over my own face as I stare in anguish at my mother and all of the pain I've caused her. "I should have been better. I should have helped you or him. I just...wanted to be a good son."

"You *are* a good son, Adam."

"To him," I reply in agony. "I could have protected Isaac. I should have stood up for him. Offered him a safe place to stay or told him that I loved him. But I just...kept quiet. You lost Isaac because of me."

I'm sobbing now, my hand soaked with my tears as I cover my face. When I feel her comforting touch on my shoulder, I force myself to look up.

"Adam, honey. I never lost him."

When I swallow, it feels like needles in my throat. I wipe my face again, staring at her in confusion because it doesn't make sense. Of course, she lost him. She's only saying this to spare my feelings.

"No, Mom..." I reply with a shake of my head. "Isaac's gone."

"No, he's not, Adam. I know...where Isaac is."

I pause, frozen as I search her eyes for answers. "What?"

"I talk to your brother nearly every day."

The muscles in my body clench with anxiety as I work to piece together what she's telling me. "You...talk to Isaac?"

Tearfully, she nods.

All these years, I had nothing but hope that my brother was still alive. Gone without a trace, he stayed frozen in time at seventeen, but now I'm racking my brain trying to imagine a twenty-five-year-old man existing somewhere just out of my reach.

"Why didn't you tell me?" I ask in desperation.

Again, her lips tighten and her brows lift. Then she strokes my hand like she's delivering bad news. Then it hits me.

"You were protecting him," I say with another cracked sob.

She doesn't have to nod for me to know. My mother was protecting my brother...from me. Because I am my father's son. Because I was so focused on being *like* him when that's the last fucking thing I should have ever wanted to be.

I burst out of my chair, dragging my hands through my hair with a feeling of panic. What the fuck is wrong with me? This whole time I thought I was ruining my reputation by rebelling against that man, but this whole time...I was *worse* when I was trying to emulate him.

It was never about the videos or the club or Sage. I never used her to get back at him. I used her...to get *away* from him. She was my lifeline. The lifeboat carrying me from the storm.

I've had it wrong this entire time.

The only *bad* thing I've ever done was try to be the next Truett Goode.

"Are you okay, honey?" my mother asks as she approaches me from behind, placing her hands on my back.

"Yeah," I reply, nodding my head. "I just...realized something."

"Adam, listen to me." With her hands on my arms, she spins me until I'm facing her. Then with her hands on my cheeks, she forces me to look into her eyes. "You're not like him, baby. You are a good man and a good son. It's okay if you were lost or if your faith in one man led you astray. I taught my boys to think for themselves, but I was afraid he already had his claws in you."

It's like being punched in the heart, having my eyes opened for the first time in my life. Seeing my family for the people they are.

Touching her wrists, I realize what it is I desperately need to know about my mother.

"Did you...know?" I ask, searching her eyes for answers.

Her features fall, guilt written across her face. "Yes. I knew about your father."

"Jesus," I reply, turning away from her. Snatching the half-full glass of wine off the table, I guzzle it down without stopping. It's not strong enough.

Turning my back to my mother and this little nugget of information I'm not quite ready to face, I head into the house and march straight up the stairs. She calls after me, but I don't stop. Even when I reach the closed French doors of his office, I tear them open and walk directly to the bottle of whiskey he keeps in the small bar in the corner.

Hands shaking, I pour myself a glass. After tossing the stopper on the floor, I throw the shot back with a wince.

Once I feel the alcohol burn my throat and warm my bloodstream, I think about the bombshells my mother has dropped at my feet.

*She knows where Isaac is.*

*She's protecting him from me.*

*She knew about my father's cheating ways the entire time.*

Was I the only one in the dark? Did I have my head so far up that man's ass that I couldn't see what was right in front of me? What would have become of me if none of this would have happened?

I would have been the next Truett Goode. Liar, hypocrite, cheater, homophobic, abusing, murdering monstrous piece of shit.

"No," I mutter to myself as I pour another shot. "No."

It burns its way down like the first one.

Before I know what's happening, I'm on the floor, my back to the wall as I sob with my head hanging between my knees.

That's not me. I never lied and I wouldn't in a million years have treated my family the way he did. I'd sooner chop my own hand off before I'd lay it on my child or a woman as innocent and perfect as my Peaches.

Thirty-seven years I devoted to that man and what do I have to show for it?

When my tears have dried and my sadness has melted into anger, I stand from the floor and walk over to his desk. Staring at the empty chair where he once sat, I think of all the things I'd like to say to him now.

Three weeks ago, he asked my mother to send me a message asking for a meeting with me. And I don't know if it's the alcohol or not, but I'm suddenly feeling ready for that conversation. But I want to go in prepared.

Making a mess of his desk, I shuffle papers from the various piles before I find the document I want.

Holding the deed between my fingers, I pull out my phone. After dialing his number, I hold it to my ear and wait while it rings.

His voice sounds weak and tired on the other side. "Adam?"

"You want to talk, motherfucker? Let's fucking talk."

# FORTY-FOUR

ADAM

My hand is clenched around the manila envelope. I've already left a fist-size indentation along the edge from clutching it too tight. With every floor the elevator passes, the tremble in my bones gets worse.

I'm about to be alone with him, and I can't seem to get the image of him with his hands wrapped around Sage's neck out of my mind.

My moral compass isn't just skewed. It's dead. The needle no longer points north. I'm not sure where it's pointing at the moment because the temptation to walk into that hotel room and end his miserable existence calls to me like a gross, violent seduction.

As the elevator chimes, I pick my head up and face forward.

Where there would normally be an entourage of assistants and security guards, there is no one. Just an empty hallway in a four-star hotel, where my father is currently hiding.

As I approach his door, I take a deep breath and look back at the papers in my hand. There aren't many in this folder, and really only one that matters. I'm not sure how I'm going to go about this, whether it be blackmail, begging, or violence, but I know which one sounds more satisfying. I also don't know what state he'll be in when I go in there. Will he be the smug, pompous, ego-inflated asshole who I sat across from four months ago?

Or will he be humbled?

I'm not sure which one I want.

It'll be a lot harder to kick his ass if he's desperate and apologetic, but not impossible.

So I guess there's only one way to find out. My knuckles rap on the door. Then I hear his footsteps heavy on the hotel carpet before the dead bolt clicks as he unlocks it. A moment later, he opens it, and then...there he is.

Standing in dirty clothes, wreaking of whiskey, gaunt and exhausted in a presidential suite...alone.

As his eyes bore into mine, I feel like I'm sharing eye contact with my real dad for the first time in my life. He's not a god or an idol, or a hero. He's just a simple man who cares about no one but himself.

With surrender in his eyes, he backs up and opens the doorway, allowing me to enter.

"Come in," he mutters with a tired-sounding rasp in his voice.

I step in with hesitation, looking around to get a sense of the scene. I'm not sure which of us is feeling more vulnerable at the moment, but I'll be damned if I'm going to let my guard down around him now.

"Where's Mark?" I ask in a cruel, sarcastic tone as I stand next to the desk against the wall. Unlike the one in his office, this desk is empty. His work is gone.

He huffs. "They think it's best if another pastor steps in for the time being. To protect the ministry's name."

A slow, dark chuckle creeps up my chest, and soon it's a full laugh, sinister and satisfying.

"I'm glad you think this is so funny," he says as he drops onto the maroon-colored sofa. As he props his feet up on the coffee table, I enjoy watching karma at work.

"Sit down," he says in a fatherly tone, and my eyes narrow at him. I don't move an inch toward the chair facing him.

"I'm here on *my* business, not yours. If you think for one fucking second I'm going to just listen to you the way I did before, you're wrong. You nearly killed the love of my life, and I will hate you for that until the day I die."

He scoffs with a smug, bitter expression. "The love of your life? Give me a break, Adam. Just because you found a good piece of ass—"

"Stop it!" I bellow, slamming my fist down hard on the desk. Emotion bubbles its way up to the surface, and I'm done holding it back. Everything this man has done to my family in the course of my life has pushed me to this point.

"Why can't you just be my father? Why did you have children if you never had the desire to love anyone but yourself? Instead of pretending to be a good man...why couldn't you just fucking *be* a good man?"

He stares at me without emotion, and, to be honest, I don't know if he has any. Maybe that's why he can stomp all over the people he's supposed to love. He feels nothing.

I toss the envelope on the table in front of him and drop into the chair, feeling defeated. I came here trying to get through to him, but it's clear I never will. The closure I want doesn't exist.

"You couldn't possibly understand how much I love Sage," I say, the boom and anger in my voice dissolved. Then I look up at him. "The love of your life is your fame and success. It's not God or faith or Mom or any of us. It certainly isn't the twins and it sure as fuck isn't Isaac."

His jaw clenches and he looks away from me at the mention of my baby brother.

"But I'll be honest. I thought for a moment it was me." I hate how desperate I sound. Sad and broken, like a puppy that's been kicked by its owner too many times. "And I lived to be your favorite. It's all I wanted in life. In turn, everyone I care about got hurt. So I'm done."

I let out a long sigh of relief. It feels like the chains have been broken, and for the first time in my life, I'm truly free.

"So what do you want then?" he asks, like not a single word I just said matters.

I laugh to myself before flipping open the envelope and shoving the deed toward him. "Sign it over to Sage. It's the least you can do for her. After what you've done."

He stares at the paper for a moment, but he doesn't move toward it. I wait in anticipation. The sooner he signs the paperwork I've had drawn up, the sooner I can get the fuck out of here.

When he lifts his eyes to my face, my blood turns cold.

"No," he mumbles, and I grow immediately frustrated.

"What do you mean, no? What the hell do you need with it now?"

"Adam, it does me no good to sign over a sex club to my son's girlfriend."

"Your reputation is already in fucking shambles. What difference does it make?" I yell.

"Listen," he says through tight lips. "I'm going to prison, probably for at least five to ten years. I don't want to see everything I've built run into the ground while I'm gone."

My mouth is hanging open as I stare at him. "And?"

"And I need you."

"Fuck you," I reply with a laugh. "You expect me to help you? Have you lost your fucking mind?"

"I want you to take the church, Adam. Take my place. Head the ministry and turn it all around before those assholes give it to someone else. I want it to stay in our name. The people still love you, son. It's not too late to turn your reputation around."

I barely even notice when he stops talking. I'm just staring at him as I realize he's finally saying the words I prayed for him to say every day of my adult life.

In my mind, I picture myself up there. At the pulpit, in front of the crowd, writing my own sermons, and hearing my voice boom through the mic as I deliver them. I see it all.

This is everything I ever wanted.

*My* way.

He's handing me the keys to the kingdom, and I'm still too stunned to even move.

Then, my eyes trail down to the open folder on the table, the deed to the club sitting there. And it all clicks into place. Everything makes sense now...and yet, nothing makes sense at the same time.

I fall back in the seat and stare up at the ceiling, and I laugh.

Because it's all so fucking hilarious at this point. And I can't stop. The chuckle turns into a mad howling and I sound downright maniacal.

"Get yourself together," he says as my cackles continue.

"It's so fucking ironic," I say through my laughter. "You can't sign the sex club over to her and the church over to me at the same time. How fucking stupid is that?"

He furrows his brow at me. "You think you can marry her? People will forget about those sex tapes you made if you come clean and ask for forgiveness, but if that club is in her name, your future as a pastor is gone. They will never accept you, Adam, and you know it."

"I don't give a shit. I just don't care because I don't want it. Not the church or the fame or the work or anything that might put me at risk of turning into you. I don't want it."

I stand from the chair and start to pace the room. I feel renewed. Turning down everything I've ever wanted is terrifying, but I feel as if I've done the first *right* thing in my life, and I'm suddenly high on it.

So I turn back toward him, pointing a finger. "And I think you're wrong. I think a lot of people would accept us. You taught me since I was a kid that that place was evil and wrong, but all you did was instill fear and ignorance. Now I truly understand. Sex and God coexist. You can have...both. You can be both."

His unfocused gaze is settled somewhere across the room as I speak, and I suddenly realize I don't want to be here anymore. He doesn't listen and he doesn't care, so there's no point.

I'll buy Sage a new club. I'll give her the world, whatever she wants. And we can finally move on without either of them, Brett or my dad.

My hand is on the door as he finally speaks.

"I'll sign it right now, and you can give her everything she's ever wanted..."

I'm frozen in place as his words hover over me like a dark cloud. There's a very obvious *if* missing from his statement, and I wait to hear it. The rustling of papers draws my attention, and when I finally turn around, he's holding a pen. Looking at me with an expression of expectation, he waits for my answer.

*Lead us not into temptation, but deliver us from evil.*

I'm not a fool. I know he's not giving me something for nothing.

But when the listless eyes of the woman I love flash through my mind, I realize he's right. I could give her everything she's ever wanted. And that temptation is the greatest I've ever faced.

# FORTY-FIVE

## SAGE

The front door of the apartment closes and Roscoe jumps from the bed to greet Adam. I keep my eyes closed on the bed so he thinks I'm asleep, and I feel like shit for it.

I can't take another moment of his guilt-ridden expression, wishing me better. His comfort and care are all just reminders that I'm not who I'm supposed to be. I'm not the shiny, smiling, happy girl I was when he met me.

My roots are showing because I need to dye my hair. My makeup has sat untouched for weeks. And my clothes have been in a constant cycle between floor to bed and back again. For a girl that lives above a Laundromat, it's sad how little I've been washing them lately.

But the one thing I can't seem to face with Adam is the fact that after all of this, for the past three weeks, he won't touch me. I'm lucky if I can get a kiss or a tight hug. I miss his hands on my legs and his weight on my body. I miss the scruff of his beard against my neck or between my thighs. I miss *feeling* wanted.

I want to scream at him. I'm in a funk, maybe even depressed, but I'm not dead. I think I just need to be royally fucked back to normal.

Obviously, that's not how it works, but it's the normalcy I crave, and I can't help but feel like he may never treat me like *me* again, and I can't bear that thought. If I'm not me, and he's not him, then who the fuck are we and what are we doing?

His movements are quiet as he slips off his shoes and pulls off his rain jacket, hanging it on the stand by the door. The floorboards creak as he steps closer to the bedroom, but just when I think he's abandoned me here to sleep, I feel his weight as he settles on the mattress next to me.

His hands wind around my waist like they normally do and his lips press softly to my shoulder.

"Where were you?" I whisper.

He doesn't answer, so I freeze before turning over. I expected him to just say something like his mom's house or the store, but the fact that he's not answering tells me that he has something to hide.

"Adam..." I say in a warning. "Tell me."

His eyes find my face and he swallows. "I saw him."

Blood rushes to my cheeks. "Why?"

"It doesn't matter. We never have to see him again."

My eyes narrow at him. "Please don't keep secrets from me. Brett did that—"

"Okay, okay. I'm sorry," he replies across the pillow, taking my hands in his.

"He asked me to take his place. He...offered me the job."

I sit up on my elbow and stare at him. "What?"

I'm searching his face for answers, desperate to know and terrified to hear his response at the same time. Would he take the job? It's what he always wanted, but now?

"What did you say?" I ask when he doesn't respond for a moment. There's an expression of hesitation on his face, like he's deep in thought.

"I told him to fuck off," he whispers, and just like that, I'm flooded with relief.

Should I feel bad for how happy I am that he turned the offer down? The last thing I want is for Adam to follow in his father's footsteps, but I still want him to have everything he's ever dreamed of.

Don't I?

He still looks so uneasy, so I nuzzle closer to him and kiss him once on each cheek. His arms tighten around me.

"How do you feel about that?" I ask, burying myself in his embrace.

"I feel good," he replies softly. "I never really wanted that job. That was his dream."

"What is your dream?"

"This," he says as he covers my body with his. My legs open and he settles himself between them. It feels so good to have him like this, but I sense there's something holding him back.

"Then touch me, Adam."

"Are you sure?" he whispers, lifting up and staring at me with empathetic eyes.

I wrap my hands around his waist and I pull him farther down. "I need you to touch me. I need to know you still want to."

At that, his expression changes into something resembling perplexity. "Are you fucking kidding me? I want you more than anything."

"My body?" I ask, and it feels like I'm fishing, but I just need to hear him say it.

"Peaches, yes." His hands drift over my breasts and down to my hips. With a tight squeeze, he looks me in the eye as he declares, "I told you, this body belongs to me. If you tell me you're ready, I'll show you exactly what I want to do with it. But only when you're ready."

My breath gets caught in my chest. Watching this modest, good man turn feral for me does something to me inside. Warmth creeps down my spine as I melt like candle wax for him.

"I'm ready," I whisper as I grind my hips up toward him.

For the first time in weeks, I feel alive again. We're connected, which means I'm not alone. He looks into my eyes like he is right now, his heart beating with mine.

His lips dive toward mine, and I moan into our kiss as my body wraps itself around him. His lips are ravenous and desperate, and so are mine. His touch and taste are so familiar and comforting to me now. I hope I always feel this way in his arms.

In nothing but one of his T-shirts and a pair of panties, he quickly swipes the tee over my head and delicately kisses his way down, placing a soft, loving press of his lips against my throat before moving down to my breasts.

As his mouth ravages each side, biting and licking the tight buds, he glances up at me and mutters darkly, "Mine."

Then he travels lower, sucking his way down my belly, sending shivers through my body. Reaching the top of my panties, he licks a long slow line across the top of the elastic band, and I tremble with anticipation.

My fingers wind through his hair. *Don't stop. Please don't stop.*

Hooking his thumbs under the hem of my panties, he slides them down my legs. Positioning himself on his knees, he holds my bare legs against his chest. Then he kisses his way up my legs, staring into my eyes as he does. The closer he gets to my inner thighs, the more I writhe with need.

Locking eyes with me, he growls when he reaches the apex. "This," he says. "This is mine."

My body hums with desire. When his tongue slides through me, from bottom to top, as if he's savoring me, I nearly cry with relief. A low growl vibrates from his mouth all the way up my spine. It awakens me. Brings me back to life.

He's here. He's mine.

I'm home.

As he continues to assault me with pleasure, licking, sucking, biting, I shut my eyes and let myself just *feel* him. He draws the orgasm out of my body like he knows exactly where to find it. Before I know it, I'm breathless and flying through the euphoria of a blinding climax.

I'm not even down from this high when he's lying on top of me, pressing his cock into me. My body welcomes him like an extension of myself.

"God, you feel so good," he mumbles into my neck. "You're like heaven."

I feel it too. This warm pleasure that only he can touch and a need that only grows with each thrust. I never want it to end.

And I need more.

"Harder," I groan, desperate for the impact of his body.

He listens to me, pounding me into the mattress.

When he lifts up, our eyes connecting as his hands intertwine with mine above my head, I feel happier than I've felt in a long time. Maybe ever. We are connected physically, mentally, emotionally.

"I want to come inside you," he says between gasps.

"Yes," I cry out, barely able to even breathe from the harsh crash of his body.

Only a moment later, I nearly scream with the wave of pleasure that washes over me. At the same time, he stills, holding me tight as he comes, filling me like he promised.

We lie here for a while, just holding each other. Carefully, he pulls out and presses my legs together. My brows wrinkle with confusion.

"Keep me there for a little while longer."

"Okay," I reply.

I don't think much about it as he settles his weight into the mattress behind me. Wrapping me up in his arms, he kisses my head and whispers, "I love you."

"I love you too," I reply before letting my eyes close and falling into an easy slumber with his body to keep me warm.

Everything feels settled and safe and perfect, so I don't dream at all. No nightmares or fears to worry me. Just the feel of him near me and his words of affection on repeat in my mind.

When I wake up a couple hours later, he's gone.

A manila envelope with my name scribbled on the front is on the nightstand.

# FORTY-SIX

Dear Isaac,

Mom won't give me your phone number or your address, but she said she would deliver this to you for me. If that's all I can have, then I'll take it. I promise this won't be a sappy, emotional letter. I know how much you hate that.

For now, I hope you're well.

And since I can't exactly ask you any details about your life, I figured I'd fill you in on mine.

I'm sure by now you've seen the shit our father is in, and you might have seen some of the things I've been up to lately (although I hope you haven't watched the videos. Please don't.)

I found someone. You'd love her. She's honest and tough and funny. Nothing like you'd expect, I'm sure, but it doesn't change the fact that she's my favorite person, period. I'm simply obsessed with her, and I could see the two of you becoming close friends. Maybe someday you will.

To be honest, I think you would have been a little proud of me for rebelling...at thirty-seven. I'm not the same guy I was when you left, and I imagine you'd be cheering me on if you were here.

Basically, you were right about our father all along. And while I can say I just found out myself, the truth is that I always knew. Even before he drove you away. Even before he started his church. He was always a monster to us, and I should have protected you sooner. I shouldn't have let that behavior slide. I should have held him accountable when I had the chance, and then maybe no one would have been hurt.

So, here it is. I'm sorry.

I'll probably say it again another thousand times and every chance I get, but I hope you know it's true. Mom said, "All men make mistakes, but good men make it right." So, that's what I'm trying to do now.

Here I sit in my favorite diner while I write this letter to you, trying to imagine you rolling your eyes as you read it. Giving me shit for trying to be such a "fancy writer." Telling me to stop trying to be so fucking righteous.

Obviously you're still seventeen in my mind. I know you're twenty-five now, but until I see you again, you're still that same sarcastic, bratty teenager I remember. Still my best friend. Still the kid I would spill my guts to, just so you could give me the worst advice possible.

And while I know you're not a kid anymore, I'd still die for some of that bad advice.

So, tell me what to do, Isaac.

With some coercion that I'm sure you would have loved to see, I managed to get Dad to sign the property title of the club over to Sage. Because she deserves it.

Because I hate to say it, he was right. I can't have the church and her—not in the ways that I want.

So I can either give up my dreams of running this place on my own, or I can give up her.

And you're probably thinking, "Jesus, Adam. How is that even a question?" I'd just like to point out that Sage has never been a bad influence on my life, but I have always been one on hers. So, I really am thinking about her in this scenario. I'm just afraid that she'd be better off without me.

With all of her brilliant ideas and good intentions, I can only imagine what she could accomplish.

I have no clue what my future holds, but I know what hers will.

According to the woman who worked at the club, Sage's ex-boyfriend skipped town and closed it down once Dad's stuff went public. Apparently, all the VIP assholes were afraid of their secrets getting out, so they pulled their patronage.

Which means it's all hers.

So who am I to interfere? Right?

Am I only being selfish if I stay? After all of this, would I hold her back?

And this is what made me think of you. I understand that I was too much like our dad to earn a place in your life, but I still want you to be happy and free and never face his judgment or bigotry again. I want all the best things in the world for you, Isaac. I hope you find love. And success.

I hope you've found a new family.

And I hope you never miss me a day in your life.

Because I understand now that loving someone doesn't mean forging a way into their life. It means being able to step out of it for their sake.

I know you may never read this letter, but I'm going to continue writing them. Maybe someday you'll write back, but it's okay if you don't.

You're free from him, and you're free
from me.

I love you, Isaac.

And I'll keep praying that there will come a
day when I can wrap my arms around you again.

Your brother,
Adam

# FORTY-SEVEN

SAGE

I'm on the verge of tears as I drive. Am I overreacting?
No.

I'm going with my gut and my gut is telling me that something is up with Adam. He's not answering his phone and he left me with the signed transfer of ownership paperwork along with a fifty-thousand-dollar check from his account and the note reading, *Your first investor.*

My heart is telling me he would never make a deal with his father for that club.

My gut is telling me to worry.

There are only a handful of places I could imagine him to be. I called his mother right away and she said she hadn't seen him. And a swing by the old church proved wrong again. Why he would go there, I don't know. But I had to at least check.

I drive around town for a few minutes, mostly worrying that he went back to his dad's hotel or he's on a one-way plane ride out of town. Of course, I'm just being dramatic now. When I look down at my phone, I realize it's Saturday, at eight in the morning.

And realization dawns.

*Of course.*

Pulling into a spot along the street, I snatch the folder off the passenger seat and fly out of the truck. As I hurry along the quiet sidewalk, I worry my lip, running my tongue over the ring as I do when I'm mostly nervous.

The bell above Sal's chimes as I enter. The crowd has already gathered in the lobby, but I push past all of them, ignoring the hostess at her stand as I take stock of the patrons at the bar. The last seat on the corner, where he usually sits, is filled—by someone else.

"Can I help you?" the hostess asks as I let out a despondent sigh.

My eyes scan the rest of the diner, landing on a dark-haired man with his head down like he's writing something.

"Ma'am?" the hostess calls again, but I ignore her, rushing toward the booth in the back where Adam is sitting alone. People are staring at me, and I get the feeling I'm causing a scene, but at the moment, I don't care.

"What are you doing?" I ask loudly as I approach his table, slamming the papers down next to his cup of coffee. The panic is coming out as anger, but I need him to assure me he didn't do what I think he did.

As his head snaps up to find me standing there, there's softness mixed with surprise in his eyes.

He reaches for my hand.

"Hey, Peaches. What's wrong?"

At the sight of him, tall and handsome and as perfect as the day I met him, I feel a swell of emotion bubble to the top. My voice cracks with my next words.

"Tell me, Adam. Did you make a deal with the devil for this?"

His shoulders fall away from his ears.

"Wha—" he starts before gesturing for me to sit down. I feel the eyes of the other diners on us as I stand there in a panic, but at the moment, I really don't care. "Sit down, Sage. Let's talk."

My eyes are stinging with tears as I stare at him. I didn't realize fully until this moment how much of a permanent fixture Adam has become in my life. Just the thought of my apartment without him leaves me feeling shattered and hopeless. It started out as a scheme, but it was never truly fake to me. From the very beginning, I felt the comfort of his voice and the safety of his touch. Even when our dating was supposedly fake, I felt the pride of having him at my side, calling him *mine*. It was reckless of me to spend even one second around Adam Goode because my heart was at risk from the moment he gave me his seat four months ago.

"Just answer the question," I reply shakily. "What did you give him to get this?"

He looks at the envelope. Then he shakes his head. "Nothing."

"What?" I drop into the seat across from him. My heart is hammering in my chest, and I'm lost in a fury of emotion. Should I be angry or confused, or relieved? Because right now, I'm all of them.

"I mean, he tried..." he says, reaching across the table to touch my hand. "He tried to blackmail me into leaving you and taking the job at his church. And in return, he would give you that."

"So how..."

"I turned him down. I left. I told him to get fucked. And then...he signed it anyway."

"I don't understand," I cry.

With a sigh, he leans back in the booth and stares across the table at me, softness around his eyes. No longer so distraught or worried. He seems at peace.

"He told me the choice was mine. Then, he tried to tell me that if I stayed with you while you owned this club, my career in the ministry would be over. He tried to tell me that you were holding me back, but I can't help but wonder...if I'm the one holding *you* back."

I lean forward, feeling the panic start to rise again.

"What are you talking about?"

"Peaches, I just want you to have everything you ever wanted." He says it so plainly, I'm sitting here wondering if he's suddenly lost his mind. My hands ball into tight fists, and I want to punch him for how stupid he's being right now.

"Are you fucking kidding me?" I reply, drawing the eyes of those around us again. "All I've ever wanted was you, you idiot. I never had a family, Adam. I've never had a place where I truly belonged. Now, I have you. I don't give a shit about the club. I just need you."

"You know it's going to be hard, right? As long as we're together, you may never get your VIPs back or your members. And you'll have to start from scratch."

I let out a long, frustrated groan. "Stop trying to be so fucking *good*. Stop trying to follow the rules, Adam. Fuck the rules. Fuck the *right* thing. And fuck the VIPs. I won't even have a VIP section at my club. And anyone who has issues with you can fuck off."

A smile stretches slowly across his face, but I still want to punch him. I want to punch his stupid, perfect, handsome face. Then I want to kiss it.

"Come here," he mutters in a low, sexy command, and I jump up from my seat in the booth and crawl into his next to him, burying myself under his arm. He cuddles me close, and I inhale the familiar scent of his cologne. His arms feel like home to me now.

"I'm sorry for scaring you," he says against the top of my head. "I just...do my best writing here."

"I thought you left me," I reply, looking up into his warm-brown eyes.

"I would never leave you like that, Peaches. I told you. I'll be here for as long as you want me to."

Closing the distance between us, he presses his lips to mine, and I just hold him there for a minute. Our mouths pressed together, content to just be touching.

Someone across the aisle clears their throat, and Adam looks up, looking offended. With a roll of his eyes, he mutters, "Prude."

I giggle as I squeeze my arms around him. "What are you writ-ing?" The yellow pad of paper on the table is already full.

"A letter to my brother."

"Did you tell him about me?" I ask.

He chuckles. "Yes. I told him all about you."

The waitress refills Adam's coffee cup and sets another on the table for me. My eyes catch on the manila envelope on the table, and it suddenly dawns on me that I finally have the club to myself. Brett is gone. And I can finally start the venture the way I want to.

"So..." Adam says as he picks up a bite of his scrambled eggs, dips them in ketchup, and feeds them to me like a child. "What are you going to name your new club?"

As I'm chewing, I furrow my brow. "What's wrong with Pink?"

He shrugs. "I thought you'd like to start fresh. Pick something you'd really like."

"Hmm..." I say, mixing creamer into my coffee. "What about...Sex Church."

He laughs, nearly choking on his waffles. "Why don't we brainstorm a little longer?"

I'm chuckling over my cup of coffee before resting my head on his shoulder. I feel his lips on my head just as I notice an older couple watching us with curiosity from across the restaurant.

I know we look like an odd pairing, but it doesn't matter to me anymore. We might be incompatible or complete opposites, but I've found a good man, and I'm not going to let him go.

I don't need him to be a hero—I just need him to be here.

# ADAM'S EPILOGUE

## THREE MONTHS LATER

"We need more plates," Sage says, rushing around me and heading toward the kitchen.

"They're stacked up by the fridge," I reply, glancing back toward the room she disappeared into. If I wasn't up to my elbows in mashed potatoes, I'd help her.

"Found 'em!" she says, jogging back out to the rec room with a stack of paper plates in her arms.

"Hey, hey, hey," I shout at her as she brushes past me. Turning with a perplexed look, she stares at me as I smile and lean toward her, waiting for a kiss.

"Can't you see I'm busy, Church Boy?" she replies, stepping closer to press her lips to mine anyway.

With a lopsided grin, I watch her walk away, delivering the plates to the end of the table, where my mother is greeting our guests.

"You're so screwed," my brother Caleb says with a laugh next to me, where he's serving gravy for the turkey and mashed potatoes.

"Screwed?" I ask.

"I give it three months before you two are married and six months before she's knocked up," he replies, shaking his head as if he knows something I don't.

"And you call that screwed? Don't let your wife hear that."

Caleb's smile falters for a moment.

"Screwed in a good way, of course. Marriage is bliss," he adds. There's no hint of a smile on his face this time.

While I focus on scooping mashed potatoes and greeting our guests, I can't help but wonder if there's more going on with Caleb than he's letting on. Dread starts to seep in through the cracks.

He and Briar were once crazy about each other, too. I remember when he brought her home. The way he looked at her like she was the most dazzling diamond this world had ever seen stuck in my memory for a long time. Briar and Caleb were the real thing.

Sage laughs on the other side of the room, and I glance up to watch her standing with Gladys, Mary, and Sylvia. When I catch her eye, she winks at me, a sly, secretive smile stretching across her face.

Being married to her would be bliss. My life is already perfect. We spend our days in *our* apartment now since I finally put mine up for sale and it was snatched up almost immediately. At night, we work at the club together, and on Sundays, we're here.

We're not holding services at the new church. Not yet, and maybe not ever. There're a lot of legalities and church property laws to get through before it becomes officially mine, but for now, the owners lease it to us for gatherings and events like today—free Thanksgiving dinner for the community.

I have no idea yet what I want to do with this place or with my life. The ministry doesn't feel like my path anymore, but I can't seem to let this place go either. I'm still so afraid of turning into my father that the idea of delivering sermons and building a congregation makes me uneasy. For now, this is enough.

Especially while I finish my book—this one exploring the deconstruction and reformation of finding yourself outside of a strict religious upbringing. It doesn't have a name yet, although Sage still insists that Church Boy has a nice ring to it.

But her name ideas have always been terrible.

This is why the club is *not* called Sex Church, but a much more appealing and equally apropos—*Sinners and Saints*. Because everyone who enters is *both*.

When the line dies down, I take a moment to glance around the room, taking stock of our first big event, and so far, it seems like a success. The rec room is full. Everyone looks happy, sated, and at ease.

In the corner, Briar set up a craft station with Abigail, where the neighborhood kids are making thank-you cards and place mats. On the opposite side, Gladys set up a free book library, a familiar copy of *The Rake and His Reluctant Bride* sitting untouched on the top.

When I feel a pair of arms wrap around my waist, I smile.

"Watching you serve those mashed potatoes is getting me hot," she whispers, and out of the corner of my eye, I see Caleb snicker to himself before pulling off his gloves and walking away.

I peel mine off as well, turning to face the pink-haired beauty trying to dirty talk me in a church. Although...I guess we've done worse here.

"Oh yeah?" I ask, looking down at her and biting my bottom lip. Reaching behind me for a spoon, I scoop up a dollop of the creamy potatoes. "Open, Peaches."

With a sultry expression on her face, she parts her lips and tilts her chin up for me.

"Good little slut," I mouth before sliding the spoon into her mouth. She closes her lips around it, letting out a hum as I pull it out. "Lick it clean," I whisper, and with a mischievous smile, she does.

"I think we need something out of the storage closet," she says with a wink.

Laughing, I lean forward and take her mouth in a kiss, trailing my hand over her jaw and holding it delicately around her throat. This girl makes me crazy.

"And what is that?" I hear my mother's voice from just a foot away, and it's like ice water over my quickly growing dick.

Clearing my throat, I pull away and glance down at what my mother is staring at in horror.

"Busted..." Sage teases.

That's when I notice the sleeve of my shirt has rolled up enough to expose the black-and-gray tattoo covering most of my forearm.

My mother approaches, practically ripping the buttons off my sleeve to see the artwork there. As far as I know, I'm the first of her sons to get a tattoo.

"What is it?" she asks, as her fingers run over the ink.

"It's a snake wrapped around a peach tree," I reply, glancing up at Sage, who's biting her bottom lip and smiling back at me.

"Why on earth did you get that?" my mother asks with alarm.

"The snake represents fresh starts and rebirth since it's always shedding its skin. And the peach tree...is personal."

At first, my mother's expression is loaded with emotion, staring up at me as she touches my cheek. Then her gaze tracks over to my girlfriend, looking more and more mischievous by the second. My mother narrows her eyes at her before wrapping an arm over her shoulder.

"You're a bad influence," she says with affection as she squeezes Sage to her side.

"Thanks," Sage replies, taking that as a compliment. "We can get you one next."

"Nice try," my mother says with a laugh.

After letting go of Sage, she wraps a hand around my arm and squeezes it. Then we gaze out at the crowd, eating the meals we provided. For a moment, the emotion is thick between the three of us, my mother at one side and the love of my life at the other.

As Sage tucks herself under my arm, nestled in with her arms wrapped around my torso, my mother smiles. Then she looks me in the eyes as she whispers, "I'm so proud of you."

And those five words alone make everything worth it.

# SAGE'S EPILOGUE

## LATER THAT NIGHT

"**E**verything looks good," I say as I hand the expense report back to Sadie. "It's so nice to have things actually add up."

She laughs as she takes the packet and drops it on the desk. The decision to keep Sadie around as manager of the club was the best decision I've made. She's clearly dedicated to making it the best it can be.

"Check this out," she says with a proud smile, pulling something from her back pocket. "Look who's officially enrolled."

My jaw drops as I stare at the college ID with her photo on the front.

"Oh my god, Sadie!" I say, snatching it out of her hands and pulling her in for a hug. "I'm so proud of you."

With a bashful shrug, she takes the ID from my fingers and stares down at it with a tight-lipped smile. "Thanks. Hopefully, with a business degree, I can really make this place even better."

"I have no doubt you're going to do amazing things," I reply, feeling so proud and excited for her. After only meeting her a few months ago, it's amazing how *right* it feels having her here with me. She cares about this club and this industry. Unlike Brett, who only really looked at the figures at the end of the day, Sadie shares a vision with me of what this place could be and how valuable it would be for a lot of people.

"Your boyfriend is here," she says, nodding toward the security camera. On the screen, Adam is strutting across the floor of the club, looking fine as hell in that black long-sleeve button-down and tight black slacks.

A moment later, there's a knock at the door of the office, and I bite back my smile as I open it.

"Can I help you, sir?" I ask, teasing him as I peek my head out.

He leans in, stealing a kiss like he couldn't go another minute without it. As he pulls away, he flashes me the camera.

"We have work to do," he says.

"Well, let's give the people what they want," I reply.

I wave back at Sadie, who shoots Adam a quick wave before we slip out of the office. "Happy Thanksgiving," he calls after her before the door closes.

My hand links with his as we walk together toward the Blue Room at the back of the club. While I'm unlocking the door with my master key, Adam crowds me from behind, pulling my hair to the side to kiss along the constellation tattoo on my neck. Goose bumps prickle every inch of my skin and my blood starts to warm up from his tender touch.

Continuing to film our videos has actually been great for the club too. After our account reached nearly two million followers and we had more fame than we anticipated, we had to decide if this was what we really wanted to do. It feels like we're too far to turn back now and I still worry that this has ruined any chance of Adam achieving his dreams. Especially after the internet proudly proclaimed him the *Porn Star Preacher*.

He's promised me he's not worried about his future—that being the *Porn Star Preacher* doesn't bother him. He wants to carve his own path instead of walking down one already paved by someone else. And he seems to really think that even being a quote, unquote "porn star" hasn't entirely ruined his chances of standing at the pulpit. If he does, I can't wait to see the congregation that flocks to listen.

He's setting up the camera on the tripod while I get undressed. We've upgraded from our phone cameras to one of those adventure-style cameras that can attach to practically anything. It has made the filming of our videos much more fun. We've attached it to the dash of his car while he enjoyed some road head. We even filmed underwater in a hot tub once. That was fun.

Once he's done, he walks over to me, pulling me close as his hand caresses my jaw and neck. Then he leans down and presses his lips to mine.

"I love you, Peaches," he whispers, and I let those words warm me from the inside out.

As I let my fingers drift over the fabric of his shirt and all the way down to his belt, I gaze up at him with adoration. "I love you too, Church Boy."

Then with a thin smile, I add, "But we're going to have to edit that out."

He laughs. "Yeah, our viewers don't want to hear that."

"What do they want to hear?" I ask.

"What do *you* want to hear?"

With a tilt of my head, gazing up through my lashes, I softly whisper, "You know what I want to hear."

Like an instinct, his hand moves from the tender spot on my shoulder to the base of my throat, squeezing hard and angling my face up toward his. "You want me to tell you what a dirty little fuck toy you are?"

"Yes, please," I reply as my toes start to curl and my thighs clench.

Then Adam winks and pecks me quickly on the mouth before shoving me to my knees.

"Get on your knees and beg me to fuck you."

Gazing up at him from the floor, I love him from this angle. So dominant and confident and nothing like the man who morphed and transformed in front of my very eyes over the span of three months.

Even as I beg him to fuck me like the dirty slut I am, I know that none of this would be possible for him without the trust between us. Adam could never be this free or liberated with anyone else, and that makes me want to be his fuck toy for the rest of our lives. I know because I feel the same way. I trust that with Adam, this is our fantasy, and he is willing to be as kinky and dirty with me as long as I know he also wants to keep me safe, loved, and protected for the rest of my life.

Both.

His hand grips the back of my head at the scalp as he drags my face closer to his crotch. "Take it out then, slut. If you want it so bad."

My fingers eagerly tear open his belt and pull down his zipper. My mouth practically waters at the sight of his throbbing cock, hard and ready for me. Thick veins travel along the length and a bead of precum waits for me at the tip.

I don't ask for permission before I lap at the slit, tasting his arousal on my tongue. With a hum, I smile up at him as he pulls my face back toward his cock.

"Open," he commands, and I do. Parting my lips and letting my tongue hang out of my mouth, I wait for him to glide the shaft along the surface. It's heavy in my mouth as he bides his time, easing it in and out. I hold out for as long as I can, my eyes starting to water every time he grazes the back of my throat. Finally, on a rougher plunge, I gag and cough, letting out a choking sound as he does it again and again.

My hand grips his thigh the way he wants me to, knowing that if it becomes too much, I can just give him a tight squeeze and he'll stop.

"Look at how much you love my cock down your throat, Peaches. I think you love it so much I should just come right here."

Unable to speak, I try to make some semblance of a hum that

sounds like *no*. He's teasing me. He must be because if he comes down my throat right now and deprives me of what I really want, I'll be disappointed.

Thankfully, he pulls himself free of my mouth just as I feel the head of his cock swell and tighten, but he stops himself before he blows.

"Get on the bed, Peaches," he barks in a rough command, clearly struggling with the close call. I scamper up on the bed. Crawling halfway to the head of the bed, I'm stopped by a rough arm sliding under my hips and dragging me back. I let out a squeal and a whimper, my fingers clutching the sheets, just as I feel his cock at my core, pressing into the already wet heat.

After easing his way in to ensure he doesn't hurt me, he pounds himself home. A satisfied and desperate moan escapes my lips at the familiar fullness he provides.

"If you want this cock so much, why are you trying to crawl away from me, Peaches?"

No sooner are his words out than his hand lands with a resounding smack across my ass cheek. I let out a shriek.

"Not trying to crawl away now, are you?" he asks in a sexy, dark tone. God, I love him like this.

My dirty, beautiful, sexy freak of a preacher boyfriend. The sweeter he is in the daytime, the dirtier he is when the lights go out, and I can't get enough. I am the only one who gets to see this side of him.

Okay, me and two million FanVids subscribers. But the point is that it's all still for me.

He smacks my ass even harder on the other side, pounding hard as my mind starts to muddle, distracted by the pleasure. Whatever spot he hits when he fucks me like this is almost literally blinding. It's pleasure and pain, and I want so much more of that hurt. Every time he fucks me like this, I feel like I might explode with sensations.

His hand reaches down to find my throat, wrapping his fingers around it as he hoists my head backward. With my ass in the air, he has me in the perfect position to gain leverage and slam into me even harder.

I feel like I'm dying the most heavenly death. Then when I don't think I can take another second, everything inside me explodes. I let out a scream as my body seizes and my limbs tremble. I want this sensation to last forever—pulsing, pulsing, pulsing.

And he relentlessly shoves himself inside me throughout the whole thing. As my body starts to recover, he continues his thrusts. That hand around my throat pulls me upright, so he can wrap his arms around my torso. Forcing my face to turn toward him, he kisses me like he's bringing me back to life.

"Your cunt is so wet for me, Peaches. I could fuck you all night. You've got another one in there for me, don't you?"

The red light of the camera blinks in my periphery. "I think I do," I reply with a wasted smile.

"I bet you do." Still moving slowly inside me, he gives me a quick kiss on my cheek and whispers, "I love you."

I laugh as I turn back toward him. "I love you too."

Our eyes meet for a moment, and it's so powerful. Two souls connecting through one look, and it's how I know this love is *real* and he is my forever. I can look into his eyes and never want to look away.

After a quick wink, he shoves my head back down toward the mattress and grabs hold of my hips, pounding harder, and I think for a moment, he might actually want to fuck all night long. With a smile, I realize I wouldn't mind that so much.

And in the corner of the room is a camera, catching every single moment.

# ACKNOWLEDGMENTS

First and foremost, I need to thank my readers and everyone who has ever taken a chance on one of my books. I'm so blessed and honored to have my stories resonate with someone else. It's what keeps me going in this crazy job of mine, so thank you. Seriously.

Okay, now here is my favorite thing to write—the list of people who dedicate time and energy to my books. It's a list over-flowing with talent and love. Everytime I sit down to work on this list, I feel like the luckiest writer in the world.

My beta readers—the people blessed *and* cursed to put their eyeballs on my writing first. You guys must like it really rough. Adrian, Jill, Becca, Amanda, and Janine. Thanks for the input, the beatings, the emojis, and the encouragement. Mostly, thanks for loving Adam, even when I couldn't.

My girls, my best friends, my soul-mates—Rachel, Katie, Gail, Ashton, Lori, Misty, and Tits. I hate to think about what this would be like without you.

The greatest assistant in the industry—Lori Alexander. No competition.

Amanda Anderson, for giving me even a moment of your time while you're out conquering the world and being an all-around badass.

My agent, Savannah Greenwell, for being an amazing agent and friend.

The rockstar, Misty, who keeps my store running and mostly for always believing in me. And for bookstore roadtrips.

The talented team at Wander Aguiar photography. Thank

you, Wander and Andrew for the stunning cover photo. You guys are stuck with me forever.

Lori Jackson and Emily Wittig, it was such a pleasure to work with you on the design of these covers.

My Salacious Sluts, and the women who keep that group going—Christine, Heather, Daniela, and Brooke.

And last, my husband for the never-ending support and love. Thanks for being my safe place to land when this job of mine shows its claws. You handled it beautifully.

# Also by Sara Cate

**Salacious Players' Club**

Praise

Eyes on Me

Give Me More

Mercy

Highest Bidder

Madame

**Age-gap romance**

Beautiful Monster

Beautiful Sinner

**Wilde Boys duet**

Gravity

Freefall

**Black Heart Duet**

Four

Five

**Cocky Hero Club**

Handsome Devil

**Bully romance**

Burn for Me

**Wicked Hearts Series**

Delicate

Dangerous

Defiant

# ABOUT SARA CATE

Sara Cate writes forbidden romance with lots of angst, a little age gap, and heaps of steam. Living in Arizona with her husband and kids, Sara spends most of her time reading, writing, or baking.

You can find more information about her at
www.saracatebooks.com

Milton Keynes UK
Ingram Content Group UK Ltd.
UKHW020816221024
2310UKWH00048B/498